Eden's Daughter
Katherine Matiko

Print ISBNs
Amazon print 9780228636083
Ingram Spark 9780228636090
BWL Print 9780228636106

Copyright 2025 by Katherine Matiko
Editor Nancy M Bell
Cover Artist Michelle Lee

Dedication

To James and Nicole

"Trust the dreams, for in them is hidden the gate
to eternity."
– Kahlil Gibran

Acknowledgements

Thank you to James Matiko and Nicole Matiko for being my first readers and biggest cheerleaders. I am indebted to those who read my manuscript and provided valuable input and encouragement – Dorothy Bentley, Barb Howard, Sheri Reed, Karen Engleson, Bonita Felton, Sheelagh Matthews, Eva Bjerreskov, Christine Chambers, and Robin Harron.

The poetry by Kahlil Gibran used throughout the book is in the public domain.

Table of Contents

Chapter 1

1974
Saskatchewan's South Country

Eden knew Donalda and Curtis were speeding along the road long before she saw them. HoundDog had recognized the sound of their truck and was baying joyously. Mother and son braked with a gravelly flourish beside the house.

Donalda leaped out of the truck as Eden's mother stepped onto the porch, shaking her head.

"Donnie, what's your hurry?" Barbie said. "The coffee's still perking!"

Eden opened the passenger door for Curtis. He slid out of the truck and stood at the tailgate, staring at the rutted driveway and rocking back on his heels. He seemed calm today.

"Mom, can we take the horses out?" Eden asked.

Barbie wiped wet hands on her jeans. She'd been rinsing a bucketful of lettuce, radishes, and onions; a nice haul for early June. May had been rainy and warm, and the garden and crops looked better than they ever had. She glanced at her watch.

"Okay, as long as you're home in plenty of time to help with supper. Dad wants to go to the dance tonight, and you'll need to clean up." She frowned at Eden's filthy cut-offs and tangled waist-length hair.

"Yay, let's go, Curt!" Eden headed toward the barn, Curtis following in a circuitous manner down the path.

"And use the bridles!" Barbie called after them. "The bridles, not the hackamores!" She turned to Donnie. "That girl would steer a horse with a ribbon if she could."

Donnie laughed. "She knows her way around horses. They'll be fine."

Eden waited for Curtis to catch up. "They didn't say anything about saddles," she whispered. "So, come on!"

Blackie and Patches were dozing in a sliver of shade beside the corral. Their bur-filled tails twitched idly at the torpid flies. Blackie looked sidelong at Eden and Curtis then gazed at the horizon as if ignoring them would make them go away.

Patches snorted a welcome when she saw Curtis, leaving the shade to greet her favourite person. She pressed her forehead against his chest with a sigh of completion. Curtis scratched behind her ear where the halter left a sweaty stripe.

Eden left them to their mutual adoration and approached the big gelding. Blackie flung his head out of reach but eventually allowed her to clip a rope to his halter. A waft of dry manure and worn leather greeted them as they walked into the barn.

Shirtless and wearing an old pair of jeans cut off at the knees, Curtis looked comfortable in the heat. The sun had brightened his hair to the colour of ripe wheat; the sparse hair on his arms stood white against his bronzed skin. Eden noticed a smattering of blond hair on his chest. That's new, she thought.

Eden hitched the horses to the tie rings and picked up a curry comb from the floor. She handed it to Curtis, who gazed at it for a long moment before swiping it half-heartedly across Patches's withers.

"Here, let me!" Eden grabbed the curry comb and scraped it across Patches's back to dislodge the dried mud and straw the mare had rolled in since their last ride.

"So, Curt, is it the coulee or the bridge today? Or both? Do we have time?" Eden glanced at the wall clock. "We have time!" she announced, deciding for both of them.

Curtis did not respond to Eden's questions or acknowledge her presence. She was used to this; Curtis had been part of her life since before they could walk or talk. Curtis learned to walk, of course—and to ride at an early age—but never to talk. Never to look her in the eye or smile.

Donnie often said that without Barbie and Eden, she would not have been able to cope with Curtis's condition. Without Barbie's sunny kitchen and bottomless coffee pot, Donnie would not have survived.

About five years after Curtis was born, Donnie and her husband Vic had two daughters a year apart. The girls were perfectly fine. Barbie said Donnie had guts, taking that leap of faith. Then again, she would point out, lightning rarely strikes twice.

Pussy brushed like grey smoke against Eden's ankle then weaved through Patches's legs to find Curtis.

"Pussy, out of there! You'll get trampled." Eden kicked at the cat, but Pussy ignored her as she purred against Curtis's leg. Her belly writhed with her latest litter; once the kittens were born, Pussy would become feral, and they would rarely see her up close.

Barbie had named Pussy as a kitten. She had named every animal on the place with a legendary lack of imagination that was the favourite family joke. With her children, Barbie had been more inventive. Her first child was River Rock; the second boy, Skylar Blue. Barbie said these unusual names occurred to her during long third trimester walks on the prairie. A third son, George James, was named after his father and grandfather. Four years later, a daughter joined the family; Barbie named her Eden Holly. And the twin sister who died at birth—Ava Marie.

Eden quickly bridled the horses and led them to the mounting block. Curtis ambled behind her, staring at the horses' swinging tails. She held Patches's bridle while Curt scrambled aboard. Blackie sidestepped when Eden attempted to get on.

"Stand still, you idiot!" she cried, flicking him with the reins. Finally, he succumbed, and they were off, taking cover behind tall caragana bushes so Barbie wouldn't notice the saddles were still in the barn.

Blackie's mood improved when they got to the road; Eden didn't have to urge him to canter. Curtis and Patches were right behind them. The sun had passed its zenith, and on the prairie, the breeze was cooler. The sky was wearing a pearl necklace of clouds strung above distant telephone wires.

The grass along the road was nearly at the horses' bellies. Soon, the men would be haying; it looked like there would be more than enough to feed the cattle this winter. Eden's father George Senior was already planning to sell some of his bales. It would help pay for the house renovations Barbie was so excited about.

Many ranchers in the district were expanding or replacing their houses; crops and prices over the past ten years had been abundant. For the first time since the land was cultivated, it was profitable to farm in the South Country. Everyone was talking about how to spend the windfall. The Pedersens were even planning a trip to Hawaii next winter. It was unheard of!

Eden didn't envy the Pedersens. She was quite certain southern Saskatchewan was far more beautiful than Hawaii. As the horses plunged headlong into the undulating waves of the prairie, Eden surfed the wind, her hawk's wing hair lifting her into the sky. Eden and Blackie, Curtis and Patches, flying close to the ground.

They pulled up at the old bridge. Patches's belly heaved—she coughed and shuddered, clattering Curtis to the bone. Blackie's ears twitched as swallows swooped near his head. Eden found it thrilling to watch the birds, circling by the hundreds, desperately trying to distract them from nests clinging to the underside of the rusting structure.

"Hey, Curt, see the birds?" she said, but Curtis was gazing at Patches's mane, scratching her neck with blackened fingernails.

"Let's go to the coulee, okay, Curty?" The unshod horses walked gingerly over the graveled grid road and into the opposite ditch, where foxtail and wild oats brushed the riders' feet. Curtis lifted his knees to avoid the tickling sensation on his bare toes.

Although Curtis never spoke to her, Eden knew that when they were together, he was at ease—on their rides in recent years, and during the many hours they spent as children sloshing in puddles, digging dirt with sticks, and climbing the bale stacks.

They walked the horses the rest of the way to the coulee. HoundDog caught up with them, her tongue nearly dragging on the ground in the heat. She ran ahead to the coulee, helpfully flushing out a family of white-tailed deer taking shelter from the sun. The doe and her fawns surged elegantly up the hill, white flags alerting the universe to the presence of a ravenous dog. Panting, HoundDog watched them flee.

The coulee was silent except for the lacy trill of a meadowlark and the startled squeak of a gopher. The riders slid off their horses, leaving them to graze in the shade. The horses could step on the reins that now drooped around their heads, and if they broke the bridles, Barbie would be furious. *We won't be here long. It probably won't happen.*

Curtis flopped down in the tall grass, carving a boy-shaped cave under the arching blue bowl of the sky. Eden lay beside him, enjoying the relief of the cool blades against her back and the vanilla scent of the clover crushed beneath them.

The grass was thick with vetch, buffalo bean, and wild rose, a bower above their heads. The rest of the world disappeared, leaving only Eden and Curtis, forgotten and free, with the hypnotic chomping of the horses in their ears and the scent of heaven in their nostrils.

Eden noticed a small cloud floating directly above them in the bottomless ocean of the sky. She blew at the cloud, and it obediently dissipated. She laughed in delight.

She sat up and looked at Curtis. His arms were lightly muscled, his waist slim and long. Eden's gaze traveled further; she was shocked to see Curtis's jeans straining at the zipper. She could see the outline against the worn denim of his cut-offs, the mysterious shape of a man.

Eden knew from observing the farm animals what must transpire for the world to recreate itself. At the age of fourteen, she grasped the mechanics of sex but not the sway of desire. After staring in fascination and sympathy, she glanced up at Curtis's face. His head twisted to the right, and his eyes were closed.

Does he even know what is happening to his body? Perhaps, she thought, although Curtis was not normal in his brain, in this particular way, he was. He could be normal in a million ways if only the rest of the world could understand him. Eden's heart broke for her friend as he lay silent and still before her.

With a sense of wonder and a surge of hope that almost choked her, she unzipped Curtis's jeans, freeing his body from its constraints. To Eden, this private part of him was beautiful, like the sky and the flowers and the fat-bottomed bee buzzing inches from their heads.

What if, she thought, *this* would bring Curtis out of his stupor? This would be the answer Donnie and Vic had sought for so many years, the secret to brushing aside the curtains in his mind. This would make him turn and smile at her. This. So simple and natural. So normal.

Eden wriggled out of her shorts and panties and pushed herself gently onto Curtis. It hurt at first, but Eden persisted as Curtis lay immobile beneath her. With a gasp, Eden lowered herself farther onto his body. There had always been a sacred place where her lost sister Ava dwelled, somewhere below her heart. Curtis now inhabited this sanctuary, a private room of pain and pleasure, safe from judgment or harm.

Ava, Eden thought, instinctively moving over Curtis's prone form. *Curtis*. When he made a soft sound she barely heard over the meadowlark's song, she grew still, suspended in a moment she knew would live in her body's memory forever. Her cloak of tangled hair encircled them as she bowed her head, focused solely on their joining, feeling the universe condense into the cool green grotto where Eden, Ava, and Curtis were one.

When she raised her head, a thought occurred to her. Shouldn't they kiss? In the movies, this didn't happen without kissing first. Maybe they had done it all wrong. Maybe *this* was all wrong.

As she leaned forward to kiss Curtis, he finally reacted. Waving his arms and crying out, he started to rise, and they were uncoupled, Eden falling backward into the grass. She quickly slipped on her clothes while Curtis scurried over to the horses. His jeans were still unzipped and partially pulled down, revealing slim, white buttocks. He picked up Patches's reins, looking agitated and uncertain.

Eden walked over to Blackie, who was indeed standing on his reins. Fortunately, he stepped away from them when she shoved him with her shoulder. She led him to a large boulder and mounted while Curtis and Patches followed, reins straggling on the ground. Patches, bless her, stood patiently while Curtis buttoned his jeans, climbed on the stone, and swung his leg over her wide back. Eden leaned down to grab the reins and hand them to Curt. He took them without looking at her.

Despite the rare opportunity to gorge on the coulee's delicacies, the horses were frantic to get going. Blackie flung his head and pulled at the bit until Eden gave him his head, and they sailed home, Patches several paces behind due to her rotund figure. This was always the best part of the ride because if the horses were reluctant to run—given their indolent natures, this was often the case—they were always more than willing to gallop home to the barn.

Today was no different, but Eden's thoughts were elsewhere. *I'm not a virgin anymore. What if I get pregnant? What if Curtis didn't like it? What if somebody found out? I would be in big, big trouble.* But no, she thought, it probably won't happen.

HoundDog appeared in the ditch, keeping up with the horses as they sprinted into the wind. Eden was horrified to see the dog's muzzle speared with porcupine quills.

"Houndie!" she cried. "Hang on. Come on, girl!"

Barbie and Donnie were in the garden, shading their eyes with their hands as they talked, when Eden and Curtis galloped into the yard, HoundDog right behind them. Eden jumped off Blackie before he came to a full stop.

"HoundDog got tangled with a porcupine!"

The women immediately turned to the dog. Donnie wrapped her arms around the hound's neck to calm her. "Oh, girlie, you're growing whiskers."

With an annoyed glance at Eden, Barbie turned toward the house to fetch pliers and antiseptic. "Where are your saddles? Where were you? Were you keeping an eye on 'Dog?"

"I don't know where she went. We were just down at the coulee for a little while."

"Okay, I want you cleaned up before supper. Your legs are filthy."

Curtis slid off Patches and followed Barbie into the house. By the time Eden settled the horses, Donnie had extracted the quills from HoundDog's nose and mouth, and the dog was lying half under the porch, eyes closed as she commenced the labour of healing.

* * *

Everything was just so *normal* about the rest of the day. Curtis claimed his favourite spot on the staircase landing, where he rocked back and forth on his bottom and stared up at the ceiling. Donnie attempted to scrub the horse off the boy, but he resisted a tad more than he usually did, twisting and crying while she swabbed him, then slumping in what Eden recognized as a sulk for the rest of the evening.

Barbie invited Donnie and Curtis to stay for supper as she always did, and this time, Vic and the girls were coming, too. Eden went upstairs to shower, nervously skirting Curtis on the landing. He didn't appear to notice she was there.

She shampooed her long hair twice, then gently cleansed between her legs where she was tender and slightly swollen. She wondered how Curtis felt. Does sex hurt boys, too? She always assumed she would wait until she got married to have sex. *But no one will ever know about this. I won't tell anybody!*

"Eden, please mash the potatoes and make the gravy," Barbie said when Eden reappeared in the kitchen. Barbie was frying hamburger patties, and Donnie was making a salad.

The door burst open to admit George Senior, Vic, and Curtis's sisters. The spacious kitchen suddenly felt smaller; George alone filled most of the room.

Eden's father was broad-shouldered and shaped like a barrel. His stomach pooched over his belt, which barely kept his jeans tethered to his narrow hips. Barbie often wondered aloud why he didn't lose weight when he stopped drinking four years ago, but his bulk defined him—he was large in every possible way.

Today, he was talking about the hay crop. "Looks like we'll have double last year," he was saying to Vic. "I'm going to start mowing in about ten days unless Krasinski starts earlier, then I'll have to get going, too." The men laughed about his longstanding rivalry with a neighbour.

"Vic, want a rye?" George bellowed as the little girls scampered to the living room where the colour television mumbled to itself in the corner. Vic and Donnie hadn't sprung for a colour set yet, so the girls were enthralled.

When George joined AA, he insisted on keeping booze in the house for company. For years, Barbie monitored the forty-ounce bottle of Canadian Club rye whisky that lived under the sink, but never once did she have reason to suspect George was dipping into it. She was finally beginning to relax; it seemed he really had quit.

"Oh, no, I'm fine," Vic said, knowing George wouldn't take no for an answer. George deftly mixed short rye and gingers for Vic, Donnie, and Barbie, then poured himself a tall glass of Coke, settling at his usual place at the kitchen table and lighting a cigarette.

"What are River and Skylar up to? Will they be home for supper?" Barbie strained to reach into the cupboard above the stove. "Eden, can you grab the seasoning salt for me?"

Eden was already taller than her mother and broader across the shoulders and hips. Like River and Skylar, she took after her father. George Junior, to his misfortune, was built much like his mother. The whole family doubted he would ever get married.

"River's at Stacey's for supper, and Skylar was in town earlier, but I don't know if he'll come home. He might go straight to the dance," George said, with an aside to Vic. "Got a new honey over to Elder Valley, might not see him for weeks!"

Barbie shook her head. "It would be nice if they would let me know. There's a phone right there on the wall!"

"What about George Junior?" George asked.

"He's been upstairs all day." Barbie took over from Eden to give the potatoes a final expert mashing. "His asthma is just terrible at this time of year," she said to Donnie. Barbie liked to emphasize the various ailments afflicting her brood in an attempt to commiserate about Curtis and his troubles. As if there is any comparison, Eden thought.

"George! Get down here for supper." George was confident his voice would carry up the stairs and to the back of the house, where his son was probably lying on his bed reading comic books. Everyone within miles could hear him.

George Junior must have been on the way because he appeared on the landing.

"Hey, there, Curt, what's happening?" he said. Curtis continued staring at his feet. George Junior walked over to the table, gave Vic a friendly poke, and sat down beside him.

"Oh, shoot, I forgot about Doris!" Barbie exclaimed. "Eden, run down to Grandma's and see if she wants to eat with us."

"Why can't George go? I'm up to my elbows in gravy here."

"Eden, go!" her father ordered, and out she went, running down the path to her grandmother's tiny house in the trees. Now in her eighties and widowed for thirty years, Doris clung to the land like a prairie cactus, stubbornly proving year after year she didn't need to move into the seniors' lodge. Eden found her on her knees pulling weeds in her immaculate vegetable garden.

"Grandma, Mom says come for supper! Sorry we're asking so late. Vic and Donnie and the kids are here, and we're going to the dance later." Eden gasped for breath.

Doris rose stiffly to her feet, reaching for the cane she sometimes used. "I'm fine. Already ate. It's almost six thirty!"

"Yeah, sorry. Curt and I went riding, and then HoundDog got into it with a porcupine and Donnie had to pull the quills out, and I think Mom got behind with supper."

"That dog! Always getting into something—if it isn't a porcupine, it's a skunk or a badger. More trouble than she's worth!"

"Okay, Grandma, I'll see you later, maybe tomorrow." Eden turned toward the path. *I'm starving! Riding and sex can really give a person an appetite.* She hid her blushing cheeks from the old woman in case she could read her mind.

Doris looked at her granddaughter thoughtfully. "Mind yourself at the dance, now. Lots of young men on the prowl; they'll be taking a look at you."

Eden smiled and waved. "I'll come over tomorrow and tell you all about them."

"Watch out for those Pedersen boys," Doris called after her. "If they're anything like their grandfather was at their age..." But Eden was too far along the path to be pulled into Doris's memory. She would hear all about it soon enough.

By the time she got back, Barbie had covered the table with steaming bowls and platters laden with more food than the nine of them could eat in one sitting. Fried hamburger patties, mashed potatoes and gravy, salad with fresh garden lettuce and homemade vinaigrette dressing (oil, vinegar, and a dash of sugar), green beans and corn from last year's garden, freshly baked bread, milk, and iced tea.

Curtis was set up with a tray in front of the television, but his sisters had to sit at the table with the adults. The television was set to a low volume so it would not disturb the diners.

"Grandma already ate," Eden announced as she slipped into her chair. Barbie rolled her eyes; they could set their watches by Doris and her routines, especially at supper time.

Eden's father was expounding about the rising price of farm equipment, Donnie was fretting about HoundDog and how well her wounds would heal, the little girls—Angela, aged nine, and Carol, eight—were smearing potatoes on one another's clothes, Vic was attentively listening to George Senior, and George Junior was shoveling food into his mouth without engaging in any of the commotion.

"Hey, George, you going to the dance?"

He looked up, startled. "What dance?" His eyes focused reluctantly on his sister.

"What *dance*? Leanne's and Travis's wedding dance! You know!"

George Junior did know; Leanne had been a classmate since Grade One. Leanne and Travis had planned their wedding mere weeks before George, Leanne, and thirty other Grade Twelve students would celebrate their high school graduation.

Word was that Leanne had always wanted a June wedding. The whole community knew the couple was five months pregnant, and that Leanne's parents had insisted they get married as soon as possible. With the bride and groom from prominent South Country ranch families, their wedding dance promised to be a big, boisterous affair. Nobody wanted to miss it.

"Don't you have to babysit?" George motioned with his eyebrows at Angela and Carol, who were now kicking one another.

Eden often babysat for Vic and Donnie, but not tonight. She wanted to go to this dance. All her friends would be there, and she even had a new dress from the Sears spring and summer catalogue, a polyester double-knit halter dress, perfect for a hot evening like this.

Now that she was almost fifteen, she was filling out a bit. She would probably never be as curvy as Barbie—certainly, she'd never be as petite—but she knew the dress was flattering.

She looked down at her plate, suddenly recalling what had happened earlier in the day. It seemed surreal; perhaps it hadn't happened at all. But the tenderness between her legs reminded her it was real.

She was simultaneously horrified and smug. If she could tell her friends—and she *couldn't*—they would have to agree she was ahead of her time. No one in their grade was even dating yet; well, except for Celeste. But she was a slut.

Eden had a disturbing thought. What if she got drunk and accidentally told someone? She glanced over at Curtis lying under the coffee table. *No one would believe me. The secret's safe with us.*

"What are you smirking about?" George kicked her under the table. "Got a date tonight?"

She kicked him back. "What about you? Who are you taking to the dance?"

He shrugged. "Not going."

"Loser," Eden said affectionately. Nobody was ever going to marry George.

Chapter 2

The sun was setting behind orange and navy stripes as George Senior, Barbie, and Eden stepped into the prickly field near the community hall. Cars and trucks lined the street and most parking spots in the field were full. As expected, everyone was coming to the dance.

Eden ran ahead, pushing through the crowd to the door. Feeling shy, she stopped to get her bearings. *Where are Louisa and Carrie?*

The first person she recognized was Celeste, who was standing with a sweaty knot of boys near the door. Then she saw her friends across the room. She made her way to them with difficulty, dodging another gang of inebriated high school boys.

"Look at those..." Louisa said, her eyes fixed on Celeste and her entourage.

"...big..." Carrie continued.

"...hooters?" Eden finished the sentence and the three of them collapsed into one another's arms, cackling like helpless hens.

Despite the well-rehearsed joke and the familiar and accepting arms of her friends, Eden felt oddly detached. Was it so funny? What would Louisa and Carrie say if they knew about her and Curtis?

The truth was everyone thought Curtis was creepy. At school, he was in a classroom with a kid named Gordie. The special education teacher taught them in the morning, and their parents picked them up before lunch. No one had ever played with Curtis and Gordie at recess. Not even Eden. Of course, Curtis didn't know how to play.

George and Barbie were surrounded by friends. Her father was a magnet at events like this; his sobriety had not detracted from his popularity. He was half a head taller than everyone in the room, and his voice could be heard in every corner.

Eden scanned the room for her brothers. Near the dance floor, River watched the festivities with an arm around his girlfriend, Stacey. She was the daughter of a local rancher and farm auctioneer; Barbie said Stacey knew the meaning of hard work. Eden's parents agreed she would make a good rancher's wife. Everyone expected them to be engaged by Christmas.

She saw Skylar with his friends—their table had disappeared beneath a brown field of stubby beer bottles. As she watched, he took a long swig, wiped his mouth, and laughed so loudly she heard him across the room. *Drunk already*. In many significant ways, he was a replica of his father. One of the girls draped her arm around Skylar's neck. Something about her reminded Eden of Celeste.

The band was assembling on stage. As the musicians picked up their instruments—banjo, accordion, saxophone, trumpet, and drums—the band leader, Dr. Christianson, announced the grand march. The bride and groom and their wedding party were arriving! Conversations gradually faded as the men and boys clogging the door made way for Mr. and Mrs. Travis Clement.

The newlyweds looked bewildered by the attention. It had been a long day following orders from both sets of parents determined to celebrate despite the scandal of the pregnancy. However, it was common for young couples, even high school students, to come to the altar in this circumstance. Eden suspected Barbie and George had River on the way when they got married twenty-five years ago.

As Travis and Leanne shuffled alone in the middle of the hall—the band was doing a credible job of "You Are the Sunshine of My Life"—George Senior and his friends weaved through the crowd collecting money in old cowboy boots. At midnight, when the revelers would pause to feast on cold cuts, buns, salads, pickles, and a wide selection of squares and cookies, the men would present the money to the happy couple. Then they could escape into the starlit night, taking their burdens and hopes to a hotel room for a one-night honeymoon. Real life started the next day, right after the gift-opening luncheon at Leanne's parents' home.

The grand march was over, and couples were swinging onto the dance floor. Eden felt a meaty hand on her arm—her father, asking her to dance.

George was an excellent dancer. Light on his feet despite his bulk, he expertly guided his daughter in a lively two-step. As they twirled in perfect harmony, Eden noticed River and Stacey dancing together, and Vic and Donnie. A glance at the corner revealed that Skylar and his followers had left the hall. George Junior was standing in the back with the other single men, holding a beer. *I knew he wouldn't miss Leanne's wedding dance.*

George Senior smelled of cologne and clean sweat—no whisky fumes, Eden noted with relief. Barbie wasn't the only guardian of George's sobriety; the whole family watched him with foreboding at gatherings like this. In the drunk days, George would be stumbling, slurring, and leaning on the arms of his friends by now. Barbie would be preparing to take him home in tight silence. These days, she didn't even take the truck keys away when they arrived at a dance—she trusted him that much now.

George twirled Eden around in a full circle, coming to a graceful stop as the band finished the song.

"They have a long road ahead of them," George said, nodding at Leanne and Travis, who were preparing to cut the wedding cake for photographs and then distribute plastic-wrapped fruit cake slices and thank you notes to their guests. Barbie had a drawer of petrified fruit cake from decades of weddings. She said it was bad luck to eat wedding cake; apparently, it was also bad luck to dispose of it.

George looked down with affection at this daughter who had grown as high as his heart in the past year. "It's a little young to start a family, don't you think?"

Eden shrugged. "Weren't you and Mom young when you got married?"

George nodded. "Yes, your mom was nineteen and I was twenty-one, so we were young. But I already had the farm and cattle. I'd been out of school since ninth grade, so I had a little bit of money. We weren't starting from scratch. The Clements don't have much money or land, so Travis will be on his own supporting a wife and kid. Don't envy him much."

He spoke so quietly Eden had to strain to hear him. "I'm glad you kids have more options now. But let this be a lesson—don't get into Leanne's position so you can take advantage of all those opportunities when you finish school. Don't settle, Eden."

This manner of talk was so unlike George that Eden took another sniff, wondering if he *had* been drinking. But before she could detect any odour over the reek of cigarette smoke in the room, George's friends swept him away, and Eden was recaptured by Louisa, Carrie, and other girls from her class. She followed them gladly to line up at the bar for pop.

Hours later, Eden watched a crescent moon keep pace with the truck as the ribbon road unfurled behind them. Insects splattered against the windshield or plummeted to their deaths in the headlights. Barbie and George were discussing the evening, laughing as they companionably shared a cigarette.

Eden was caught up in her own thoughts— Leanne's swollen ankles revealed briefly when Travis removed her blue garter with his teeth and tossed it into the crowd (George Junior caught it, which was hilarious!); Celeste leaving the hall with Jason Pedersen and never returning; Skylar's brief reappearance after an obvious necking session with the girl from Elder Valley; River and Stacey's entwined hands as they politely bid Barbie and George good night.

Eden was thinking about love, about what her father had said about options, about Curtis. As she nodded into sleep, she thought about her sister Ava and the place where she—and now Curtis—lived forever, deep in her body.

When they pulled into the yard, George Junior's blue truck was parked by the house. River and Skylar weren't home, no surprise there. Eden gazed up at a shimmery spray of stars, the silver droplets so close she could feel their cold sparks. A cricket chorus ushered them into their waiting beds.

The sun was already up when the telephone on the kitchen wall startled them awake. It was their ring on the party line—long, long, short; long, long, short.

Eden heard her father's ponderous step in the kitchen, his hoarse, sleep-heavy voice answering the phone, a long silence, and then his anguished cry shaking the house.

"Barbie!"

* * *

Skylar rolled his truck driving his girlfriend home to Elder Valley. He missed the turn, and the truck flipped end-to-end, plowing into a wheat field. The police had to use the Jaws of Life to pry him out of the crumpled cab.

A passing farmer found the girl, Jennifer Miller, sprawled and weeping in the mangled field. He held her while the sun rose on a perfect South Country morning, but by the time help arrived, her life had seeped into the cool mercy of the earth.

All summer, on their way to Regina to visit Skylar in the hospital, Barbie and George laid flowers at the small white cross Jennifer's parents placed where their daughter died.

The English family sat in the back row at the funeral, flattened by sorrow into cardboard cutouts of themselves. At the reception, to be polite, they nibbled on open-faced buns topped with egg and tuna salad, then slipped away to drive the lonely road home, where they each sought solitude—Barbie and Doris in their gardens, weeding by hand; George Senior in the pasture, checking the cattle; George Junior on his bed, reading; and River in the shop, tuning his truck. Eden went to the barn to fling her arms around Patches's neck, sobbing to the beat of the horse's steadfast heart.

As Doris noted on the way home, no one had spoken to them at the funeral.

It was a summer of silence. George's booming voice faded. Barbie's light dimmed. Few vehicles disturbed the dust on the gravel road leading to the English's yard; no one spilled out seeking conversation and coffee or a well-timed invitation to supper. HoundDog, healed and contrite from the porcupine encounter, rarely barked.

River and George Junior were seldom home. River was busy establishing his own farm and George Junior had taken a job at the lumberyard in Everview, finding this easier on his inflamed lungs than haying or summer fallowing. Eden, too young for a summer job and largely ignored by her mother, went on long rides, giving Patches and Blackie their exercise by turns.

Only reckless gallops across the fields, her hair billowing behind her like the horse's tail, lifted Eden from the dispirited atmosphere of her home.

She found herself spending more time with Grandma Doris than she usually did. It was difficult to tell if her presence was welcomed or merely tolerated. Doris was a loner.

On the day Eden turned fifteen, she wandered listlessly down the path to see what her grandmother was doing. She never looked forward to her birthday.

Barbie often spent the day crying for Ava; the only time in the year she indulged in obvious grief for her lost baby. By the time the family gathered for a perfunctory birthday celebration, Barbie was typically lying on her bed with a wet dish towel over her eyes.

The boys would try to jolly things up, and George Senior would give her a gift—this year, she was hoping for a cassette recorder—but it was shaping up to be another non-birthday. Earlier that day, Barbie and George drove to Regina to bring Skylar home from the hospital. He had been in the rehabilitation wing for ten weeks.

Doris was in her kitchen making crab apple jelly. Eden flopped on the couch, resting her head on one of Doris's crocheted pillows. At this time of the day, Doris liked to reminisce about the journey she made—all on her own—from North Dakota to the South Country with a team and wagon and three cows to join Grandpa James on his homestead. Doris had left her mother and siblings to come to the land James had staked out, to marry a man she barely knew. She was sixteen. Once they got a shack built, her mother and younger brothers joined them in Saskatchewan.

The five of them lived together in the two-room shack that first brutal winter, heating it with wood from the coulees and coal from a neighbour's mine. In the spring, Doris gave birth to Irma, her first child. Irma was buried five days later in the community cemetery a mile from the homestead. It was a story Eden had heard a thousand times.

Today, though, Doris sank into her armchair and said, "You look like death warmed over."

"Do I?" Eden pushed herself into a sitting position. "I don't know. I feel like I have the flu."

"Come here and let me feel your head. No, you're not hot. You look pale, but you're obviously eating. Put on some weight, I see."

Eden was self-conscious about her weight. She favoured her father but dreaded becoming a large person like he was. She had to admit her t-shirts were tight. She needed to go on a diet before school started.

Doris looked out of the window, a little tremor in her mouth as she gazed at the lilac bushes bordering her yard. At this time of year, they were flowerless and turning yellow. Beyond the yard, the barley field was a sea of tufted golden waves.

"You know, it's been in the family for a long time," she said. Eden had no idea what she was talking about, but prepared to listen politely, like she always did.

Doris looked at Eden with softened eyes. "Your great-grandfather—my father—drank himself to death. I'm not sure I ever told you that. He left Mother with three children and no money. Thank God my Jim came along when he did. And Jim liked his drink, too. I always thought the Depression saved him. We didn't have money for liquor or anything else. We ate what we could raise on the farm, and that was it. But your Daddy—he carried on the family tradition." Doris chuckled ruefully.

"Dad quit drinking. He goes to AA."

"Oh, I know it, thank the Lord. But now Skylar... well, he's in line for a lot of trouble in life if he doesn't watch out. It's so much easier to be an alcoholic now than it was in the Depression. Everyone has money."

Eden thought about Skylar in the hospital, pinned down by tubes and plaster, his eyes glazed with pain. His vacant stare made her wonder if he even recognized her. He was paying a steep price for pushing away from a groaning table of empty bottles and driving through the night with one hand on the steering wheel and the other wrapped around his girl.

People in the community blamed Skylar for Jennifer's death. Louisa had filled her in during a long telephone conversation recently.

Doris turned her eyes to Eden, the softness gone. "You don't have to mope around about Skylar, you know. He just needs more time. I don't buy that brain injury nonsense. Brains heal, just like bones. He's a tough character."

Eden was less than certain about that. Although she had only seen Skylar twice since the accident, she had heard Barbie and George talking late at night. They were worried Skylar would never be the same.

She heaved herself off the couch and raked her hair off her face. "I think I'll give Blackie a run. See you later at dinner, Grandma?"

"Oh, that's right, it's somebody's birthday, so they tell me. Take your present up to the house now, so I don't have to carry it when I come over."

Doris reached behind the armchair for a large, loosely wrapped gift tucked under a pile of crocheted afghans. It was soft and pillowy; another afghan, Eden guessed. *Oh, well. Another non-birthday gift for another non-birthday.*

Eden had hoped to invite Louisa and Carrie for supper, but that wasn't going to happen. There was too much going on—Skylar was coming home, River was fencing, and her father was trying to get the grain truck and combine tuned up and ready for harvest. The crops were ripening rapidly, and, with all the trips to see Skylar, George was running behind. Eden knew better than to even ask.

She stopped at the house to deposit her new afghan beside the television, where family birthday gifts were traditionally placed before opening. No other gifts had accumulated there. *Sigh.*

Blackie was hard to catch; Eden had to entice him with a handful of oats. She slipped the hackamore bridle over his ears and buckled it under his jaw to give him a break from the bit. Barbie wasn't around to object and probably wouldn't have noticed anyway.

This might be a good year, Eden thought as she neck-reined Blackie out of the yard. Everyone might leave me alone now that I'm fifteen. That would be nice for a change. She felt woozy as Blackie walked away from the yard. She'd been dizzy all day. *Must be the heat.* She didn't urge Blackie into a gallop.

"Let's just take it easy today," she said, patting his slick neck. The horse rotated his ears conversationally, listening to her voice and snorting from the dust. HoundDog was following at a distance, burying her nose in gopher and badger holes, looking for trouble.

When she got back to the yard, Eden was surprised to see so many vehicles. Mom and Dad were home, and there was Donnie's car, and George Junior's truck, but whose truck was that? Everyone was admiring a gleaming bronze Ford truck with white sides and hood. Skylar was leaning on his crutches, looking gratified and confused. Slipping off Blackie, Eden approached the group, letting the horse graze near the house while she held the reins.

"Insurance just came in, so we thought we'd pick it up today," her father was saying to Donnie, who looked admiringly at the truck and sidelong at Skylar; he had lost thirty pounds and looked like a starving waif. There was no Skylar-swagger left in the boy.

"What do you think, Sky?" Barbie asked, hand on her son's arm.

George Junior slapped the fender. "Excellent wheels, man. Soon you'll get back on the horse, eh?"

Skylar limped painfully to the porch. HoundDog nearly upended him, but Donnie quickly intervened, distracting the dog as everyone moved toward the house. Eden twitched the reins to pull Blackie from the tender grass. In protest, he emptied his bowels in a steaming heap by the step.

Patches stood anxiously at the fence, yearning for her equine companion. Eden opened the gate to let Blackie into the barnyard, pulled the bridle off the miscreant, gave him a scolding slap on the rump, and went with resignation to the barn to get a shovel. *Fun times at the English household tonight. Big birthday celebration. Yay.*

When she came into the kitchen, she noticed Donnie had prepared supper. Barbie was sitting at the table with a rye and ginger, and George Junior was setting the table. No Curtis this time; Donnie had left the kids at home with Vic, knowing Barbie and George would be exhausted and Skylar overwhelmed after his extended hospital stay.

Eden leaned into Donnie's birthday hug for a couple of moments longer than she had intended. She was so tired, and Skylar looked so completely wrecked. Donnie's plump arms were a balm for the soul on this non-birthday to beat all non-birthdays.

How nice of her to make supper. Eden could see an iced cake with candles in a pan on the counter. She glanced into the living room. *Nope, no more presents. Just Grandma's afghan.*

Skylar and George Junior sat down in front of the television. It was six o'clock, time for *The Wonderful World of Disney*. Tinkerbell was lighting the top of the Disney castle, and the familiar theme song filled the house. Skylar stared at the television, mesmerized. A small smile teased his lips. He had always liked *The Wonderful World of Disney*.

Eden's father whistled the tune as he came out of the bedroom in his work clothes.

"Doris should be here right away," he said to Donnie. "Let's eat so I can go milk." Thanks, Dad, Eden thought. I won't take up much of your time opening presents, so you can go do your chores. George turned back to the bedroom and returned carrying an unopened Sears package, which he placed beside the television.

"Happy birthday, kiddo." He patted her on the head. "Fifteen, wow. Barbie, our baby's grown." Barbie took this as a cue to start weeping about Ava.

Eden helped Donnie put the food on the table—a huge lasagna she had brought over, fresh corn on the cob, peas, and carrots, and a Caesar salad, Eden's favourite. Eden was so hungry she felt like throwing up. *Give me food, now!*

Doris stepped into the kitchen. Her cane clomped on the floor as she approached Skylar; he barely acknowledged her. Doris had not seen Skylar since the accident—she was disinclined to go to the city for any reason.

"Well," she said, "you've got yourself into a pickle. But you're in one piece. Just be grateful for that." Skylar merely shrugged. He and Doris were not close.

"And don't feel too bad about that girl. People may blame you, but everyone's time is coming. Only God knows when."

A horrified silence gripped the room, then George Senior exclaimed, "Donnie, where's your drink?" and Donnie said, "Supper's ready!" and Barbie said, "Eden, come here, honey. I haven't given you a birthday hug!" and George Junior urged Skylar to hobble to the table, and even River showed up at the last minute, filthy and ravenous.

They were all together again, and it wasn't a complete non-birthday after all. Donnie presented the cake with a dramatic bow and, as per tradition, Eden cut and served it after blowing out all fifteen candles in one puff.

After dessert, she opened her presents—a mauve chenille bedspread with an embossed daisy pattern from Doris (not an afghan!), and a cassette recorder with four tapes, a head cleaner, and an earphone. This outfit was even nicer than Louisa's!

She was excused from dishes—Barbie and Donnie wanted to talk, and Eden wanted to try out her new recorder. She smuggled the radio from its usual place on the refrigerator and spent the evening in her room, hitting the record button when her favourite songs came on. She cried a little, listening to a Cat Stevens song, thinking about Jennifer Miller, who had danced for a very short time on this earth and was now gone forever. *Forever*. It was unthinkable.

And Curtis? Their time together in the coulee had not changed him. He was still buried deep in a jumble of thoughts, oblivious to the touch of a loving hand.

Eden tossed and turned under her new bedspread. It was gloriously soft and luxurious, but much too heavy for a muggy night like this. She could hear Barbie and George talking in the living room.

"Shush, now," George said, and Eden knew without seeing them he was holding Barbie on his lap. She was so tiny; he often held her like a child during times of sorrow, or playfulness, or even while watching their favourite television program, *The Carol Burnett Show*.

Eden knew this was a private moment, but she listened, nonetheless. She could hardly avoid listening.

Barbie was crying about Ava, and also about Skylar. Her two lost babies.

"There's just... nothing there," Barbie said. Eden imagined her face buried in the shoulder of George's plaid work shirt.

"Not yet. Give him time. The doctor said brain injury takes a long time to heal."

"Some things never heal," Barbie said. "You know who he reminds me of now? Nobody more so than Curtis."

George paused. Perhaps he agreed. He said, "Nothing holds an English down for long. He'll find his way back. Good old-fashioned work will help, once he's on his feet. We'll have him picking bales before you know it."

"I just worry so much about all of them."

"Barbie, you always say lightning never strikes twice. They'll be okay."

Chapter 3

It was the first day of Grade Ten. Eden felt drained all summer, but now she was bursting with energy. The summer from hell was over; things could only get better.

When the school bus pulled into their yard, Eden and George Junior stepped on. George was training to work as a bus driver, so today he was shadowing Lance, who was nearing retirement.

George was beloved by the kids on the bus. "Sir Joimes!" they all cried. George acknowledged them with a regal wave, then took a seat behind Lance. They called him Sir Joimes because his middle name was James. *Shades of Barbie, but with more imagination.* Eden had a nickname, too—or, at least, Jason Pedersen thought so.

"Frenchie," he said with a nod when she sat down in the middle of the bus. He called her Frenchie because her name was English. *Please.* Eden ignored him. He thought he was so smart in tight Wrangler jeans and cowboy hat, a western shirt with two snaps undone.

Curtis was on the bus today. On good days, Donnie put him on the bus in the morning and then drove into town to pick him up after his class. Curtis hated it when other kids sat with him; he was known to kick if people got too close. He didn't want Eden or George to sit with him, and his sisters sat near the front with their friends, so he sat alone.

Having a seat to himself was only a big deal when the bus was filled to capacity, which was always the case on the first day of school. When the bus was full, students had to triple up in the seats built for two, and sometimes that led to fights. It always led to a busload of complaints.

Eden was Curtis's defender on the bus, whether she wanted to be or not. No one else would retaliate when books or garbage were thrown at him, spit back when kids spat on him, and respond with cutting comments when the taunting grew too intense. Over the years, kids learned not to mess with Curtis. Now, they just messed with Eden.

"Hey, Frenchie." Jason wouldn't let up until he got a rise out of her, but she was determined not to respond today. "Why don't you sit with your boyfriend? He looks lonely."

Jason Pedersen, you are in Grade Eleven. Grow up already. She hunched down in the seat, gazing at the crystalline September sky and the pregnant swaths of wheat, barley, and oats. A million dollars in the field just waiting for rain, hail, or snow to wash it all away, as Eden's father often said. The farmers were in a race against nature at harvest time; often, they came in on the losing end.

The bus lumbered along the blacktop, bulging with kids, backpacks, jackets, crayons, scribblers, books, new clothes—some kids had new clothes on the first day of school; others wore hand-me-downs for their entire school careers—squeaky clean running shoes, old stinky shoes, old resentments, new hatreds, unrequited loves, belly laughs, and outright spite. Spite was Jason Pedersen's specialty.

"Hey, Frenchie, you screwed him yet?" Eden cringed but didn't let it show. "Your little retarded boyfriend?"

With no response from Eden, Jason turned to Curtis. "Hey, Curtis, how's the pussy? You like licking pussy?"

The other boys were roaring, practically rolling in the aisle. *So funny, Jason. I've heard it all before.*

Still, it was hard to sit through this, especially after what had happened in June. Eden prayed Curtis didn't understand this dirty talk. Soon the bus would be turning into Carrie's yard, and she would join Eden in her seat. The torment usually eased off then.

Jason stood up, reached across the aisle, and flicked Curtis on the ear. Curtis screamed and thrust his head between his knees. Eden whirled to her feet and kicked Jason in the abdomen. She'd been aiming for his balls.

Jason collapsed into his seat. Eden was tall, strong from riding, and fast as a rattlesnake. And she'd given it everything she had. She *hated* Jason Pedersen with every molecule in her body. She would have *killed* him if she could.

The kids were still sniggering, but more quietly. They watched warily, wondering what would happen next. Did Eden have the upper hand? What would Jason do?

It took Jason a couple of moments to catch his breath, but when he straightened up, he had a wicked grin on his face. He wasn't going to let her win.

"Frenchie, Frenchie, what? You gonna kill me?" he said. "Another English killer on the loose? How's *Skylar* doing? He in jail yet?"

Eden was still standing, her mouth gaping. Even Jason Pedersen wouldn't say something like that! But he had. Before she could respond, an unearthly howl filled the bus, stopping every conversation. It even reached the men in the front. Lance signaled right to bring the bus to a stop.

Curtis was screaming in a way only Curtis could— mouth wide open, wordless, harrowing, horrible. Eden hadn't heard him scream that way since they were little kids. He flapped his arms and twisted his torso, striking the kids in the seats in front and behind him. The kids ducked down, and everyone looked scared.

George marched down the aisle. Curtis continued screaming, and George had to shout to be heard.

"What's going on?" he asked Eden. He looked at Jason. "What did you do, asshole?"

Jason stood up but, despite George's diminutive size, he was cowed. "Nothing. This retard is screaming. It's nothing to do with me."

Eden sat down. She knew the code well. No one in authority cared what one kid said to another. They might care about kicking, but she knew Jason would never say anything. She would never tell her parents or Curtis's parents. There was no point.

Lance joined them to assess the situation. Curtis was still screaming, and Eden was staring out the window. The other kids were trying desperately not to make eye contact. Everyone was uncomfortable with the screaming, which Eden and George knew could go on for hours.

This was a setback for Curtis. He had been successfully riding the bus most mornings for several years now. Lance decided to turn around and take Curtis home. The students would be late for school on their first day, but there was no help for it. He used the two-way radio to tell his supervisor about the delay. The kids on the bus sat quietly during this exchange; the little kids held their hands over their ears to muffle Curtis's cries.

When they finally made it to town, Eden noticed Jason held his ribs as he stepped off the bus. *Hope you're hemorrhaging, you jerk.*

She and Carrie slipped into their new homeroom and took seats at the back near Louisa. The teacher was babbling about how high school students, although they enjoyed new privileges, also had additional responsibilities.

At lunch, the girls retreated to the shady park across the street to eat and smoke. Louisa supplied cigarettes smuggled from her dad's pack. They felt very grown up; as high school students, they were allowed to leave the school grounds without permission. The drama and fury of the morning bus ride started to fade from Eden's thoughts.

Jason wasn't on the bus after school. Maybe he had to go to the doctor, Eden thought with a qualm. *Nah, he's tough as nails and would never admit to being hurt by a girl. I could get in trouble, but it probably won't happen.*

As the bus rumbled down the highway, stopping every few miles to expel hyper, grubby kids into sweltering farmyards, huge clouds amassed in the northwest, frothing like whipped cream edged with coffee.

When Eden entered the kitchen, Barbie said, "Can you take River some supper? You can take Dad's truck; he's working in the shop."

Barbie waved her hand through steam; she had a large quantity of Okanagan peaches blanching on the stove. Sweat was running off her face and dampening her short cotton dress.

"Can I take Patches? I can put the thermos in the saddlebags."

Barbie nodded distractedly. "Yes, yes, but get going. River has had a long day already and he wants to stay out there until dark."

Eden quickly changed out of her school clothes and ran to the barn. When she was back at the porch, Barbie placed George Junior's old Mickey Mouse lunch kit in one saddlebag and a thermos of coffee in the other, giving Patches an affectionate slap on the hindquarters.

"Watch the weather, okay?" Barbie looked at the sky. "I think the clouds are moving to the east, so you should be alright."

River was fencing two miles south of the yard on one of his recently purchased quarters. He wanted to run cattle on the quarter; the hay had been taken off, but there was enough new growth and water in the dugout to keep his small herd going for a few weeks.

As she and Patches drew near, Eden saw River standing in waist-high grass, driving a post into the ground with brute force. His truck was backed up to the fence to keep the posts and tools handy.

Fencing was arduous work on a hot day; River looked up eagerly when she hollered at him, throwing his work gloves on the ground beside the truck. HoundDog loped up to him, tongue dripping; River scratched the dog's ears.

Eden pulled Patches close, and River unlaced the saddlebags. At that moment, the wind changed direction, slapping them with cold relief from the muggy heat. They looked up at the sky; the whipped cream cloud was roiling but still far away.

"They might get hail in town," River said calmly, gazing at the cloud. The wind accelerated, dashing the tall grass against the barbed wire. HoundDog was snuffling along the fence, eagerness and joy evident in her upright tail. She must have found a terrified creature to harass, Eden thought.

They heard thunder as the hulking clouds began competing for position in the greenish sky. As they watched, sheet lightning streamed to the ground like an illuminated waterfall.

Patches pranced and turned; she hated storms. Eden tried to rein her in and noticed the horse's hair standing at full attention on her neck. She whinnied and tossed her head. As River reached up to grab the bridle, molten fire seethed along the barbed wire fence, scorching their faces with a blast of white heat.

Patches reared up, knocking River to the ground and dumping Eden in the dirt beside the truck. Eden heard an anguished yowl from HoundDog and a horrified screech from Patches as she galloped back toward the yard, empty stirrups flapping against her belly.

Eden's arms and legs were tingling painfully. When the next thunderclap came, she rolled toward the truck, her hands pressed tightly over her ears to protect her throbbing, numbed eardrums.

It was impossible to know if she was crying because the storm suddenly discharged a fire hose in her face, and she struggled to breathe. Her scream was drowned in icy water that flooded her mouth and sinuses.

She could feel River's hands pulling on her arm, but couldn't see or hear him. He opened the truck door and hauled her behind him into the cab, using all his strength to slam the door against the deluge. It was so dark and noisy in the rocking truck they could barely see one another or hear the other speak.

"HoundDog!" Eden screamed, and River said something—she couldn't make it out. She looked out of the window for the dog, but all she could see were dung-coloured streams of water on the glass.

River and Eden sat in soggy shock, as every few seconds the lightning revealed and then hid the storm from view. The rain turned to hail, slamming so hard against the windshield that River held the glass to prevent it from buckling inward. The glass shattered into a web of tiny prisms, but fortunately the windshield held, and they were protected, at least for now, by River's battered old Ford.

Eden was frantic with worry about HoundDog. She prayed the dog had scurried under the truck after the lightning strike and before the hail. The rain and hail were easing up, and she pressed her face against the back window, wiping it with her arm to clear the condensation. *Where is that dog?* Donnie said she had nine lives, like a cat; Eden hoped frantically it was true.

"Let's get out of here!" River cranked the ignition, but the motor wouldn't turn over, and within seconds the engine flooded. They took deep gulps of air, watching the storm pass and wondering what to do next.

"Stay here." River opened the driver's side door and walked behind the truck. Rain was still plunging down, but he was already soaked to the skin. In a moment, he returned, carrying a charred odour into the cab.

He turned to Eden with an ashen face, and she knew. HoundDog had been killed by the lightning. She had been standing right beside the barbed wire fence. She was burned. She was toast.

When George Senior's truck appeared over the hill, moving gingerly across the white slushy field, River and Eden were walking hand-in-hand, soaked, bereft, and shivering with shock. The sun was shining like nothing had happened; the storm clouds were shaking hands and congratulating themselves somewhere to the east.

They climbed into the warm, smoky cab. "Dad, we have to go back and get HoundDog," Eden said through tears. George looked at River, who shook his head solemnly.

"I'll go back for her after I get you home to Mom," George said as he cranked the truck around.

Chapter 4

Eden was in no shape for school the next day. Her face looked severely sunburned, and her hair and eyebrows were singed. Every muscle in her body was sore, and her heart was battered and broken.

If only she had called HoundDog away from the fence. If only she had taken the truck instead of riding Patches; HoundDog would not have followed the truck. Grandma Doris was right—HoundDog always looked for trouble. This time, trouble found her.

When she came downstairs mid-morning, Barbie was on the phone with Donnie, Skylar was watching television with his cast resting on the coffee table, and George Senior and River were out in the fields, checking the hail damage.

"George buried her in the shelter belt," Barbie was saying. "She looked like..." When she spotted Eden coming into the room, she abruptly changed the subject. "I think I'll take Eden to the doctor today. She seems okay, but you never know. Yeah, that was a close call if there ever was one. Okay, talk to you later."

Barbie hung up and turned to her daughter. "What would you like for breakfast? Eggs? French toast? Porridge?" She knew Eden loved porridge.

Eden shrugged. "Nothing, just juice," she said, going to the fridge. Barbie placed her hands gently on Eden's burned face.

"You and River are red today." She peered into Eden's eyes. "Are your eyes sore?"

"Everything's sore, Mom," Eden said, pouring Tang into a tall glass. She sank down dejectedly at the kitchen table.

"I'm going to call Dr. Christianson and ask if he can see you this afternoon," Barbie said, turning back to the telephone. Eden finished her Tang, then slipped on her rubber boots. She wanted to check on Patches.

The old horse was enjoying the cross draft in the barn, looking lazy and content. Blackie was nearby, pulling on a bale that George Senior had dropped into the corral for the horses. He wanted to keep them in the corral temporarily as a precaution. He was worried Patches might spook and try to jump the fence in the barn pasture, but at the moment Patches was dozing, her eyes half closed, one rear hoof cocked in pure relaxation.

What if we lost Patches, too? Eden thought. What if she ran toward the fence, instead of back to the yard? It was too horrifying to contemplate.

Back in the house, she sat sullenly beside Skylar—who was watching *Mister Rogers' Neighborhood*—waiting for Barbie to get ready to go to town.

"Does River have to go to the doctor, too?" Eden called out to her mother, who was in the bedroom changing her clothes.

"River is twenty-five years old and doesn't listen to me anymore," Barbie said. Eden could see her brushing her hair in front of the dresser mirror. "But you, my girl, do as I say. Let's get going."

Driving to Everview in Skylar's new truck was a treat. He couldn't drive it yet and took little interest in it, but Eden was charmed by the new vehicle smell and the spotless interior. She knew that wouldn't last long.

"Now, Eden," Barbie was saying, "be sure to tell the doctor everything you are feeling. Are your ears okay? Do you have a headache? Where does it hurt? Tell him everything, okay?"

Eden shrugged. "Sure." Her eyes welled up as she thought about HoundDog. *How are we going to go on without HoundDog?* She was feeling shaky.

"It's normal to feel a bit shaky after an experience like that," Barbie said, reading Eden's mind in the annoying way she had. "Don't be too hard on yourself. Let's stop at the school and pick up some homework for you. Maybe you can stay home for the rest of the week."

"Mom, I don't need to stay home. I'm fine."

"You were nearly electrocuted. Let's see what Dr. Christianson says."

The Saskatchewan Wheat Pool, United Grain Growers, and Pioneer grain elevators cast vigilant shadows over the deserted streets as they drove through town. They pulled up beside one other vehicle parked in front of the medical clinic.

Eden sat in the waiting room reading *Ladies' Home Journal* while her mother spoke with Mrs. Samuels, the receptionist. The women were comparing notes about the hail damage when Dr. Christianson's office door opened. Eden was startled to see Celeste and her mother, Odette, walk through the waiting room and out to the street. Celeste glanced at Eden, then looked away quickly. Eden shrugged and went back to her magazine.

"Okay, young miss, I hear you had an exciting evening," Dr. Christianson said to Eden, motioning for her to enter his office. Barbie and Eden sat across from him while he asked questions about the lightning strike and storm that Barbie answered to the best of her ability, even though she wasn't there, thought Eden, with an internal eye roll.

"Eden, let's give you a quick check-up," Dr. Christianson said. "Mom, can you wait outside for just a minute?"

Eden moved to the examination table, where she endured poking and prodding. The doctor used a light to examine her eyes and ears, took her blood pressure, then listened to her heart with a stethoscope. Eden flinched when he placed the cold instrument on her chest.

"A little sore here, is it?"

"Ouch," she said, as he pressed harder.

"Are your breasts tender?"

"Kinda," Eden said, embarrassed.

"Well, that's common at your age. How old are you now? Fourteen?"

"I just had my fifteenth birthday." Eden winced as he moved the stethoscope to various locations on her torso.

"And how are your periods?" The doctor pushed her shoulders downwards to indicate she should lie on the table.

"They're good," she said.

"When was your last one?" the doctor asked, tapping on her abdomen with two fingers and pressing tender spots near her pelvis.

Eden thought about it. "Well... I'm not sure. Back in the spring."

"Spring? Are you sure? Well, irregular periods are pretty common at your age, too." He motioned for Eden to sit up. "Any other pain? How have you been feeling lately?" he asked, regarding her through smudged glasses.

"Well, I've been tired this summer, but I don't think that has anything to do with almost getting hit by lightning."

"Really? Tired in what way?"

"I guess just tired and not feeling like doing too much."

"Your brother was in an accident, wasn't he? It's been a tough summer for you folks. But I think I'll run a few tests, just to see if anything else is going on. Mrs. Samuels will take a blood sample and a urine sample, and then you can go. I have some cream you can take home that might help soothe your reddened skin."

After enduring more poking and mastering the gymnastics moves required to urinate into a plastic cup, Eden joined her mother in the waiting room. As they were preparing to leave, Dr. Christianson opened his door.

"Barbie, could you step in here for a moment, please?"

Resigned, Eden picked up the magazine again, opening it randomly. As a child, she knew better than to predict how long she would have to wait for the adults to finish their conversation. It was possible the doctor wanted to speak with Barbie about Skylar and his recovery.

She looked at a headline in the magazine, "Can This Marriage Be Saved? I Was Terrified to Tell My Husband I Was Pregnant." As she reached involuntarily to touch the tender place above her pubic bone—the secret place she now shared with her sister Ava and Curtis—she perceived another entity there, too. With a surge of great tenderness, horror, and tentative joy, she knew she had a little daughter.

When Dr. Christianson's door opened and he gestured for her to enter his office, Eden was already crying. She was terrified and overjoyed; exhausted and energized. She wanted to run from the room to embrace the endless prairie skies; she wanted to curl into a ball on the worn, brown carpet of the doctor's office.

Barbie was pale. She did not reach for Eden or look with sympathy upon her tears. Eden could feel her mother's anger and disbelief as clearly as she could see her own clenched, white-knuckled hands as she looked down at her lap.

Dr. Christianson took his seat and cleared his throat. "Eden, it looks like you might be pregnant," he said, peering kindly through his thick lenses. "Is that possible?"

Eden shook her head, wiping tears with the back of one hand and raking her hair away from her face with the other.

"Eden!" Barbie said. "Is it possible?"

"I don't know."

"What do you mean, you don't know! Is it possible or is it not?" Barbie's voice was getting louder with each word, and Eden was sure Mrs. Samuels could hear from the other side of the door. But then she remembered—Mrs. Samuels already knew she was pregnant.

Dr. Christianson said to Barbie, "We will confirm the urine test at the lab, but these days the office tests are pretty definitive. I could also detect the pregnancy when I did the pelvic exam."

To Eden he said, "We need you to think very carefully about when you had your last period."

Eden cupped her baby with both hands, lovingly, defensively. "Um, I think it was in May because I remember that I had bad cramps in math class, and I went to the office to get some pills from Mrs. Michelchuk."

"May!" Barbie exclaimed. "How is that possible? Why didn't you tell me, Eden?"

"I don't know."

Barbie threw up her hands.

"Well," the doctor said, addressing Barbie. "If she's only about fourteen weeks along, there is still time to terminate, but we'll have to act quickly."

"Terminate?" Eden sat up straighter and stared at the doctor. "What do you mean?" She turned to her mother, but Barbie wasn't looking at her daughter.

"How do we go about doing that?"

"There is a committee in the city that will look at this case and I know one of the doctors. I can try to expedite their decision, but in this case, given Eden's age, it probably won't be a problem. I can make a call today."

"M-o-o-o-o-m!"

"Hush now, Eden. We'll talk about it on the way home. We have to see what your dad thinks."

"Mom, no!!" Eden flailed at her mother, striking her with an open hand. "No! I don't want to. No!"

"I will have the lab report back by the end of the week, but we should get going if this is the route you want to take."

"Please contact your friend and I'll call you tomorrow." Barbie rose to go. "We will go up to Regina as soon as you can make the arrangements."

Mrs. Samuels glanced up apprehensively as Barbie and Eden quickly passed her desk; neither of them looked at her. As soon as the truck doors slammed and they were alone, Barbie grabbed Eden's shoulders and looked piercingly into her tear-streaked face.

"Eden, who did this to you? What happened?" Eden shrugged off her mother's hands. "Eden, talk to me. Who was it? Did someone hurt you?"

"No. I don't know."

Barbie backed out of the parking stall, driving carefully down the street as she tried to control her shaking hands. Soon they were on the highway, headed toward home.

"You have to tell us, you know. Whoever did this has to take responsibility."

Eden stared out of the window at the bountiful fields and robin-egg sky. The world looked exactly as it did when they drove to town. This seemed impossible. Everything had changed.

"Eden, it's 1974," Barbie said, staring straight ahead at the trembling horizon. "Women have options now that were unheard of when I was your age. You don't need to have a baby at fifteen. Especially if you were... taken advantage of."

"But, Mom, I don't want to take away the baby. It will hurt! I'm scared." Eden wailed, slamming her hands against the dashboard. "I won't!"

"It won't hurt that much. They will make it easy on you, I hope. It will hurt a lot less than raising a baby at fifteen, with no job, no husband, and no help. You need to finish school, for God's sake! And I'm not raising your baby. I won't!"

Eden was silent, wiping her tears with the backs of her hands and drying them on her jeans.

"And you have to tell us who you were with," Barbie said. "We'll talk about it later." She pulled into their yard. "I'm going to the field to talk to Dad. There are carrots to clean on the counter."

Eden ran into the house. She looked at the dirt-encrusted carrots for a second, then rushed out the door and down the path to Doris's house. For a moment, she sensed HoundDog rising from the shade of the porch to follow her, but when she looked back, she saw only a sparrow hopping along and pecking the ground. It made Eden cry even harder.

Doris was sitting in a rickety kitchen chair that she kept in the shade beside her back door. Eden burst around the corner and stood before her grandmother, her hair a knotted mass around her shoulders.

"Okay, then, come on in for some iced tea," Doris said, laboriously pushing herself to her feet and shaking her head. Eden followed humbly, sniffling.

Doris lifted the powdered iced tea carton from her cupboard, added cold tap water to two tall glasses, and stirred the sweet brown liquid until the powder had dissolved.

Eden had stopped crying. She looked fiercely at Doris as if anticipating her lecture. She knew she wouldn't get sympathy from this old woman; perhaps she would get understanding. She might gain an ally. It was worth a try.

"So, you're pregnant?" Doris asked as she handed a dripping glass to Eden.

"How did you know?"

Doris shrugged. "I could see it, even if no one else could. But I didn't want to believe it was true."

Eden sipped the restorative drink. Powdered iced tea was the flavour of summer in Doris's house; it was the aroma of normalcy. It tasted so good—Eden felt calmer.

"Mom wants to terminate my baby in the city," Eden said. "I don't even know what that means. Does it mean killing it?"

"That's exactly what it means," Doris said, deeply shocked; it wasn't easy to rattle the octogenarian. "And that will happen over my dead body. That is an abomination against God."

Doris fretfully straightened canisters and other homely items on her counter, her face flushed. *Yes. Grandma's on my side.*

"You know that I got married at sixteen." Doris had recovered her equilibrium.

Eden nodded; yes, she had known that fact from the moment she could sit on her grandmother's lap and listen to her stories.

"And I was pregnant before I turned seventeen. I wasn't much older than you are now. You are young, but not too young to be a mother. And I know what it is to lose a baby. I still think about Irma every day. How much different life would be if my daughter had lived."

Doris had two sons after Irma died. She always managed to imply that they were a disappointment to her.

"At least you were married," Eden said.

Doris looked at her. "Yes, at least I had that. But this is 1974. Women's lib and all that. Women can make their own way now." She shook her head. "But for you… I don't know how things will be for you. It's a new world and yet it's not."

"Mom says she doesn't want to raise another baby. But I'll do it! I'll raise her. She's mine!" Eden started crying again, moving to the couch and plunking down on her favourite pillow. She wrapped her arms around her middle, washing her little daughter in waves of sorrow, panic, and love.

"I don't know how you got into this predicament. All I know is that God wants this baby to be born. He wants all babies to be born. Especially when all odds are against them. And believe me, Eden, your baby will live. You will make sure of that."

George Senior appeared at the back door. "Eden, come home right now," he barked through the screen.

Doris stepped forward and looked her son directly in the eye. "Now you go easy, George. Remember, nobody's perfect. Least of all you."

"Yeah, thanks for the reminder, Mom. Come on, Eden." George held the door open, and Eden reluctantly stepped through it. She was dreading the next few hours of her life.

When they got back to the house, Barbie was sitting at the kitchen table biting her nails. It was getting close to supper time, but there was no sign of food preparation. Skylar was in his bedroom, River was eating at Stacey's, and George Junior was working an evening shift at the lumberyard. Thank God, Eden thought. She did not want her brothers to know she was pregnant; it was so embarrassing.

George sat down beside Barbie and took her hand. Barbie started biting the nails on her other hand. Eden stood awkwardly, not sure what to do. She wanted more than anything to go out to the barn to see Patches and Blackie.

"Sit down and tell us what happened," George said in a quiet tone. He was trying to go easy.

She sat down but said nothing. What could she say? Curtis could tell no one what happened and neither could she. No one would ever understand.

A tickle of excitement was growing under her breastbone. It wasn't going to be fun having a baby—it was very painful from what her mother said about childbirth—but, in some mysterious way, she would have her womb sister Ava back. She could even name the baby Ava. In the end, it would all be okay.

"Who did this to you?" George roared, his resolve to go easy lost in his rage and worry. "Who were you with?"

He turned to Barbie. "Who was she with?"

"George, this kid hasn't been out of our sight all summer. She hasn't even been on a sleepover for months, you know that. She's been here in this house every day and every night. I have no idea!"

"Honey," George said, lowering his voice. "Did someone force themselves on you?"

Eden felt she should say something. "No."

"Eden, do you have a boyfriend we don't know about?" Barbie asked.

"No."

"Was it one of the neighbour kids?" George asked. "Was it Jason Pedersen?"

"Dad! No! I hate Jason Pedersen with every molecule in my body. I would never let him..."

"It was Jason Pedersen," George said to Barbie as if that settled it. Everyone knew Jason's reputation.

"No, it was not!"

"I'm going over to the Pedersens right now." George stood and knocked his chair over with a ringing clatter on the linoleum floor.

"Dad, no! That's ridiculous."

"Then you tell us right goddamn now who it was!"

"George! Come on, sit down." Barbie reached over to pick up the chair. She started to cry.

"It doesn't matter," Eden said. "It really doesn't matter at all."

She pushed away from the table, slammed the screen door, and fled to the barn. She needed to hear the soothing rhythm of Patches's mother heart; she needed to see Blackie toss his shaggy head at her approach and then pretend to ignore her while never taking his eyes off her. Maybe she'd go for a ride. Was riding dangerous for babies? There was so much she didn't know.

What she really wanted was to lie in Barbie's arms on her bed, talking and snuggling like they did when she was little. She feared her mother was lost to her forever. Her mother was angry with her and didn't want to raise her baby. She would have to do it herself. But how? Maybe Doris would let Eden live with her while she raised little Ava. But Doris was eighty-two and grouchy. She wouldn't want a baby around, either.

Eden felt utterly alone. But she wasn't really alone. She had her little one. She had Ava.

* * *

Barbie had forbidden Eden from going to school that week, so the two of them harvested and froze all the corn and beans from the garden and canned eighteen quarts of tomatoes. Eden could feel Barbie's anxiety bubbling red-hot below the surface like the pot of tomatoes. She hoped she wasn't around when it boiled over.

"I can feel the baby moving," she announced to her grandmother one afternoon.

Doris glanced at Eden's stomach. "How far along are you?"

"About three months."

"That would put you full term around February. Worst time to have a baby. All the roads will be blocked, and you won't get to the hospital in time."

Eden shrugged. At least Doris was willing to acknowledge her baby existed.

"Maybe in your day, that would be a problem. But this is 1974. We have highways and snowplows. Bombardiers and ski-doos. I think it will be okay."

Doris smiled a little. "Yes, you are an optimistic person, I'll say that about you. Too bad you've ruined your life already."

The rest of the family was furious with Eden for not naming the father of her child. Her brothers tried to pry it out of her. River's wide, kind face—still flushed from the lightning strike—hardened when she rolled toward the wall and turned on her cassette recorder as he stepped uninvited into her bedroom. He threw up his hands and left the room.

George Junior was more persistent. He came upon her in the barn after a hard ride on Blackie. Both girl and horse were dishevelled and sweaty, tousled manes falling in their dusty faces. Patches was yearning over the corral fence; she blurted a greeting when she saw George. He ignored her—he wasn't a horse person—and absently stroked Blackie's withers with a curry comb. Blackie twisted his neck, revealing menacing yellow teeth, but Eden gave him a slap.

"Blackie! No biting."

"Where'd you go today?" George asked offhandedly.

"Just down to the coulee for a while." Eden had been spending a lot of time in the coulee, lying in the grass where Ava was conceived, watching the clouds and thinking, What am I going to do? What now, little Ava?

"You know, things would probably go a lot easier for you if you told Mom and Dad who the father is." George was watching Blackie out of the corner of his eye, but the horse was now sharpening his teeth on the trough.

"I don't think there's anything that is going to help things go easy for me in the next little while. And the father is nobody's business but mine."

"That is absolutely untrue, Eden," George said. "This is affecting everyone."

"Yeah, and Skylar rolling his truck and killing Jennifer Miller affects everyone, too. Guess the heat's off him for a while; now it's all about me. Nice for Skylar."

"Mom and Dad have been through a lot lately. I'm worried about Mom. She isn't taking this very well. And Dad? Who knows where his head is? I was just hoping you could reconsider this vow of secrecy or whatever it is. If you're getting an abortion, it won't matter anyway."

"I'm not getting an abortion."

"If you told us who it is, maybe the guy's family will talk Mom out of the abortion. Maybe they will help. Or maybe the baby could be put up for adoption."

George had another thought. "Does the guy know about the baby?"

Eden tugged Blackie's head a little too hard and turned him toward the corral. "Let's just pretend there is no guy, okay?"

George released a skeptical puff of air with his lips. "South Country's first immaculate conception."

Chapter 5

Eden felt a rising panic and had to ask her mother to pull over so she could vomit in the ditch. Barbie stared straight ahead while Eden crawled back into the cab, then yanked the truck into gear and proceeded along the highway without a word. They had an appointment at the abortion clinic, and Barbie didn't want to be late.

Eden was thinking about Grandma Doris as they drove. Her grandmother appeared at the kitchen door last night in a final attempt to dissuade Barbie from taking Eden to the city. Although her words were meant for Barbie, she addressed her son directly, ignoring her daughter-in-law. The women had identical scowls on their faces.

"Every human life is created by God. Every conceived baby has an immortal soul." Doris's hand was shaking on her cane as she glared at George. "And this particular baby is a member of the English family, like it or not."

George looked at his mother helplessly; his bluster had collapsed like a hot air balloon without a flame. He seemed a smaller man; Eden wondered if he was losing weight.

"Doris, this isn't a baby," Barbie said. "It is a clump of cells with no brain. And Eden has her whole life in front of her. She will have many babies when she grows up and gets married. She's just a child herself. In this day and age, children do not need to give birth to children."

Doris turned to Barbie then, her sagging, lined face red and furious. "When children have sexual intercourse, then those children must accept the consequences. It's not this little baby's fault that..."

"That *what*?" George shouted. "That someone in this community took advantage of *my* baby and is getting off scot-free? We won't have a reminder of that staring us in the face for the next twenty years! This is in Eden's best interests so she can move on with the rest of her life!"

None of the adults acknowledged Eden's presence in the room. She was the calm in the center of the hurricane; while chaos swirled around her, she kept moving, slowly and surely, to a place of determination.

She knew the little girl curled inside her, silent and beautiful as Curtis on the day she was conceived, would one day sing the song her father had bequeathed to her. She would inherit the honeyed sunshine, the scent of crushed grass, and the contentment of birds in the coulee. She would be as pure in spirit as the act that had created her.

But she also knew instinctively that the adults in her life would sully the memory of that moment. She would never tell a living soul about that day. It was hers alone to treasure. And Curtis? Did he have a memory to cherish? It seemed unlikely.

Eden rarely saw Curtis now. Donnie and Curtis had stopped spinning into the yard, a spray of gravel announcing Donnie's arrival to share her burdens with her best friend. Barbie and Donnie spoke on the phone, and occasionally Donnie and Vic dropped in for coffee, but Curtis was never in tow. They had hired an aide to take Curtis for drives and into town for ice cream or to the swimming pool. They hoped it would move Curtis toward living a more independent life.

Since their ride to the coulee in June, Eden and Curtis had not ventured onto the prairie for a freedom gallop, with no decisions to make except whether to go north, south, east, or west. In this and so many other ways, Eden's life had changed. She wiped a tear now, thinking about this lost sweetness in her life.

Barbie was a driving machine, heading for the city and an end to this nightmare. When she noticed Eden's tears, she said, "It's not going to hurt, don't worry. They will give you a sedative and, hopefully, you will sleep right through the procedure. Soon this will all be over, and you can get on with your life."

Eden felt a bitter surge of hatred for her mother. *She* hadn't tried to kill any of her children. *She* was pregnant at nineteen, only four years older than Eden was now. But she had George in the wings, a protector. No one was going to protect Ava if Eden didn't do it. They were alone in the world.

Barbie and Eden found the clinic on the hospital's fourth floor, arriving an hour early for the appointment. It was the longest hour Eden had ever endured. Her fidgeting infuriated Barbie.

"Could you please tie your hair back? Get it out of your eyes, please."

Eden's heart was thumping alarmingly, and she had to leave her seat twice to use the toilet before the nurse called her name. Barbie rose to join her, but the nurse held up her hand.

"We'll call on you in a moment to sign the consent forms," she said. "We just want to talk to Eden for a few minutes."

Barbie sat down reluctantly.

The nurse read a long list of questions from a form on a brown clipboard. Eden answered them as well as she could, sitting on the padded examination table, unable to control the tears that dripped off her nose as she stared down at her knees.

The nurse handed Eden a hospital gown. "Slip this on and the doctor will be in to examine you and talk to you about the procedure. This will be over before you know it."

She clicked the heavy door closed behind her. Eden peeked through the window in the door. She couldn't see anyone nearby, so she slipped out, moving along the corridor away from the waiting area.

When she had visited the washroom earlier, she noticed an emergency exit sign; the door opened easily when she shoved it. Within seconds, she was flying down a stairwell, clutching her hair with one hand to keep it out of her eyes while she concentrated on her feet.

The grubby stairwell circled down to a door labelled parking. Eden pushed the door open to discover a concrete parking garage. She dashed across the garage toward another set of stairs that led to the street.

She hit the pavement running. Buildings towered above her—like a white-tailed deer, she sought cover in the deepest shade of this concrete forest.

She slowed to a walk when she noticed that her frantic running was drawing attention. She ducked into a small alley between two buildings to catch her breath. *What now?*

Clutching her abdomen, Eden slid down against a brick wall, trying to slow her heartbeat and suppress a surge of nausea. Across the alley, she noticed an opening beneath a low overhang, behind two large metal garbage bins. Although the bins stank and the space behind them was littered with beer bottles and other garbage, she crept under the overhang. Here she felt safe, at least for a moment; on top of everything, she could feel approaching rain.

It was the first storm since the lightning strike that killed HoundDog. Eden didn't want to take any chances. She shuddered and shut her eyes. Soon, rain soaked the alley, bringing cooler air with it, but under the overhang, Eden was dry and warm. She leaned her head against the concrete building and tried to relax.

"Whoa! Hello!"

She opened her eyes to see two tall men crawling into her hiding place. She was trapped in a corner with no way to escape. The older of the two slid down the wall beside her. His long, jean-clad legs prevented her from making a dash for it.

"What's up, little daughter?" His smile revealed two missing front teeth. Eden was horrified; she curled into a terrified ball around her baby.

"'White Girl on the Run. Two Indians Charged with Kidnapping.' I can see the headlines now," said the younger man. "Let's get outta here."

"We're not going to hurt her, are we?" the older man said with a wobbly grin. "Hey, what's your name?"

Eden stared at the garbage bin in front of her. "Eden."

"Say what? I'm an old man—speak up!"

"Eden!" she yelled, looking defiantly at the man.

"Okay, okay. Eden, I like that. My daughter's name is Meadow Starlight. She's about your age. My old lady likes weird names."

The younger man snorted. "What old lady? You ain't had an old lady for years!"

The two chuckled sadly about that, then the older man extended his hand. "Name's Kakeesheway, pleased to meet you." Eden tentatively shook his dry, cracked hand. "Speakin' of weird names, eh?"

"Yeah, it means He Who Eats Young Girls for Breakfast," the other man said.

"Don't listen to him! It means He Who Has a Loud Voice. But everyone just calls me Harry."

"Come on, let's get going," the younger man said.

"What's your hurry? It's rainin'."

The young man sat down with a grunt. "Let's go get a drink, man."

Eden prayed they would leave so she could escape.

"Got any money?" the young man asked Eden. She shook her head.

"She ain't got money," Harry said. "She's just a kid, right?" He looked at her intensely. "So, little daughter, who you hidin' from? You in trouble?"

Eden shrugged. "Yeah."

"Well, join the fuckin' club. 'Scuse my language, ma'am." Harry bowed respectfully. "You just hang tight. Porgie here and me, we'll take care of you."

"Porgie?" Eden couldn't help but smile. Weird names.

"Short for Georgie-Porgie, puddin' and pie, right, Porgie?"

Porgie grunted again. "Yeah, it's an old Indian name, sacred to my people."

"My dad's name is George." Eden was warming to the conversation. "And my brother's."

"Whoo, really?" Harry said. "Well, where are they? They're not taking very good care of you, little daughter."

"I ran away." Eden's eyes filled with tears against her will.

"You ran away from home one time, didn't you, Porgie?" Harry kicked his companion gently in the thigh. "You were about five years old. Found you in the bottom of the dugout. Lucky for you, it was dried up." Harry rocked with laughter at this memory.

Porgie didn't laugh. He stood up. "Look, the rain stopped. Think I'll go for a little walk around the neighbourhood."

"Bring some lunch. I think Eden's hungry, right?" Harry nudged her with an elbow. Eden had to agree.

After Porgie left, Harry took a nap, head slumped on one shoulder and long legs stretched out. Eden looked him over—dark, grey-streaked hair braided down his back, a ratty green ski jacket with a broken zipper, worn Wrangler jeans, and a faded Pink Floyd t-shirt. Black scuffed cowboy boots. He reeked of stale sweat and cigarettes. She could quietly step over his legs and slip away, but she felt too exhausted to move. She even took a little nap herself, resting her head on her bent knees.

She woke when Porgie returned with paper-wrapped cheeseburgers and a plastic cup filled with Coke.

"Lady at McDonald's bought us these." Porgie proudly set the feast at Harry's feet.

"Thank you, that looks delicious. But I've got to go to the bathroom," Eden said, urgency overcoming her embarrassment.

"Go over there." Harry tilted his head to the left while he unwrapped the burgers. Eden squeezed past the men and walked deeper into the alley, looking for a place to pee. She found another garbage bin and squatted behind it. Others had been there before her. The stench brought the nausea back in full force.

She knew eating would help the queasiness, so she walked back to the men. She could escape, but where to? They didn't seem surprised when she returned. She gratefully devoured the burger, even consenting to a sip of Coke from the straw both men had already used.

"Now, for dessert." Porgie triumphantly produced a handful of cigarettes.

"Whoop!" Harry grabbed one and lit it with a pink lighter. He kindly handed the cigarette to Eden, who accepted it tentatively. She smoked sometimes, but was it good for the baby? She took a deep drag. It made her think about smoking with Louisa and Carrie in the park across from the school. What were her friends doing right now? She thought about it; they were in math class. Her life had changed so drastically in the past week that the first day of school—only five days ago—felt like years in the past. Tears threatened to surface again.

"So, Eden," said Harry, who was passionately savouring his cigarette, "what do you know?"

"I almost got hit by lightning on Monday."

She told them the whole story, and they listened raptly, laughing in the right places, when she told them about Patches's wild gallop with the stirrups slapping her round belly, and moaning in sympathy in others, when she described HoundDog's horrific end.

Porgie then told a long story about getting caught in a punishing hailstorm while hitchhiking. When he approached a parked semi-trailer to seek shelter, he was told by the driver to crouch beneath the truck. The driver wouldn't let him into the cab. Porgie seemed unperturbed by this harsh display of inhumanity.

Next, Harry pulled away his coat and shirt to reveal a ragged scar on his shoulder from a cougar that jumped out of a tree and attacked him. Porgie pointed out a scar on his hand where his index finger had been sewn back on after it was nearly severed by an axe. Harry pulled off his boot, peeling off holey socks to reveal a scar on his foot where a rattlesnake bit him.

Eden had nothing to contribute to the scar competition—the best she had was a triangular scar on her knee where she fell on a broken beer bottle in Grade One—but she was impressed by every gruesome story the men could offer. Her tears were forgotten.

The day was fading, and the men were restless. "Let's go," Porgie urged, and Harry finally relented.

"Little daughter, if you want to stay here for a while, we'll be back. Nobody will find you here. Otherwise, it's been nice knowin' ya."

"Okay, I'll just stay here. Thanks."

"Don't mention it." The men disappeared and Eden dozed fitfully in her dank corner.

It was dusk when Harry and Porgie returned with sandwiches from the Sally Ann and a mickey of rye in a brown paper bag. Eden ate a sandwich but refused to sip on the rye. She felt nervous about the alcohol, but the men were blurring around the edges like indistinct shadows on the concrete wall. They laughed at their private jokes, drifted off to sleep, and then woke to drink some more. Soon, it was pitch dark and getting cold.

"You cold, little daughter? Here, take my coat." Harry gallantly handed her his greasy jacket, and she was grateful for it. Her teeth were chattering so loudly that she could barely talk. The damp night and events of the day were taking their toll. She wrapped her arms around Ava and slept as well as she could.

* * *

The sun was shining when Eden woke up. Harry and Porgie were snoring beside her. She stepped over their legs to relieve herself in the alley. The men were arguing loudly when she came back.

"She ain't coming with us today," Porgie was saying. "She'll cramp our style."

"She'll be a big help," Harry said. "She has the right look."

"People see a white girl with us, and they'll call the cops for sure."

"She looks Native. Look how dark her skin is."

"The hair's all wrong. It's too light and curly to be a Native chick."

Harry looked at Eden's greasy locks. "Hmm, you have a point. Give her your bunny hug, and she can hide her hair."

"Absolutely not!" Porgie said. "My mama gave me this bunny hug for my birthday."

In the end, Porgie pulled off the black hooded sweatshirt he was wearing under his jean jacket and handed it angrily to Eden. *As if I asked to wear the filthy thing! It smells like pigeon shit in an abandoned farmhouse.* She pulled it aggressively over her head; Harry was right, the hood was large enough and the sweatshirt long enough to cover her waist-length hair. Porgie and Eden followed Harry grumpily into the street.

Harry picked up a piece of cardboard he spotted in the gutter. "Perfect for our sign." He fished a pen out of his pocket. "Eden, I bet your handwriting's better than mine. You can make our sign!"

They found a sunny spot near the entrance to Eaton's and Eden got to work.

"Let's say 'Hungry Need Food'," Harry suggested, but Porgie thought it would be better to say, 'Homeless Please Help.' To stop their bickering, she wrote,

63

'Hungry Please Help,' and added a peace sign at the bottom, an artistic flourish she thought up on her own. The men gushed about the peace sign. *You'd think I'd painted the Mona Lisa.* Eden rolled her eyes.

Harry carefully spread a wrinkled western-style handkerchief on the sidewalk to collect a windfall from the shoppers lining up before the store opened at ten o'clock. None of them even looked their way. No one smiled or nodded. For the first time in her life, Eden felt invisible.

Occasionally, Porgie would say, "Bless you, ma'am," as another shopper passed without acknowledging them. They had disappeared in a puff of the smoke Harry was generating from one of the few remaining cigarettes.

Eden was careful not to make eye contact with anyone, keeping her head down and her face deep inside the hood. Every time someone looked right through them, she fell deeper into a well of shame. Sleeping rough was one thing, but begging was entirely another. Ava deserved so much better. This was no life for the two of them. But where could they go? How could she keep her baby safe? Despair dripped out of her eyes onto the cold concrete. She wiped her snotty face with the dirt-stiffened sleeve of Porgie's bunny hug.

A vehicle pulled up to the curb. Eden recognized George Junior's rusted blue truck. George leaned over to push the passenger door open, then sat back and stared straight ahead.

"You know that guy?" Harry asked.

"It's my brother, George."

"He gonna beat us up?" Porgie asked worriedly.

"No, I don't think so. But I'd better go home." She stood up and took a step forward, but Porgie yelled, "Hey, my bunny hug!" She whipped off the sweatshirt, handed it to him, and looked down at the men.

"You guys rock," she said.

"G'wan," Harry waved her toward the truck. "You know where to find us if you ever need us."

Eden climbed into George Junior's truck and slammed the door. He jerked the truck into gear and drove forward without a word. She sat silently beside him, her arms wrapped around her middle.

"I will not have an abortion. I will not kill my baby."

"Yeah, we get it."

George started to cry. "I've been driving around this godforsaken city all night. River and Stacey have been driving around all night. Mom looked for you in Skylar's truck until three in the morning, then she went to a motel in hysterics. The police are looking for you. Where the hell were you?"

"I was with a couple of guys named Harry and Porgie."

"Those Native dudes? Are you absolutely crazy, Eden?"

"They were okay. They didn't hurt me."

"Did you have sex with them, Eden?"

"George! Of course not. What do you think I am? I'm not a slut."

George sobbed so hard he couldn't speak. Eden had never seen one of her brothers cry. Not as an adult. It was horrifying.

"Look, I had sex once by accident in June. And now I'm pregnant. That doesn't make me a slut and it's no reason to kill a little baby. I know it's made life complicated, but is it really that big of a deal? Babies are conceived every minute of every day. I know I'm young, but everyone is just going to have to get over it. I'm not the first person this has happened to, and I won't be the last. Take a chill pill."

George hiccupped a laugh through his tears. "Take a chill pill, she says. You have no clue, Eden. You are living in a fantasy world. And on top of all that, you really, really stink."

They laughed, which helped lighten the mood until they pulled into the Holiday Inn parking lot, where

Barbie, River, and Stacey were speaking with two police officers. They all turned to stare as George and Eden walked toward them.

"I take it this is your daughter, Mrs. English?"

Barbie didn't speak or move, but Stacey, attempting to alleviate the mounting awkwardness, emitted a little squeal and ran over to hug Eden. River gave George a congratulatory clap on the shoulder.

Barbie turned to the officer. "Thank you so much for all your help. We are so sorry to have troubled you with this."

"Ma'am, that's what we're here for. This kind of thing is more common than you would think. Glad she's okay."

Eden climbed back into George's truck. River and Stacey took the lead with the others following in a convoy that soon left the city streets behind. Eden dreaded seeing her father, but was glad to be on the open prairie again. When they got home, she would take Patches out for a leisurely ride to clear her head.

A thought was nagging at her. "Where's Dad?"

George shrugged. "When Mom called to tell us you'd gone missing, he just left the house. I don't know where he went. I headed straight for the city, and River went to get Stacey, and then they headed out. I'm not sure what happened to Dad."

"Should... should we call him?" Eden asked in a small voice.

"Mom tried, but there was no answer at home. I hope he's not driving to the city now. We'll watch for him on the road."

George rubbed his face and the top of his head vigorously with one hand. He was obviously struggling to stay alert. For Eden, it was impossible to resist sleep; her head bobbed with the sway of the truck, her face hidden by a veil of hair.

She knew this was unfair. George stayed up all night looking for her, and now he had to drive for three hours to get her home safely. She added this to a long list of things she felt guilty about. But she saved her baby's life. In time, when they met Ava, everyone in her family would agree she had done the right thing.

When they finally got home, they discovered George Senior, Skylar, and Loren from AA at the kitchen table, hunched over an overflowing ashtray as if warming themselves at a campfire. Skylar and Loren were drinking coffee. The forty-ounce bottle of Canadian Club was open on the table and George Senior held a glass of the amber liquid in his right hand.

Relieved tears filled her father's red-rimmed eyes when Eden walked in. Loren and Skylar turned mournful faces toward her; clearly, they were grieving George's sobriety.

Then everyone's eyes whipped to Barbie. She screeched like a tortured animal and ran back outside. They listened to the tires spinning on gravel as Skylar's truck sped from the yard, then looked wretchedly at one another.

George Junior threw his jacket on a chair. "I'm going to bed," he announced, trudging with his boots up the stairs. No Barbie to tell him to take his boots off and hang up his coat.

"Daddy?" Eden was still standing in the doorway.

"You go get cleaned up." Her father swayed as he stood. "Loren'n I are going for a little drive to check on the cattle. Comin', Skylar?" The men shuffled out of the kitchen, Skylar taking up the rear on his crutches.

Eden dumped the whisky in her father's glass down the drain, then shoved the bottle under the sink, slamming the cupboard door to keep the demon in its lair. The kitchen was a mess, with dishes and garbage everywhere. I'll clean all this up for Mom, she thought. Instead, she stood mindlessly under a hot shower, then crawled beneath her chenille bedspread and dropped like a rock into a deep cavern of sleep.

"Eden, get down here!" It was Doris, calling up the stairs. Eden stumbled down to find her grandmother leaning on her cane, looking bedraggled. "Let's get this kitchen cleaned up and make supper for the men. Hop to it!"

It didn't take Eden and her grandmother long to clean up the mess. Eden buried her forearms in soapy water to wash the dishes while Doris wiped the table and counters.

"These damned cigarettes!" Doris emptied the overflowing ashtray into the garbage. It was unusual to hear Grandma Doris swear, but these were unusual circumstances; Barbie rarely relinquished her kitchen. Eden ached for her mother.

"Enough of that sniveling. Let's see what there is to eat."

Doris opened the fridge door and pulled out leftovers—boiled potatoes to slice and reheat in a frying pan, a handful of sausages to warm up with the potatoes, a few carrots. Doris ordered Eden out to the garden to pull more out of the dry soil.

Within minutes they had the carrots peeled, sliced, and simmering on the stove, and the leftovers warming on the back burner. Doris sent Eden to her house to grab a loaf of fresh bread, the can of powdered iced tea—Barbie appeared to be out of iced tea—and the puffed wheat cake sitting on her counter. A feast awaited, but there was no sign of the men. Or Barbie.

Eden clutched her stomach; the hungrier she felt, the more nauseous she became. Doris looked at her for the first time since they began making supper.

"So, you still have your baby," Doris remarked, not unkindly. Eden nodded, a defiant tilt to her chin.

"Good for you and good for this innocent child. But you know you can't keep the baby. Not at fifteen. And not in this community. We still have some standards of decency in the South Country."

Eden turned on her grandmother. "Leanne Clement gets pregnant in Grade Twelve and everyone is over-the-moon happy about it. Big wedding, big wedding dance, presents. She is two years older than I am. It's just so unfair!"

Doris drained the carrots, her wrists trembling with the weight. "It's nothing to do with fairness. Neither one of you girls should be in the family way. Young people today think God's laws don't apply to them."

George Junior chose this moment to descend the stairs, refreshed from his nap. The other men pulled into the yard; George Senior noisily sent Loren on his way, slapping the hood and hollering at him like nothing was amiss.

George's face fell when he walked into the kitchen and remembered Barbie wasn't there. He went directly to the sink and extracted the whisky bottle from behind the garbage can. Everyone stared as he poured himself a generous helping.

"Drink, anyone?" George waved his glass, sloshing a few drops onto the counter. "Oops, better not let Mom see that!" He swiped the spill with his shirt sleeve, sat down heavily at the table, and lit a cigarette. "Where's the goddamned ashtray?"

Chapter 6

Changing before gym class was a nightmare. Eden felt eyes on her as she pulled her top over her head; her breasts were spilling out of her bra. It took several excruciating minutes to button her shorts. She felt like a Goodyear Blimp.

Everyone was standing on the volleyball court when Eden finally walked out of the girls' locker room. Eden loved volleyball; she delivered a mean spike and was usually picked first for teams. Today, however, the teams had already been selected, and she had to sit out the first round.

The only other person sitting it out was Celeste. Eden deliberately sat on the other side of the court. She wasn't in the mood for Celeste and her inane chatter today. She watched the girls' game and half-watched the boys playing on the adjoining court.

Eden's team cheered when she stepped up at the teacher's nod. Celeste joined the opposing team. When Eden executed her trademark spike, Celeste threw her hands protectively over her head.

"Aw, come on, try to return it," someone said.

"Waste of space," someone else muttered.

Eden caught Celeste's eye and grinned.

While the other girls were stripping down for their mandatory showers, Eden changed into her street clothes in a toilet cubicle. Anxiety fluttered under her sternum; it would soon be impossible to hide her pregnancy. It was best to tell people about it before they could see it with their own eyes.

"Meet you at the park?" she said to Louisa and Carrie, who were drying off.

"Sure," Louisa said. "I have cigs."

"Great," Eden said unenthusiastically. Smoking did not appeal to her these days.

Eden grabbed her lunch from her locker and headed out to the park. She noticed Curtis and his aide, Jonathan, getting into Donnie's car in the parking lot. Jonathan was driving Curtis to school, attending class with him, and then taking him home. It must be a relief for Donnie not to drive into town every day, she thought.

Feeling a pang of loneliness for Curtis, she waved hesitantly, but he didn't see her or was unable to acknowledge her. A single tear trickled down her cheek, which she furiously swiped away. No weeping for the past; she now had Ava to protect. Curtis would have to be all right without her.

Eden settled under her favourite tree to wait for Louisa and Carrie. She peeked into her lunch kit; Barbie had packed peanut butter sandwiches, a slice of hillbilly cake, and an apple. Eden started with the apple.

Soon her friends joined her, laughing and damp from the shower. Eden felt a surge of love for them. They had been close friends since Grade One. Louisa was quickly surpassing Eden in height; she was a dark-haired, olive-skinned beauty. Carrie was short and curvy, a freckle-faced, brown-eyed blonde. *Ava, meet your favourite aunties.*

She girded her heart with all the courage she could muster and took a deep breath.

"I have something to tell you guys, and you have to promise not to say anything to anyone, at least for a while."

The girls looked at her sharply, attuned to her every mood. They knew immediately that something big was afoot.

"Well, what is it?" Louisa asked. "Don't keep us in suspense."

"Spit it out!" Carrie said. "Let me guess, you have a new horse."

"No, nothing like that. I'm pregnant."

The ensuing silence seemed endless. As one, the girls looked down at her stomach, then rested their eyes on her expanding chest. Eden held her breath.

Finally, Louisa looked deeply into Eden's face and snorted with laughter. "You?" she said incredulously. "You've never even kissed a guy, at least last I heard."

"Quit shitting us, Eden," Carrie said, chortling along with Louisa. While amused, she looked pale and shocked. What a thing to kid around about!

"I know, I don't have a boyfriend or anything, but... well..." Eden watched their amusement go up in smoke like the smouldering tip of Louisa's cigarette. They knew her well enough to know she was telling the truth.

"Then, how? I mean, who?" Louisa was rigid on the grass, her cigarette forgotten.

"I have decided not to reveal the father of my child," Eden said stiffly. "It isn't important. The important thing is that I have a little baby on the way, and I want to keep her and raise her myself."

"But... how?" asked Carrie. "You don't have a job. You're only in Grade Ten. You're even too young to get married, aren't you?"

"What about your career?" Louisa asked. "You want to be a veterinarian. You want to travel. Now you can't." She looked truly stricken.

Eden raked her hair impatiently. "I know the timing isn't great, but everyone's just going to have to roll with it. Sometimes, babies just want to be born! And they don't ask their parents if it's a good time or not. If they did, no babies would ever be born."

Her friends were silent. The cool breeze lifted their hair, and drops of rain splashed on their skin. The girls gathered their lunches before the waters broke from above. An oppressive silence settled on their shoulders like a heavy drizzle.

At the door, Louisa stopped and turned to Eden.

"Well, see you around," she said, walking into the school with Carrie and leaving Eden alone in the doorway. Feeling slapped, Eden let them get a head start before retrieving her biology textbook from her locker.

Eden was unable to concentrate in class, seething one moment and silently weeping the next. Carrie and Louisa did not look at her for the entire hour, nor did they wait for her when they moved to another classroom for French.

Eden fared better during French; it was one of her favourite subjects. As she conjugated verbs, she managed to stop thinking about the fact that Louisa and Carrie were no longer speaking to her.

When Eden climbed onto the bus, she noticed Carrie sitting in their usual spot. Eden slipped into a seat near the front behind Angela and Carol. The sisters regaled her with questions about the lightning strike. The bus swayed into motion to begin its bone-rattling journey along the dusty grid roads.

Eden glanced back once to see Carrie in deep conversation with Jason Pedersen. There was a flirtatious tilt to her friend's head as she listened intently to whatever nastiness Jason was spewing. Eden turned back to Curtis's sisters with a toss of her own head. *Damn them all.*

Eden stared blindly into the rainy afternoon. Right now, they are shocked out of their skulls, but they will eventually be happy about the baby, too, she thought. Everything will be back to normal tomorrow. *Can a baby have two godmothers?* Eden thought there must be a way. She relaxed for the rest of the trip home. It was going to be okay.

But when she stepped into the kitchen, Barbie and George were sitting at the table. George had a drink. It was not okay.

"Sit down, please, Eden." Barbie gestured with her coffee cup at a chair. Eden glanced at her father, who did not meet her eyes. She sat reluctantly.

"I've been on the phone all day, and it looks like Wheatland Manor can take you this week," Barbie said.

"What? What's that?"

"It's a home for pregnant teenagers and unwed mothers. Kind of a boarding school. It's in the city. We will leave in the morning, so start packing."

"But... why?"

"Because you will be better off there than here in this nosy, judgmental community, that's why!" Barbie walked to the counter, scrubbing it fiercely with a damp dishcloth.

"I don't want to leave, please, Mom, please. I can do my Grade Ten by correspondence, so I don't have to go to school when I get big. I'll help around here a lot, you'll see. Dad! Please talk to her!"

George took a swallow of his whisky, then looked at his daughter for the first time. His eyes were bloodshot; from alcohol or crying, Eden couldn't tell. She felt a pang of guilt for putting him through this, then a flash of disgust that he had to resort to drinking because things were slightly complicated at the moment.

"It will be for the best if you go to Wheatland," George said gruffly. "I think they run a pretty good ship. And it won't be forever; just a few months."

"You mean... I'll have the baby there? But that's a long time! I don't want to live there all winter, please. I'll do anything you say..."

But Eden knew she would not do everything they asked her to do. She would not hurt Ava no matter what her parents wanted.

Barbie was scouring a frying pan with a Brillo pad, her back to the kitchen table. "You will have good medical care there, you can work on your high school classes, and you won't have to endure... well, you'll be with girls in your situation, and I think that will be better all around."

"Better for you, you bitch!"

George turned to her with a drawn face. "Go to your room right now and never let me hear you speaking to your mother like that again."

"Don't tell me what to do with a drink in your hand! Talk to me next time you quit."

Eden ran out the door. She paused beside the porch for a moment, seething and gasping for air. She yearned to bury her face in Patches's dusty neck but noticed Skylar limping slowly from the barn on his crutches. To avoid him, she turned down the path to Grandma Doris's house.

The rain had stopped, but the air was cool. Summer had abruptly abdicated, bowing out in a shower of regretful leaves. Doris was in her kitchen, baking muffins. The familiar smell of her house—vanilla, furniture polish, and stale clothing—encircled Eden like a comfortable old quilt. Eden sank onto one of Doris's chrome-legged chairs and dropped her head onto her arms on the yellow Formica tabletop. The table was strewn with toast crumbs and felt sticky. *Is Grandma losing her eyesight?*

"Mom wants to send me to the city to a home for pregnant teenagers," Eden said morosely, her nose inches from a smear of—was it jam?

Doris opened her wobbly oven door and arthritically placed a pan of muffins on the middle rack. Eden noticed from the corner of her eye that Doris's hands were shaking. Her grandmother grabbed a tea towel—hand embroidered with the day of the week, Monday—then sat at the table, wiping her veiny hands with the towel. When Eden sat up, Doris was blotting her eyes. Eden was disconcerted; Doris never cried.

"I lost a baby too, you know." She sniffled. "Her name was Irma."

Eden looked at her grandmother in shock. The Irma story was well-known family lore.

"Well, *my* baby will be okay," she said. "I think she's pretty healthy; I can feel her moving more every day."

"Yes, but you will lose her in the end." Doris buried her face in the towel. "It will amount to the same thing. You will never forget her, though. She will always be with you."

"That's just bullshit. I want to keep my baby. No one can love her the way I do."

"That's probably true." Doris rose to check on the oven. Her old stove was prone to losing heat; a quick brush of her hand on the glass door assured her the appliance was working. "But you can't take care of a baby by yourself. You know that, Eden."

Eden grabbed the tea towel and wiped her own eyes. "Grandma, will you help me? I can live here with you and take care of you and do housework and weed the garden and help you make preserves—you can teach me!"

"Sorry to tell you this, but my helping days are over. I raised two sons and worked side-by-side with my husband on the ranch—I'm worked right out, Eden. I'm worn out."

Doris looked elderly and forlorn, leaning against her counter. She turned to fill the kettle, which came noisily to life on her stovetop.

"I'll run away again if they put me in that home," Eden said, tossing her hair behind one shoulder. "I won't stay there. No one can make me."

Doris's glowering expression was more like the grandmother Eden had known all her life. "You are to stay at that place, take good care of yourself and that baby, work on your studies, and do what you are told. Do you hear me? Under no circumstances are you to run away. That could mean death to your baby and to you. Pregnant women need to stay safe and be careful. You wanted to have this baby, now act like a mother."

She was so angry that Eden felt fearful. *Don't have a heart attack or stroke!*

Eden shrugged. "Are those muffins done? I'm kinda hungry."

After tea and muffins—Eden and Doris passed the tea towel back and forth to wipe the Monday blues away—and a few stilted words of farewell, Eden walked up to the house. Barbie had unearthed the suitcases from the basement and set them outside of Eden's bedroom door. She pulled them into her room and started to pack.

* * *

Eden was surprised and relieved when Donnie showed up early the next morning to drive them to Regina. She suspected Barbie had invited Donnie to serve as a buffer between them. Donnie fulfilled her purpose by chatting breezily with Barbie in the front seat of her Pontiac sedan while Eden sat in the back, staring at the rain-saturated prairie. Harvest in the South Country was at a full stop.

After a quick lunch at the Esso service station—hot turkey sandwiches and mashed potatoes with canned peas—Donnie parked in front of Wheatland Manor.

"This must be the place. Wow, what a beautiful house!"

Wheatland Manor was shaded by ancient cottonwood trees arching over a quiet downtown street. Some of the neighbouring turn-of-the-century houses were lovingly tended, and others were crumbling and sad. The two-storey brick Manor flaunted blinding white trim and a spacious veranda. They walked through the tidy front yard and rang the doorbell. After an agonizing minute or two, Eden heard multiple locks disengaging. A whiff of mildew seeped past the gaunt, middle-aged woman on the threshold.

"Mrs. English." She extended her hand to Donnie.

"Oh, no, I'm just a family friend." Donnie moved back, stepping on Eden's foot as Barbie rushed forward to take the woman's hand.

77

The woman laughed heartily. "So good to meet you. And you must be Eden."

Eden ignored the proffered hand. She had no intention of making this easy on anyone. She had no intention of staying in this musty hellhole. Barbie poked Eden painfully in the back, urging her into the foyer.

"I'm Mrs. Maitland, the matron." She shut the door firmly behind them. "Let's sit in my office. Would you ladies like tea?"

Mrs. Maitland marched toward the back of the house while Barbie, Donnie, and Eden settled uneasily in high-back chairs in front of a large, orderly desk. At one time, the room must have been the front parlour. Large bow windows allowed dim light into the room through thin lace curtains. A ficus tree in a brown ceramic pot drooped elegantly in the corner. The mildew smell was apparent even here.

Mrs. Maitland returned with a tray of sturdy mugs, a squat brown teapot, and a bone china plate of sugar cookies. Barbie and Donnie politely took mugs, and Mrs. Maitland filled them with strong steaming tea. Eden refused refreshment. Her stomach was still churning from greasy gravy, soggy peas, and nerves.

Mrs. Maitland smiled warmly at Eden. "I know this is a big adjustment for a girl of your age. So many of our girls are homesick at first. But it's only for a few months! You'll be home before you know it!"

She pulled a file folder from the top drawer of the desk. "Now, Mrs. English, I just want to check all the details from our telephone conversation to make sure I have it right. You say that Eden is about three months along. Is that correct, Eden?"

Eden stared stonily at the woman. Barbie quickly filled the silence.

"Yes, the doctor estimated that she would be due in late February or March." A flush rose in her cheeks.

"We will have the residence doctor conduct a full examination next week," Mrs. Maitland said. "We offer the best care here at Wheatland. You have nothing to worry about."

She rose to her full height, walking around her desk to the door.

"I will let you say goodbye now, and then I'd like to show you to your room, Eden. And Mrs. English, I know it may be tempting to check in, but we find it best if families give the girls time to adjust before visiting or calling. The very first weeks can be tough, but then we all settle into a busy time, focusing on what is most important—having a healthy baby, doing our schoolwork, and helping with chores. The time just flies!"

She stepped out of the office, leaving Barbie, Donnie, and Eden staring at one another. Eden burst into tears, and Donnie scooped her into a hug. Eden clung to Donnie's round shoulders, memorizing her spicy scent as a defence against the fusty stench of this horrible place.

When Donnie released her, Barbie stepped forward to give Eden a hasty hug.

"I want you to be brave and good. Do what they tell you to do, and soon this will all be over." She looked into Eden's eyes. "And don't even think about running away. Dad and I implore you—stay here where you are safe. You can write us letters or even call once in a while."

As Mrs. Maitland escorted Barbie and Donnie to the door, Eden stroked her abdomen. *It's okay, Ava. I've got you. Sleep now, little baby.*

In her room, Eden looked with distaste at the pink, flouncy ballerina bedspread and matching ruffled pillow sham on her narrow bed. The room was cold and dreary, and the silky bedspread did nothing to warm it up.

An identical bed across the room looked unused. Perhaps she wouldn't have a roommate; she prayed that she wouldn't. Eden walked over to the dormer window. It overlooked a rain-soaked vegetable garden in the backyard. The window was sealed, so no escaping from there. Eden knew the front door was secured but hadn't had a chance to explore the rest of the house. Soon she'd get the lay of the land and decide what was next for her. She knew she couldn't stay in this prison, but had no idea where she would go if she escaped.

She thought of Harry and Porgie. Were they out there somewhere? Would they welcome her back into the concrete crawl space they had shared only a few days ago? Eden shivered; it was unseasonably cold. It was hard to imagine sleeping outdoors tonight.

Eden lay on her chilly bed, curled herself around Ava, and willed herself to sleep. It had been an early morning, so sleep came easily. When she opened her eyes, a stout woman with a ruddy face was at the door.

"Wake up, sleepyhead! It's almost time for supper." The woman walked briskly into the room and yanked the curtains shut against the late summer daylight.

"I am Mrs. Kravchenko, the night manager. Everyone just calls me Mrs. K. Freshen up, comb your hair, and come down for supper. The dining room is on your left at the bottom of the stairs."

Eden went to the bathroom down the hall, splashed water on her face, and looked at herself in the mirror. The drastic lighting and yellow walls cast deep shadows under her eyes and a greenish tinge to her cheeks. *It doesn't matter what I look like here.* Eden's hair was bushy because of the dampness and dishevelled by her nap; she ignored it and set out to find food.

When she entered the dining room, three girls were sitting at the large oak table, and two others were carrying steaming platters from the adjoining kitchen. They all looked at Eden with frank curiosity.

"Everyone, this is Eden," said Mrs. K, setting a basket of buns and a pitcher of water on the table. Eden's stomach contracted with hunger. She took a seat, boldly staring back at the others. All five of the girls were showing signs of pregnancy; two of them looked like puffballs about to pop. None of them smiled.

"Introduce yourselves, please," Mrs. K commanded.

"Dorothea."

"Samantha."

"Josey."

"Mandi."

"Charo."

Everyone cracked up at that. "Linda, please use your real name!" Mrs. K tutted.

"Yeah, you look about as much like Charo as Mrs. K does," Samantha said. The girls chuckled maliciously. Linda tossed her head and reached for the salad.

"Is Eden your real name?" Mandi stroked the top of her balloon belly. She was wearing a bright orange maternity top with cap sleeves.

Eden shrugged. "Yep, that's my name." She reached for the cabbage rolls, which smelled divine.

"You don't look pregnant," Mandi observed.

"Yeah, most people come here when they start to show," said Linda. "What's your hurry?"

"Girls, leave Eden alone," Mrs. K said. "She's only just arrived."

Eden looked down at her flat stomach. What *was* she doing here?

No one spoke to Eden again as they worked through generous helpings of roast beef, cabbage rolls, salad, buns, and canned fruit salad for dessert. The girls snickered over private jokes; Eden preferred to tune in to her own internal misery. When they finished eating, three of the girls cleared the table and went into the kitchen to wash dishes.

"Josey, please show Eden the donations cupboard and help her choose some items," Mrs. K said.

Josey, a short redhead with a pixie haircut and large aviator-style glasses that slid down her tiny nose, gestured for Eden to follow her. She too wore a voluminous maternity top over black Fortrel slacks, although her baby bump was smaller than Mandi's.

"Never mind them." Josey hitched up her glasses with her middle finger as they walked into the hall. "Linda and Mandi think they're king shit, but they're just scared pitiful little girls."

Josey herself looked like a little girl, standing no higher than Eden's shoulder. "My parents hid me away at home until I started to show, and then they brought me here. I'm giving my baby up for adoption. My boyfriend broke up with me when he found out I was pregnant. What's your story?"

Eden thought Josey would be better named Nosy. She declined to answer.

Josey went on. "I'm eighteen. How old are you?"

Eden felt trapped. "Fifteen," she said diffidently.

"Oh, boy, you're really in trouble. Yikes, fifteen. I've never met anyone that young here. Shit. Wow. Fifteen. Crap."

Josey pointed at a closet. "Here's the donations cupboard. Loads of maternity clothes here. Some of them are nice." She twirled to show off the pleated seersucker blouse that hung to her knees. Eden was appalled but tried not to let it show on her face.

She pulled out a pair of maternity slacks, holding them up to her body. The legs were six inches too short. *I'll just wear my jeans unbuttoned a little longer.* A chambray top with contrasting floral print patch pockets caught her eye.

"This looks like it might fit," Eden said, to be polite. She held it to her nose. "It stinks, though. Everything smells musty in this place."

Josey shrugged. "Monday is laundry day, Tuesday is ironing. Just throw it in your clothes hamper and it will get washed next week."

"So is Wednesday mending and Thursday…?" Eden thought hard about Grandma Doris's tea towels. What was Thursday?

"You got it," said Josey. "This place is a time warp from the Fifties. Including a strict taboo on premarital sex."

Josey winked, and Eden blushed.

Chapter 7

Eden was an automaton during her first weeks at Wheatland Manor; her legs felt heavy and artificial, and her hands were no longer fully connected to her brain. Every task required a concentration of will that she did not possess.

Getting up in the morning was the biggest challenge of her day. Mrs. Maitland made sure she was on time for breakfast by throwing the covers off her shivering body every morning at seven o'clock.

After breakfast, each girl was assigned chores. Eden, being a farm girl, was delegated to help with the garden. This was a good arrangement because Eden knew exactly what to do with the ripening vegetables. She was more familiar with the processes of canning and freezing than either Mrs. Maitland or Mrs. K. Her time in the garden was the only opportunity she had to be outdoors. Here, the murky soup in which she swam thinned and brightened. Occasionally, the sun broke through.

It was here that she fantasized about running away from the Manor. She thought often about Harry and Porgie, envying their freedom but not their living arrangements. It occurred to her that no one was watching her closely while she was digging potatoes and carrots; it wouldn't be difficult to walk away. But her leaden legs and disembodied hands prevented it. That and the prospect of the next hot meal; Eden was always ravenous.

Mandi's due date was September 25. This was well known to everyone because she spoke of it daily—the end of her prison term and the beginning of parole when she moved back home with her religious parents. The night before her due date, Eden was awakened by a piercing scream. Mrs. K rushed to Mandi's room in a fluster. Eden lay tense in her bed, listening.

"It hurts, it hurts, it hurts." Mandi was sobbing like a little girl with a skinned knee.

Eden could hear Mrs. K muttering and soothing. "Hold on now, hold on. It's just getting started. I'll make you some tea."

"Fuck tea. I want to go to the hospital now! This fucking hurts!"

"Watch your language, young lady," Mrs. K sputtered. "No need to talk like a sailor."

Mandi screamed for several agonizing seconds. Eden had her head buried under her pillow when the door burst open, and Linda walked into her room.

Linda was next in line to give birth. She rolled clumsily into the bed across from Eden, grunting as she struggled to pull the covers over her bulk. Linda was carrying a lot of weight; Eden suspected most of it existed before her pregnancy.

"Mrs. K kicked me out," Linda explained in a loud whisper. "I don't think I'll be getting any sleep in here either," she added, as Mandi emitted guttural grunts and high-pitched squeals. Eden and Linda lay side-by-side, listening to the caterwauls.

"God, it must hurt like hell," Linda said into the darkness. "But then again, Mandi's a drama queen," she added, laughing. Eden laughed too, agreeing. She could see Linda's silhouette against the weak glow from the streetlights. She was lying on her back, stroking her swollen abdomen mechanically. Eden clutched her own middle, silently soothing Ava and urging her to go back to sleep.

Mandi exploded again into screams, followed by swearing. Mrs. K was losing her patience. "This is what happens when young girls don't keep their legs crossed," she spat at Mandi, every word clearly audible through the thin wall. "Let this be a lesson to you!"

Eden and Linda turned to one another in the dark, shocked. Then Linda laughed again.

"Mrs. K probably hasn't had sex for twenty years," she said. "She's just jealous."

Eden blushed invisibly in her bed. She had never discussed sex with anyone before coming to Wheatland Manor; not with her mother nor with her friends. But these girls talked about it all the time, it seemed.

Linda glanced at the small table between the beds. "Nice doily," she commented. "I've counted thirty-two doilies in this place, but wow… this is one of the nicest ones."

Eden snorted in her balled-up sheet. Grandma Doris would be in doily heaven at Wheatland Manor. Eventually, she drifted off to sleep despite the battleground racket next door.

In the morning, after Mandi was examined by the doctor and finally permitted to go to the hospital, the war-weary survivors gathered at the breakfast table to spread dread on their toast. They, too, would be called into action whether they were ready or not.

One afternoon in the middle of October, Eden was working on her correspondence courses at the dining room table. She was soaring through English and social studies but floundering in math and chemistry without a teacher. Despite her struggles, she enjoyed her schoolwork. It reminded her of her old life; she often thought about Louisa and Carrie as she worked through her lessons. Did they know where she had gone? Did they miss her?

She looked across the table at Dorothea and Samantha, who were working on their Grade Twelve courses. Mandi and Linda were long gone. Once a resident of Wheatland Manor delivered a baby, it was the last anyone saw of them. No one came back for a fond farewell.

A loud knock on the front door roused Mrs. Maitland, who hurried out of her office to peek through the side window. Unannounced visits were rare. Eden perked up her ears when the matron unfastened all the locks and opened the heavy door. Was that a familiar voice? Was that George? Eden ran to the door, trying to glimpse past Mrs. Maitland's tall frame.

"Visits need to be pre-arranged, I'm afraid," she was saying to a polite George Junior, who was planted firmly on the veranda, legs apart and a determined smile on his face. The English are stubborn, Eden thought. Stand aside because George isn't going anywhere. She ducked around Mrs. Maitland and launched herself into George's arms.

"All right," Mrs. Maitland said reluctantly. "You may visit here on the veranda, but you are not to leave the premises."

Over George's shoulder, Eden saw Skylar on the lawn, a huge grin on his broad face. He nearly knocked George over as he vaulted onto the veranda and swept Eden into a fleshy bear hug. Eyebrows at her hairline, Eden looked inquiringly at George. Skylar had never hugged her before. George shrugged and grinned.

"Hey, Eden," said Skylar, "you're so nice and fat!"

Eden laughed and stepped away from Skylar's arms. "And you don't have your cast anymore. You look good."

"Yeah, Skylar got his cast off a couple of weeks ago and the doctors have given him the all-clear to get back to work, right, Sky?" George said.

A sudden realization clutched at Eden's throat. "A couple of weeks ago? You mean Mom was in Regina a couple of weeks ago?"

George's shoulders twitched with embarrassment. "Well, Mom and Dad both came up with Skylar. He got to drive his new truck for the first time."

Since arriving at Wheatland Manor, Eden had shed dull throbs of despair, boredom, anxiety, and loneliness with every heartbeat. These feelings were part of the landscape, like the doilies she moved aside when she dusted the mismatched wooden furniture on cleaning day. What she felt now was not smothered by the dank atmosphere of the old house; this emotion was white lightning travelling along a fence line.

"Mom and Dad didn't come to see me. They haven't written. They haven't called."

Although she remained calm, fury lit every nerve cell in her body, resurrecting the girl who urged an unpredictable black horse to run at full throttle and kicked foul-mouthed shitheads in the stomach on the way to school.

Visiting hours at Wheatland Manor were Friday evenings and Saturday afternoons. Most of the girls received regular visitors; Mrs. K or the weekend supervisor, Mrs. Thompson, would bring tea and cookies to the tiny visiting room when family members arrived. Boyfriends were strictly forbidden. The girls were restricted to fifteen-minute phone calls in the evenings, to give others a chance to make calls if they wished.

Eden received no visitors or telephone calls. In her misery, she accepted this as part of her banishment. Now, she refused to accept it.

"We got a new puppy," Skylar announced, trying to break the tension.

Eden looked at him blearily, then smiled. "No way! What kind?"

"It's another hound. He's pitch black and a little rascal," George said.

"Black? Uh, oh, Mom won't be able to name him Blackie, 'cause that name's taken," Eden said.

"She named him Barker," Skylar said happily.

"Barker. I like that. Like Bob Barker from *The Price is Right*?"

"No, it's because he barks a lot," Skylar said.

Eden motioned for her brothers to sit in the wicker chairs. She wanted to warm herself in the sweet glow of their homely faces for as long as possible.

"So, what brings you to the city?" she asked. "How is combining going?"

"We're a long way from finished," George said. "The rain just won't quit. Things are starting to dry out now. We came up for a machine part and to see Grandma Doris, too."

"What do you mean? What's happening with Grandma?"

George glanced at Skylar, who was gazing adoringly at Eden and seemed oblivious to her pain. "Well, she's in the hospital. She had a heart attack."

"What the shit! No one told me." Eden jumped to her feet and started pacing. Her brothers looked mildly shocked; they had never heard her swear before.

"Am I no longer a part of the English family? What is going on? What's wrong with Mom and Dad?"

"Eden, sit down for a second," George said. "I know this really sucks, but Mom and Dad are in a bad way. Dad is drinking like a fish. Some days he doesn't even get up to go to work. River and I are doing everything, and I had to quit my job at the lumberyard. Mom is trying everything she can to get him back to AA, but all they do is fight. You're lucky, actually, that you aren't there so you don't have to hear them every day."

"And it's all my fault!?" Eden said, tearing her fingers along the length of her hair.

"I think it's just a combination of everything that went down this year," George said. "Dad has a hard time staying away from the booze at the best of times. You know that."

After the boys clumped noisily down the wooden steps and slammed the doors of George's old truck, Eden remained on the veranda, grieving their absence. An old man raking leaves next door watched them leave, then turned his rheumy eyes to her, pointedly staring at her midsection. She stared back, lifted her middle finger, and reluctantly returned to the house.

Eden slipped upstairs to her room. She had cried copiously into the slippery fabric of the ballerina bedspread over the past six weeks; today she did not cry. She stared at the stained ceiling until Mrs. K called for her to clean up her books from the dining room table and come down for kitchen duty. Although reluctant, Eden's legs were no longer leaden, and her body obeyed her more readily. Eden had finally awakened after a long stupor; she vowed she would never go back to the shadowy existence she endured in her first weeks at the Manor.

The next morning, Eden was cleaning up the garden wearing a coat she found in the donations cupboard—a maroon boucle knee-length wool sheath with a tiny mink collar. Eden thought Doris would love this coat despite the body odour emanating from the stained silk lining.

It wasn't the best garment for hauling garden refuse in a wheelbarrow, but it was warm. Eden steered the wheelbarrow behind the garden shed, dumped the dead plants in the compost pile, wiped her hands on her thighs, and walked down the alley toward the center of town.

"Doris English, please," Eden said to the young woman at the hospital reception desk.

"She's on the cardiac ward on the third floor." The receptionist barely looked up from her registration book. Eden was relieved; she feared that a fifteen-year-old girl wearing a matronly wool coat would attract attention.

She clutched Ava as she rode up in the elevator; only six weeks before, she and Barbie had stepped into the same elevator on the way to the abortion clinic. Eden started to sweat in the heavy coat.

It wasn't difficult to find her grandmother. As she stepped off the elevator, she saw Doris's name beside a door and recognized her bare feet sticking out from under a blue sheet. Eden tiptoed past a white-haired woman sleeping in the bed beside Doris and peeked around a curtain partially shielding her grandmother.

Doris was awake. She impatiently pushed aside a food tray trolley and reached out to Eden. Eden sobbed and rushed over to her grandmother, noticing that her face was grey and pinched. Intravenous tubing dangled from one of her arms and a heart monitor bleeped monotonously in the corner.

Eden stood awkwardly with her head on Doris's flat breast for a long moment. She relaxed for the first time since coming to the city.

"Sit, girl, sit down right here." Doris patted the bed beside her. Eden gingerly accepted the invitation as she unbuttoned the maroon coat.

"Grandma, what happened?" Eden wiped her tears on the coat sleeve.

"Oh, my age is just catching up to me, that's all. My heart is getting tired. So am I, frankly."

"No, Grandma, you have lots of energy left in you. I know it!"

Ignoring that comment, Doris reached up to touch Eden's face. "And how are you making out?"

"I hate it here. I just want to go home." Eden sounded to herself like a petulant little girl, but she couldn't help it. She was desperate to get away from Wheatland Manor.

"Are they treating you right? Are you eating well? How are you feeling?"

"I'm okay, I guess. I just want to go home and see everyone. No one has come to see me except George Junior and Skylar yesterday. They told me you were here."

Doris looked at the snow-heavy sky. She was silent as she gathered her thoughts.

"Your parents are going through a very hard time right now," she said weakly. "Your father is ill, and your mother blames him for it. The crops have failed. Skylar is coming around. Luckily, he's forgotten all about drinking and chasing girls. River can't wait to get out of the house and start his own family. He spends most of his time at Stacey's. George Junior is running around trying to do all the work and keep everyone happy. You'll have to forgive them all, eventually."

I'll never forgive them, Eden thought.

"What about Patches and Blackie? How are they doing?"

Doris snorted. "I never go to the barn, you know that." As the two of them chuckled softly, Doris's roommate stirred. A buzzer blared, and a nurse appeared in the doorway.

"I'm sorry, visiting hours begin at one o'clock," she said officiously, glaring at Eden. "And only adults are allowed on the cardiac ward."

Eden looked at Doris, whose eyes crinkled at the corners. "I thought I looked older in this coat," she said, leaning over to kiss her grandmother's cheek. "I'll come back another time."

The creases around Doris's eyes deepened, but she said nothing, leaning back against her pillow and shutting her eyes.

Eden took the stairs down to the street, vividly remembering her flight down the same staircase a few weeks before. She retraced her steps from that day, stopping in front of the overhang, and peering behind the garbage bins to see if Harry and Porgie were home. The space held only empty beer bottles and fast-food wrappers.

She walked dejectedly down the street, not wanting to return to Wheatland Manor but not sure where she could go. And she was hungry again. It was lunchtime. Mrs. Maitland probably knew by now that she had fled the property.

She noticed Harry trudging along the sidewalk across the street. Eden jaywalked to where he was rifling through a garbage can.

"Hey, Harry!" Eden was thrilled to see him. He stared blankly at her, reeking of booze and sour clothes. Then his face brightened.

"Little daughter," he said, flashing his gap-toothed smile. "You're back."

He glanced down at her stomach, revealed behind the unbuttoned maroon coat. "Still in trouble?" he asked.

Eden shrugged. "If you call having a baby being in trouble." She pulled her hair from underneath the coat and tossed it over her shoulder.

"I s'pose everyone thinks you're way too young to be a mother," Harry remarked, looking over Eden's shoulder. "But you'll be a good mama. Don't let them take your baby away. They do that, you know. Even to white girls."

"Well, they're not taking my baby away from me! There will be hell to pay if they do," Eden said defiantly. She could see Harry was losing interest.

"Got any money?" he asked, attempting to focus on her face. When she shook her head, he shuffled off without a backward glance.

* * *

Agatha Browne, a social worker from the Department of Social Services, was a tightly wound brunette of about forty-five, Eden guessed. She was wearing a tight black Fortrel business suit, which did nothing to disguise her thick waist. Her brown hair was tightly curled, and she wore wire-rimmed glasses on her short, sniffly nose.

Eden disliked her immediately.

Eden and Agatha were sitting with Mrs. Maitland in her office reviewing Eden's "case" when the doorbell rang.

"I'll just step out for a moment," Mrs. Maitland said. "We are expecting a new girl today. Go ahead and get to know one another!" She strode out of the office in two long steps, leaving Eden and Agatha sitting in the uncomfortable high-back chairs.

Eden was picking at her thumbnail; she didn't look up when Agatha spoke.

"Now, Eden, I'm going to set up a schedule whereby we will meet twice a month between now and your due date—what is it? Oh, yes, I see it is estimated to be March 1," Agatha said, referring to her notes.

"I understand from the doctor's report that you aren't sure of the date of your last period?" She looked over the top of her glasses at Eden. "It would be helpful if you could pinpoint the date of conception. At your age, I assume that wouldn't be difficult?"

Eden focused on her fingernails, which were cleaner than they used to be. She was never able to entirely eradicate the horse dirt from under her nails when she lived at home.

"And I see that you have not revealed the name of the father," Agatha went on. "You are legally bound to name the father on the baby's birth certificate. I will bring some paperwork on my next visit, and we can go over some things that you will need to decide before the baby is born."

Eden looked up then, alert to a new danger.

"Don't worry right now." Agatha placed her hand on Eden's forearm. "You have lots of time to make the right decisions for yourself and the child. I understand you have been seeing Dr. Andrews, who is a wonderful doctor. You will be in good hands when the baby comes."

Although she was trying to appear compassionate, Agatha effused gleeful superiority. Eden shuddered and, as politely as she could manage, extricated her arm from Agatha's grip.

"Thank you," she muttered, praying for an excuse to end the meeting. Agatha answered her prayer by standing abruptly.

"All right then, I will see you in two week's time." She stuffed her papers into a brown leather briefcase. Eden slipped from the room and bounded up the stairs, hoping for a few minutes alone before she had to help in the kitchen.

She burst through her bedroom door and shrieked; her heart caromed against her breastbone like a bowling ball. Celeste Tremblay was sitting on the bed, wearing a white coat and surrounded by dilapidated suitcases and cardboard boxes tied with baler twine.

"Oh, my blessed Jesus!" Celeste exclaimed. "There you are! Everyone is wondering where you went."

Eden was unable to find her voice. She stroked her belly, soothing Ava. *It's okay, little one. It's only Celeste.*

"Are you... pregnant?" Eden said finally, moving to her own bed and sitting down with a dumbfounded thump.

"Oh, yes, five months along," Celeste said cheerfully, shedding her coat to reveal a perky baby bump under a frilly maternity top. Her breasts, always prominent, now filled the room with maternal promise.

"The story was that you had moved to the city to live with your uncle and aunt, but nobody really believed that. It just didn't make any sense." Celeste was regarding Eden with a mixture of warm familiarity and long-suffering apprehension. Eden had never willingly consorted with Celeste at school.

"But now I see what's going on. You are having a baby, too!" Celeste seemed unable to suppress her joy at seeing a familiar face. Eden felt the same way—she had a strong urge to clutch Celeste to her own swollen breasts and plant a slobbery kiss on her blonde, curly hair.

"Yeah, I sure am." Eden's heart, now beating calmly, had thawed imperceptibly; she hadn't noticed before this moment how icy her soul had become since arriving at Wheatland Manor.

"Well... that's nice," Celeste said, uncertainly. "I mean, I think babies are nice, whether they are planned or not. My mom's having another baby, too. We are due about one month apart. That's why I came up here. *Maman* said we can't have so many babies around our house! I'm giving this one up for adoption."

Celeste was the oldest of a long succession of Tremblay children. They littered the school playground, a tumble of ruffians who, with their gaggle of little friends, were forever underfoot. Were there six or seven of them? Eden had never bothered to count.

"Aren't these ballerina bedspreads just darling?" Celeste stroked the satiny, pilled fabric. "I can't wait to sleep in my own bed. My little sister is such a kicker!"

Eden was still speechless but warming to this new roommate. She just seemed so happy about the whole situation. But then, Celeste was a simple person. *Simply chatty*. Eden had been living in her head for so long that she felt now like a meadowlark heralding spring.

Celeste pushed the buttons of a suitcase with her thumbs to click it open. Reams of fabric spilled out— maternity clothes of every colour, style, and vintage.

"*Maman* had all these in the attic, just waiting for the next baby, I guess," Celeste said with a grin. "She and Papa... well, they're affectionate."

Celeste pulled a transistor radio from the bottom of the case. Things are looking up, Eden thought. She watched in fascination as Celeste spread everything on the bed. Stuffed animals. Books. A Bible. A rosary. Shoes, boots, slippers. A fluffy pink housecoat. And her proudest possessions, hair clippers and stylist scissors.

"I'm going to beauty school after high school. I already cut everyone's hair at home." Celeste set the tools on the bedside table. "I thought I could get some practice with all the girls here. What are they like? Have you made any friends?"

Eden had to admit that she hadn't. Mandi and Linda left to have their babies, and two other young women arrived at Wheatland Manor to take their places, but Eden kept to herself. Josey was the closest thing to a friend she had; she regularly took it upon herself to instruct Eden on the intricacies of surviving life in a home for unwed mothers.

She remembered one piece of Josey's advice that suddenly seemed highly relevant. "Mrs. Maitland doesn't like it when people get too chummy," Eden said. "You're the first roommate I've had, and I want to keep you. Let's pretend that we don't know each other, okay?"

Celeste beamed. *Honestly, the kid has no pride.* Eden guiltily recalled how often she and her friends had mocked Celeste. Gratitude for Celeste's forgiveness overwhelmed her, and her eyes filled with unwanted tears. Celeste noticed them and smiled kindly.

"No problem. Who are you again?"

Eden laughed at the lame joke, wiping her nose on the hem of her top. "Right now, I don't have a friggin' clue."

Celeste chatted with all the girls over supper, finding out more about them in an hour than Eden had gleaned in the previous two months. She raved about the dinner of roast chicken, mashed potatoes, and Brussels sprouts. Eden was simultaneously amused and appalled as she ate quietly at the opposite end of the table. Mrs. K looked bemused, and some of the girls exchanged glances, but in the end, everyone seemed more relaxed and friendly. Before the meal concluded, Celeste talked everyone into getting haircuts.

"Only if that's okay with you and Mrs. Maitland," Celeste said fawningly to Mrs. K, who had to laugh and shake her head.

"I can't see why not as long as you clean up all the hair. If the weather is good, you can do it out on the veranda, maybe on Saturday."

At bedtime, Celeste donned a voluminous flowered flannel nightgown that fell below her knees. She looked like one of the overstuffed square pillows on Grandma Doris's couch.

Eden had already changed into threadbare cotton pajamas scrounged from the donations cupboard, shivering as her body slowly created a warm pocket in the polyester sheets. The ballerina bedspread did little to hold the heat, and Eden felt perpetually cold. Celeste would be warm and toasty, though. Eden looked enviously at her nightgown.

Celeste sat on her bed and pulled on a pair of men's work socks. This procedure was hampered by her round belly and, when she finally accomplished it, she asked, breathlessly, "Does it... smell funny in here?"

Eden laughed. "Yeah, this house smells like an old lady's armpit!"

The girls giggled, and Celeste started brushing her hair, electric sparks springing from her brush despite the dampness of the room. Eden watched her sheepishly; she had not brushed out her own hair for days. Without Barbie to nag her about it—and to attack the tangles when she felt Eden needed to be more presentable—Eden didn't give her hair much attention. Now she scraped it away from her face, lying back on her pillow to watch Celeste's toilette.

Celeste glanced at Eden, then looked politely away, seeming to brace herself for her next remark. "Would you like a haircut on Saturday? I think I have a couple of appointment times available."

Eden would have snorted, but she was trying to be on her best behaviour on their first night as roommates. *Appointment times?* "Um, I guess you could take a few inches off the bottom."

Celeste's eyes lit up. "Oh, great. I'll pencil you in at two-thirty." With a flourish, she notated the appointment in a green exercise book on her bedside table. "And a few layers would help you manage that gorgeous head of hair. It's going to look *darling*."

Eden cringed but smiled when Celeste pulled her transistor radio out of her bedside drawer. She tuned the radio through loud static until she found 620 CKCK. The announcer was introducing Paul Anka's newest hit, "Having My Baby."

Eden and Celeste clapped their hands over their mouths to control their giggling; Eden motioned violently for Celeste to turn the radio down. She obligingly adjusted the volume, humming along with a dreamy expression on her face.

"That's how I want my husband to feel when I'm expecting his baby," she said, cuddling a homemade Raggedy Ann doll.

"What husband?" Eden asked sharply.

"Well, I don't know who I will end up marrying, but I hope it's Jason Pedersen."

"What!? Why the hell would you marry *him*?"

"Everyone knows you hate Jason," Celeste said, a knowing smile on her lips. "But he's not that bad, really, Eden. As far as I'm concerned, he's the sexiest boy on this planet. Have you noticed his jeans?"

Eden was suddenly transported to another time and place. She remembered the feeling of her foot slamming against the strong muscles of Jason's stomach and the shocked expression on his face as he sat down abruptly, as if the bus had knocked him off his feet.

Perhaps if she'd kicked him in the crotch, Celeste wouldn't be pregnant right now. Then she remembered seeing Celeste leave Leanne's and Travis's wedding dance with Jason; a fatal blow to his testicles weeks later would have been too late. The deed had already been done.

"So, are you and Jason going out?" Eden asked tentatively.

"Oh, yes, for quite some time now." Celeste crawled under the covers. "But he wanted to keep it a secret, just between us. He said his mom doesn't want him to date until he's in Grade Twelve."

Horrified, Eden said nothing.

"He always used a rubber, but that one night—it was the Clement's wedding dance—well, we kind of forgot about the rubber. And that's all it took," Celeste said serenely, stifling a yawn.

"Does Jason know about this?" Eden asked.

"Oh, yes, my parents and his parents had a big talk, and they all decided to send me here until the baby comes. It's too bad that it had to happen before we got married, but it will be okay in the end. This way, I can finish school and get my hairdresser's. I'd like to have a salon in my house so I can stay home with my kids when we get married."

"Has Jason... proposed to you?"

"Well, not in so many words. But we're young, right? There's time."

From her breathing, Eden assumed Celeste had fallen asleep. Eden was on the precipice of sleep herself when she heard Celeste sobbing quietly in her bed.

Hush, Eden said silently, to both Celeste and Ava. Go to sleep now. Sleep well, little one.

Chapter 8

Eden tentatively opened the visiting room door and was immediately swept into a muscular Donnie-hug like no Donnie-hug before it. Eden relaxed into Donnie's arms, inhaling citrus shampoo and ironed cotton.

"Your hair! I just love it!" Donnie brushed her hands over Eden's smooth locks. "What, layers? It looks gorgeous. Did you go to a hairdresser?"

Eden shrugged, embarrassed. "No... a girl here cut it. I feel kinda naked, actually."

Celeste had trimmed Eden's hair to her shoulder blades and performed magic that made it easier to comb out tangles. On Celeste's advice, Eden had taken to swooping it to the side instead of parting it arrow-straight down the middle. Celeste declared she looked "less like a hippie" this way.

"Wow, she's good!" Donnie gestured for Eden to sit across from her. "Other than amazing hair, how are you doing?"

Eden glanced at her baby mound. "Okay, I guess."

"Can you feel it kicking?" Donnie reached forward as if to touch Eden's abdomen, then drew her hand back respectfully.

"Oh, yes, constantly. She's a little tiger, always on the prowl."

"Just like her mama, I suppose. You think it's a girl?"

Eden shrugged again. She knew it was a girl.

"What brings you to the city?" Eden asked, eager for any news of home.

"Well, it's Curtis." Eden noticed Donnie's eyes were red-rimmed and her heart stumbled.

"Is he okay?" Fear clutched at Eden's stomach. Ava executed a sympathetic somersault punctuated by sharp kicks to the ribcage, making her gasp.

"Yes, he's fine... probably more than fine." Donnie fished a soggy tissue out of the sleeve of her black cardigan sweater. "But it's hard to tell with Curtis."

Donnie and Vic had decided to move Curtis to a group home in the city, where he would partake in recreational and occupational therapy, including a daily excursion to the sheltered workshop to sort recycled bottles. Curtis had been in the group home for two weeks, and Donnie had come to the city to check on him.

"He just wasn't doing well at school." Donnie moved the shredded tissue from one hand to the other. "He wouldn't get on the bus anymore, for one thing. And Gordie has left the special education class, and they couldn't justify running it just for Curtis. We think that more structure will do him good. But he doesn't like change, as you know."

"How's he settling in?"

"He didn't seem to recognize me when I stopped in this morning. He wouldn't hug me or anything." Donnie started to cry. "I think he's okay, but I don't know. I miss my boy so much." She buried her face in her hands. Eden felt at a loss. *What can I say?*

"Vic and I won't be around forever to take care of him," Donnie went on. "He needs to have some independence. He's not a child anymore. He's almost a man."

Although Eden had long ago decided she would never tell anyone who had fathered her child, she was gripped now with an almost irresistible urge to tell Donnie. Maybe it would help her to know that she was going to be a grandmother and would soon have another little child to love. For the first time, it occurred to Eden that Ava might turn out like Curtis.

Was his condition hereditary? Eden tasted yet another bitter flavour of fear.

Donnie was gathering herself, wiping her eyes and nose with the tissue, then using her cardigan sleeve to finish the job. She inhaled deeply and looked around the tiny room.

"It's stuffy in here," she remarked, her pretty nose and the creases around her eyes crinkling in mild revulsion. "Why does it smell so nasty? Let's go for a walk!"

Eden jumped to her feet, eager for an outing. "I'll grab my coat upstairs! But we'll have to tell Mrs. Maitland."

"I'll do that while you get your coat." Donnie shrugged her ski jacket on. "Bundle up, it's a chilly day."

Eden pounded up the stairs and pulled the maroon coat off a hook on the wall. Donnie raised her eyebrows when she saw the coat, but made no comment as they pulled on boots and mittens and opened the heavy front door.

Cold streamed into Eden's veins as she gratefully inhaled the crisp air and a brilliant, cloudless sky. Ava kicked excitedly. Let's get going, she seemed to be saying.

Donnie and Eden marched along the sidewalk, their boots crunching in the snow. The frost-covered trees, yearning for their brothers across the street, created an archway of sparkling, mingled fingers. Eden laughed with delight when the trees released a shower of snow on their shoulders, like confetti at a wedding.

"There, that's better," Donnie said, laughing too. "There's my girl." She linked her arm with Eden's as they turned the corner and walked out of sight of Wheatland Manor.

"It's so Christmas-y," Donnie said, looking at the trees, then at Eden. "Will you be coming home for Christmas?"

Eden's mood dived from the tops of the trees to the trampled snow in the gutters. It hadn't occurred to her to wonder about Christmas. Where *would* she spend Christmas?

She stopped walking abruptly and looked into Donnie's concerned eyes. "Well, I haven't heard from Mom and Dad since I got here. No calls, no letters, no visits. Nothing. So, it's hard to say about Christmas."

"Oh, Eden." Donnie took her arm again and steered her further along the street. "You know, I haven't seen much of your mom since we dropped you off that day. I miss her too."

Eden missed home. She missed the farm's hopeful bustle, the raucous men perpetually smoking and joking at the kitchen table, the tantalizing smells of Barbie's baking and cooking, her usually good-natured and largely ignored nagging and scolding, and the quiet dark refuge of Grandma Doris's house, blinds pulled tight against scorching sun or winter blasts.

She missed the wind in her face as she urged Blackie into a gallop and the reverence she felt when she found Pussy's latest litter in the bales, carefully observing the mewling, tangled mass of kittens from a distance so Pussy wouldn't feel compelled to move them (but she always did). But did she miss Barbie? Bitterness stung the back of her throat, and she swallowed hard.

Donnie went on. "I'm not sure I completely understand what's going on, but I think your mom is overwhelmed right now. She's really worried about your dad and also furious with him. And Skylar's almost a different person entirely, as you know."

Eden remembered the feeling of his massive arms as he lifted her off her feet with his hug. If that moment of pure joy was an indication of change in her brother, it was a definite improvement over the sullen, arrogant Skylar she'd known all her life.

"River and Stacey haven't made it official yet, but it looks like she'll get a ring for Christmas, and they want to get married next summer. River can't wait to get out of the house, it's pretty obvious." Donnie smiled. "I'm not sure your mom is ready to let her oldest son go. I can totally relate to that."

"Well, I'm her kid, too. I'm still a member of the family, last time I checked. Why don't they care about me?"

Donnie was silent as they turned onto a snow-gilded street lined with well-kept historic houses. "You know, there were many times, especially in the last few years, when raising Curtis meant I barely paid attention to Angela and Carol. I left them to their own devices way too often. That's probably why they are so bratty," she said, with a quiet chuckle.

"It doesn't mean I don't love them every bit as much as I do Curtis. But I guess I sense that they are going to be okay, even without my full attention. Your mom knows you are in a safe place right now and that this will soon be over. Then you can get back to school and go on with your life. Your mom will come around, you'll see."

Come around? Eden imagined Barbie melting at first sight of her little granddaughter, clasping them both to her heart and apologizing through tears of regret. She mentally brushed this fantasy away like a wisp of snow tumbling from the trees. She had to come up with a plan because Barbie wasn't going to come around.

"Maybe I could come live with you guys after the baby is born," Eden said, hope rising as the thought suddenly occurred to her. "I could help with the girls and on the farm. The baby and I could stay in Curtis's room!"

Donnie looked stricken. "Well, Curtis will be coming home on holidays and hopefully for a few weeks every summer. We need to keep his room ready for him. And Eden... aren't you giving the baby up for adoption?"

"No, I am not giving my baby up!" Eden waved her arms, and a flock of chickadees rose in alarm from a nearby tree. "I don't care what anyone says. This baby is mine and I'm keeping her! No one can love her as much as I do."

"That's true," Donnie said calmly, "but take it from me. Raising a child is no easy thing. You don't want to do it alone."

Eden spun and ran awkwardly back to Wheatland Manor, tripping in the coat, the mink collar strangling her. She pulled at the collar to loosen it as she ran full tilt into the wind, tears streaming towards her ears.

At bedtime, Eden and Celeste listened to the radio as they always did. Celeste was full of news about the girls and staff.

"Did you know that Mrs. K was a teen mother, too?" Celeste said. "She gave her baby up for adoption twenty-five years ago, and now she has three other kids. The youngest one is still in high school. She lived here at Wheatland Manor—back then, the girls got to take care of their babies until someone came along to adopt them. She says she was holding her baby right up until the very last minute when the adoptive parents came to get him. He was three months old."

Celeste paused for breath. She turned to look at Eden, who was silent in her narrow bed.

"Was that Donalda Hughes I saw earlier?" Celeste asked. "Curtis's mom, right?"

"Yeah, Donnie is my mom's best friend. She stopped in because she was up here in the city today."

"That's nice!" Celeste exclaimed, the sympathy in her glance revealed by the faint glow of the transistor radio.

Celeste had been at Wheatland Manor for two weeks but had already received visitors—an aunt who lived in Regina, a family friend who had come up for a doctor's appointment, and her mother, who took the bus to the city and planned to come every other weekend unless the roads became impassable with winter storms.

Celeste and her mom, both glowing with pregnancy, spent the afternoon giggling and visiting in Celeste's and Eden's bedroom, with special dispensation from Mrs. K since most visits were restricted to the visiting room under strict orders from Mrs. Maitland.

Eden had skulked around downstairs that afternoon, waiting impatiently for Celeste's mother to leave so she could fling herself onto the ballerina bedspread, put her head under the pillow, and block everything out.

"I think that would be really, really hard, giving up your baby after taking care of him for three months," Celeste went on, settling herself on her left side and arranging her flannel nightgown in comfortable folds around her legs. "It's got to be better when they just take the baby away before you even see it. Before you have a chance to... start loving it."

The little catch in her voice betrayed her for a moment, but she quickly regained her loquaciousness, pushing back the room's silence with a babbling stream of chatter that Eden quickly tired of but never stopped being grateful for.

* * *

Agatha Browne was talking, but Eden wasn't listening. Her mind was careening from one bleak possibility to another. She caressed her abdomen, trying to soothe an agitated Ava.

"In this envelope, there is a brochure that I encourage you to read before our next appointment," Agatha said, hauling Eden up from an eddy of anxiety. "It outlines the adoption process quite clearly. Please let me know if you have any questions after you finish it."

Eden didn't lift her hand to take the envelope, so Agatha set it on the table beside them. They were sitting knee-to-knee in the visiting room—Agatha's pudgy legs were clad in checked wool slacks due to the plunging temperatures.

Agatha went on. "It's not too early to be getting the paperwork in order. It will help to alleviate any stress when the baby comes. You will want that time to be as *painless* as possible," she said with a little smirk. Eden rolled her eyes.

Agatha sniffed self-importantly and leaned back in her chair. "I understand from Mrs. Maitland that you haven't been in touch with your family during your time here at Wheatland Manor. I must say that is rather unusual. I gather that you and your parents are estranged?"

Eden squirmed. Agatha leaned forward, a well-rehearsed pucker of concern appearing between her eyebrows.

"Although it is unusual, it is not unheard of. A teen pregnancy can be terribly hard on a family. I will contact your parents and recommend family counselling." She pulled a battered day timer from her briefcase. "Let's see—perhaps it would be best to schedule it in the New Year. December is such a busy time for everyone!"

Eden smiled as she imagined her father attending a family counselling session, his massive frame bludgeoned into a tiny chair, work-scarred hands folded meekly while Agatha pontificated from behind a polished oak desk.

Agatha noticed the rare smile. "Yes, that's a great idea. I'll call them this afternoon. Now," she added, her sincere expression unwavering, "will you be going home for Christmas and, if so, how will you get there?" She referred to her notes. "Your home is about three hours from Regina?"

"I don't think my parents want me to come home," Eden mumbled into her chest.

"Oh, I'm sure they do! They haven't seen you for a few months; they'll be anxious to spend some time with you. I'll ask them about it when I call. Wheatland Manor either shuts down or runs a skeleton staff over Christmas; it's very uncommon to have a girl spend Christmas here. You might be all alone if you do!"

Colour drained from Eden's face as she raked her hair from roots to tips. *I won't be alone. I'll have Ava.* She straightened her back and looked directly into Agatha's eyes.

"I'll be alright alone," she said firmly. "And I'm not giving my baby up for adoption. I won't be signing any of your paperwork."

Agatha's face sucked up the colour that had leached from Eden's cheeks.

"Look, Eden." Agatha packed up her briefcase and pulled on her coat. "If you care about your baby's welfare, you will sign those papers. There are families in this province lining up to adopt babies like yours. If you love your baby, you will let it go to a loving home with a mother and a father and food on the table. Can you offer your baby that? Can you even feed your baby when it comes?"

She stood and looked down her dribbly nose at Eden. "Think about that when you read the information I'm leaving with you. Think about doing what is best for your child."

With another sniff, she was gone. Eden felt bolted to her chair, unable to heave herself to her swollen feet. Finally, she climbed the stairs to the meager comfort of her bedroom.

Actually, she thought as she lay shivering on her bed, her room was more comforting now that Celeste shared it. Celeste's possessions overflowed from her side, littering Eden's with an array of childish detritus. Celeste even put a Donny Osmond poster over Eden's bed. Eden hated Donny Osmond but was oddly soothed by his bland, handsome smile.

She was trying to sleep, wishing fervently for one of Grandma Doris's maligned afghans, when Celeste burst into the room. Eden could tell without opening her eyes that Celeste was startled to see her there and was now desperately trying not to wake her up. Celeste stealthily opened the closet door, rummaged in the boxes on the floor, then sat on her bed with a creak of ancient bedsprings.

Eden kept her eyes closed as long as humanly possible, then opened them imperceptibly to see what Celeste was up to. With her curly hair in two ponytails on the top of her head, Celeste looked like a great horned owl on a perch.

"Hi!" Celeste said, beaming. "Wakey-wakey!"

Eden rolled onto her back with a groan, looking into Donny Osmond's cow-like eyes.

"God, I hate Donny Osmond," she said, taking up their favourite joke. "He looks like a Ken doll."

"Yes, the best kind of man there is. Dick-less!"

Eden and Celeste were highly amused by off-colour jokes, and this one had them rolling in their beds with suppressed laughter. Eden suddenly sobered.

"I just met with Agatha. She is pushing me to sign adoption papers. At least this time she didn't ask me who Ava's father is."

Celeste looked sidelong at her. This was a touchy subject for Eden, one she rarely raised. Celeste was uncharacteristically silent, waiting.

"Have *you* signed the papers?" Eden asked.

"Oh, yes, weeks ago. *Maman* was here and we signed them together since I'm a minor."

"Maybe if my parents don't come to the city to sign the papers, I won't have to put Ava up for adoption." Eden sat up. "It won't be legal!"

Celeste looked doubtful. "Mrs. Maitland said I could have signed them without my parents' consent, so I don't think that would work." Then a thought occurred to her.

"Josey is giving her baby up, but she says she can't go home because her parents don't want her back. She says she's going on welfare. Maybe you and the baby could go on welfare, too."

"Why didn't I think of that? I'll have to ask Agatha about that! Wow. Maybe."

Eden contemplated this possibility for a moment, then looked at Celeste.

"Agatha said Wheatland Manor closes at Christmas, and everyone goes home for the holidays. But I don't think I can. I don't think Mom and Dad want me home." She swallowed a stinging lump of tears.

"Eden," Celeste said gently. "Call your mom and ask. You can call collect. They will accept the call."

Celeste had suggested this before, but every time Eden passed the telephone in the hallway, her heart convulsed, and she broke out in a sweat.

"Yeah, maybe one of these days." Eden swung her legs ponderously over the edge of the bed. "I'm on kitchen duty, so I'd better get down there."

* * *

Josey went into labour on the morning of Celeste's sixteenth birthday. She and Eden were in the same grade at school because Celeste had repeated Grade One to improve her English skills. The Tremblay family spoke French at home.

Josey walked restlessly throughout the house wearing a plaid men's housecoat, her short red hair sweat-spiked all over her head. She clutched her huge belly with every contraction, resting her head on the wall while breathing deeply.

Eden avoided her as much as she could, but Celeste walked beside her, holding her hand and making encouraging noises. Finally, Dr. Andrews showed up, declaring within minutes it was time for Josey to head to the hospital. Wheatland Manor thrummed with subdued excitement.

"Josey won't be back, you know," Eden told Celeste. "We'll never get to see the baby or even see Josey again. This was her last day here."

"Oh, she has promised to write and tell me what she had and how it went."

Celeste started to open her birthday cards. "Isn't this one cute from *Maman* and Papa? Look at the kittens!" She balanced the card on a pink doily and tucked the rest into the frame of the bureau mirror.

"It must be so weird when the baby comes out," Eden mused, stroking her belly. "I mean, now our babies are part of us but after they are born, they are their own person."

"They'll always be part of us," Celeste said sadly.

"I've always felt something was missing inside me, ever since I was a little kid. You know I was born a twin, right? But now that I've got *my* Ava, I don't feel that way anymore. It's like I just had to wait a few years to get my sister back."

Eden glanced over at Celeste to see how she was taking this. Celeste looked blankly at her for a moment, then laughed.

"Wow, that's really messed up." She looked at the poster. "Donny, Eden needs therapy, preferably physical therapy!" Both girls laughed at that.

"Agatha says she is going to call my parents and recommend family counselling." Eden was still shaking her head at the vision of her father in a therapy session. "I better not tell anyone about my crazy ideas; they'll put me in the loony bin!"

A few evenings later, Eden walked to the telephone and dialled zero without completely deciding to do it. When the operator answered, she recited her home number and asked to place a collect call. A clammy sweat rose on her forehead as she listened to the crackling line during the endless seconds it took for the call to go through.

"Yeah, hello?" Barbie always sounded disgruntled by a call, as if she had better things to do than chit-chat on the telephone.

"Collect call from Eden," the operator said tonelessly. "Will you accept the charges?"

There was a silence, and Eden considered hanging up as she wiped her slick forehead with the back of her hand. Then Barbie said, "Yes, Operator, I'll accept the charges."

"Hi, Mom," Eden said, a little girl whine rising unbidden at the sound of her mother's voice. To her shame, a sob bubbled up from the deep place where Ava was peacefully sleeping.

"Oh, hi, Eden. Are you okay?"

"Yeah," Eden said morosely. "I just thought... it would be nice to talk."

"We heard from your social worker—was it Miss Brownley? She gave us a bit of an update. She said you are doing well physically, but perhaps not so well mentally. She said you are resisting her efforts to set up an adoption. Is that right, Eden?"

Hair rose on the back of Eden's neck like porcupine quills. All little girl impulses evaporated. "I will not be giving Ava up." As soon as she said it, she realized her mistake.

"Ava? What the hell are you talking about?"

"I mean, I don't want to give my baby up. I want to keep it." Barbie was silent on the line, but Eden could hear her breathing unevenly.

"Mom, can I talk to Dad?" Eden suddenly craved a dose of George Senior's jovial bluster.

"Your father is sleeping," Barbie said tersely. "He is usually in bed right after supper these days. Eden, he drinks from morning until night. You have no idea."

"Is it... I mean, it's not my fault, is it?" Guilt thrust a fresh wound into her heart.

"Between your situation, Skylar's injury, a lousy crop, and major tension between your father and River right now, it has been a trying time for him," Barbie said. "But it really comes down to his decision to drink or not drink, and he has no right making any of these things an excuse for his behaviour. He has to grow up and take responsibility for himself."

Barbie paused. "But I do think it's best that you are in the city, so he doesn't have to be continually reminded of what I suppose he thinks of as his failure to protect you from the predator who made you pregnant and who you insist on protecting!"

"I was going to ask if I could come home for Christmas, but I suppose that's out of the question."

"Well, Grandma Doris is sleeping in your room because we need to keep an eye on her at all times. She isn't doing the greatest, and we've got her on a waiting list for the care home in town. You can just imagine how much fun it is having her under our roof twenty-four hours a day."

"Poor Grandma." The sob was threatening to burst out again.

"So, really, Eden, there's no room here for you this Christmas. You are better off there until the baby comes, then you can come home if you want to."

Eden didn't exactly slam the receiver down, but she did replace it decisively without another word, spinning abruptly to go to her room.

Mrs. K was standing behind her with a resolute expression Eden knew well. As Eden swerved to avoid her, her belly struck the woman's arm. Before she realized what was happening, Mrs. K had captured her in a doughy embrace.

Eden froze, wondering how to break away gracefully.

"There, there," Mrs. K said. "You will come home with me for Christmas and that's that." There was the sob. *That is so kind.*

"Thank you, Mrs. K," Eden mumbled into the shoulder of her house dress; it smelled of garlic and onions. "But I'll be okay here."

"Nonsense. I will speak with Mrs. Maitland and Agatha Browne in the morning. I know staff are discouraged from getting involved, but honestly, I've rarely come across a family like yours in all my years at Wheatland Manor. Imagine not letting you come home for Christmas!" She released Eden and huffed back to the kitchen.

The girls were watching television in the residents' lounge. They all turned to gape as Eden sprinted past the open door. Despite her cumbersomeness, she took the stairs two at a time and flung herself on her bed.

She wasn't surprised when Celeste appeared in the doorway, rushing to wrap her arms around her. Unlike Mrs. K's overtures, Eden was grateful for Celeste's gentle hand on her hair, smoothing it back from her tears. It reminded her of Barbie's efforts to help her sleep after a nightmare when she was a child.

Eden sat up and wiped her face with the backs of her hands. Celeste handed her a tissue, and she blew into it with a honk. *That's enough now. Enough of that.*

"Well, you tried," Celeste said. "Good for you; it's all you can do. Now we can make plans for Christmas!" She squealed and clapped her hands.

"What do you mean?" Eden said, hiccupping as her sobs subsided.

"You are coming home for Christmas with me. I have already talked to *Maman* about it, and she's all for it. She loves a full house at Christmas."

Full house? Isn't the Tremblay household full to the rafters every day of the year? Eden had to smile. Yes, she thought. Celeste's home would provide shelter from the prying world and escape from this mouldy old house for a few days. *Yes, thank God.*

Chapter 9

It was nearly dark when they arrived at the Tremblays' farmhouse. Before Eden knew what was happening, an army of children descended on the Impala station wagon. Eden, Celeste, and her parents Odette and Denis—and all their suitcases and packages—were unceremoniously dumped inside the front door. Someone peeled off Eden's coat, and one of the children tried to pull off her boots, causing her to tumble backward until Denis gallantly caught her by the shoulders.

"*Attendez!*" he admonished. "Let the girl get her bearings, you pack of wild animals!"

A broad woman with grey curls approached from the kitchen, wiping her hands with a stained dish towel. She chattered in French with Odette, then turned to Eden.

"*Bonsoir*, Miss English, so very nice to meet you!" she said warmly. "I am Celeste's old aunt, here to make supper for you all. I hope you like *tourtière*."

"Um, I... sure, thank you." Eden didn't know where to turn or what to do as members of the Tremblay clan darted from room to room.

"Eden, bring your suitcase into my room." Celeste grabbed her hand. "I'll show you where we are going to sleep." Celeste led Eden into a bedroom crowded with bunk beds, a small double bed, two dressers, and a toy chest.

"Gisele, Amelie, Lucie, pick up your toys!" Celeste barked at the little girls who had followed them. "How are we supposed to unpack our bags and settle in? Ooh, what's this?" Celeste fell to her knees and picked up a doll from the floor.

"That's mine!" The littlest girl Lucie snatched the doll from Celeste's hands. "For my birthday!"

"Oh, it's so cute! What is her name?" Celeste scooped Lucie and the doll, holding them precariously in her lap. Lucie burst into laughter, her pearly teeth showing as she rolled her head against Celeste's belly.

"Celeste, *ton bébé est si grand!*" she said, wriggling against her sister.

Ava could hear the high-pitched prattle of the little girls; she began to pound on Eden as if demanding to join the party. The girls darted around Celeste like curious barn swallows. Eden sank to the bed, gratitude rising like spring sap as she recalled the empty corridors of Wheatland Manor.

"*Le temps de manger!*" roared Denis, and it seemed to Eden that horses were galloping through the house as the family gathered in the kitchen. Everyone squeezed around the wooden table except Celeste's brothers, Gilbert and Alain, who sat nearby at a shaky card table.

After a prolonged prayer led by Denis in French—unfamiliar with this ritual, Eden followed the crowd and bowed her head—the *tourtière* was served, along with fresh bread and salad.

Tourtière was a meat pie that Eden found spicy but delicious. Celeste's aunt watched her devour her first helping, then reached across the table to give her another piece immediately.

Like at home, there was no shortage of food here. Memories of her mother's wonderful cooking and the banter around the English family table—not as rowdy as this one, but still lively and laughter-filled—darkened Eden's mood like a storm cloud over the sun.

Odette noticed the tiny tear in Eden's eye. "*Ma chérie*, you are welcome here," she whispered into Eden's ear with a whiff of Chanel No. 5 and red wine. "Do not despair."

After dinner, Celeste's aunt departed, and Odette, Celeste, and Eden cleaned the kitchen while Denis and Gilbert, the eldest of the brothers—he was fourteen—

smoked at the table. The rest of the children dissolved into the now-quiet house.

"It is the three pregnant ladies that do all the work around here," Odette complained, hoisting her belly around the room as she wiped the counters and tables.

She took a swipe with the dishrag at Denis's smirk; he intervened by grabbing her arm, and before Odette could say another word, she was sitting on his lap, trapped in a human vise. The ensuing struggle drove Gilbert from the table, and soon Celeste and Eden were alone, surrounded by tilting towers of plates and bowls.

"This always happens," Celeste murmured to Eden. "I am glad you are here to help me, at least. Gisele! Come dry dishes!"

The rest of the evening passed in a blur. All Eden could recall later was the sweet, sweaty body of the youngest Tremblay—one-year-old Hugo had found a pocket of warmth in her lap and refused to leave it, sucking passionately on his thumb while fighting sleep as long as he possibly could. Finally, Odette said to Celeste, "Take that boy and put him to bed *tout de suite!*"

Celeste plucked Hugo from Eden's lap and nodded for her to follow. In her parents' bedroom, Celeste changed him into a flannel sleeper and placed the inert little body into a wooden crib beside the bed.

Eden wondered where the new baby would sleep; in fact, she wondered where everyone would sleep in this tiny house. She discovered that Gilbert and Alain slept in the attic accessed by a ladder on the living room wall. Gisele, who usually slept in the double bed with Celeste, crawled groggily into the bottom bunk with Lucie.

"No one ever sleeps with Amelie," Celeste explained as she watched her sister climb the bunk bed ladder. "She snores!" The girls laughed loudly while Amelie haughtily plumped her pillow, turning her back on the hilarity.

Eden looked askance at Celeste's bed. "This is a double?" she remarked, wondering how she, Celeste, and their babies were going to lie down together in it.

"It's called a French bed," Celeste explained. "Appropriate, *non*? Come on, squeeze in!"

After negotiating, elbowing, shifting, and giggling, Eden and Celeste settled into a tenable sleeping arrangement—Eden faced the wall, her back snuggled into Celeste's, who faced the bunk beds. Ava administered the occasional jab, rebuking her mother for such a long, arduous day. Eden closed her eyes.

"Do you believe in aliens?"

"What?" *Here we go.* Celeste rarely stopped talking, even at bedtime.

"I think if aliens invaded the Earth, all the countries would have to join together to fight them away. We would become one great big country, and then we would have no more war among us. We would have world peace."

"Wow, that would be nice for a change," Eden muttered, barely moving her lips. Except for a little smile.

"I would hate it if my baby had to go to war."

"I am pretty sure your baby is a boy. I can see why you might worry."

"How do you know these things?" Celeste asked in wonder. "How do you know you have a girl?"

"I don't know how I know. I just do, especially with Ava. She's a girl, for sure."

Celeste became quiet, and Eden slipped gratefully off the cliff.

"Do you believe in God?"

Eden's eyes flicked open. She stared for a moment into the womb-like room, listening to Amelie snore rhythmically and Denis snort erratically across the hall. *I wonder if he drinks. He snores just like my dad.*

"I kind of do," Eden said, thinking about the swirling, sweeping prairie and the thrill of galloping with her horse through the wild grasses. The pure wind that restored the gasping horse and blew her cares away. The vast sky that smiled upon her, sheltering and guiding as she rode.

"I do, too. But it is hard to believe in God when you think about aliens. You know?"

"It's probably one of those things it's best not to think about too much," Eden said. "Can we sleep?"

Celeste fidgeted as she sought a comfortable position. After she had become still, Eden said, "I think I owe you an apology." Eden could tell that Celeste heard her; her stillness grew wary and questioning. She did not speak.

"I wasn't very nice to you at school," Eden said softly. "I was a real bitch, to be honest. You are a great person, and you come from a really nice family. So, I'm sorry."

Celeste continued to lie preternaturally still. Then she called out, "Donny, where are you when we need you! Eden needs physical therapy again."

"Shut up, you idiot! You'll wake the house." Eden poked Celeste with her foot, and the girls—well-practiced in stifling giggles—stuffed their mouths with the sheet, snorting and gasping, then slowly settled down to sleep.

***

The next day was Christmas Eve. Celeste's aunt—actually, it was Odette's aunt, Sylvie—returned early in the morning to help Odette make the Christmas Eve supper. The women blocked the door to the kitchen with a small table, which allowed them to shout orders to the others while preventing all but Hugo from entering their workspace.

Hugo crawled back and forth from the kitchen to the living room and down the hallway, searching plaintively for his siblings, who tended to ignore him. Eventually, he sat under the table, sucking his thumb voraciously and watching all the festivities; in time, he curled up and took a long nap on the floor.

While the women cooked, the others decorated a tree that Denis and Gilbert cut from the shelterbelt behind the house. The tree was lopsided, but Celeste and Gisele skillfully tied the branches together to give it a traditional Christmas tree shape.

Eden helped by surreptitiously rehanging ornaments that Lucie and Amelie had hooked to the bottommost branches. The little girls didn't notice; they shrieked with delight whenever another glass ornament was removed from its wrappings. In the end, the tree drooped impressively with ornaments and tinsel. The lights, however, would not be plugged in until after midnight Mass. This was a strict rule.

By now, Eden thought, Barbie's Christmas tree would be standing dejectedly in the corner, long since decorated and taken for granted. Eden wanted to help decorate the tree when she was a little girl, but Barbie was always in a hurry, quickly doing it herself and grumbling about the lack of interest George Senior and the boys were showing in the task.

"They seem to think Christmas just happens, like that," she would say, snapping her fingers. Barbie looked at photos from *Good Housekeeping* or *Redbook* to guide her tree-decorating efforts, and every year ordered new ornaments from Sears to add to the design. As a child, Eden sat at the foot of this wonder for hours, watching the sun animate the sparkling baubles and poking the wrapped gifts with a careful finger until her mother told her to stop.

There were no gifts under the Tremblays' tree; apparently, presents would appear magically while everyone was at Mass and could not be touched until after the feast to follow. Eden wondered if the family stayed up all night on Christmas Eve.

Excitement was beginning to overtake the homesickness that hit Eden like an avalanche earlier in the day. Even Alain, who considered himself much more mature than Gisele, Amelie, and Lucie, was bouncing on his tiptoes, socks trailing off his feet as he ran from room to room in a fever of anticipation. The little girls chased him relentlessly until he fell to the floor and let them jump on him. The noise rattled the rafters. Hugo slept through it all.

This, Eden thought. This is the kind of family I want.

Somehow amid the melee, Celeste found time to cut the kids' hair—except Alain, who would not sit still, and Lucie, who ran howling in search of her doll when she saw the scissors—and then put a French braid in Eden's hair.

"French braid, French bed, am I seeing a pattern here?" Eden asked, submitting to Celeste's firm fingers. She loved the result; for the first time in many months, Eden took a good look at her ears, which she had always considered to be one of her best features.

Celeste rummaged deeply in Odette's tangled jewelry box to find a pair of tiny clip-on earrings for Eden. Eden felt self-conscious but also very alluring as she examined her new look in the dresser mirror, twisting around to admire the back of her head and her elegant ears.

At supper time, platters of sandwiches and cookies appeared on the doorway-blocking table. Everyone took small plates of food and glasses of purple Kool-Aid into the living room to consume carefully. After supper, Denis, Sylvie's husband Claude, who had arrived at some point, and Gilbert chased the children from the armchairs and sat down with cigarettes and glasses of whisky to admire the tree and stretch their long legs into the room.

Claude pulled a harmonica from his shirt pocket and soon all the kids were leaping and twirling in the middle of the room, while the men kept time with their feet and the women hollered from the kitchen to keep it down, for cripes sake! For Eden, sitting unnoticed in the corner, it was a glory.

The festivities continued throughout the evening. Eventually, Hugo and Lucie were put to bed, and Amelie fell asleep at her father's feet. He extended his legs to provide dubious protection from the gyrations of Alain and Gisele, who seemed tireless. Yes, Eden thought, we are staying up all night.

Around ten o'clock, the men left to hitch up the team. Denis's Impala would not start; the men had spent much of the day trying to get the motor to turn over in the blasting cold. The only alternative was to hitch the stone boat to the horses to take the family to Sainte-Marie, a tiny village about two miles away.

At around the same time, the bundling process began. The family put on almost every article of clothing they possessed to brave the daunting night. Eden wore all the clothes she had brought, plus an old sweater of Odette's under the maroon coat, carefully wrapping her French braid in a plaid scarf.

Sylvie and Claude were staying behind with the sleeping little ones; they obsessively checked that everyone's coats and boots were buttoned and secure. Finally, the clot of children burst from the house, brightening the night with colourful mittens, scarves, and toques, their laughter floating in a billowing fog above their heads.

Amelie had been awakened for the excursion; it was her first midnight Mass. Once Odette and Amelie were settled on old quilts in the high-sided stone boat, the rest of the children, including Celeste and Eden, crowded around them. Looking up at the shimmering Milky Way, Eden wondered how two horses could possibly pull them all.

With an impatient shake of their harness, the massive draft horses strained in tandem, and the stone boat leaped forward. Denis, Gilbert, and Alain walked beside the horses, expertly guiding the swaying barge and its priceless cargo along the misty river road to Sainte-Marie. It did not seem to touch the ground.

The prairie sank fierce teeth into the exposed parts of Eden's face, but she felt warm enough under the quilts with the squirming children. The full moon followed them, worriedly peering down from among a billion quivering cousins. Eventually, they pulled up in front of the church, the light from its open doors casting a welcoming carpet for their frozen feet.

A babble of laughter, the homely smell of wet wool, and a waft of incense filled the air as they lined up to enter a pew near the front. When Eden and Celeste peeled off their outer layers, the volume in the room dipped—everyone had noticed their pregnancies. Within seconds, the chatter resumed, but Eden felt as if she had stripped off all her clothes. Her naked ears reddened in embarrassment and defiance.

Gilbert squeezed beside Eden, his cold coat brushing her arm and bringing relief from the dormant volcano inside her. He wiped his nose on his mitten and grinned at her. Then he tilted his head to peer closely at her ear.

"Your ears are very beautiful," he said under the noise in the room, his green-eyed seriousness seeking her cynical brown gaze. Eden had to laugh. *Yes, with these magnificent ears, I will go far.*

The Mass was conducted entirely in French. Eden grew drowsy as the priest murmured in his white robes, but she was held firmly upright by Gilbert's hard arm on her left and Celeste's soft one on the right. At the end of the service, ushers ceremoniously lit candles row by row. When the electric lights came down, the worshippers gasped in awe as the stars inside the little wooden church soared to greet the stars keeping watch above.

Tears rolled down Eden's cheeks; she rubbed Ava affectionately, not caring who saw her caressing her child. Like baby Jesus in the crèche, this little one was loved and wanted despite the circumstances of her birth.

After saying *Joyeux Noel* to dozens of neighbours and relatives, the family wedged themselves back into the stone boat, survived the bumpy ride by singing rowdy renditions of "Mon Beau Sapin" and "Vive Le Vent," admired brilliant waves of wrapped gifts washing up under the glistening tree, and—once the men had unharnessed and fed the horses—savoured an exquisite meal with more dishes than Eden could count.

Christmas Day had arrived. *Joyeux.*

Chapter 10

1975
Regina, Saskatchewan

A warm January wind was moaning in the eaves when Celeste screamed and lurched to a sitting position on her bed.

Eden could see her silhouette swaying against the streetlight glow on the lace curtains. She switched on the overhead light—Celeste was clutching her back with both hands, leaning forward as much as her pregnancy would allow.

Eden gasped when she saw blood seeping into the sheet beneath Celeste, soaking her flannel nightgown. "Oh, my God!"

"My back hurts so much, Eden." Celeste's head was bowed so Eden couldn't see her face. "It hurts. *Mon Dieu*, help me."

Mrs. K flew into their room. "Calm down, sweetheart," she said to Celeste. "We will call an ambulance right away."

She looked at Eden, arms around Celeste's shoulders and face grim. "Call the Operator. Tell her it's an emergency at Wheatland Manor."

Eden took the stairs three at a time, forgetting she was pregnant and should be more careful. As she waited at the door for the ambulance, two girls joined her in the chilly foyer, clutching one another's hands in concern and for warmth. Eden did not indulge in the hand-clasping; she stared ferociously into the street, willing the ambulance to materialize in the starless night.

Celeste's cries filled the corners of Wheatland Manor like rising floodwaters. Eden feared she would drown in her anxiety, but within minutes the ambulance pulled up, its throbbing lights piercing her eyes as she peered into the darkness.

Two uniformed men rushed into the house with a stretcher, leaving it in the hallway as they clomped up the steep stairs. One of them carried Celeste down carefully as Mrs. K fluttered behind him, waving Celeste's white coat like a flag of surrender. The paramedics strapped Celeste to the stretcher, covered her with the coat, and wheeled her to the ambulance with impersonal efficiency.

"Wait, I'll come with you," Eden cried, running onto the veranda in her bare feet. "Celeste, I'm coming! Hang on, don't worry!"

"Oh, no, you don't." Mrs. K's fist was a steel vice around Eden's arm. "Come back inside. She is in good hands."

"But she's all alone!" Eden stumbled into the house with a twist of Mrs. K's no-nonsense arm. "She can't be alone right now. She would never leave me all alone, never!"

With a forlorn bleep, the ambulance pulled away from the curb, making a U-turn toward the hospital.

"Come, girls, I'll make us tea." Mrs. K encompassed them in a sweeping gesture that wagged her underarm flesh. "It will be morning soon, so come along."

But Eden turned back to the stairs.

"Okay, then. Shirley, put the kettle on, and I will be right back." Mrs. K followed Eden to her room, stripped Celeste's bed of its bloody sheets, and bustled out, leaving Eden curled up protectively around Ava and shuddering with shock.

Eden knew as soon as she opened her eyes that she had slept through breakfast; it was the first time she had been allowed to sleep in. She listened to the muffled sounds of the house—the vacuum cleaner whining in the hallway, girls murmuring as they worked on their school assignments, and the jarring ring of the telephone in Mrs. Maitland's office below.

Celeste's cheerful chirp was missing from the homey hum of the Manor. Although Eden had not expected to hear her voice, she found herself listening for it in the same way she saw HoundDog hovering at the edges of her vision when she did chores in the barn or rode Patches in the pasture. There, but not there.

She shrugged on the frilly blue housecoat she had found in the donations cupboard and walked directly to Mrs. Maitland's office door.

"I just got off the phone with Dr. Andrews," Mrs. Maitland said, not waiting for Eden's question. "Celeste will be okay, don't worry. She might need to stay in the hospital for a few days, though. She's been through a lot in the last few hours."

"And... and the baby?"

"Eden, that is confidential information, you know that." Mrs. Maitland stood to leave the room. "I'm afraid I can't divulge that information at this time. I believe you are long overdue for study time. Please get dressed and join the others."

The chill Eden felt as she dressed did not stem from the chronically frigid temperatures at Wheatland Manor. *There's something wrong.* Mrs. Maitland had not returned to her office, so it was easy for Eden to slip out the front door carrying the maroon coat.

A chinook wind was lapping the snow like a thirsty dog. Eden was grateful for the warm wind because the coat no longer buttoned up over her waistline. She hurried along the familiar route to the hospital.

She decided not to stop at the reception desk but instead followed the clearly marked hallways to the maternity ward. She peeked around the corner; the busy ward clerk did not raise her head. Behind her was a whiteboard with 'Tremblay 6' written in bold red marker. Eden straightened her back, tucked the coat around Ava, and walked with contrived indifference to room six. No one even glanced at her.

Curtains encircled Celeste's bed. Eden opened them hesitantly and gasped. Celeste was lying under a sheet, stomach almost flat, hair and face the same institutional grey as the pillowcase under the fluorescent lights. Her eyes stared sightlessly like the marble angel guarding the Catholic cemetery outside Sainte-Marie.

"Celeste!" Eden reached for her flaccid hand; Celeste flinched and looked away. There had been tears, but now only salty rivulets marked her pale cheeks.

"Oh, honey, what happened?" Eden said.

"It's over," Celeste said. "It's over now."

"Good. I'm glad it's over."

"I always knew I would have to give my baby away," Celeste whispered, "but I wanted it to live. I wanted it to live its life, you know?"

"Oh, Celeste, I'm so sorry."

"The placenta came apart, and my little baby died. He died."

"There wasn't anything you could have done differently."

"I know."

"It was a boy. See, I was right."

"*Oui.*"

Eden wanted to kiss Celeste's cheek and lie down beside her, but she remained sitting on the edge of the bed, helpless.

"Jason Pedersen," Celeste said abruptly. "He did not even send a card on my birthday. It was on my birthday that he... that we first... you know. Now he does not have time for me. Now I hear he is dating Carrie Klein."

Eden started at the mention of her friend's name; her once-friend, she reminded herself.

"That girl should run far away from him," Celeste said. There was no hint of irony or humour in her voice; there was no sign of Celeste in this lifeless form on the bed.

The curtains parted with an authoritative rattle, and Dr. Andrews and a nurse walked into the space.

"Eden English, what are you doing here?" Dr. Andrews said harshly. "Celeste needs to rest. Please get back to the Manor!"

Eden stood and stared at the doctor. "Will she be alright? Tell me she will be okay!"

"Yes, yes, of course. But please... I don't believe you have permission to be here. It is not visiting hours, so off with you!"

Eden looked at Celeste, who had closed her eyes. With a final squeeze of her hand, Eden fled the room, taking the stark emergency exit stairs to the concrete parking lot, then down one more level to the street. Bare trees swung wearily in the strong breeze. Eden took a big breath. *What now?*

She had no choice but to go back to Wheatland Manor. Her stomach reminded her that she had not eaten breakfast, and she felt nauseous. As she turned toward the Manor, she nearly collided with Porgie.

"Whoo, mama, you're a mama!" he exclaimed, drawing back to behold her protruding stomach.

"Hi, Porgie," Eden said with a smile. "How is Harry?"

"Aw, he sobered up and moved back north. Crazy asshole!"

"How about you? You doing okay?" Eden asked, gagging slightly from Porgie's stench. He was still wearing the black bunny hug beneath a tattered Hudson's Bay blanket coat. He was a multi-coloured bright spot on a dreary day.

"I got beat up bad yesterday, see?" He pointed to a yellow bruise beside his eye. "You got any money?"

"Nope, sorry. I live in a home for pregnant teenagers. They don't pay well over there."

"You look ready to pop. Well, gotta get going. See ya around town." Porgie wobbled off.

That night, Eden stared into the fathomless dark for hours. Ava fluttered questioningly, then fell asleep.

Celeste's boxes and suitcases were stacked in the foyer, waiting for her parents to pick up. Mrs. K left the Donny Osmond poster over Eden's bed.

Up until now, Eden's greatest fear was that her baby would be taken from her. Now, her biggest fear was that Ava would die. She could hear echoes of Celeste's cries and see the bloodstained sheets on the inside of her eyelids when she tried to sleep. For the first time, she began to fear the birth itself. She knew it hurt, but hearing Celeste in agony terrified her.

She walked over to Celeste's bed, pulled back the ballerina bedspread, and crawled between the laundered sheets. There was no trace of Celeste's baby powder scent. She was truly gone.

***

Eden's pain began in the first week of March. She was sitting at the dining room table working on math. Math was the last subject she needed to complete Grade Ten. She had advanced to Grade Eleven subjects and already had her English and social studies credits. She squirmed in her chair, trying to soothe the cramp in her abdomen. Ava was very, very quiet. She suddenly realized that she hadn't felt Ava move for a long time.

Mrs. K hustled into the room. "Girls, put your books away. Study time is over, and it's chore time." One or two of them groaned. "None of that!" Mrs. K said, scowling.

"Mrs. K, I think there's something wrong with my baby," Eden said. "She hasn't moved today."

"Well, you are close to your time. Babies like to rest before the big day. Do you feel any pain?"

"Yeah, a bit. Like cramps."

"Go lie down. I will excuse you from chores today."

Eden went to her room, but she didn't lie down. She paced, feeling more cramps and remembering

131

Celeste's desperate pain. This wasn't like that at all. *Hang on, Ava. We'll get this over with as quickly as possible.*

But it wasn't quick for Eden. All night, the cramps surged and retreated, permitting spurts of blessed sleep and then snatching it away again. In the morning, after Dr. Andrews probed with a gloved finger while she white-knuckled the examination table, Eden resumed her restless pacing and waiting. She was a long way from the delivery room, as Dr. Andrews put it.

Eden had written to Celeste twice with no response. Celeste loved writing and receiving letters; her silence told Eden she was still grieving. Celeste wasn't there to help Eden scale this wall of sheer pain. Eden felt she could never reach the top alone.

Shortly after lunch, Agatha Browne came into the house in a puff of snow. "Beastly weather," Agatha remarked, brushing her brown coat with red hand-knitted mittens. Eden tried to retrace her steps to the kitchen, but Agatha spotted her at once.

"Eden, a moment, please." Agatha gestured to the visiting room. Eden shuffled in, one hand on her back. A contraction was twisting her uterus like a wringer washer squeezing a sheet.

"Dr. Andrews tells me that you are in labour," Agatha said without preliminaries. "I have the adoption papers here for you to sign, and I strongly recommend that you do it now before you go to the hospital."

She thrust the papers into Eden's hands, who dropped them as another strong contraction crashed down on her. She sank into the chair and breathed heavily, not looking at Agatha. With each contraction, she burrowed deeper into a hot tunnel where the rest of the world did not exist.

"Eden, look at me!" Agatha exclaimed. "A couple is waiting in a hotel room right now to take your baby to their wonderful home. They have been waiting to adopt a baby for several years. These are your baby's parents. You can't raise it yourself. You know this. Sign the papers now!"

Eden raked her sweat-darkened hair away from her face with both hands. "No," she said. "I want to go on welfare and take care of my baby myself. I want to get a job and take care of her. I am her mother."

"We have been all through this, Eden. You can't go on welfare unless you have no other means of support. And your parents want you to come home after all this is over. You have their support, so you can't go on welfare. Can't you understand this?"

Anger and desperation flooded Eden's pain-addled brain. "No! Leave me alone! Don't talk to me again!" She left the room abruptly.

Dr. Andrews dropped in after office hours, examined Eden, and declared she should go to the hospital for the duration of the labour. "No point in you getting up in the middle of the night," he said to Mrs. K.

"Oh, that's nothing new in my line of work." Mrs. K laughed flirtatiously. Eden glared at them. *I'm having a baby over here, if you don't mind.* With Mrs. K's help, she packed her suitcase, and Dr. Andrews drove her through the snow to the hospital in his Lincoln.

As she laboured throughout the evening and into the night, Eden retreated into her body. She emerged from her cave only when the nurse strapped a monitor over her belly to check the baby's heartbeat or encouraged Eden to use laughing gas to ease the pain. The gas did nothing to soften the bludgeoning contractions, but Eden obediently inhaled until she lost patience and pushed it away.

It was the first time since she found out she was pregnant that she didn't feel Ava's presence. Her little daughter was about to tear herself away to live her own life. Eden was on this frightening journey alone. Even Ava had abandoned her.

At one point, Eden surfaced from her lava bed of pain to see strangers gathered around her. They lifted her to a stretcher and took her to a cold lonely place. Here, although she wanted to pace around the room, they forced her to lie back with her feet in metal stirrups.

"No, no, I can't!" she screamed, churning the frigid air with her legs and arms.

She heard voices but couldn't understand the language. When Ava entered the birth canal to begin her slow, burning journey into waiting hands, Eden screamed. The separation was far worse than the birthing. She screamed and screamed until the nurse gave her an injection, and then she slept.

* * *

Eden opened her eyes. She was lying on her side. After a moment, her father's feet came into focus. His scuffed cowboy boots extended into the room, and his head was tilted against the tall back of a green padded chair. His mouth was partially open. He was asleep.

How long have I been sleeping? Memories of the previous night lashed her face like icy water. She sat up abruptly and looked down at the pale-yellow hospital gown she was wearing. Her body was flat. *Ava!*

"Dad!" Eden shouted. Her father leaped to his feet, his greying hair a wild halo around his head.

"Where is my baby?" Eden started to climb out of the bed, but George Senior grasped her shoulders and held her down on the mattress.

"Hold it, sister. Let's just hold on for a minute." Her father bent down to look into her eyes. "Your baby is going to a good family. This is the only way, Eden. You've got to accept it."

"But I'm her momma." Eden began to moan, an unearthly crooning that frightened her.

Barbie rushed into the room, strode over to Eden, and shook her arm with a heartless hand. "That's enough now. People are resting here. Keep it down."

Eden wrenched her arm from her mother's grasp, and reached out to her father like a toddler. George picked her up, carried her over to the chair, and rocked her tenderly. Barbie busied herself by sorting through the items in Eden's suitcase.

"But Dad, I didn't sign the papers. The... adoption papers," Eden sobbed. "So, they can't take Ava away from me!"

Barbie swung around furiously at the mention of Ava's name. George gave her a dagger look, then hitched Eden closer to his chest.

"Don't worry, it's all taken care of. You don't have to worry about anything. We'll take you home and you can see Patches and Blackie. And we have a surprise for you that I think you're gonna like."

"I already know about Barker," Eden said into his neck.

"This is an even better surprise. You'll see."

"Why?" Eden shifted so she was sitting upright on George's lap. "Why can't I keep my baby? Can I see her?" She started wailing again.

"You know why, Eden," her mother said, her voice rising to be heard over Eden's sorrow. "You are fifteen years old. You can't be a mother to that child; you never could. You are a child yourself."

"Shush now," George said, over and over, to Eden and to Barbie. "Shush." Eden could smell liquor like faded perfume on his leathery skin. There was booze in every cell of his body. It was a familiar smell that reminded her of childhood.

A nurse slipped into the room. "Good afternoon," she said. "Dr. Andrews will be here shortly. Eden, do you need to change your pad? Come on, let's go to the washroom."

Eden followed the nurse meekly into the adjoining toilet room. When she emerged, Dr. Andrews was talking with her parents.

"She did pretty good, all in all," he was saying. "A little hysteria at the end. It had been a long day for her. She was in labour for about thirty-six hours."

George winced and looked at Eden, who was standing motionless at the door.

"Is there anything we should know before we take her home?" Barbie asked.

"I am writing her a couple of prescriptions, and I'll check her stitches now. I think she is ready to go home. Isn't that right, Eden?"

"Not without my little girl," she said flatly. She had an overwhelming urge to run throughout the hospital until she found Ava, then escape with her down the emergency exit stairs. It was the only way her baby would survive. She had to save her. She took one step towards the door, but Barbie grabbed her with that iron hand again.

"The doctor wants to examine you, so Dad and I will wait outside," she said.

"I know this is a tough one, but it really is for the best, you know," Dr. Andrews said as he squinted at her perineum. "You have your whole life ahead of you. Finish high school, pursue a career. You can have more children when you are older. In the end, you will see that this was the only way to go."

Eden was silent.

"I'm going to write you a prescription that will help dry up your milk and another one for an antibiotic that I want you to take until all the pills are gone." He handed her two slips of paper. "And one more thing. Here is the form for your child's birth certificate. Please fill it out; I will wait until you have finished it."

There was information about Ava on the form.

Gender – Female

Weight – 7lbs 2oz

Length – 19 inches

Date of Birth – March 5, 1975
Time of Birth – 2:35 am
With a shaking hand, Eden filled out the rest.
Name – Ava Celeste English
Mother – Eden Holly English
Father – A friend
Dr. Andrews raised his eyebrows when he read what she had written. "I'll write you one more prescription for birth control pills. Do you know what those are?"

"I'm not a fucking idiot," she said.

The doctor did not speak or look at her again. He left the prescription on the bedside table. *Good riddance, right, doctor? On to the next promiscuous teenager.*

Barbie entered the room. "Okay, let's see what you can wear home. These maternity pants will do for a day or two. Dad's gone over to Wheatland Manor to pick up your things."

Eden slipped on the pants, leaning on the bed for support. She tried to put on her bra, but her breasts flopped uncontrollably, like unbaked loaves of bread on her chest. She tossed the bra aside and pulled the maternity top over her head. It fell loosely around her waist. She forced her swollen feet into her winter boots.

Barbie glanced at the prescriptions, then put them in her purse. "We will get these filled before we leave the city."

Barbie and George had borrowed Donnie's car. Eden stretched out in the back seat, her depleted body sinking into the plush upholstery. Her breasts were becoming more tender by the second, but she welcomed the pain; soon, all evidence that Ava existed would be gone.

Barbie twisted around in her seat. "Honey, I know this is hard for you. Remember, I lost a baby, too. But *my* Ava died. That's a harder thing. We all experience hard things in life, and we just have to keep going. We have to put it behind us." Eden closed her eyes. George turned into a small town along the highway to buy a mickey of whisky for the drive home.

Wild barking greeted George Senior, Barbie, and Eden as they pulled into the yard. A black coonhound writhed and slobbered when they opened the car doors. The dog growled menacingly at her. George Senior kicked vaguely in the dog's direction. "Get out of here, stupid dog!"

Barbie and George grabbed Eden's suitcase and headed into the house. Eden stood for a moment looking at the house, barn, and bare trees cowering under the brooding March sky. So familiar, yet the ranch felt like an alien planet. *I don't belong here.*

Skylar and George Junior were sitting at the table when she entered the kitchen. Skylar took two giant steps to engulf her in a smothering, unwanted hug. Eden yelped as her breasts were crushed against his hard chest. Skylar released her, but his smile didn't dim.

"Hi, little sis," he said fondly.

"Hey, Eden, glad you're home," George Junior said, with an uneasy glance at his mother, who was clearing up the coffee cups and filling the sink with sudsy water before she took off her coat. George Senior set the mickey on the table, reached for a glass from the cupboard, and slumped wearily into his chair.

Eden stared at the new avocado-coloured appliances in the kitchen and harvest gold wall-to-wall shag carpet in the living room. She walked mechanically across this unfamiliar terrain to her bedroom. She sat on her beloved chenille bedspread and touched the cassette recorder on her bedside table in wonder.

She lay down, pulling her knees into a fetal position. *Ava. I never got to hold you. I'm sorry. Where are you, baby?*

Barbie entered her room to cover her with an afghan. "Have a little rest, then you can help me with supper. We'll get you back into a routine before you

138

know it. And take your pills," she added, handing Eden the prescriptions and a glass of water. "You'll feel better."

Eden didn't reach for the pills or acknowledge her mother, so Barbie placed them on the bedside table and left, leaving the door slightly ajar.

Later, Eden heard Donnie and Vic arrive—her father's loud "Come in!" followed by his heavy footsteps to the door; her mother's undecipherable murmur and Donnie's "She'll be alright, just give her time..."; the clatter of cups and the aroma of coffee perking. The coffee smelled delicious. Eden wasn't even slightly nauseated. She was ravenous. She walked into the kitchen, and all chatter ceased.

Donnie hugged Eden gently, aware of her breasts. "Sweetie, you're home. It's going to be alright now." Eden held her for a moment, tears rising uncontrollably. She still had no words.

"Have a cookie!" her father yelled, gesturing with a white plastic container full of peanut butter cookies for Eden to sit down and join them. Eden took a cookie but remained standing near the stairs. She wondered where George Junior was.

As if summoned, her brother appeared at the top of the stairs. "Is it okay if I take Eden out to see what's in the barn?" he asked his parents, who shrugged and waved them toward the door. Eden found her old barn coat on its usual hook in the mudroom and followed George Junior while eating her cookie, relieved to escape the tension in the kitchen.

She couldn't walk fast because of her stitches, so George slowed his steps to match hers. He looked at her with concern, clearly uncertain what to say.

Barker was following them, more or less. He stopped frequently to bark—at a crow in a tree, loose barbed wire waving in the wind, the shadow of the barn. The cows stared at them from the corrals, hooves buried in churned manure, straw strands poking from their jaws. Their pregnancies were obvious; soon it would be calving time. Life had not stopped just because Eden had lost her child.

George stepped aside dramatically to reveal a yearling filly in the stall, scouring the trough with her lips. The filly's head shot up as they approached, then she relaxed and leaned out to nibble George's coat sleeve. She was a beautiful bay mare with white feet and a diamond-shaped star on her forehead. Eden was astonished.

"Yeah, Dad was on a tear a few weeks ago and didn't come home for a few days," George said. "Mom was going crazy. Then he comes home with a horse trailer and this little beauty inside. Mom named her Diamond."

"Is she... Mom's horse?"

"No, she's for you. Not sure why he picked a horse as a peace offering."

"Is she broke?"

"No, Dad said you'd have to do it."

"Oh."

Eden reached for the horse, who nosed her hand for oats. "Where's Patches and Blackie?"

"They're in the barn pasture. Let's go get them."

Eden and George waded through aging snow until they saw the horses in the far corner of the pasture. When George whistled, Patches disentangled herself from Blackie and plodded in their direction. She stood for a moment with enquiring nostrils, then rested her head against Eden's body with a satisfied snort. *There you are.* Blackie made his way in their direction, wondering about oats. The four wandered slowly back to the barn.

Patches's winter coat was falling out in clumps, revealing smooth hair beneath. Eden grabbed a curry comb and groomed her with practiced strokes. George left to water and feed the cows.

Eden buried her face in the solid comfort of Patches's neck and sobbed into the horse's wind-brushed hair, gulping for breath. Patches stood patiently, head low and ears laid back, while Blackie and Diamond touched noses through the stall boards, their tangled black tails dangling near the floor.

Chapter 11

In the following weeks, Eden spent most of her time in the barn with the horses. Her parents decided not to send her back to school until September; she had passed her Grade Ten correspondence courses with high marks. Her Grade Eleven studies came to a halt because Barbie and George felt Eden should not advance too far ahead of her classmates.

Eden shrugged when they shared their decision. She did not have the energy to deflect the stares and whispers that would surely follow her along the corridors. She had no desire to go back to school.

March brought both unseasonably warm weather and blinding snowstorms as the prairie moved reluctantly toward spring. On days when the horses huddled against the barn or haystack, enduring the cold, Eden would finish her chores and walk over to Grandma Doris's lonely little house to search for vestiges of her grandmother among the faded surfaces. She found them in the limp clothes hanging in the closet and on the patchwork quilt-covered bed where Eden would lie wrapped in the gaudy colours of Doris's favourite afghan, staring at the ceiling.

For Eden, the future was a listless river trickling through dead grass and colourless gravel. A barren landscape, an endless winter. Eden did not have the strength to slog through this stream of hopelessness for the rest of her life. And she could not shake the conviction that Ava was unsafe.

Her body healed rapidly after Ava's birth. "She looks good as far as the stitches are concerned," Dr. Christianson said to Barbie after examining Eden. "It would probably be best for her state of mind, though, if she keeps busy. Will she be going back to school?"

"Not until September," Barbie said curtly. "She'll be quite busy enough on the ranch, especially now that spring is coming."

"Well, she should be out and about with her peers. It's time to move forward, right, Eden?" Eden shrugged. Dr. Christianson exchanged a sympathetic glance with Barbie and rose from his chair to dismiss them.

"Can we go see Grandma?" Eden asked as they climbed into the truck.

"Oh, I suppose so. I'll drop you off and go get groceries while you visit with her."

Eden entered the care home hesitantly. She scanned the terrain of bobbing grey heads in the lounge until she saw Doris dozing in a corner, a red and purple quilt over her knees.

"Grandma?" Eden touched her hand. Doris looked up with a vacancy that shocked Eden. *Just like Skylar after the accident.* Everything had been taken from Doris; her vitality, her memories, and her purpose. She was a withered husk, scraped out and abandoned, left to die. Eden felt the same, except she had to endure a swirling burden of resentment and regret that mingled in the empty space where Ava used to live.

She wearily closed her eyes and held her grandmother's hand until Barbie pulled up in front of the picture window and honked the horn.

Eden found it difficult to concentrate on conversations—table talk at mealtimes, instructions and orders from her mother, Barbie and Donnie laughing and gossiping over afternoon coffee. Curtis, Donnie said, was doing well in the group home and had become the resident garbage man. He loved taking out the garbage and would leap to his duties whenever a piece of trash was tossed away.

"It keeps him busy," she said, chuckling and shaking her head.

Eden drifted away from the kitchen. Talk of Curtis made her think of Ava, his little daughter, alone in the world. She drifted from kitchen to bedroom, and back again, gazing inward, until Barbie said, "For God's sake, Eden, go out to the barn!"

Eden put on her high-top rubber boots and waded through the spring run-off to the barn pasture where the horses were munching their way through an oasis of scattered bales. She grabbed the cheek strap of Diamond's halter and urged her toward the barn. Eden tied her to the stall, scattered a few handfuls of oats in the trough, and began her ritual. While Diamond teased the oats from the deep crevasses, Eden stroked her legs, hooves, hindquarters, tail, belly, and the tender insides of her thighs and groin.

Then she stood on tiptoes to lean across Diamond's withers, putting her full weight on the filly. Diamond had disliked this part of the routine at first but was now used to the feeling of Eden's body draped over hers. Eden didn't know exactly how to break a horse, but this seemed like a good start.

Eden's father grunted with amusement when he walked into the barn and saw her sprawled across the horse. Then he stopped and looked more carefully.

"That's a good idea you've got there, Eden," he said. "Good girl."

Eden wasn't sure if he was addressing her or the horse. He reached over to scratch under Diamond's forelock, brushing the black mane out of her eyes.

Eden slid off the horse and regarded her father. It occurred to her that every time she saw George Senior now, she asked herself whether he was drunk or sober. The question was a horsehair blanket flung between them, a thick curtain of doubt, guilt, resentment, and fear. Eden wondered if her father sensed the same barrier when he looked at his little girl, pregnant at fourteen, a bereft mother at fifteen.

Drunk. Pregnant. Irrefutable.

Squirming under the intensity of her gaze, George Senior turned away. "Turn on the pump and water the cattle. River's tied up in town and I'm doing his chores. When you're finished, help me shovel feed, okay?"

Gladly, Eden thought. Anything to prolong her time in the barn.

The tension in the house simmered like a watched kettle. It boiled over spectacularly one evening when Eden was in bed, listening to the radio, missing Ava, missing Curtis, missing Celeste. She even missed Donny Osmond.

George Senior was sitting in his usual spot with an open bottle of whisky and a glass. Eden could hear his voice, then her mother's voice, then his. Murmured, subdued. The simple kitchen sounds that had lulled her to sleep for years—plates rattling, cabinets opening and closing, lighter flaring as George lit a cigarette. Another day's work done.

Suddenly, her mother screamed. "You filthy drunk!!"

And then the crash of George's bottle shattering on the kitchen floor.

It was deeply shocking. Eden felt like she had in first grade when she wet her pants in school; there was no way to put this right, to put it back. Barbie—the mother she knew—would never soil her spotless kitchen. There would never be an end to her mother's embittered plodding from one day to the next; from one farm wife's task and one sarcastic comment to the next, Barbie would keep on. Until that moment, Eden had not realized how much she had counted on that.

It was silent in the kitchen, so Eden peeked around her bedroom door. George was sitting alone at the table, sipping from his half-filled glass. Barbie was nowhere to be seen. An amber ocean was widening on the floor. Islands of glittering glass reflected the overhead light.

Eden took a step out and her father shouted at her, "Stay away, you'll cut your feet! Let the bitch clean up her own mess."

Eden hesitated. The pool was quickly approaching Barbie's treasured carpet. She looked around for something to stem the flow, settling on an afghan draped over the back of the couch. The synthetic fabric did little to absorb the liquid that threatened to take over their home. The foul sap that had blood-poisoned her father and brain-injured her brother had spread to every corner of their lives.

When George Junior appeared at the top of the stairs, followed anxiously by Skylar and reluctantly by River, Eden walked back into her room and shut the door. *Let the men clean up for once.*

When she walked into the kitchen the next morning, the floor was immaculate. Barbie and Donnie were baking for a baby shower that they were hosting for a young woman in the district. Barbie did not meet Eden's eyes.

"There are suitcases and boxes by the back door," she said as she separated eggs for the angel food cake. "After breakfast, please take them over to Grandma's house. I'm not sitting around here watching him drink himself to death night after night. I'm going to sleep at Grandma's."

Eden made several trips down the path with the boxes. *Wow, Mom means business. These are all of her clothes.*

When she was finished, she found the horses standing lethargically near the barn. Feeling lethargic herself, Eden decided not to work with Diamond today. Instead, she brushed her with her mittens and murmured into her soft, swivelling ear. *You're a good girl. That's a girl.* Patches lumbered over and pushed her nose between Eden and Diamond, demanding her share of the love. Eden had to smile as she rubbed Patches's neck.

Pussy suddenly appeared around the corner of the barn. Eden hadn't seen her since returning to the ranch. The cat was heavily pregnant again, barely able to waddle. She rubbed against Eden's legs and weaved through Diamond's. Diamond brushed her nose against the cat and snorted violently, flinging her head up and nearly knocking Eden off her feet.

Barker was barking maniacally, and when she went into the barn to investigate, Eden saw him throwing himself against the slatted fence surrounding the bale stack. Eden glimpsed a flash of black. *One of Pussy's kittens must have lived through the winter.* When the cat scrambled out of the bales, another reflected flash caught Eden's attention. A mickey of rye tucked between two bales at eye level. Eden decided to take it; her father was unlikely to complain if his hidden booze stash went missing. Nothing would be said.

The horses were wandering back to the barn pasture, so she followed them until she found a dry patch of ground beyond view of the barn and house. Eden had never tasted liquor; she wondered what the fuss was all about.

She spat her first mouthful on the ground; it burned her esophagus and brought tears to her eyes. When she carefully swallowed a second sip, the alcohol tingled in her veins, spreading heat to her clenched stomach and exhausted brain. It tasted dreadful, but it felt like relief.

Although the relaxed feeling was pleasant, the whisky only served to bring Ava to mind more vividly. She drank the liquor and mourned her baby, envisioning, as she always did, her adoptive home. Another mother, a father. Perhaps a brother or sister. Or no, Ava might be an only child. Only kind people who couldn't have children of their own would adopt, right?

She closed her eyes and saw Ava lying in a bassinet, waving her arms and crying. *Are you hungry, little one? Someone, feed this hungry baby!* Was she lonely?

Did she miss her real mother and wonder what had become of her?

When she rose to go back to the house, she stumbled and fell, smearing her hands and jeans with mud. The bottle was empty. The world tilted again, and Eden's stomach heaved.

Barker loped over to look at her with his head cocked.

"Come here, you stupid dog. Help me!" Eden leaned on the dog to find her feet, which seemed to exist in another dimension. The dog twisted away from her as she closed one eye to estimate the distance to the house. She just wanted to lie down on the chenille bedspread and sleep.

Barbie and Donnie looked up in surprise when Eden crashed into the kitchen door frame. "What's the matter with you?" Barbie said. "We could use your help decorating these cookies."

"'m sick," Eden said, staggering toward her bedroom. As she turned the corner into the living room, she vomited profusely on the harvest gold carpet, then looked blearily at the chunky mess as if not comprehending where it had come from. Barbie screeched and ran over with tea towels.

"Oh, my God, you reek of whisky," she said. "Go to your room right now!"

The women turned their attention to the carpet, and Eden flopped down on her bed with a groan. In a second, she was asleep, her sodden brain mercifully deadened to visions of a hungry, lonely baby.

Eden searched the bales fruitlessly for weeks, looking for her father's hoarded whisky. One day, it came to her. When the men didn't want to take off their boots and coveralls to walk through Barbie's kitchen to the bathroom, they used the old outhouse beside Grandma Doris's house. She opened the creaky door and squinted into the cobwebbed corners. There, tucked in the gap between the sloping roof and plywood walls, was a nearly full twenty-six-ounce bottle of Canadian Club. *Bingo!*

Eden tucked the bottle under her coat and walked to the barn. She found a loose floorboard in the tiny tack cupboard, shoved the bottle into the soft dirt under the floor, and replaced the board. A swift brush with her mitten over the disturbed dust made her cache invisible.

Eden spent a lot of time in the barn with Diamond that spring. She liked to pull out the bottle when no one was around, sipping while she groomed and trained the young horse. She never drank much; the memory of vomiting on her mother's carpet was still fresh in her nostrils. But furtive sips softened the ragged emotions she felt whenever Ava came to mind. Time spent with Diamond and her bottle each day girded her for the upcoming sit-down meal at suppertime.

Barbie slept in Grandma Doris's house every night, but spent her days at the main house, cooking for the men as calving season blended into preparations for seeding and haying, supporting the perpetual cycle of a farm family once again hoping for a better year.

Supper was always ready by six o'clock sharp, and the men were always there to eat it, washed and famished. Every night, as George Senior reached under the sink for his bottle, Barbie would fill a plate for herself and take it down the path to Doris's house, Barker trailing her closely. The woman and dog would disappear into the house, not to emerge until daybreak.

Meanwhile, it was up to Eden to finish putting food on the table and clean up after the meal. She felt it was fair payment for a break from Barbie's acerbic comments or sullen silences. However, her father's slurred outbursts, River's snarling replies, Skylar's vacant stares, and George Junior's placating comments were a recipe for indigestion. Eden was grateful for the fortifying properties of Canadian Club rye whisky.

River proposed to Stacey at Christmas, as everyone expected. Their wedding was planned for August. Last year's substandard yields set him back financially, but he had sold his calves in the fall and put a down payment on a quarter section of land near Stacey's family farm. Together, they were fixing up an old farmhouse on the place, replacing rotting floorboards and repairing the leaky roof. Eventually, River hoped to farm full-time with Stacey's father; he made no attempt to hide his impatience to be rid of the English household as soon as possible.

Over supper, he kept the guilt cup topped up. *You sound just like Mom,* Eden thought, nurturing the little buzz she still felt from the whisky while ducking the barbs flying across the table. George Junior frequently threw himself in front of the verbal spears, trying to deflect them. Eden was never sure who he was protecting, her father or River.

***

One evening in May, Eden was lying on her bed, recording songs from the radio on her cassette player, when she heard a vehicle enter the yard. Probably Vic or Loren, she thought; then she heard a familiar chirp at the door.

"Hi, Mr. English, how you doing?" It was Celeste!

Eden flew out of her room and swept Celeste into a ferocious hug, her now small breasts pressed against Celeste's ample ones. Two men stood in the doorway behind Celeste—her brother Gilbert and a mountainous figure she recognized as a Boucher from Sainte-Marie. Maurice.

Celeste tilted her head back and laughed with all her white teeth showing. *She's better. She's back.*

"Hey, girl, get dressed. We're going to the show tonight. Want to come?"

"Show?" Eden felt disoriented. "You mean... a movie?"

150

"Of course I mean a movie!" Celeste said. Gilbert and Maurice looked uneasily at George Senior, who was glowering as he sipped his whisky.

"Okay... yeah, sure. Let me get changed!" Eden raced back to her room, frantically considering what she should wear to a movie. She grabbed her old jeans from the closet and struggled into them; a snug fit, but they would do. She changed into a tight purple t-shirt and added a white cardigan. She looked at her face in the mirror—clean—and considered her hair; it would take too long to comb out.

She reappeared in the kitchen, breathless. Celeste laughed again. "*Ma chérie*, you can comb your hair in the car! Come on, we'll be late!"

George Senior heaved himself out of his chair, swaying ominously. "Eden, get back in your room. You're not going anywhere with this... these...!"

At his full height, Maurice was as tall as her father. "We will have her home before midnight, Mr. English. Don't worry about a thing."

Before George Senior could say another word, Celeste and Eden were out the door, with Maurice and Gilbert close behind. George stood on the porch watching as Maurice turned his Buick Skylark around in the yard and accelerated with a little jet of gravel at the gate.

"Nice car," Eden said, settling herself in the tiny backseat while attempting not to brush against Gilbert, who was studying the back of Maurice's head. Maurice and Celeste were clasping hands passionately while Maurice navigated the twisting gravel road with his left hand on the steering wheel.

"Isn't it *darling*?" Celeste said. "Maurice just bought it off a guy in town. We love it!" she said with a fond and proprietary glance at Maurice. He may not be as handsome as Jason Pedersen, but he's way nicer, Eden thought.

"How're you doing?" she said to Gilbert, forcing him to look at her. He jumped a little.

"*Tres bien*," he said with a tight smile. *Relax, buddy.*

When they were several miles away from the English's yard, Maurice pulled over and jumped out, returning with four brown beer bottles from the trunk. He used one bottle to pop the caps off the others, handing them in through the window.

Eden noticed that Maurice and Gilbert nestled their bottles in the crotch of their jeans, taking large gulps as they sped along the highway. Eden sipped—*Yuck, what's the big deal about beer?*—then reached forward to touch Celeste's bottle with hers.

"To us," she said.

Celeste glanced back; Eden could see pain embedded in her steady blue gaze. "Here's to us and Donny Osmond," she said, toasting the air.

On Main Street, dozens of teenagers congregated outside the café while others walked in groups toward the theatre. Eden glanced at the marquee as they drove slowly along the street—*The Return of the Pink Panther.* She shrank back into her seat, shame dampening her mood.

She sank a bit deeper when she noticed Louisa lounging against the brick facade of the café, leaning her length against Leonard Walsh, a boy in Grade Eleven. Carrie was there too, openly smoking a cigarette. All three turned their heads, spilling disdain into the street as they watched Maurice's car coast by. Eden broke into a cold sweat.

Celeste turned to look at Eden, then glanced at Maurice. "Let's not do the movie," she said. "Let's get more beer and head out to Sage. It's too nice out to sit in a stinky movie theatre."

Maurice shrugged, then parked in front of the bar and went in for off-sales. With a screech of tires against the pavement, they headed out of town toward Sage Coulee, a hangout of renown that Eden had heard about but never seen.

There were already half a dozen vehicles parked on the bluff above the coulee when they arrived. Celeste handed Eden one of two blankets from the trunk; the boys carried the beer and a cassette player as they walked down the path into the coulee.

Eden looked warily at the teenagers sitting by the creek. Most of them were in Grade Twelve; the boys greeted Maurice and Gilbert with a hoot or a wave. They settled on the blankets and sipped on their second beers of the night. Eden felt giddy after her long isolation and the speed with which she'd been rescued from it.

Celeste and Maurice picked up a blanket and walked along the coulee into the shelter of a chokecherry stand. Eden sat silently beside Gilbert, watching the creek trickle past them and nervously peeling off the soaked label of her beer bottle with her thumbnail.

Gilbert plucked grass to make a whistle with his thumbs, which he demonstrated with enthusiasm. Cut the crap, kid, Eden thought. She didn't want to draw the attention of the older kids sitting nearby. She wanted to melt into the ground.

After a third beer and wearied by Gilbert's fidgety silence, Eden joined the growing circle around the fire; Gilbert meekly followed. She saw Melanie O'Connor from her class and waved tentatively to her across the leaping flames.

Melanie and Eden began chatting easily. Eden relaxed as she sipped her beer and watched the pink sky above the coulee slowly transmute to midnight blue.

It was nearly dark, and the fire was roaring when a stranger walked down the path to join the party. Melanie's chatter stopped in mid-sentence, and everyone standing around the fire watched the tall man swagger over to them. He was greeted by the boys standing across the fire from Eden and Melanie; the vision of his arrival was immediately obscured by sparks and smoke.

"The Jesus freak," Melanie breathed.

"Jesus freak?" Eden squinted through the smoke for a better look at him. "What do you mean?"

"Oh, that's what we call him. Doesn't he just look like Jesus with that beard and long hair?" Melanie said. "Sometimes he even wears sandals with his jeans. He's been working at the Turners as a hired man. His cousin is Eric Baronowski. Dad hates him, says he's a draft dodger from the States. But he would hate anyone with hair like that." Melanie chuckled, then turned to talk to the person on her left.

Eden stepped closer to the fire, reaching for its warmth. Gilbert whipped off his jean jacket and placed it on her shoulders. She smiled her thanks. *What a sweet kid.*

Eden experienced the rest of the evening in short bursts illuminated by the fire as it danced in the dark. The beer had taken a grip on her, and the world shrank, reduced to the small patch of grass between her outstretched legs and the fire. She didn't know who was sitting on either side of her. She couldn't see them clearly, and she couldn't hear them. She existed only within the guttering licks of the fire.

The Jesus freak materialized out of the smoke as he collapsed his long legs to sit beside her on the ground. He extended his hand.

"Monroe," he said. "Not sure we've met." She placed her cold hand in his, mesmerized by the reflection of the fire in his aviator glasses. He pushed them higher on his nose.

"Want a toke?" he asked, presenting the joint she now saw glowing in his hand. Eden shook her head, looking down with embarrassment. The skunk smell of the weed threatened to overtake the woody aromas of the fire.

"What's your name?" he persisted, taking a pull from the joint and holding it deep in his lungs as he spoke.

Eden looked into his eyes. "It's Eden."

"Ah, a beautiful garden," Monroe said. "The garden at the beginning of time. Did you know sadness is but a wall between two gardens?"

Chapter 12

"Irene Murdoch took her case all the way to the Supreme Court, and look where it got her!" Donnie sounded exasperated as she tossed the magazine on the table in front of Barbie. "*Status of Women News*. Where did you get this?"

"From my lawyer," Barbie said. "Keep it. A little bedtime reading for you."

She was calm but cold as glaring ice. It was rare for Barbie and Donnie to quarrel. Eden was at the counter stirring cake batter and, as usual, the women ignored her.

"And a woman lawyer yet," Donnie said. "How do you ever expect to win a case against George?"

Barbie shrugged. "I have worked as hard as he has, and as long, to keep this ranch afloat. Harder in fact, if you look at what he has contributed in the last year. And don't tell me that my work is worth less than his. The lawyer thinks I have a good case, especially since we started from nothing as young kids and built everything together."

"Um, I think George had the land before you got married. This is his father's homestead, is it not? I just worry you have heartache and financial pressures ahead if you proceed with this." Barbie was silent for a long moment. Then Donnie spoke again. "Would it be so bad to stay with George? Maybe he'll go back to AA. You could learn to work as a team again."

Barbie tossed her head as if to shake Donnie's words out of her ears. "We bought two quarters about ten years ago. But, of course, *my* name's not on the title. Women are going to have to start waking up and pretty damn quick. It's a new world, Donnie."

"How much do you think you can get if you go to court and win?" Donnie asked, inhibitions thrown aside.

"About a hundred thousand. Split it right down the middle."

"And where will you live?"

"I'm thinking Regina."

Donnie wiped her eyes on the tissue she kept tucked into her shirt sleeve. "Gonna miss you, lady."

Barbie squeezed her hand. Both women were crying and laughing a little at the spectacle they were making. Tears were rare in the South Country.

Eden scraped the batter into a blackened cake pan and placed it in the oven. "I'm going out to work with Diamond," she announced, walking past the women into the mudroom. "Mom, check the cake in half an hour."

God, I need a drink, she thought. Sadly, her tack room cache was empty, and she hadn't found George's new hiding place.

River and George Junior were in the corral, shovelling straw-laced manure into a heap in the center. The cows and calves were in the spring pasture, and it was time to clean up the barn. They didn't notice Eden's approach, but she could hear them clearly.

"You know Dad will have to sell the land to pay Mom out, right?" River said reproachfully. "There's no other way. Once Dad pays the debts on this place, he'll have nothing left. Nothing."

George was wheezing and rubbing his allergy-aggravated eyes with his dirty coverall sleeve.

"Maybe you don't want to farm," River went on, "but what are me and Skylar supposed to do? Skylar's not going to be able to do much of anything without help. Are you going to look after him for the rest of his life? I'm sure the hell not going to."

George glared at him, leaning on his shovel. "Guess you've got your life all planned out perfect, don't you?"

"Not really." River heaved another heavy shovelful of manure. "I was kind of depending on ranching with Dad for another couple of decades. Stacey's real upset."

"Do you really think Mom will go to court?" George asked. "I think she's bluffing. Anything to get Dad back to AA."

"I don't think you really know our dear mother," River said. "When has she ever backed down about anything?"

George Senior pulled up with the front-end loader, parking the tractor at the open corral gates. With the edges scraped clean, he could now scoop up the manure and dump it in the field behind the barn. Eden could no longer hear the men talking over the belching motor. She grabbed a rope and went to find Diamond.

On Saturday night, Celeste and Maurice showed up after supper to take Eden to town. George Senior was again belligerent.

"Don't worry, Mr. English," Maurice said with a respectful smile. "I got her home by midnight last week, and I'll do it again. We'll keep her safe, right, Celeste?"

Gilbert wasn't in the back seat waiting as Eden had expected. "Where's the kid?" she asked as she crawled into the Buick.

Celeste snapped the folding front seat back into place. "He's home tonight. Said he didn't want to hang out with us anymore. Not sure what's got into his *petite tête*."

"I think he wants to practice his *English* but he's too shy," Maurice said with a twinkle, his tanned left arm resting on the open driver's side window. Celeste glanced back at Eden and raised her eyebrows.

"Don't be daft," Eden said, attempting a British accent gleaned from *Monty Python's Flying Circus*. Everyone laughed.

"I wonder if Monroe will be out tonight," Celeste said, lighting a cigarette and offering it to Eden. Eden inhaled awkwardly, tears streaming down her face. Apparently, she had forgotten how to smoke while living at Wheatland Manor.

"Now look what you've done to my mascara!" she said accusingly to Celeste.

"You're all dolled up for the Jesus freak!" Celeste squealed happily. Eden handed the cigarette back to her.

"He's cute alright, but I think he writes poetry. He's kinda creepy."

"More like sexy," Celeste said with a knowing smile. "Did you get a look at his jeans?"

The girls dissolved into helpless giggles while Maurice hummed a tune under his breath, taking the curving gravel road at top speed.

It was difficult to talk from the backseat with the windows open and the prairie flowing by. Eden leaned back in her seat and allowed Ava into her mind. She had learned to block thoughts of her lost baby, except late at night just before falling asleep. Then, in the slumbering house, grief would boil up from the craters gouged out by Ava's absence, and she would fling her body against the mattress in a futile battle with the thieves. Agatha Browne. Dr. Andrews. Barbie. George. Rage would replace the grief and inflame the wounds. She often didn't fall asleep for hours.

Now, in the clouds of dust billowing from beneath the tires, Eden could clearly see her child.

A three-month-old baby, sucking her hand, alone on a blanket on the floor. She was wearing a pink sleeper. Her eyes were darting from side to side, looking, looking. Her legs were kicking listlessly. She was unwell.

Eden gasped and clutched her stomach. Celeste looked quizzically at her, then turned to Maurice and smiled at him with a trust Eden doubted she would ever feel again. Not living among thieves.

Maurice didn't even turn toward town this time. "Maury, aren't you going to take us to see *Shampoo*?" Celeste said sweetly. "Please, Maury, please..."

Maurice shrugged, grinned, and turned down the dirt road toward Sage Coulee.

There were a dozen cars on the bluff and a fire roaring when they walked down the path into the coulee. Gnats congregated over their heads, and the sky was a blue flannel blanket settling down to sleep. The air smelled of emerging crops and newly minted leaves. Eden could hear the ooo-wah-ooo ooo ooo of a mourning dove in the trees.

The first person Eden saw as they approached the fire was Monroe, sitting on a rock and strumming a guitar. As they settled on a blanket, Monroe began to play the haunting chords of "Stairway to Heaven." Celeste handed Eden a beer, which she accepted without taking her eyes off Monroe. His hair swung to his shoulders, and his glasses glinted in the setting sun.

"My favourite song," Eden whispered, ignoring Celeste's giggling nudge.

The chatter around the fire ceased as Monroe played. The sun tipped below the edge of the coulee, allowing the fire to illuminate Monroe as he tapped his sandaled feet and cradled the guitar on his lap, his hair falling forward to hide his face.

Everyone clapped when he finished; he nodded modestly, then leaned his guitar against the rock. Someone handed him a beer, and he melted into the crowd of young men across the fire from them.

"*Ma chérie*, you are in heaven right now," Celeste said, grinning in delight. "He'll make his way to you, never fear."

When Monroe approached about half an hour later, Celeste and Maurice quietly melted into the shadows, leaving Eden with an empty beer bottle and a fluttering stomach. *He's gorgeous. What can I say?*

"That was really good," Eden stammered. "I mean, I really liked your... I mean, the guitar..."

Monroe smiled beneficently. "Your body is the harp of your soul; it is yours to bring forth sweet music," he said, offering her a drag on his cigarette. Eden took it, trying not to cough but failing miserably. Monroe helpfully thumped her on the back, his hand lingering as her spittle flew into the air.

Despite the sputtering start, Monroe stayed by her side for the rest of the evening. They spoke little, for which Eden was grateful. Many eyes were on them, and she could sense whispering among the others. It was possible some of the girls would have traded places with her.

Eden felt self-conscious and also brazen. She drank the beers that magically appeared before her and smoked Monroe's cigarettes, mastering her gag reflex. It made her feel sophisticated and older. *You're a fifteen-year-old kid who's never been kissed. And you've had a kid of your own.*

"I hear you had a kid." Monroe was reading her mind. Eden bristled but then relaxed.

"Yeah, but I had to give her up for adoption," Eden said, watching Monroe for his reaction.

"Your children are not your children. They are the sons and daughters of Life's longing for itself," Monroe said with a serious expression.

"Life's longing for itself. That's beautiful." She wiped an unexpected tear from her eye.

Eventually, someone brought him the guitar, which he strummed sitting cross-legged on the ground, looking at Eden for inspiration.

"Do you know "Band on the Run"?" she asked, and he strummed the opening chords. The night drifted on as Eden drank and watched the stars eclipse the untended fire. Rock me gently. Time in a bottle. Contentment in a stubby brown bottle on a starry, starry night.

Celeste and Maurice appeared at her elbow. "Time to go home, Cinderella," Celeste said, laughing up at Maurice and Monroe, who had sprung to his feet to tower over her. Eden stood obediently and nodded to Monroe.

"Thanks for… the songs," she said.

"Don't mention it," he said with a little wave.

"Come on, pumpkin girl, let's get you home." Celeste supported Eden as she stumbled groggily up the hill.

* * *

Barbie and Eden had a busy week, baking bread, cinnamon buns, apple pies, matrimonial cake, and Neapolitan bars. Tomorrow was branding day, and there would be hungry men to feed.

"For Lord's sake, tie your hair back, Eden," Barbie barked as she pounded the bread dough with unwarranted ferocity. "You'll have hair in the batter. We'll have to get you into town for a haircut next week."

Eden spied an elastic hair tie with pink plastic baubles in the debris on the counter. The house now reflected Barbie's state of distraction. Without her diligence, every corner of the kitchen was littered with crumpled envelopes, rusty nails, greasy John Deere ball caps, bits of baler twine, coins, and dust. Eden pocketed the coins whenever she saw them; it was her only source of cash.

"And you could probably use some new clothes." Barbie regarded her daughter as if she hadn't looked at her in months. "Let's go to town and do some shopping. What do you think?"

Eden shrugged as she whipped the cake batter into submission. She glanced into the yard where Barker was yapping at a hapless gopher scurrying from one hole to another. Barker easily caught the rodent, crunched it between his teeth, and spit it out. *Stupid dog is good for something after all.*

Barbie stopped kneading the dough and looked at Eden, demanding an answer.

162

"How come you're leaving Dad?" Eden turned from the window, her cheeks flushed.

Barbie slowly wiped her floury hands with a tea towel. She walked over to the table and sat down, stretching her stiff neck by rolling her head from side to side.

"Is it because of me?" Eden asked, immediately furious at herself for putting this thought into words.

"Do you mean, did Dad start drinking again because you got pregnant? Or because Skylar rolled his truck and a girl died, and now he's almost unrecognizable? I don't know," Barbie said thoughtfully, as if she'd never pondered the question before. "Honestly, I think it was just a matter of time."

Barbie walked to the counter, sprinkled the dough with flour, and placed a clean tea towel over the yeasty mound.

"When Dad got sober about..." she calculated, "... five years ago now, I told him that I would leave if he ever started drinking again. I know some wives of alcoholics say that but don't mean it. I meant it, Eden."

Barbie opened the drawer under the oven and drew out the old bread pans, as familiar to Eden as the gentle lines at her mother's eyes and between her brows. While Eden considered her mother to be old as dirt, she knew that Barbie, at forty-four, looked younger than most South Country wives. For one thing, she refused to cut her hair short, twist it into pink sponge rollers, and then cover it with a headscarf to go grocery shopping, a common sight in the community. Her light brown hair fell in natural waves to her shoulders and was usually tied up in a high ponytail. Even after having five children, she was trim and fit. George Senior could almost encircle her waist with his hands. It was something he used to do often, marvelling.

"Maybe that makes me a hard bitch, but I won't watch him drink himself into the grave. I won't."

"But what will happen to Dad? How will he manage if you leave?"

"Maybe he'll find himself another wife."

"Mom!"

"You kids are grown now. Well, the boys are. I know you're still a kid, but..." Eden was startled to see Barbie wipe a tear, leaving a stripe of flour on her cheek.

"I know I've been hard on everybody, especially you, Eden. But I... want to survive. I need to survive this, for myself. I don't have any other choice."

"Dad might stop drinking again. He might, any day!"

Barbie tucked a strand of hair behind Eden's ear. "I hope he does. I really do." She looked searchingly into Eden's eyes. "I knew your father was an alcoholic in high school. And there were many times that I wanted to break up with him, but it was hard to do. I loved him a lot. And then I got pregnant with River."

Eden stepped back in surprise, and Barbie turned away. "So, of course, we got married, because that's what you did back then. But when *you* got pregnant at such a young age... well, I just couldn't stand the thought of you being trapped like I was. I didn't think there was any reason why you couldn't be free to live a different life."

Eden said, "There is one big reason. I want my kid. Being her mother is the only life I want. And you took that away from me."

Eden felt an overwhelming craving for a drink. If she had a beer right now, she would gulp it in seconds. Only one more day until she was in Sage Coulee again, a cold beer in hand. She broke out in a sweat.

Barbie looked sadly at her daughter, then lifted the tea towel to check on the dough.

After supper, George Senior asked Eden to catch the horses and put them in the corral for the night. She grabbed a bucket from its nail in the barn, walked to the granary, and unlatched the door. The evening sun slid on a beam of oat dust, landing on pillows of grain festering with mice and bird droppings. Eden coughed as the musty odours congealed in the back of her throat. Sparrows hopped from beam to beam above her; one swooped down to see what was going on.

As she leaned in to scoop oats into the bucket, she spied the brown neck of a whisky bottle poking out of the grain. *Aha!* Eden grabbed the bottle, hid it in the bucket, then rushed to the tack room to stash it in her hiding place.

With a skip in her step, she walked through the corrals to look for the horses in the barn pasture. They were tucked behind the hill, grazing in a lap of purple clover. The waning sun cast long equine shadows against the hill; she watched her own leggy shadow approach the horses like a stalking petroglyph.

When Eden shook the bucket, all three horses looked up. Diamond was the first to take the bait, making her way over to nudge her nose into the pail. Patches and Blackie ambled over, too; Blackie laid his ears against his skull and Diamond leaped away from the pail. They all knew who was boss.

"Aw, Blackie, I'm the boss," Eden said, scratching behind his ear as he nibbled the oats. "You know that, right, buddy?"

After she lured them into the corral, she started the pump to fill the trough. The horses slurped giant mouthfuls, swished the cold water between their yellow teeth, then spit it back into the trough.

Eden had one arm draped over Patches's withers and the other over Diamond's. In a rare show of affection, Blackie stretched his neck toward her, nibbled gently on her arm, then spit water on her hand.

"Thanks, guy, I needed that." Eden smeared horse spit on her already-filthy jeans. For the first time since Ava was born, Eden's heart was at peace.

And she could have a little drink before bedtime.

Barbie was in the kitchen at five-thirty the next morning and everyone was at the table by six. She served pancakes, sausages, and steaming coffee. Vic appeared in time for a plate and soon Garth Pedersen showed up, too. He tied his quarter horse Shelby to the barnyard gate; the horses were calling plaintively to one another in the still morning air.

Eden slipped out to saddle Blackie and Patches. She left Diamond in the corral; the yearling trotted anxiously along the fence, her piercing whinnies answered earnestly by Shelby. Everyone was excited on branding day.

When George Senior and the rest of the men strolled into the barn, the horses were ready. Eden's father cinched the saddles a couple of notches tighter than Eden had done. Patches let out a startled squeak and an extended fart. She knew from experience what was ahead.

River was riding Blackie and George Junior took Patches, wheezing as he climbed up on her back.

"Need a stool, little feller?" Pedersen bellowed. "I think there's a ladder in the shed."

Everyone, even George Junior, laughed as the three riders set off, followed by George Senior in his truck with Skylar, and Vic in his own truck. Together, they would bring the cows and calves back to the barn. It was seven o'clock; if all went well, they'd be back with the herd by ten.

Eden watched them wistfully as they headed south to the pasture. *I'm a better rider than any of them, but I have to stay home and peel potatoes.* But at nine-thirty, she would be excused from kitchen duty to wait for the men and cattle at a tricky juncture in their journey. The cattle tended to bunch up where two fences formed a bottleneck; Eden's job was to wave the cattle through the open gate. Without this encouragement, the cows could turn back into the herd and create a dangerous, moiling mess. It had happened before, adding hours to a long day.

When Eden got back to the house, Donnie had arrived, and the midday meal was well underway. A massive beef roast was in the oven, and pots were at the near boil on every stove burner.

Neither woman commented when Eden slipped back outside. She meandered to the barn as Barker ran circles around her, barking. She threw a stick for him, but when he ran to fetch it, he was distracted by two robins sitting on fence posts. Oh, Dog of Very Little Brain, Eden thought, shaking her head.

It was going to be a long wait until the men got back. To pass the time, Eden decided to have a sip of her concealed whisky. *Just a nip.* After a few swallows, Ava came to mind, as she always did, but Eden forced herself to think about something else. Someone else. Monroe.

As she thought about Monroe and sipped her whisky, the time passed quickly. Suddenly she could hear cattle bawling and men shouting. *They're early!* Eden ran into the corral, remembered to go back and hide her bottle, then sprinted at full speed toward the south gate. Cattle were already streaming into the barn pasture when she took her post. She waved and yelled to keep them headed in the right direction.

River galloped up on Blackie, in a black mood. "Where the hell were you?" he yelled, pulling Blackie around sharply. *Easy on that bit!* "You can't be depended on for shit!"

"Screw you," Eden yelled, standing back from the stampede of agitated cattle. The dust made her eyes stream, and she roared in frustration as some of the cattle tried to double back.

Garth, River, and George Junior worked the horses hard to keep the cattle funneling through the gate, while the men in the trucks held the rear. Eventually, all the stragglers were in the pasture.

George Senior pulled up. "Sleeping on the job, were you?" he said mildly, while Skylar looked smug. It was all she could do not to scratch their eyes out.

Eden refused to jump into the truck bed for a ride to the barn. By the time she got there, the horses were tied to the corral fence, heaving and lathered. The men were on foot, using whips to separate the cows from the calves. It was grueling work, but eventually the calves were in the corrals and the cows were in the pasture.

"Unsaddle the horses," River snarled at her as the men dusted themselves off and headed for the house. She angrily pulled the saddles off, left them in a tangled heap, watered Blackie and Patches, and put them in the stalls. She watered Shelby and tied him to the corral, loosening his cinch as he waited for the trip home with Garth later in the day.

Eden was embarrassed. She was angry. She didn't want to walk into that house and listen to conversations that she could never be a part of because she was a girl. Before heading to the house, she had one more stiff drink from the bottle. To fortify herself.

The men were sitting at the table when Eden walked through the kitchen door.

"Wash up, you're covered in dust," Barbie ordered, placing a bowl of mashed potatoes on the table as the men began to dish up. Donnie leaned on the counter with her coffee cup; the women would eat after the men.

Eden turned toward the bathroom and tripped on a pair of boots by the door. She flew forward, landing hard on her knees. There was a stunned silence, then guffaws. No one laughed harder than George Junior. For once, he wasn't the brunt of the joke.

Barbie laughed too, helping Eden up. "Can you turkeys please leave your boots on the porch? How many times do I have to..."

Her hand froze on Eden's bicep. She stared hard into her daughter's face, then dropped her arm like it was a hot branding iron.

"Wash up and go to your room," she said flatly. "Don't come out until I tell you to."

Many hours later—after the fuzzy round scrotums of ninety-seven calves were sliced open, and the testicles snipped out and thrown to the dog; after one hundred and eighty-nine calves were flipped, held down, branded, and vaccinated in a proficient but profane assembly line of sweating men; after Vic and Garth were fed, thanked, and sent on their way—the screaming began.

River left right after supper to go to Stacey's, so he missed the worst of it. When Barbie showed no signs of abating, George Junior and Skylar slunk out and drove away in Skylar's truck. In her room, Eden gritted her teeth and vowed to endure it. She had little choice.

Besides, the whole miserable mess was her fault.

"Where are you hiding the booze, George? This is the second time I've seen her drunk. Do you have no shame? Your fifteen-year-old daughter is stumbling around drunk. You're so drunk yourself that you hardly notice. And obviously, you don't care."

I think he has plenty of shame, Mom. He's drowning in shame. Ease up on him, please.

"You are a sorry excuse for a father, do you know that? And people wonder why I'm leaving you. And I am leaving you, never doubt it for a minute!"

George had been silent. Eden could hear the clink of his bottle against his glass as he topped up. Finally, he spoke in a low tone that she could barely hear.

"Then go, you bitch. Get off this farm tonight. We'll be better off here without you. It's no goddamn wonder I drink, living with you for the past twenty-five years. Go!"

Eden ran from her room then, her wind-mangled hair falling over her frantic eyes.

"Mom, Dad, please! I won't drink again, I swear." Eden raised her hands toward each of them like a hockey referee. "Just shut up!"

At that moment, a car drove into the yard. Maurice and Celeste were here to take her to Sage Coulee. Eden dashed to the door, but Barbie's clasp on her arm stopped her. When Celeste and Maurice walked in, Eden and Barbie were screeching like magpies as Eden thrashed to break free from her mother's lock on her wrist.

They turned their wide eyes to George Senior.

"Come on in and have a drink. Join the party," he said, gesturing with his glass at the empty chairs around the table.

Barbie seemed to grow several feet taller as her outrage filled the room. She dropped Eden's wrist and stalked toward Celeste and Maurice.

"You! You are never to set foot on this property again. You are not welcome here. Eden will be going nowhere with you."

Maurice had stood up manfully to George Senior, but he'd met his match in Barbie. He and Celeste backed out of the doorway.

"I will phone you, *ma chérie!*" Celeste called over her shoulder, looking frightened. And they were gone.

* * *

Eden was standing on Main Street clutching a small suitcase when Celeste and Gilbert pulled up in the Impala. She jumped into the back seat, looking around to see if anyone was watching.

"What a bummer. George Junior just dropped me off in the street!"

"How did you get away from the house?" Celeste backed the car up and headed toward Sainte-Marie.

"Mom was out, so I just left a note to say I was staying overnight at your place. I was so afraid I would miss the grad party!"

"Well, do not worry. We are going to the Quonset party, right, Gilbert? Maurice will take us! Get ready to party 'till the sun comes up!"

Later, as Celeste was detangling Eden's hair, she said, "Tonight is the night. I can feel it in my bones. The night for Eden and Monroe to finally get together."

Eden rolled her eyes. For all she knew, Monroe had already returned to his mysterious origins. *I barely know the guy*. But nerves tickled her stomach as she lined her eyes with bright blue eyeshadow.

That evening, Maurice, Celeste, Gilbert, and Eden drove around town drinking beer to kill time before the party. The forty-two graduates of 1975 were attending a dinner with their parents in the Catholic church hall, then partaking in graduation ceremonies in the school gymnasium. Earlier, the graduands had draped the room in gold and silver streamers, and fashioned banners and an archway with gold and silver paper flowers. For one exquisite evening each year, the smelly old gym became an ethereal portal to adulthood.

She envied the kids who would soon escape the South Country to study or work in the city. Many of the boys were headed to Alberta to work on the oil rigs. This mass exodus was becoming more evident every year—young people weren't staying in the district to farm anymore.

"It's our turn to graduate in just two years, hey, Eden?" Celeste said as they watched formally dressed teenagers cram into cars and head out of town. Eden shrugged. She dreaded going back to school.

"It will be so much fun," Celeste went on. "I can already imagine my dress. *Maman* is going to sew it for me. And I have my grad escort right here." She smiled at Maurice, who beamed back. *These two are making me slightly ill.* Or was it the bottle of lemon gin they were sharing on the way to the party? By the time they drove ten miles out of town and parked beside the Quonset, the grad party was rocking.

The graduates, who had replaced their floor-length, floral-patterned gowns and three-piece suits with jeans and bunny hugs, were settling in to celebrate until morning. Already, the din in the metal building made it impossible to talk. Five-foot speakers throbbed; the cigarette smoke atmosphere alone was intoxicating.

Everyone from the age of fifteen to twenty-five and from miles around came to the grad party. Eden saw

George Junior in the crowd; even River and Stacey were there, sitting primly on a straw bale as they sipped their beers. She spotted Melanie O'Connor and weaved through the throng to join her Sage Coulee companions.

Melanie handed her a mickey of rye, and Eden took a long, deep swallow. The burn along her esophagus was an old friend. The room began to sway. The music grew louder. Eden's vision became a pinpoint of brilliant clarity in a mélange of blurred colours and dizzying movement. She was gloriously, utterly drunk.

And then there was a time of unremembering.

She came back to herself in the thrall of an expert, inquiring mouth. To the smell of Old Spice aftershave and the taste of cigarettes. To hardness and softness, a probing tongue that became the center of the universe. My first kiss, she thought unsteadily, unwilling to pull away. Unable to.

Then he leaned back and looked into her face; a cocky gloat, a familiar grin. "Frenchie," he said. "Come on. Let's get outta here."

Jason Pedersen had pushed her against the Quonset wall, the steel ribs of the structure biting into her back. She felt queasy.

"No!" she screamed, pushing weakly against his chest. "Let me go!"

"Asshole, get your hands off her!" Eden wasn't sure who had spoken, but she used the distraction to wrench herself out of Jason's grasp and stumble blindly toward a cluster of onlookers.

To her left, she saw Gilbert, who looked ready to tear Jason Pedersen's limbs off. To her right stood Monroe, eyes amused behind his glasses. He opened his arms as she swayed indecisively. Then, as if it were preordained, she floated into Monroe's arms and away from the South Country.

Eden's memories of the rest of the night were patchy. She did know that she spent hours leaning against Monroe, who kept one arm firmly around her waist while using his other hand to smoke, toke, and drink beer.

While she was unsteady on her feet, he was firmly planted in one of the dim corners of the Quonset. People came and went; conversations ebbed and flowed. Eden felt safe and sleepy encircled by Monroe's denim shirt sleeve, her nose near his heart, arms around his waist. She inhaled the musky smell of his skin, revealed along with a tuft of brown hair by his unbuttoned shirt collar.

All of this came back to her as she rolled over to encounter Celeste sleeping beside her. They were back at the Tremblays'. Gisele and Lucie curled together in the lower bunk, and Amelie snored quietly above.

A baby's cry pierced the quiet house. The newest addition to the family, Felicia, was awake and, consequently, so were the rest of the Tremblays.

Eden sat up, reeling slightly in the bed. Pain hit her head like a baseball bat when she opened her eyes to see Hugo standing on tree trunk legs in the doorway. His diaper hung to his knees, and his intent was clear.

"Help," Eden said softly, sinking back into her pillow.

"Hugo, get off! Go away." Celeste swatted at her brother as he grabbed the blankets to scramble onto the bed. "Oh, shit!" she said, rolling onto her back and clutching her head.

"Watch your language!" Gisele grumped at her sister, dashing to the bathroom before anyone else could get there.

Hugo triumphantly climbed onto the bed and jumped up and down in the small space between Eden's and Celeste's legs. Both girls roared at him in unison, "Stop, Hugo!"

Odette appeared in the doorway, holding Felicia and looking amused. "Celeste, up you get now. Change Hugo and feed him his breakfast. Eden, you, too. No lying around this morning, there are chores to do!"

"*Maman*," Celeste said weakly. Hugo jumped on her stomach. "Aaack, *bébé*," she squawked, tossing him onto Eden's stomach. Hugo squealed with glee.

The frenzy that was breakfast at the Tremblay's had subsided. Eden and Celeste sat at the kitchen table, sipping black coffee while Odette and Gisele washed the dishes, their ears tuned to the conversation as the girls relived the night.

"When he held his arms out to you, that is a moment I will never forget," Celeste said, her eyes sparkling despite her malaise.

Eden looked up cautiously. Had Celeste seen her with Jason? Unwanted memories flooded back as she re-experienced the kiss; she doubted she would ever forget it, despite the bitter rancour she tasted whenever she thought about Jason Pedersen. If she'd been sober, she would have kicked him in the ribs again.

"And the look on Jason's face when you went to Monroe," Celeste went on. "That is not something he is used to. He is used to girls coming to him. It was perfect!"

Gilbert and Alain banged into the house with manure on their boots. Gilbert glared into Eden's bloodshot eyes, kicked off his boots, stalked into the living room, and snapped on the black and white television. Eden raised an eyebrow and looked inquiringly at Celeste.

"Oh, he is just in puppy love," Celeste whispered. "You don't want to rob the cradle. You have a new man now."

"Oh, I don't know about that," Eden said. "I'll probably never see him again."

That evening, after Maurice and Celeste drove Eden home and her hangover had mostly subsided, Monroe drove into the English's yard in a rusted Dodge Dart. Eden was walking back from the barn, and George Junior and Skylar were sitting on the porch steps, picking their teeth after supper and enjoying the mild weather.

Eden's heart almost stopped as her brothers rose to greet the visitor. They were discussing the relative merits of the Dart when she approached, regretting her holey jeans and mud-splattered rubber boots.

"Ah, beauty is eternity gazing at itself in a mirror," Monroe said when he saw her. George Junior couldn't hold back a scoffing snort. Skylar stared hard at Monroe as if he planned to punch him.

"Hey," Eden said, coming up to Monroe and steering him subtly away from her brothers. "How did you know where I live?"

"Oh, I have my sources. Want to come for a drive?"

At that moment, Barbie and George Senior stepped out of the house. They glared down from the porch; for once, they were acting as one.

"Can we help you?" George Senior grunted.

"Hello, sir, my name is Monroe, and I've come to invite your daughter for a drive in the countryside," Monroe said calmly. Eden was impressed with his composure. *How old is this guy?*

"Well, that's not happening, Mr. Monroe," Barbie snarled. "Eden was out last night without our permission, so I'm afraid she won't be going anywhere for a long, long time."

Monroe smiled pleasantly. "Well, I certainly respect your wishes. If Eden were my loved one, I would protect her with every ounce of my being."

George Junior snorted again. His father stepped off the porch, his bulging stomach poking combatively toward Monroe's concave one. Eden wanted to fling up an arm to protect Monroe, but he didn't need protection, as it turned out.

"Get this rust heap off our land and don't come back," George Senior growled, his whisky breath drifting over to Eden and Monroe.

"Dad! It's okay. He's a friend of mine!"

"In the house!" George Senior roared, but Eden stood her ground.

"I'll see you later," she said to Monroe, touching his sleeve. Monroe bowed his head and saluted her with two fingers. He looked at her with meaning, then turned to her father.

"Mr. English, it has been good to meet you finally, and I hope we meet again under better circumstances."

With difficulty, he pulled the warped driver's door shut and wobbled out of the yard in the Dart, which looked like it needed towing to the dump. Eden fondly watched his progress along the gravel road.

"Hippie freak," George Junior said. "Why are you getting mixed up with him, Eden? Nobody around here knows where the hell he came from. He's probably a draft dodger. Freaking coward."

"Maybe standing up for what he believes in makes him a hero. Ever think about that?"

George Junior snorted again and went into the house with Skylar. George Senior and Barbie were still on the porch, staring at Eden.

"Well," she demanded, "can't I have a boyfriend? What's your problem?"

Barbie said, "Go to your room and I'll tell you what my problem is!"

Eden stomped into the house, leaving her muddy boots in the doorway to aggravate her mother.

A couple of hours later, Barbie opened Eden's bedroom door. During the first hour, Eden listened to her parents blaming one another for her moral decline. George had been too deep in the bottle to notice his daughter. Barbie had been too busy with the house, garden, and three sons to nurture a little girl. And around. And around.

During the second hour, the house was eerily quiet. Eden reveled in her daydreams about Monroe and the family they would raise one day. *They* wouldn't ignore their children. *They* wouldn't fight loudly for hours while their children lay in their beds, cowering and trapped.

"Eden." Barbie closed the door behind her. "Sit up. I want to talk to you." Eden reluctantly slid into a seated position, drawing the bedspread to her chin.

"Is this Monroe person the father of your child?"

"No!! I just met him a few weeks ago. That's ridiculous!"

"Then I want you to tell me who is. Once and for all."

Eden realized that whenever Barbie and George looked at her, this question clouded their vision. With every sip of George's whisky and every punch of Barbie's bread dough, this mystery floated into their minds. When they went to town, they looked at every man with suspicion. The unknown identity of Ava's father was a heavy rock slowly sinking their family to the bottom of the sea.

Eden envisioned Curtis, his head twisted away from her while she challenged his silence in the tall, waving grass; as she tried to break through to him, to show him what love was. She rarely regretted this moment, because Ava was the result, and Ava was meant to be born.

"I can't tell you. Ever."

Barbie drew a ragged breath. "We don't want you seeing this Monroe. For one thing, he's too old for you. We don't know anything about his family. You don't know him at all, Eden."

"How can I get to know him if I can't see him?"

"You are only fifteen. Time enough for dating when you are older. And we don't want another pregnancy, do we?"

"No," Eden said in a small voice.

Barbie's face flashed with anger, indecision, judgment, and concern. It occurred to Eden that, every day, vengeance and self-preservation fought love and duty beneath her mother's workaday demeanour. Here stood a woman deciding by the minute whether or not to tear her family apart. She turned abruptly and left the room.

Chapter 13

"Tell him to drive west five miles from the Pedersen's turn-off, then turn right on the grid road and go about three miles to the school."

"Okay, okay, let me write this down." Celeste dropped the receiver; Eden could hear her rustling through papers. She looked nervously out of the window. Barbie was still in the garden, hacking weeds with a hoe.

"Okay, say that again," Celeste said breathlessly. Apparently, finding a pen and paper at the Tremblays was a challenge. Eden smiled at the thought as she repeated the directions.

"Tell him three o'clock Sunday. I'll be there with one of the horses."

"Okay! How romantic! A secret love affair."

"Don't get all excited. It's not that big a deal," Eden said, the Monroe-flutter swooping beneath her heart.

Sunday took an excruciatingly long time to arrive. Eden's heart rattled in her chest as she caught and saddled Blackie. She had considered taking Patches but liked the picture she had in her mind of riding up to Monroe on a glistening black steed.

"Now, listen," she said in Blackie's ear. "No shenanigans. Lots of fresh grass in the schoolyard to keep you busy while we... talk."

Oh, my God, what am I doing? Fear and desire stabbed her lower abdomen, and her mouth turned to dirt. She rode slowly along the gravel road until they were out of sight of the house, then dug her heels into Blackie to gallop all the way to the abandoned school.

Blackie's sides were heaving when they arrived—according to her watch, an hour early. *Idiot. What's your hurry?* As she led the horse over to a grassy patch near the outhouses, she was slammed with an Ava-vision. These visions couldn't be summoned, she had discovered. They came to her completely unbidden and at the most inconvenient times.

Ava was lying in a basket beside a tilled garden plot. A woman walked into a weathered outhouse at the edge of the garden and closed the door. Ava kicked her legs out of her thin blanket. She shrieked when a large dog shoved its slobbery snout into her tiny torso. She cried and cried in a breathless, scratchy voice. No one came to her.

Eden wiped tears from her eyes, then looked up to see the Dodge Dart sail over the hill in a ripple of dust. She pushed Ava to the back of her mind.

Monroe shed the car in one smooth motion. In the next, he lifted Eden into his arms and kissed her with her feet dangling above the ground. It was a nice kiss—awkward due to her lack of purchase, but nice. The memory of Jason's kiss rose like a snake along her spine, but she shook it away with a toss of her tangled skein of hair.

"Hello, fancy meeting you here," she said, laughing and feeling foolish for saying the first thought that popped into her head. Monroe laughed too and set her on her feet.

"Ah, beauty shall rise with the dawn from the east," he said, holding her hands and gazing at her.

"Are you for real?" Eden said, releasing his hands. "Did you make that up?"

Monroe grinned, his eyes sparkling. "Not me. Somebody a lot smarter than me."

He drew a tattered blanket from the back seat, slapping it against his legs to tease out the dust. Carrying a case of beer and the blanket, they walked to the shade of the school, away from the road.

With the blanket spread out, the tall grass created a green screen to conceal them as they leaned against the rotting boards of the old school. Monroe opened two beers and draped his arm across Eden's shoulders. Her heart was still thrashing around in her chest, but she liked the clean soap smell of his checked shirt. She rested her head against his shoulder and sighed.

Blackie crunched grass across the schoolyard while Monroe rolled a joint and Eden told Monroe her parents had attended school here back in the day.

"We could probably pry the door open and go in if you want." She tried to inhale the harsh smoke without coughing when he handed the joint to her.

Monroe slipped his hand under her blouse and cupped her breast.

"I like it here just fine," he said. He carefully extinguished the joint in the dirt, put it safely aside, and gently drew her down to lie beside him.

This is when I'm supposed to say no. A tear escaped the corner of her eye when she realized with certainty that she wasn't going to turn Monroe away. She thought of Curtis and their encounter in the coulee. She thought of Ava, the beautiful child she had never seen. She thought of her father's whisky bottle on the kitchen table and her mother's unearthly scream as the bottle shattered on the floor.

Eden closed her eyes and wrapped her arms around Monroe's shoulders. *I don't want to think about any of that anymore.* When Monroe unsheathed a condom, tears came again to her eyes.

"Hey, don't worry," he said, noticing the tears. "I'll go easy." When he was finished, he smudged her tears with his thumb, pulled his jeans back on, and reached for the roach.

"Have a toke, it'll help," he said, and for the first time, Eden relaxed into the soft arms of the marijuana. Her sharp edges softened as she leaned back to gaze at the cloudless sky and listen to the rhythmic chomping of Blackie's teeth on the grass.

Later—she wasn't sure how long they had been lying there—Monroe said, "Even if I didn't know you'd had a kid, I'd know now."

Eden turned to look at him. "What do you mean?" She thought of the stretch marks on her abdomen. Had he noticed them?

"You're loose, you know. You're looser than most people. Guess that happens when you have a kid."

Eden looked into the sky. Her bruised heart urged her to gallop away on Blackie, yet she stayed put, as if planted in the ground. Her limbs were liquid from the pot. She was too tired to get up.

She shrugged. "Yeah, maybe. That's what you get."

***

It was Eden's sixteenth birthday. River and Stacey's wedding was the next day. "We'll celebrate your birthday the weekend after the wedding," Barbie had said within the prenuptial pandemonium. Sure, you will, Eden thought. She knew that wasn't going to happen.

Stacey asked Barbie to make squares for the midnight lunch at the wedding dance, and Barbie was embracing the challenge. She and Donnie worked all day yesterday, making peanut butter chews, fudge squares, and date loaf. Today, Eden was her helper.

"Don't eat that!" Barbie said as Eden sampled a walnut slice. "I'll have to take out the seams on your dress!" Eden shrugged and took another piece. Opportunities for revenge were sweet. Barbie glared at her.

The counter was covered with cooling walnut slices, chocolate coconut macaroons, lemon lace cookies, and River's favourite, chocolate chip crunchies. They were all impossible to resist.

Only butter tarts and rocky road squares remained on Barbie's list. Eden hoped to squeeze in a ride before supper, her own private birthday celebration with Patches under the denim-blue August sky.

She thought about her dress. It was so beautiful—a soft green sleeveless gown with a wide flounce on the skirt. Both Barbie and Eden had fretted that the full-length dress would be too short for Eden, who was still growing. She now stood a full head taller than her mother, and her waist was two sizes larger.

Barbie was wearing a yellow-and-white floral print full-length empire dress with a matching bolero jacket. George Senior had barked when he saw the bill from Sears—almost one hundred dollars, including their new white sandals. Barbie ignored him. She, too, relished revenge.

"So, about your hair for tomorrow..." Barbie began, but Eden cut her off.

"I told you Celeste is going to French braid it for me," she said impatiently. "And no, I don't want to trim it."

"I'm sure Celeste could trim it before she braids it." Barbie looked dubiously at Eden's tangle. "Just a little?"

Eden ignored her mother as she took the cookie sheets out of the oven and set them on the stove burners to cool. *I won't have to listen to this nagging much longer.*

As Eden caught and saddled Patches, she tried to forget this was their last ride. After a gallop in the south pasture, she pulled the mare to a standstill to gaze at her favourite view; from here, she could pretend they lived before the land was parcelled out, fenced, and settled. From this vantage point, she saw only golden grasslands rolling to the edge of infinity.

When she got back to the yard, Eden leaned her head against Patches's cheek to say a quiet farewell. The horse twitched her ears as if to ask what was wrong. *Everything's wrong, girl. That's why I'm going.*

The other horses were already deep in the barn pasture, nibbling on the dry grass and switching their tails at the flies. Eden raised her hand to them, then walked to the house.

Only Celeste knew about Eden's plan to leave the South Country with Monroe. The burden of this secret had been too much for Eden to bear alone all summer. To Eden's surprise, Celeste tried to talk her out of it when she arrived to style Eden's hair the next day.

"I know you and Monroe have been spending time together and I know he is very romantic and sweet, but do you really know him so very well?" Celeste yanked on Eden's hair in a business-like fashion.

Romantic and sweet? Eden rolled her eyes. She was getting to know the real Monroe, who was decidedly less romantic now that they had been together for a couple of months. Still, he wanted her. He wanted her to live with him up north.

"How well did you know Maurice when you started going out?" Eden asked.

"Well, we grew up together, for one thing. And we aren't planning to live together until we get married after I finish school. What about school, Eden?"

You're sounding more like Barbie by the second. "I can't go back to school here, I just can't. Everyone knows what happened. I hate the way people look at me."

"I have learned to ignore them. They don't know anything, those people," Celeste said passionately. "You and I understand, but they don't."

"I'm a little nervous about going away," Eden admitted. "But I've done it before. I lived in the city for six months, and no one in my family—except George and Skylar that one time—even came to see me. I got used to not having a family."

"*Ma chérie,* you have family with me. I am your sister now," Celeste said. "And I am going to miss you *tellement.*"

"I'll write every week, I promise. Don't cry. This is the best thing for me. An adventure!"

"Your *maman* and papa are going to go bananas. They will come looking for you."

"I'm not going to tell them exactly where I am. I'm not even sure where Monroe lives. Somewhere up north."

Monroe was cryptic about his northern home. He had been in Canada for almost ten years and was twenty-eight years old. This came as a shock to Eden—he was twelve years older than she was.

"What do you see in me?" she asked him once. "I'm a baby compared to you."

"I see everything in you. You are a duckling, becoming a swan. As soon as you're 'legal,' I am going to take you away from all this." (This was said in one of his more romantic moments.)

Monroe was uneasy living so close to the United States border. He had been staying with his uncle and aunt for almost a year, but it was time to go home. He said he didn't want to go home alone.

He deplored Canada's two-faced ways—selling arms and resources to the United States and helping to fuel its war in Vietnam while harbouring those he called "renouncers" of the war.

"I renounce that evil war," he was in the habit of stating, usually after they had sex and then smoked up close to the old school where passersby couldn't see them. The conflict was over, but the United States would never recover from the divisions the war had wrought, he said. He wanted to live as far away from government control as he could get. The lonely north of Canada was "utopia."

This talk of politics and war was new to Eden. She didn't really understand it. Monroe said that was a consequence of living in the backwaters of North America.

"Where we're going, all of that won't matter," he said. "The bombs will never find us there. Or the radiation, if we're lucky. When everything's blown to shit, we will live off the land, like the Natives used to do. That's all we'll need."

Monroe said the north was the safest place to be when the Soviets bombed the Minuteman ballistic missile silos buried all over Montana—not as far north as the 55th parallel, the location of one of the United States early warning lines, but somewhere in the middle.

Eden listened to this in shock. No one had ever told her about missile silos in Montana. The horrifying risk of nuclear devastation was never discussed at the English's supper table. Everyone went about their business as if the world was not about to end. Eden thought she should warn them, but her relationship with Monroe was a secret, and she didn't want to bring suspicion upon herself. She admired Monroe's knowledge of the world and was grateful they were going to a safer place.

After Celeste left, Eden and her mother had fun getting ready for the wedding. Barbie was in a giddy mood and never once criticized Eden's hair. Wisps were escaping, but Barbie merely wet them with a washcloth and pinned them carefully in place.

"Gorgeous," Barbie exclaimed when Eden put on her dress. "You look like a model. So statuesque!" She looked up into Eden's face. "And so grown up!"

Eden struggled not to cry. She knew this day meant a lot to her mother. While Barbie wanted it to go well for River and Stacey, she also hoped the celebration would redeem the English's position in the community. After Skylar's accident and Jennifer Miller's death, Barbie felt excluded. People had been cold. Eden knew the feeling; most people in the South Country knew she had a baby. It had been a hard year for Barbie and George.

Eden didn't want to think about how upset Barbie would be when she left with Monroe. But her parents would get over it eventually. She would write to tell them she was okay. It was harvest, the busiest time of the year. Would Barbie stay to help with harvest, or would she leave soon, too? It was impossible to imagine the ranch without her mother.

When they walked out of her parents' bedroom dressed, coiffed, and lipsticked, George Senior let out a low whistle. He looked smart in new jeans, shirt, and vest, with a shoestring tie and his good cowboy boots. Only a slight scent of whisky—George had promised River he would not drink on this day. Eden prayed this would turn out to be true. *Please, God, don't let him drink.*

George extended an arm to his wife and the other to his daughter, and together they walked out to the truck, the women holding their skirts high. Even the truck was clean and shining. Barbie scooted over on the bench seat to sit beside George before Eden could slip in ahead of her. George and Barbie smiled at one another. Eden shut her eyes and committed this moment to memory. Then she remembered what she was about to do that evening. It might be the last straw between them. *At least I won't have to witness the carnage.*

They were arriving early to meet Donnie, who had offered to drive Grandma Doris to the ceremony. The family had decided that of all the day's festivities, Doris would enjoy the church service the most.

"You look fantastic!" Donnie said as Eden jumped into her car. "What a perfect dress!"

"Thanks." Eden blushed and looked down. *Donnie is so sweet. I am going to miss her so much.*

"Everything okay with you?" Donnie asked, a frown between her eyebrows. "You look... I don't know... tense."

"Yeah, I'm kind of nervous about the wedding," Eden said. "I haven't seen many people since... well, you know. Everybody's going to be looking at me."

"No way, they'll be looking at Stacey. If you feel uncomfortable, just come find me. We can sit together and imagine everyone naked. That's always fun."

Eden snorted, thinking of the grizzled farmers and stout farmers' wives who would attend the wedding.

"Besides, you'll be going back to school soon," Donnie said. "You might get some looks, but before long, everyone will forget about it. Life goes on, right?"

Eden smiled wanly. As they parked in front of the care home, they saw Doris standing with two staff members at the door. Eden's grandmother was wearing a flowered dress and a straw hat pinned with lavender, pink, and white sweet peas.

Her hands shook as she clutched Eden's arm. "Where we going now?" Doris said, alarm in her eyes. "When we coming back?

"We're going to see River get married, Grandma. You don't want to miss that, do you?"

Doris allowed Eden and Donnie to guide her to the passenger door. With difficulty, they lowered her into the seat. Eden crawled into the back. As they drove, Doris reached back to squeeze Eden's hand.

"My baby girl," she said. Tears threatened to wreak havoc on Eden's makeup. Donnie handed her a tissue.

Eden was glad they had seated her grandmother in the church ahead of the other guests. As people began to file in, Doris twisted her head around and glared at them. Eden held her hand and put her arm around her.

"Don't worry, Grandma. These are all good friends of ours."

Doris sniffed. "Since when are the Krasinskis friends of ours?" she said, but then forgot about any longstanding resentment because River was walking up the aisle with Barbie on his arm and George Senior close behind.

Skylar and George Junior, River's best man and groomsman, joined River at the front once Barbie and George Senior sat in the front row on the right. The organist began to play.

"Who's that?" Doris pointed aggressively at River.

"That's River, your grandson. He's getting married," Eden reminded her.

Eden was startled to see her brothers in their rented black tuxedos, even though she was expecting it. The suits transformed them from scruffy labourers to sophisticated bachelors. River and George Junior looked nervous, but Skylar was radiant. *You'd think he was getting married.* He beamed at the crowd.

An usher led Stacey's mother, wearing a fuchsia and white floral dress with stylish puff sleeves, to the front pew on the left. Stacey's maid of honour and bridesmaid, in identical blue satin gowns with white fabric flowers pinned between their breasts, paced slowly up the aisle.

The moment had arrived. The organist began to grind out the wedding march at a high volume, and everyone stood up. Doris, who was shorter than Eden remembered, teetered on her toes to see what was going on.

Stacey and her father materialized at the back. Her blushing face was concealed by a white floppy hat—the latest style for weddings. She scanned the room anxiously for River, who watched her approach, emotion trembling in his tanned face. Tears streamed down her cheeks as she moved slowly up the aisle, her gaze anchored to her betrothed.

There wasn't a dry eye in the room.

The sun shone brightly on the wedding day until late afternoon, when soft, steady rain began to fall on the parched prairie. The rain guaranteed a large attendance at the wedding dance, which was open to one and all; no personal invitation required. The community hall, bedecked with crepe-paper streamers taped to the edge of the stage and along the swooping arches of the ceiling, was thronged with people.

Eden was standing with Celeste and Maurice when she felt a prickle on the back of her neck. She turned to see Louisa and Carrie standing across the room, pretending they hadn't been staring at her. They had probably been ogling Celeste's dress, which left nothing to the imagination in terms of her bust size. Eden glared at them, and Celeste laughed.

"Let them look, *ma chérie*," she said. "And who do we have here? Looks like Jason has a new woman."

Jason Pedersen weaved through the crowd, pulling a slender girl by the hand toward the bar. All drinks were on the English family tonight, which was George Senior's contribution to the festivities.

"Who is it?" Eden asked.

"I don't know, but I hope she doesn't get pregnant tonight." Celeste tossed her blonde curls and looked up at Maurice, who was lighting a cigarette.

"One for me, too, *mon amour*," she said, slipping Maurice's pack of Player's Light from his shirt pocket. He obliged by gently placing a cigarette in her mouth and sensuously lighting it while staring into her eyes. Eden turned from this nauseating display of adoration and scanned the room for Monroe.

Maybe he won't show up. Perhaps their escape was a lovers' fantasy—pillow talk on a dusty blanket brushing flies, mosquitoes, and ants away from their bare skin. But there he was, standing at the back, peering over the chattering, laughing crowd. When his eyes met hers, he winked behind his glasses. His hair had grown even longer, but his lovely brown beard was trimmed close to his face. Eden felt weak in the knees.

Celeste, of course, didn't miss this subtle exchange.

"Promise me that you will write and tell me how you are," she said, clutching Eden's arm. "And remember, you always have a home with us."

Eden noticed Denis and Odette dancing the polka to the rousing tunes of Dr. Christianson's band. Odette looked beautiful, so slim after all those babies. Denis twirled her proudly across the wooden floor. *I want Monroe to look at me like that.* Tears welled up as she realized that any chance of having a South Country wedding would be dashed when she and Monroe pointed the Dodge Dart north.

They planned to slip away after the garter and bouquet toss, just before the midnight lunch. Barbie would be helping to serve the lunch, and George would be preoccupied, hopefully sober, as he watched the proceedings surrounded by a pack of his friends. No one would be at home yet. They would drive to the English farm, grab a few belongings that Eden had secretly packed, and head north using back roads so they wouldn't run into anyone on the highway.

Eden knew she would be missed if she didn't stand among the other unmarried girls when Stacey threw a bouquet—specially ordered just for this purpose—into the crowd. According to custom, the girl who caught it would be the next to get married. Usually, girls scrambled for the bouquet, and the competition could get quite heated.

Eden did not plan to reach for the prize, no matter how close it came to her. Monroe did not believe in marriage. He called it *bourgeois*, which Eden took to mean old-fashioned. Considering her own parents' marriage, she tended to agree. What was the point if it led to such unhappiness?

When Stacey and River stood on stage and Stacey turned her back to toss the bouquet, Eden hovered behind the eager girls who had gathered at their feet. Celeste was in front, laughing and talking with the others. Stacey threw the flowers with all her farm-girl strength, and the coveted item landed in Eden's arms before she could step away.

Everyone laughed and cheered, including George Senior, who hooted above the crowd, "Thas ma girl! But not for a few more years, fellas!"

Eden's father was standing unsteadily between Vic and Garth. They appeared to be holding him up. Horrified, she scanned the buffet tables where Barbie was rooted to the floor. Mother and daughter shared a panicked glance, then Barbie started walking resolutely toward the men.

"Sheesh leaving me, ya know," George said loudly to anyone inclined to listen. "Jus' up and walkin' away from it all." The room grew quieter as Barbie approached.

Time to vamoose. Eden watched as Monroe disappeared through the double doors at the back, then she quickly walked to the side door, taking the bouquet with her. They climbed into the Dodge Dart wordlessly. After agonizing seconds waiting for the Dart's motor to turn over, they headed west along the empty highway.

The skies had cleared, and the full moon had nearly obliterated the stars by the time they pulled up to the house. Monroe followed her in, looking around with interest while she ran to her bedroom, hung her dress neatly in the closet, changed into jeans and a bunny hug, and pulled her suitcase and a couple of boxes from beneath her bed.

She grabbed a note from her bureau drawer and propped it on her pillow. As an afterthought, she arranged the bouquet beside the note. She did all this without emotion. She had rehearsed it a thousand times in her mind. It was all going according to plan.

She had bid goodbye to the horses. She had said farewell to the trees in the shelter belt and the ripening vegetables in the garden. She had even said goodbye to Barker, who was at that moment yapping incessantly at Monroe's car. In her note, she simply said she was starting a new life and not to worry, she would write soon.

In the postscript, she asked her parents to stay together if they loved one another. "You will always have my love," she wrote, swallowing the bitterness that burned the back of her throat whenever she thought about the baby that her parents—for once in their lives united in purpose—had taken from her. At the time of writing, she even meant it.

"My house says to me, Do not leave me, for here dwells your past. And the road says to me, Come and follow me, for I am your future," Monroe said, taking the boxes and leading her out of her home.

You are my future, Eden thought, watching his long back bend into the trunk as he placed all her worldly belongings there. She took one last breath of the prairie perfume—ripening grain and rain-soaked soil—then curled into the passenger seat and settled into the now-familiar skunk scent of weed. She didn't look back.

"Pure Colombian Gold, babe!" Monroe said several hours later, with a familiar squeeze of her bottom. "Our ticket to the good life."

They had stopped to stretch their legs at the side of the road. Eden stared at the boxes of bagged pot stuffed into the Dart's trunk behind her suitcase. The moon was still bright, but she couldn't see what Monroe was so excited about. She didn't share his enthusiasm for weed, especially at three in the morning. It gave her a raw throat and zonked her out for hours. She turned her face away as he handed her the joint he had just rolled.

"How much longer until we get to your place?" she said, wrapping her arms around his waist to soften the blow. He hated it when she turned down a toke.

"What's your hurry?" Monroe said as he inhaled deeply.

"Well, we could get caught with this stuff and thrown in jail," Eden pointed out. "I mean, where did you get it, anyway?"

"Ah, the secrets of my trade." Monroe stepped away from her embrace. "For me to know and you to find out. Besides, there are no cops on these roads at this time of the night. One of the things I like best about Saskatchewan."

Eden awoke when Monroe stopped the car to jump out and fiddle with the windshield wipers. A slow rain was falling. Eden pulled down the sun visor and squinted at her reflection in the dirty mirror. As she suspected, her wedding makeup had rubbed off except for the mascara that smeared her eyes and cheeks. She used a licked finger to repair the damage.

Monroe got back into the car. "*Voila!*" he said, as the windshield wipers sprang crankily to life. "You just got to know how to baby this girl." He patted the Dart's dusty dashboard, then nuzzled Eden's neck.

"Just like I know how to baby you, right, babe? We'll be home very soon," he said, with a meaningful look. Eden felt gross and miles from romantic. She shrugged and pushed him away. Monroe laughed.

"No more blankets on the ground and mosquito swatting for us," he declared. "We have our own place to do whatever we want." Eden smiled. She couldn't wait to see her new home.

The windshield wipers were squawk-squealing hypnotically as they approached the town. Eden saw the road sign. Prince Albert 10. *Okay, this is where I live now. Cool.*

The sun was shoving aside low clouds on the eastern horizon, and the rain was tapering off. Eden squinted through the windows as they drove into town, hunching down in her seat in response to Monroe's rising tension. There were no cars on the streets—yes, one, an RCMP cruiser on the main drag. Monroe abruptly turned onto a sleepy side street lined with tiny, wood-framed houses.

"Is this your street?" Eden asked. Monroe was leaning over the steering wheel, searching for something in the gloom. He swerved into an alley, killed the engine, punched the headlights, then leaned back, forehead glistening.

Eden thought about the bags of high-priced marijuana in the trunk. Her armpits dampened as her heart danced the polka in her chest.

"They don't know this car, so we should be okay if we just lay low for a few minutes." Monroe craned his neck to look toward the street. Eden said nothing, her mouth as arid as summer fallow fields in August. She could smell her armpits now. From the corner of her eye, she saw the cruiser gliding silently along the empty street. A caragana bush partially obscured Monroe's car. The cruiser moved on.

Monroe turned the ignition, and the car coughed to life. They proceeded slowly down the alley, highly conscious of the Dart's propensity to backfire. Soon they were weaving through shuttered streets and back to the highway, driving away from town.

"We'll take the scenic route," Monroe said, relaxing a little. He patted Eden's knee. "Almost home."

After turning repeatedly along narrow country roads, Eden realized they were approaching Prince Albert again. Streetlights were self-extinguishing as they drove up to a trailer park near the town. Drowsy lights bloomed behind droopy kitchen curtains, and red brake lights flared as an old pickup truck coasted down a driveway. They passed three small trailers tucked among a thick stand of spruce trees. Monroe parked beside a fourth. They were home.

Pitted by hail and corroded with age, the faded white-and-blue mobile home crouched in the cool morning air, lonely and unloved. Withered leaves crowded the unpainted plywood skirting and heaped in front of the cinder block steps at the narrow door. Monroe dug into his jeans pocket, triumphantly producing a key.

"Wait," Eden called as he flung the door open. "Shouldn't you carry me over the threshold or something?"

Monroe turned to stare down at her, pushing his scratched glasses up his nose with his forefinger. "Chickie, we aren't married and never will be, so shut up about that," he said. "And you're far too hefty for me to haul up these steps. Get real."

Eden carried herself across the threshold, staring in dismay at the crowded space—two pleather beanbag chairs, a cinder block and wood plank bookcase, a tiny black-and-white television on an overturned red plastic milk crate, scratched and dilapidated stove and fridge—pink, she noted—chipped counters, and a hinged table attached to the wall that could be pulled up when required.

She moved through her new home in a daze, noting the stained green fixtures in the bathroom and a wood-panelled bedroom at the back, dwarfed by a double mattress on the floor covered by old sleeping bags.

The trailer reeked of stale cigarette smoke and weed, an odour that seemingly didn't diminish with time. She turned to Monroe.

"Yeah, I hear you," she said, looking him in the eye. "Time to get real."

Chapter 14

1979
Prince Albert, Saskatchewan

Eden admired her new haircut in the rearview mirror. Finally, she thought, my hair is in style. While she would never be able to fashion it into the Farrah Fawcett swoop the hairdresser had accomplished, her untidy tresses, now expertly layered, had never looked better. *In my humble opinion.*

Eden shuddered, anticipating Monroe's probable reaction to her new look. He would say they couldn't afford it. He would be right.

Damn it! Eden turned sharply into the trailer park. *I pay the bills around here! I deserve a haircut at least once a year.*

She noticed Monroe had returned while she was at work. He'd been off on one of his "sales trips," meeting with associates around the province who sold the weed and hashish he unloaded several times a year from the back of a truck in the middle of the night. He stored the stash under the trailer in airtight plastic containers.

She had grown used to living above the bald evidence that could send them both to jail. She was too busy keeping body and soul together to worry about it much. Despite the astronomical value of the drugs under the trailer, Monroe and Eden lived in poverty. Monroe was inhaling the profits, it seemed. That was always his excuse not to spend money.

He liked to think that nobody would suspect him of being a drug dealer living in a backwater shithole such as this. However, the disguise was not enough to permit Monroe a sound sleep at night. He needed his dope to do that.

Monroe was driving a Chevrolet pickup these days, while she crept along in the Dart. Monroe spent long days under the hood, keeping the old girl going. She wheezed and squeaked now, protesting most vehemently when turning left. Eden devised a route between home and work that required only right turns. She had to smile. It was ridiculous.

The Chevy was parked by the trailer, and the trailer door stood open. The first thing Eden saw when she stepped in was Monroe's glasses, scattered in three pieces on the counter.

"Oh, Monroe! Not again," she exclaimed, gathering up the tattered lenses and earpieces. "I don't think I can patch these up one more..."

She stopped short. Two men were sitting in the beanbag chairs, looking up at her like hungry puppies. Two men she did not recognize.

She was so disoriented that she had to grab the counter to steady herself. One of the men was Monroe's buddy Kevin, and the other was Monroe. Both men had shaved off their long hair and beards.

They laughed hard at her reaction while she unpacked groceries with her back to them to regain her composure. Inexplicably, she fought to hold back tears.

Monroe jumped from his chair like an awkward grasshopper and grabbed her shoulders to force her to look at him. She twisted her face away, struggling to break free.

"Eden, did you get a haircut?" Monroe asked, tilting his face to look into hers. "Let's see, something is different! You look fantastic!"

Eden wiggled out of his grasp. Without his beard, long hair, and glasses, Monroe looked like Don Knotts, but with less chin. She had never noticed that he had protruding ears. It was almost as shocking as the day she learned his real name was Alfie Baronowski.

Monroe was the town where he had grown up in Michigan.

Eden refused to call him Alfie. She had to admit he looked like one now.

"All I can say is 'why?'," she said, glaring at both men, who were still laughing.

Monroe shrugged. "The heat's getting a little too hot. Cops everywhere. Thought I'd create my own little disguise." He reached for his fixings to roll a joint. "Kev is trading trucks with me. No one will know us now."

Kevin rubbed his hands over his bald scalp. "I feel naked," he said with a lecherous glance at Eden. He was always lusting over Eden. "Come here and rub my head. It's soft as a baby's ass end."

"Rub your own head," she retorted, opening the fridge hopefully. It was almost empty. She checked the cupboard over the fridge; half an ounce of Canadian Club remained in her bottle. And no money until payday to buy more. Like Grandma Doris once said, it was hard to be a drinker when you were broke.

"C'mon over here," Monroe said, gesturing with his doobie. "Have some smoke."

Eden ignored him and walked to the table. Among the junk mail she found a letter addressed to her. She didn't immediately recognize the handwriting. *Mom? Celeste? It wasn't George Junior. God, it was River!*

It was the first time since she left the South Country that River had reached out to her. She tore open the envelope to find a baby announcement. River and Stacey were the proud parents of an eight-pound, eleven-ounce boy named Daniel George English. River hadn't scrawled a personal note on the card, and there was no photograph, but Eden's mood soared at this news. She longed to hold this little nephew to her heart.

She was immediately slammed into a powerful Ava-vision. *A small girl was wearing a cotton dress, and her bare feet were dirty and cold. The girl was sucking her thumb when suddenly an adult hand smacked it out of her mouth. The little girl started to cry, then stopped abruptly and ran down a dingy corridor.*

Ava's fourth birthday was in three days. As her birthday approached, Eden had been having daily visions about her daughter. They were phantom glimpses; she was unable to pull back far enough to see the whole picture. She merely felt the little girl's despair like a punch in the solar plexus.

Eden walked to the bedroom and sank down on the mattress. She could open canned beans for supper. She had brought milk and bread from the store. She didn't have the energy to prepare the meal.

Monroe and Kevin's giggles and skunk smoke drifted to her from under the door. She felt vaguely nauseous. The smoke did that to her, but could it be… no, Eden thought, not that. She and Monroe had dispensed with condoms long ago—she told him she was on the pill, but she wasn't—but no pregnancy had resulted. Eden craved another child, but something told her it wouldn't happen here. Perhaps it would never happen.

* * *

A few days later, Eden finished her early shift at the grocery store and hung up her apron in the staff room. She was exhausted and footsore from standing all morning at the cash register. She needed new shoes; the only runners she owned were worn and saggy. Gone were the days when she could shop from the Sears catalogue and her mother would order—usually—anything she wanted.

Eden hadn't heard from Barbie for a few months. She knew her parents' long-awaited court date was coming up soon, so she assumed her mother was distracted. Barbie lived in Regina now, where she worked for an abused women's shelter. She was a vocal proponent of reformed matrimonial property rights; her upcoming court case was generating a lot of interest. Last week, Eden saw Barbie interviewed on television, her ghostly image flickering beyond reach on Monroe's tiny television.

When Eden pulled into the trailer court, she noticed activity next door—another ramshackle home that had been unoccupied for a year. A brown pickup truck was tucked under the trees, and boxes littered the doorstep. Eden shrugged. The trailer park crowd tended to be antisocial. She didn't know any of their neighbours. Monroe liked it that way.

Monroe wasn't home. Eden looked around the trailer, thinking she should clean up. Instead, after swishing a dirty coffee cup under the tap and sniffing it, she opened the overhead cupboard, pulled out a mickey of rye, and poured herself a drink. *Ahh, time to relax.*

A movement outside the window caught her attention. A toddler was wandering around out there. There was no one else in sight. *Can't they watch their goddamn kids?* Eden smiled. There was her father, talking in her head.

Carrying her drink, she stepped out to get a better look at the child. The little boy startled, then howled. He was short and very wide. His tree stump legs reminded her of Celeste's brother Hugo back in the day. Grapefruit cheeks squeezed his slitty streaming eyes.

"Ermy-erm!" the child cried, pounding the air with his fists.

"Say what?"

"Ermy-erm!" he shouted again, glaring at her accusingly.

Eden laughed, which did nothing to alleviate the tantrum. The trailer door burst open, and a short, curvy woman stepped out. She, too, reacted like a startled deer when she saw Eden. She rushed to the little boy, a waterfall of black hair hiding her face as she bent down to talk to him.

"Squirmy Worm is in the house. Come on." She hoisted the tiny sumo wrestler onto her hip in a practiced manner. Eden noticed her smooth, muscular arms. *She's a weightlifter for sure with that kid around.*

"He's pretty darn cute," Eden said.

"Sorry, he doesn't usually make so much noise. He's just confused because of the move. He lost his favourite toy."

"It's a *worm*?"

"Yeah, we call him Squirmy Worm. He's stuffed," the young mother said, forgetting for a moment to be wary.

"Ermy-erm?" the baby asked plaintively.

"Here, I'll hold him while you go get it," Eden said, reaching for the boy. He sniffled.

"Um, it's okay," the woman said. She carried the baby into the house. Eden watched them go, sipping her drink. Soon, the woman and her son returned. The boy was clutching a googly-eyed worm—*could it be a snake?*—while his mother wiped his face with a tissue. The toy, grimy with love, looked like a prize from the carnies at the fair.

"I'm Eden." She reached out to shake the woman's hand.

"I'm... um... Penny... I mean, Meadow!"

"If I get to pick, I choose Meadow," Eden said. "That's a pretty name." *Meadow. Where have I heard that before?*

A red-headed man walked out of the trailer. He nodded to Eden, then said to Meadow, "I'm heading to town. What do you need at the store?"

As they discussed the shopping list, Eden stared at the amber liquid in her cup. Their exchange was so domestic, so Barbie-and-George. It didn't sound like a conversation she and Monroe had ever had. The man jumped into the brown truck and backed out of the overgrown driveway.

Meadow smiled shyly. "Do you have kids?" she asked, shifting her offspring from one hip to the other.

Eden could feel the whisky in her stomach. "Yeah, a little girl. But she doesn't live here. I had to give her up for adoption." She had never discussed this with anyone before. In the South Country, it was a forbidden topic, and here, well... no one cared here.

Eden was surprised to see tears in Meadow's dark eyes—just for a moment—then she tossed her hair away from her face and said, "Yeah, me too. Two of my kids are in foster care." She brushed her nose against the baby's cheek. "But I'm keeping this one. No doubt about that."

Two! Eden was appalled. *I would never survive two*.

"Hey, you want a drink?" she asked, gesturing with her cup.

"No! Thank you. We don't drink." Meadow looked trapped and took a step toward her trailer.

"Hey, no problem. Can I make you tea or something?" Eden thought feverishly, trying to remember if they had tea.

"That would be okay," Meadow said hesitantly.

"Okay, don't move, I'll be right back. I'll just put the kettle on." Eden bounded into her trailer, setting her cup down with a slosh. She looked at the whisky, then impulsively dumped it down the drain. *Now, why would you do that? What a waste*. She set the kettle on the burner and began to rummage in her cupboards. *Yes, Red Rose tea, hooray*!

When she returned with two steaming cups, Meadow and the baby were sitting on the metal step of their trailer, cuddling and laughing. Eden's heart constricted and tears clumped in her throat. She had thought she was immune to young mothers with their babies by now, after working in the store for the past three-and-a-half years.

Meadow looked up, her smile revealing a deep dimple in her left cheek beside a gap in her mouth where a molar should be. She had grapefruit cheeks when she smiled, too. Eden handed her a cup and leaned against the trailer. She was tongue-tied all of a sudden.

The little boy wriggled out of his mother's arms and wandered over to a clump of grass taller than he was, clutching the worm possessively.

"What's his name?" Eden asked.

"Chance," Meadow said. "He's my second chance."

As they gazed at Chance—he tried to eat a small stone, but his mother yelled at him, and he dropped it at once—Eden stole sidelong glances at Meadow. *She can't be much older than I am.*

"So, you married?" Meadow asked. She blushed as if it was out of character for her to ask personal questions.

"Nope. Monroe doesn't believe in marriage," Eden said. "He's kind of a hippie. But you'd never know it because he shaved off his beard and long hair. Now he looks like a soldier or something." *Draft dodger.*

Monroe pulled up in Kevin's green Ford. He didn't glance over at them as he stomped into the trailer and slammed the door. Eden could hear him hollering for her, assuming she was in the bedroom.

"I'd better go," she said to Meadow.

"Thanks for the tea, it's good." Meadow handed her the empty cup. Chance toddled over to look up at them.

"You be a good boy," Eden said, patting him on the head. "Take care of that worm."

"Where were you?" Monroe asked, sinking into a beanbag chair. He reached for his worn copy of *Jonathan Livingston Seagull* and his wrapping papers.

"Just welcoming our new neighbours."

Monroe shrugged. "Don't get too friendly. It was nice having that place empty for a while."

"She's Native. The guy's white. They have a little boy."

"Well, there goes the neighbourhood." Monroe was joking. He thought Natives got a bad deal in Canada, and it was worse in the United States, he often said. Monroe was against oppression of all kinds, especially government oppression. It was something Eden liked about him.

Eden started making supper—Kraft Dinner with sliced tomatoes—while Monroe watched her contemplatively through a haze of smoke. "I miss your ass. You used to be such a cute, round little thing."

Eden glared at him. He often bemoaned her new figure. She had lost twenty-five pounds since moving here. "I'm skinny because there isn't enough to eat around here. You need to get a job."

"Hey, I've got a job that pays plenty," Monroe huffed. "Come here and have a toke."

Eden waved dismissively through the smoke. She considered pouring another whisky, then decided not to. She looked at Meadow's doorway from the kitchen window.

"Then why don't we have more food around here? I can't pay all our bills with part-time hours at the store, and they won't give me more hours. You know that!" This was such an old quarrel that neither she nor Monroe had the appetite to resume it.

"They deem me mad because I will not sell my days for gold, and I deem them mad because they think my days have a price." Monroe had a remarkable capacity for pulling relevant Kahlil Gibran quotes out of thin air. This talent had lost its ability to charm Eden years ago.

"Here's your KD. I'm going to lie down, so just leave me alone."

Monroe shrugged and grinned, turning on the television. Eden spent the evening dozing on the mattress, listening to the muffled voices of *The Dukes of Hazzard* and *All in the Family*.

* * *

A week later, outside the optometrist's office, Eden stared at Monroe in dismay. His new glasses were yellow-tinted oblong wire rims; the latest style, he claimed. They were so large they dwarfed his lower jaw. With a receding chin and clipped hair, he looked like a pair of glasses walking around without a face. Eden shook her head.

A ruckus at the hotel drew their attention. The men standing on the sidewalk outside the bar were displaying impressive signs of intoxication for four o'clock in the afternoon.

Monroe lit a cigarette and handed the pack to Eden.

"You know those guys?" Eden asked, pulling a slender cigarette from his pack of Export As. They stood together smoking under an awning.

"Yeah, some of them," Monroe said. "They work over at the mill."

The laughing men were distracted by a truck passing slowly by. Eden realized with a jolt that it was Meadow in the brown truck. She was peering into the group of men as she drove past.

"Hey, Pocahontas, your old man ain't here," one of the men called out.

"Yeah, Princess, come on and have a drink with us!" another said.

Meadow hastily cranked up her window and pulled away. Eden could see Chance standing on the seat, staring out of the rear window at the men. A short, powerfully built man wearing a Prince Albert Pulp ball cap stepped into the street to watch her go.

"Goddamn squaw," he said distinctly. "What self-respecting white guy would screw around with that piece of shit."

205

The men moved along the sidewalk, headed to another bar. The short man stayed in the street, animosity seething from his red, contorted face.

"Wow, that guy has a thing for Native chicks," Monroe observed.

"A thing. You mean he likes them? Sounds to me like he hates Natives."

"I didn't say he doesn't hate them. I know guys like that. They are full-fledged morons. Come on, let's go home."

Eden was worried about Meadow. Why was she driving around looking for Kyle? He worked graveyards at the mill and tried to sleep in the trailer during the day. It was Meadow's job to keep Chance quiet. They spent their time outside, hunting for bugs and trying not to eat rocks. Eden joined them when she could.

On the way home in Monroe's truck, Eden looked at Celeste's slanted handwriting on the fat envelope she had found in their mailbox in town. A lonely tear slipped from Eden's eye, which she dashed away impatiently. She glanced at Monroe; he hadn't noticed the tear.

After a quick supper—Spam on white bread with canned peas—and watching *Three's Company* with Monroe, Eden decided to step outside to open Celeste's envelope. A wedding invitation was wrapped inside the three double-sided foolscap pages of her letter.

Celeste graduated from high school last year and had just completed her cosmetology training in Moose Jaw. She and Maurice were getting married in September. Celeste wanted Eden to be her maid of honour.

Successive waves of elation and fear swept over Eden. She wanted to be there for Celeste, but her heart couldn't bear seeing her father in the grip of his addiction, the indifference of her brothers—except George Junior, it would be good to see him—and the glaring absence of Barbie in the farmhouse kitchen.

She was certain Monroe would not attend the wedding or give her the money to go on her own.

She almost sank to her knees in the weedy dirt, clutching Celeste's letter to her breast. Instead, she walked back into the trailer and collapsed on the mattress in the murky light of the back bedroom.

Eden never found the courage to discuss the incident in town with Meadow, but later that spring, sitting with her on a plaid blanket in the shade of the trailer, Eden asked, "Why did you say your name was Penny when we first met?"

Meadow froze, a frown etching deep rivulets between her dark eyes. She didn't speak, and Eden wondered if she had overstepped a boundary. Finally, she looked into Eden's eyes.

"When I was three, I was put in a foster home. My foster mom gave me the name Penny. It was my real mom who called me Meadow."

Eden didn't know what to say.

"I met my birth mom a few years ago, just before she died. She said she named me Meadow Starlight. I like that better," Meadow said.

"How did you find your birth mom?"

"My birth father found me. He works at the Friendship Center in Regina, and one day I was in there and he just took one look at me and knew I was his daughter." Meadow's eyes were shining. "I didn't believe him at first, but he did some research and proved he was my dad."

"Wow, that's amazing," Eden said. "Bet you look just like your mother. Pretty, like her."

Meadow blushed. "That's what he said."

A silence fell over them. A meadowlark's call—three pure notes followed by a cascading warble like water tumbling in a stream—broke the calm. Eden spotted the small brown bird sitting on the wire fence behind the trailers.

"I love the meadowlark's song," she said. "Makes me homesick."

"Why don't you go home?" Meadow asked. "I mean, for a visit, eh?"

Eden shrugged. "I guess I could, but it would take money for the bus. I'm pretty sure my vehicle wouldn't make it that far." They both laughed; the Dart squatted in the driveway like an elderly dog waiting to die.

"Take Monroe's truck," Meadow suggested. "He could go, too."

"Yeah, like that's ever gonna happen," Eden said, squirming under this gentle examination of her situation.

When Grandma Doris passed away a couple of years ago, Eden begged Monroe to attend the funeral with her. He flatly refused, and she couldn't find the fortitude to go back to the South Country without him. Missing her grandmother's funeral was among the slate of sorrows only a stiff drink could allay.

Chance waddled toward the blanket, a tuft of wild oats dangling from his mouth. Meadow pulled it out, pried his lips open, and stuck her index finger between his jaws.

"Ouch, don't bite, you little devil!" Meadow exclaimed, pulling her finger free. Chance laughed with his mouth wide open, helpfully revealing that nothing remained to choke him, at least for the moment.

Eden was broadsided with an Ava-vision that left her sweating. *A little girl was sitting on the floor under a table. She reached out for something on the floor and promptly put it into her mouth. She started choking and crying. No one came to help her. Eventually, she coughed out the morsel—it looked like a piece of dry dog food.*

"Eden, what's wrong?" Meadow asked. "You're white as a ghost!"

Eden started to cry. "You'll think I'm bat-shit crazy," she said, wiping her nose. "I get these weird visions, kind of like dreams. I see my daughter Ava in these dreams, and she doesn't look good. She looks completely neglected."

Meadow took a deep breath. "You're probably just worried about her."

"Yeah, I know. But I've been having these visions ever since she was born."

Eden stood abruptly on the blanket and brushed the front of her jeans. "I'd better get going."

Meadow called out before Eden disappeared around the corner of her trailer. "I have nightmares, too, you know, about the two I gave up. But they happen at night, usually."

Eden gave her a weak smile. It was good to know someone understood, at least a little.

Chapter 15

"Kyle keeps taking off on me."

Eden and Meadow were walking in the trailer park holding Chance's pudgy hands. He was doing that thing kids do—swinging both feet off the ground and laughing uproariously. Eden thought her arm might pop off.

Eden looked at Meadow. She was not prone to sharing personal information, and Eden knew by instinct not to ask questions. She noticed now that Meadow was crying behind her curtain of hair.

"For weeks now, he leaves town right after his last shift, before his days off," Meadow continued. "Then he comes home just in time to start his night shifts again. He won't tell me where he goes!"

Meadow wiped her eyes angrily. Chance disappeared around the corner of Eden's trailer.

"He says Chance isn't his. But he is! I can't help it if he looks so Native. He's just like me. At my foster home, they always said they wouldn't adopt me because I looked so Native. They adopted a little white baby instead, right before I left."

This was such a fount of information that Eden was stunned. "Is that why you left?" she asked hesitantly.

"No, I knew they'd kick me out when they found out I was pregnant. I was partying too much back then to care. I was just a pay cheque to them, me and the five other Native kids they were fostering. I hitched to the city and lived downtown for a few years."

Eden thought about Harry and Porgie and their lair behind the garbage bins. She shivered. Meadow's tidy trailer was a palace in comparison.

"So... what are you going to do?" she asked. Monroe had been away for a few days on a sales trip, but Eden didn't doubt that he would come back. You had to give him that.

Meadow shrugged. "Maybe get a job, but what am I going to do with Chance?" She glanced around. "Where *is* Chance?"

They sprinted to the driveway between their trailers. No sign of the kid. Panicked, they circled and screamed his name. Eden thought her heart had stopped, but then she heard a husky giggle. She followed the giggle to the weedy no-man's land behind her trailer. Monroe had left garbage there—a broken lawn chair, boxes of empty whisky bottles, and rusted car parts from the Dart. She knelt and peered into a narrow gap in the plywood skirting.

"Here he is!" she called to Meadow, pulling the baby out. It was a tight squeeze. Chance was still giggling.

"Bad boy!" Meadow lifted him from Eden's arms. "You scared Mommy half to death. Never do that again!"

Meadow and Chance turned toward their trailer, and Eden heard the door slam. Something caught her eye as she tried to close the gap with her foot. She knelt again to investigate.

Normally, Eden never looked under the trailer. It gave her the creeps with its mouldering stew of cobwebs, insects, and mud, and Monroe had forbidden her to go near his stash. Eden had no problem obeying; she tried not to think about the fact they were harbouring illegal drugs and could be thrown in jail any second. But now something shiny lured her in for a second look.

It was a green metal box with a combination lock. Eden pulled it into the light. *What the hell?* The lock was just like the one she used to have on her school locker. She jiggled the lock, and it sprang open. *Monroe! You forgot to lock the box. Typical!*

Shaking her head, she cautiously disengaged the lock and opened the lid. The box was full of cash. Twenties, fifties, hundreds. Hundreds and hundreds of dollars. Probably thousands. With trembling hands, Eden locked the box, shoved it under the trailer and pushed the loose plywood into place.

She walked inside, sat down on one of the beanbag chairs, and stared at the blank television set for a long time. Finally, she got up and poured herself a double.

Monroe lied to her about the money he was making selling pot. He made her pay rent from her meager salary. He made her buy groceries, gas, booze, and supplies. He paid for nothing. And they had nothing—two vehicles ready for the scrap yard, furniture she was sure the Salvation Army would reject, worn clothes, holey shoes. Monroe contributed only cigarettes and weed to their household. She even paid for his new glasses!

She looked around with disgust. Barbie and George wouldn't let their dog live in a dump like this. She thought about HoundDog and a tear rose and fell from her eye. Nothing had been the same since HoundDog died in the storm and she and River were almost electrocuted. That lightning bolt split her family apart.

A voice in her head reminded her that she was already pregnant when HoundDog died. Jennifer Miller was already dead. The rift already existed. Lightning had struck their family, and only scattered remnants remained.

She looked at Monroe's guitar leaning in the corner under a layer of dust. She remembered when he sang "Killing Me Softly" in the flickering Sage Coulee firelight. He had looked deeply into her eyes as he simply sang her life with his words. It was the most romantic moment of her life, and she doubted anything would surpass it. But it had been a year since Monroe picked up his guitar. Most of the time, he was too stoned to play. When he was straight, he was sarcastic, crabby, and paranoid.

And now he had lied to her again. They had plenty of money, at least enough to buy new shoes and warm winter coats. Maybe a reliable car so she could continue to work at the grocery store for three dollars and sixty-five cents an hour for the rest of her life!

She wanted to throttle Monroe. To kick him in the ribcage and shake him until his bald head rattled. To pack her paltry belongings and hitchhike back to the South Country. That would show him!

Eden plotted her escape from an existence that wasn't anything like the life she had once imagined with Monroe. For years, she refused to admit to herself that she had made a huge mistake. But now she couldn't deny that she had nothing to look forward to except her next drink. Her escape plan fizzled like her fury, drowned in whisky and tears.

When Monroe burst in about an hour later, Eden had decided not to mention the money. And she had decided not to leave him. Where would she go? To go back to the South Country would be admitting defeat to the whole community. To go to Barbie in Regina would be condoning her mother's decision to leave the ranch. She wasn't sure she would be welcome in either place.

"Chickie, what's for supper?" Monroe said, dumping his backpack on the floor for her to clean out. He opened the fridge with difficulty—the handle had fallen off, so he had to pry the door open by squeezing two fingers between the rubber seals—and stooped to look in.

"There's shit to eat in this house!" he exclaimed. "What have you been doing while I was gone? You work in a frigging grocery store, for Christ's sake!"

Eden lifted her mug of whisky in a toast. "Welcome to my world," she said.

* * *

Several weeks later, Eden and Monroe were sleeping it off—they had crashed on the mattress after toking and drinking more than usual—when Eden heard a loud shout. She glanced at the alarm clock. It was two in the morning.

The commotion sounded like a pack of drunken men. "Hey, Squaw, com'n out and party!" a man's voice called out, punctuated by wild hoots and a revving engine.

"What the shit..." Monroe sat up groggily. The trailer park was usually a graveyard at night. Mostly seniors lived there.

Eden looked out of the kitchen window. There were lights on in Meadow's trailer, and a souped-up truck idled in the driveway with its headlights off. Eden could just make out the chrome exhaust stacks in the moonless night. Kyle's truck was gone. He was either working or away on one of his mysterious absences. Meadow and Chance were alone.

As Eden watched, a man pounded on the trailer door. "Come on, bitch, open up!" Eden recognized the man. She had seen him on the street, staring at Meadow while she drove by looking for Kyle. It was the day Monroe got his new glasses.

"Monroe, we have to call the cops! These assholes are going to break Meadow's door down!"

Monroe snatched the telephone receiver from Eden and slammed it into its cradle. "No cops, are you crazy? We can't have cops crawling around here!"

"We have to do something! Monroe, go out there and tell them to get lost!"

Monroe shrugged and yawned. "Nothing we can do. Let the Indian take care of herself."

Eden pounded on his chest as hard as she could. "Meadow and Chance are all alone. Get the hell out there and do something!"

Monroe swerved back to the mattress, falling onto it like a felled log. Eden continued watching anxiously, gnawing on her fingernails. The man was pulling on the door latch now; Eden feared he was strong enough to peel it back like the lid of a sardine can.

Then she heard sirens. Someone had called the police, thank God! She heard a call from the truck, "Come on, man, let's get out of here!" With one final tug at the locked door, the man jumped back into the truck. It backed up with a belch of exhaust and roared away.

Within minutes, a police cruiser pulled up. "The police are here!" Eden shouted to Monroe. He stumbled up and lit a stick of incense, which he believed would mask the smell of marijuana smoke that clung to every corner of their home.

"Get away from the window!" he shouted, grabbing Eden's arm and painfully dragging her toward the back of the trailer. "It's not our business!"

"Ouch, let me go, you pig!" Eden said, wrenching her arm away. She stood back from the window but could still see Meadow's door. The police officer knocked, and Meadow cracked the door open, holding Chance on her shoulder. Eden could hear Chance howling, but not what was said by her friend and the officer. Soon, the officer drove off in his cruiser.

All was quiet.

Eden looked at Monroe. "You are a sorry excuse for a man. I wish I had never met you."

Monroe's beardless face was pallid in the dim light. "Hey, you know where the door is. Get out if you don't like it here."

He went back to the mattress and pulled a stained sleeping bag over his shoulders. Eden slept restlessly in a beanbag chair for the rest of the night.

Eden knocked on Meadow's door the next day after an early shift at work. It had been a tough shift after her night on the beanbag chair and all the whisky she consumed the evening before. There was no answer, so Eden called out, "Meadow, it's me. Are you okay?"

Meadow hastily ushered Eden inside. Chance was sleeping in the playpen in the living room. Meadow looked haggard; her hair was unwashed, and she wore oversized sweatpants and a saggy tank top. She plugged the kettle in.

"What happened last night? Who were those guys?" Eden asked, gratefully sinking to a kitchen chair. She was still hungover.

Meadow shrugged with her back to Eden. "I know one of them. He works with Kyle. I hate him!"

"Why is he bothering you? What's going on?"

"How did he find out where I live?" Meadow turned to Eden, eyes glistening. "I was scared shitless that he would break down the door."

"Is Kyle away again?" Eden asked, and Meadow nodded.

"He's supposed to be back the day after tomorrow. I don't know what to do."

Eden thought about it. "I can sleep over here with you guys tonight. Would that help?"

Meadow smiled. "And bring your shotgun?"

"We don't have guns. Monroe is a pacifist—he doesn't believe in them. But if I sleep here, maybe you'll feel better? At least until Kyle gets home?"

"Okay, thanks, Eden." Meadow started sobbing, and Chance woke up whimpering. Eden left them weeping together, Meadow's hair falling across their tear-streaked faces.

Monroe made a big fuss about Eden sleeping over at Meadow's.

"It's just for a night. She's really jumpy after those guys tried to break down her door." Eden put her pyjamas and toothbrush in a grocery bag. She looked at her hairbrush but decided not to bring it. She liked travelling light. "It's a sleepover. Chance will love it!"

"Stay away from those two," Monroe growled. "Those guys from the mill won't stop harassing her, and before you know it, there will be a whole squadron of cops around here. God, maybe we should find another place to live!"

Eden looked sideways at Monroe. Surely, he didn't mean it. He had a sweet deal with the landlord; Monroe supplied all his weed and hashish with the understanding their monthly rent would remain at fifty dollars. The same man owned Meadow's trailer, charging one hundred and fifty dollars a month for the family to live in a drafty box. Fortunately, Kyle made a good wage and always paid the rent.

Eden and Meadow sat in pyjamas under a blanket watching television after Chance went to sleep. Meadow had popped corn in her special blackened corn-popping pot.

Eden remembered evenings when Barbie made popcorn and they would sit together on the couch, feet on the coffee table, watching *Little House on the Prairie*. Eden's mother said she liked looking at Little Joe Cartwright. Eden, in junior high at the time, had to agree that the lead actor was very cute with his dark curly hair.

Tonight, a rerun of *Dawn, Portrait of a Teenage Runaway* was on. Eden settled down with pleasure; this was one of her favourite movies, and Meadow's television set was so much better than Monroe's.

Meadow brusquely turned off the television.

"You don't like this show?" Eden asked, perplexed. "I've seen it about five times."

"I used to turn tricks when I lived on the street," Meadow said in a flat voice. "Believe me, real life is nothing like this movie. Maybe that guy from the mill knows me from then. I don't know. He seems kinda familiar."

"He's a racist shit-for-brains idiot," Eden said.

"I don't have a good feeling about this, Eden. I was so loaded in those years that I don't have many memories. That's probably a good thing," she said with a sad smile. "But I have a feeling Kyle's not coming back, and they will take Chance away from me. Something will take Chance away from me."

"You're a good mom," Eden said. "They won't take him away. Maybe I can help get you a job at the store. Maybe we could arrange our shifts so one of us is always home to take care of Chance. Don't worry."

Meadow grinned, revealing her missing molar and the dimple in her left cheek. "Why do you even hang out with me? Can't you see I'm a drunken Indian?"

Eden looked into Meadow's bottomless eyes. "I didn't know any Native people when I was a kid. There weren't any in our school, anyway. Sometimes I'd see them at the rodeos or whatever. You're like the first Native I've ever met. And you're cool." There was that dimple again.

"Have you had any weird dreams lately?" Meadow asked. "One of those visions or whatever?"

Eden frowned and leaned back against the couch.

"Yeah, there's one I had a few days ago. So, this little girl—I'm sure it's Ava because she always looks the same in these visions—is running around barefoot in a garden. There's this old outhouse on the edge of it. She starts picking peas, and then someone yells at her, and she runs with a handful of peas and goes into the outhouse. She starts chewing the peas without shelling them. That's it. Weird, right?"

Meadow shook her head as if to clear it of a bad memory.

"The thing is, I'm pretty sure Ava is hungry," Eden said. "I don't know where she is, and I don't know how to begin looking for her."

A few hours after they went to bed, a bang against the trailer jerked Eden from her sleep on the couch. Another bang! Chance started to cry in the bedroom.

"Meadow!" Eden ran to the door. Someone was jiggling the latch. She dragged the kitchen table to block the door as Meadow appeared; together, they moved it into place. They stared wildly at one another as the man from last night—it had to be the same guy—

started to wrench the door open. He was using a crowbar!

"Call the police!" Eden screamed. "Monroe, help us!"

She launched a high-pitched screech that might have roused the dead but was unlikely to summon Monroe, who was undoubtedly cowering under the sleeping bags.

The man at the door was ominously silent. No hollering and hooting this time. He was focused on his mission. In a second, the flimsy door creaked open, bent and useless. The stocky man knocked the table aside like cardboard. Meadow dropped the phone and ran down the short hall to the bedroom.

The man stared at Eden, obviously surprised to see her there.

"Get the hell out of here!" Eden screamed at him, hair wild and eyes like forked lightning.

He stepped around the table toward her. Eden summoned every ounce of hatred she had ever felt for another human being—Jason Pedersen, Monroe, George Senior, Barbie, Agatha Browne—and, conjuring the exact moment on the school bus when she had kicked Jason, aimed her bare foot at the man's groin.

When she kicked Jason, she had been in top shape from riding every day. Now, although she was taller, she was weaker. She had not been astride a horse for almost four years. Her blow grazed his upper thigh, which merely surprised him. He continued to approach her. She jumped on his chest, wrapped her arms and legs around him, pulled his hair, and screamed like a cougar.

Knocked off balance, the man flailed, trying to scrape her off. The intruder toppled backwards, and Eden heard his head slam to the floor. She pushed away just as Meadow ran from the hallway and whacked him in the face with Chance's umbrella stroller. Chance's high-pitched screams added to the mayhem.

Panting, Eden and Meadow looked down at the man. Eden wondered if they had killed him, but within seconds he stirred and struggled to sit up. Meadow brandished the stroller and Eden started screaming again, wordless anger flowing from her mouth like a dam breaking.

The man raised his hands and crawled to the door. "Bitches," he muttered as he lurched to his feet and disappeared through the ruined door frame. Eden didn't stop screaming until she heard the man's truck drive away.

They sat in the living room, wrapped in blankets and teeth chattering. "I won't go to the police. Don't even ask me again," Meadow said, stroking Chance's hair. The baby had finally calmed down and was sleeping uneasily in his mother's arms. "They will take Chance away from me if I do." She kissed his sweaty head.

Eden didn't understand. Meadow was threatened twice by a random white guy determined to rape her. She had been abandoned by her partner, another useless white guy. What had Meadow done to deserve that?

Although she hadn't spoken, Meadow knew what Eden was thinking.

"You're white. If you went to the police, they would do something to help. If I went in, they would just look at me like I wasn't their problem. They would look up my record and figure I had a bad trick last night. And then they'd call social services and take my baby."

Eden ran her fingers through her shock-deranged hair. There was dried blood under her fingernails where she had scraped the intruder's scalp. She hoped he was bleeding to death.

Cold air drifted in from the broken door, which Eden had tried but failed to bend back into shape. It helped a little when she hooked a blanket around the door frame. Then she turned to Meadow.

"So, what are we going to do?"

"We? This isn't your problem, eh."

"Well, I can't just sit back and watch you getting attacked. He might be back tonight. And you don't even have a door that locks." Eden glanced in the direction of her own trailer. "Pretty sure Monroe won't take you in, sorry." She shrugged.

Meadow's dimple showed, which meant an inward smile. "That's okay," she said.

"Do you think Kyle will come back this time?"

Meadow took a deep breath. "Dunno. Maybe not."

Eden wanted to scream. She had to be at work by noon. She felt at a complete loss.

Meadow looked up shyly. "I could go to my dad, I guess. I mean, he said I could if I needed to."

Eden's mind whirled. "Okay, we'll take the Dart. Don't laugh, the old girl hasn't let me down yet. You could leave a note for Kyle in case he comes back. You could say you went for a visit. You could say a bear tore the door open!"

"Whoa!" Meadow *was* smiling this time. Then a tear trickled down her cheek as she gazed at the home she had created. "What about your job?"

"Shit!" Eden grabbed her hair. "I'll tell them I have a family emergency. That I need a few days off. I've never taken any days off since I started!"

They tried to sleep, tossing and turning until the sun came up. When Eden stepped into her trailer, Monroe was sitting in a beanbag chair. He looked at her accusingly.

"What was all the hollering last night?"

"That creep came back," Eden said. "But we screamed, and he ran away like the chicken shit he is."

"Look, that's the last time you hang out with those people. Natives are trouble, there's no way around it. They are cop magnets. We're lucky no one called the cops last night."

"You're probably right," Eden said, heading for the shower.

Monroe looked stunned. "That's my girl. Agreeing with me for once!"

Eden emerged from the bedroom with wet hair and wearing clean clothes. She carried a backpack, which was unusual for a workday. But Monroe probably wouldn't notice. He had already lit up a joint.

"Hey, where you off to? I thought you worked the late shift today."

"Nope, that got changed. I switched with Gerta. She has some school thing she has to attend with her grandson tonight. I'll bring supper home."

Eden felt a twinge of guilt. Then she remembered the money box under the trailer and all the other secrets Monroe had kept since the day she met him. She tried to get out the door unobtrusively with the backpack, but, of course, today he was noticing everything.

"Why you taking a bag?"

"Just to put groceries in. Paper bags always rip!"

She moseyed down the driveway, swinging the backpack by the strap, and opened the Dart's groaning driver's side door. Monroe did not follow with more questions.

When she turned toward the highway, Meadow and Chance were standing by the road. Meadow held a backpack and a diaper bag. Chance had Squirmy Worm. They both looked crushed. Eden pulled over, and they climbed into the Dart.

Eden stopped at the store to tell them about the family emergency and ask for a few days off. The store owner wasn't happy about it, but when Eden reminded him that she had worked for more than three years without time off, he begrudgingly agreed.

"But no vacation pay!" he grunted, turning back to the grocery cart he was using to restock shelves.

The next stop was the bank—Eden withdrew seventy-six dollars, leaving five dollars in the account and trying not to think about how small her pay cheque would be at the end of the month. Meadow had thirty-nine dollars from her grocery money; Kyle had a bank account, but she didn't. He gave her cash for groceries, she said. They had one hundred and fifteen bucks to get them to the city.

"Plenty of money for gas," Eden said, trying to brighten the mood.

Once they filled up and headed south, Eden began to relax. The forest gradually thinned, and soon they were on the prairie, skimming along the highway under the smoky dome of a late summer sky.

After a stop to settle Chance on the back seat under a blanket, Meadow's head began to droop, and soon she was deeply asleep. They were all exhausted after last night. Eden was tired, too, but she stayed alert, conscious of her precious cargo.

It was exhilarating to be driving on the prairie for the first time since she and Monroe came north. She pushed any thought of the consequences of not telling Monroe she was leaving to the recesses of her mind.

The baby remained sleeping, but eventually, Meadow straightened her back and stared out of the side window for a long time. Eden honoured her silence. Finally, Meadow spoke.

"If you turned east here, you would get to my foster home in a couple of hours. It was a farm, but I'm pretty sure their main income was maintenance payments from the government. That's why they had so many foster kids.

"Myrtle used to scrub us down when we went to school or when social services was coming. Otherwise, we didn't take baths. They didn't have running water, and it was a big ordeal to heat water for the tub. So, yeah, we were dirty little Indian kids most of the time.

"The boys were expected to work in the fields, but usually they just played around in the yard because Bernie was lying on the couch listening to Myrtle scream at him about drinking. My job was to pick weeds in the garden and cook supper. It was a big job making meals for eight people every day. But I did learn how to make bread and lots of other things. Myrtle was good at coaching from the kitchen table. She pretty well had me doing everything around the age of ten. My favourite was working in the garden. I loved it out there, away from them."

Eden said, "Now I see why you ran away."

"Yeah, nothing to stay for. After sixteen, they couldn't force me back. I think I let myself get pregnant just to make it final. The father of my first kid was one of my foster brothers.

"Most of them were getting ready to leave around the time I did. I think that's why Myrtle and Bernie adopted. I heard her say they needed someone to take care of them in their old age. I remember when they brought that baby home. She was so small and cute. White, of course. She used to cry and keep us all up. I'm not sure what made Myrtle think she was up to raising a baby.

"Anyway, I didn't wait around to see how it all worked out."

Hearing this, Eden prayed that Ava had a loving family. But her visions were telling her otherwise. It was difficult to brush them off as mere anxiety about her daughter's safety. They left her sweating and nauseous. They made her wonder if she was losing her mind.

***

Eden, Meadow, and Chance pulled up in front of the Indian and Metis Friendship Center in a one-storey brick building near downtown.

Ghost tracks traced her spine when they passed Wheatland Manor and the hospital on their way to the center. The curtains were drawn at the Manor, and Eden shivered, remembering its musty halls and damp bedding. The hospital was a looming reminder of

224

running down the stairs to save her baby and later pushing her into the world, only to surrender her to strangers.

As they pulled up, a cluster of young Native men turned as one and stared at them. Eden reluctantly turned off the Dart's engine. She was never sure it would start again. The car coughed once and died gratefully.

"Thanks, girl," Eden said, patting the dashboard. "Just one more trip back home."

Meadow stared at the building, ignoring the young men.

"I can't go in there," she declared. "There might be social workers, and they will take Chance away from me!" Chance started to cry; she lifted him from the back seat into her lap.

Eden took a deep breath. "Okay, I'll go in. What's your father's name? Maybe they know him."

"Harry Bird. Last I heard, he works here."

Eden walked nervously past the men, who squinted and grinned at her. She stepped into the Friendship Center and was immediately draped in a grey blanket of cigarette smoke. A lively game of bingo was going on. The caller, a tall man wearing a denim shirt, stood on a stage before a throng of women hunched over many rows of bingo cards. Eden stood at the back, looking for someone to ask if they knew Harry Bird.

Spotting a kitchen, she walked over to the serving window and peeked around the large coffee urn on the counter. Two women stood there, looking surprised to see her.

"Um, do you know a Harry Bird?" Eden asked shyly.

"Yeah, he's here. He's calling bingo," one of the women said. She wore a large apron tied around her thick waist. "Wanna cup of coffee while you wait?"

Eden gratefully poured coffee from the urn's spout into a Styrofoam cup and topped it with a large heap of Coffee-Mate.

"Bingo!" Someone shouted gleefully and everyone in the room groaned. Eden stood with her back against the wall, trying to disappear.

After a murmured consultation with his helpers, the man in the denim shirt announced the name of the bingo winner, climbed down from the stage, and headed for the kitchen. The woman in the apron scuttled over to him and pointed at Eden. The man turned toward her with a gap-toothed grin.

Of course, it was *her* Harry.

"Can I help you?" Harry said, obviously not recognizing her.

"Harry, it's me. Eden!" She was unable to contain her excitement.

"Huh?" Harry said, his brow crinkling. "Who?"

"You know, the girl who ran away and you found under the overhang? You and Porgie? A few years ago. You helped me."

"I did? Well, that was nice of me!"

"It doesn't matter!" Eden exclaimed. "Meadow is here. Meadow and Chance? They're in my car."

Looking alarmed as well as baffled, Harry hurried toward the door with Eden on his heels. He flung the door open and rushed to the Dart. Meadow opened the door and placed Chance into her father's open arms.

Tears in his eyes, he looked back at Eden.

"Thank you, little daughter," he said.

Harry led the way to his cramped office behind the kitchen. He bounced Chance on his knee while Meadow explained what happened. Chance gave Squirmy Worm's head another thorough going-over with his teeth. Eden sipped her coffee.

"And how do you know this young lady?" Harry asked Meadow, tilting his head toward Eden.

"We're neighbours," Eden said. "Friends, too."

"Well, I am much obliged to you for bringing Meadow and Chance to the city." Harry said he was taking his daughter and grandson to the house he lived in and invited Eden to stay, too.

"No, I better be going. I was thinking of going to see my mom. She works at the women's center. She'd be pretty mad at me if I didn't stop in."

"Oh, yeah, what's her name?" Harry asked.

"Barbie English."

"Barbara English is your mother? Will wonders never cease! I know your mom really well. She helps our clients out all the time. She's freaking amazing. Do you want me to call her and let her know you are coming?"

"No, I'll just surprise her." Eden's stomach clenched nervously. She hadn't seen her mother in nearly four years.

"How's Porgie?" Eden said, to change the subject.

Harry's smile disappeared. "Well, Porgie passed," he said.

"Oh, no, what happened?"

"He was in the drunk tank and when he sobered up the RCMP took him out of town and dumped him on the side of the road. He froze to death out there."

Horror and fierce anger swept over Eden. She clenched her fists as if to take revenge, but there was no visible enemy, no one to kick or scratch. Her fury meant nothing to a society that didn't care. Then an Ava-vision crashed into her, overtaking her shocked mind and forcing tears to her eyes.

A little girl was sitting in the dirt beside two large black-and-white border collies panting in the shade of an outhouse. The outhouse door slammed open, hitting the child in the face. A man shouted at the girl as she began to shriek, blood gushing from her forehead. She ran into the garden, hands covering her face. The corn stalks towered over her head and hid her from view.

"Shit," Eden said.

"You okay?" Meadow asked.

"I know it's a shock," Harry said.

"You had another vision, didn't you?" Meadow said.

Eden could only nod.

When Harry handed Chance back to his mother to speak with a man at his door, Eden told Meadow about the vision. Meadow blanched.

"Did you say border collies? Black and white?" Meadow asked quietly.

"Yeah, they had to be. They were just like Vic's dog Blazer," Eden said. "Why?"

"Now, don't freak out," Meadow said, rising to pace around the small room. Chance perched on her hip, sucking his thumb. "But that sounds just like Myrtle's and Bernie's place."

"That's impossible," Eden said. "I mean, how could that be?"

"I had a funny feeling when you talked before about an outhouse beside a garden. But Bernie always had border collies. Always. That's Myrtle's and Bernie's place. I swear it."

"No," Eden said. "I don't believe it!" She rose too, wanting to run out of the room. "Ava can't be there! Do you remember when they adopted the baby?"

"Well, it was in the spring of 1975, the year I left. I'm freaking out here!"

Harry returned to his office, stopping short when he saw the astonished look on their faces.

"Hey, now, I know it's terrible news. Us Indians are trash in the eyes of the police. But we are going to take the cops to court!"

The girls stared blankly at Harry. Like an automaton, Eden hugged Meadow and Chance. "You know my phone number, right?" Eden asked Meadow. "Call me when you get settled." Meadow nodded. Eden knew it was unlikely that she would, due to the high cost of long-distance calls.

She felt numb about this farewell, going through the motions of taking her leave. All she could think about was Ava and the blood on her forehead as she ran crying into the corn.

Eden still remembered a time when she would run to her mother at the least twinge of pain. Skinned knees, a wood tick latched in her armpit, an upset stomach. She even turned to Barbie when playground politics left her without a playmate in elementary school. This instinct still lived in Eden's heart, and she wanted nothing more than to throw her arms around her mother and grasp what comfort she could find there.

But when she pulled in front of the women's center—the sign said Women's Emergency Center and 24-Hour Crisis Line—the memory of Barbie's betrayal and rejection during Eden's pregnancy pushed aside her need for comfort.

Eden wanted to tell her mother that she now knew where Ava was, even though it was impossible, but she also knew her mother would recoil from such a revelation. There would be no help coming from Barbie. Eden needed to tell someone else.

As she sat in the Dart—she left it running, but noticed the gas tank was almost empty—she asked herself who she could tell. Monroe was the only one who might listen to her. Although he had never been supportive of her in the past, he was her partner, and they lived together. Monroe was all she had.

What she really needed right now was a drink.

Eden signalled and pulled away from the curb. The Dart shuddered as if grasping that another long journey lay ahead. After buying gas and a coffee, Eden steeled herself as she passed the government liquor store and turned toward Prince Albert without stopping. Monroe and whisky waited for her at home. She had to keep it together long enough to get there.

Back on the prairie, the sunset exploded in lavender, navy, and yellow all around her. Tears poured down her face and dripped from her chin as she drove into the night.

She thought about Meadow's shocked face when she realized that her foster home was the farm in

Eden's visions. She remembered the feel of Chance's soft cheek as she kissed him goodbye and Harry's clear-eyed, toothless grin as he walked toward her, full of confidence and peace. She envisioned Porgie's frozen body. For many people in Saskatchewan and indeed, Canada, his life held no more value than a deer carcass kicked into the ditch.

And she thought about her little girl, neglected and alone.

At that moment, she felt too defeated to figure out how she would get Ava back, but she knew she must. She needed to save her baby before she died in that hellhole. But for now, all she wanted was Monroe, whisky, and their smelly old mattress on the bedroom floor. She drove until stars, cold and impersonal, pierced the moonless sky.

At one point, she pulled off the road and slept, leaning the driver's seat back as far as it would go. The sun was coming up as she pulled into town, reminding her of the morning four years ago when she and Monroe had fled the South Country, and she looked at all the sleeping houses, wondering which one was theirs. She had been so naive.

Monroe would be surprised to see her at this hour and might be angry that she hadn't told him where she was going. But early morning was a good time to talk to Monroe; he was straight in the mornings. He would listen to her this time. He would care. She couldn't wait to see him.

When she pulled up to the trailer, she noticed the truck was gone. *He must be off on a sales call.* Feeling more exhausted than disappointed, Eden opened the cupboard door above the stove and pulled down her bottle of Canadian Club. She gulped down the remaining ounces straight from the bottle. Then she flopped onto the mattress, fully clothed and with her runners on. Blessed oblivion.

Eden woke up stiff and parched. The stench from her mouth made her gag. She hadn't eaten for more than twenty-four hours. She wrenched her depleted body from the mattress and stumbled into the bathroom.

She noticed Monroe's toothbrush and razor were gone, then remembered he was out on a delivery. I've got time to pull myself together, she thought. When she went into the main room, she saw that his guitar was missing. So were *Jonathan Livingston Seagull* and *The Prophet* by Kahlil Gibran. That struck Eden as highly unusual. Anxiety congealed in her stomach as she searched for something to eat. She had Rice Krispies but no milk.

She looked at Meadow's trailer from her kitchen window. It seemed deserted, no sign of Kyle. She decided to raid the fridge over at Meadow's. The trailer door was still twisted and useless. The incident that led to the broken door felt like a lifetime ago. She pushed the door open and looked around.

Her throat tightened as she spotted the playpen in the corner, the neatly folded afghan on the couch, the polished counters, and the empty kitchen sink. The house smelled faintly of baby powder and Meadow's earthy scent that reminded Eden of a fall day on the farm.

Eden opened the fridge door. *Right on!* Milk, half a loaf of bread, a few eggs, cheese. Eden gathered the morsels up and took them back to her dingy quarters. She enjoyed an omelet and toast, plus a bowl of Rice Krispies for good measure.

She was contemplating a shower when a niggling thought made her go back into the bedroom. She opened the closet's sliding door—limp clothes on hangers and others heaped on the floor where she had kicked them. Her clothes. Monroe had taken everything he owned.

In disbelief, Eden grabbed a large screwdriver from the junk drawer and walked behind the trailer. She used the screwdriver to pry the plywood skirting open, peering into the dank, dusty space. She could see nothing. Swearing, she ran back inside for the flashlight, which revealed exactly nothing when she used it to probe the dark depths under the trailer.

No plastic containers filled with marijuana and hashish. No cash box. There was nothing there.

Monroe was gone. Porgie had been murdered. Ava was in danger. And there was nothing she could do about any of it.

Eden sat in a beanbag chair. She needed a drink more than anything else in the world. The Canadian Club was gone, and she was too exhausted to go into town. She remembered a secret supply that she had vowed not to touch unless it was an emergency. Hiding booze made her think of her father, who, of course, was a raging alcoholic. Eden did not consider herself to be an alcoholic, but the irony had not been lost on her when she had hidden the twenty-six of rye a few months ago. Now she was glad that she did.

It was no easy feat hiding a bottle of booze in the trailer. There was just nowhere to hide. But Eden had thought of a place Monroe would not go. She had placed the bottle in a large box of sanitary napkins that she kept in the bottom drawer of their built-in dresser. She yanked the drawer open and grabbed the box; fear snagged her when she realized that the box held only sanitary napkins. Monroe found her stash!

Frantically, she pulled out every drawer, throwing the contents on the mattress and the floor. Finally, she stood on the milk crate they used for a bedside table to search the high shelf in the closet. Her unopened twenty-six had been pushed against the wall; Monroe's battered copy of *The Prophet* was propped against it.

This was his gift to her after four years together. This was his final message.

His farewell.

Eden grabbed the bottle and staggered in grief and relief to a beanbag chair. She drank the whole bottle before sunset.

The next morning, shaking and reeking, Eden crawled into the Dart, praying it would start. With many loud complaints, the engine turned over. Wincing in the sunshine, Eden drove into town, where she purchased as much whisky as her remaining cash could buy. She carried the bags of clinking bottles into the trailer and carefully lowered them to the kitchen floor.

She wasn't sure how many days had passed when the telephone rang. She ignored it, but the caller persisted. To end the godawful noise, Eden pried herself from the beanbag chair and lifted the receiver. She stared at it as if unsure of its purpose.

"Eden?" said a tinny, faraway voice. "Eden, is that you?"

Eden held the telephone to her ear, listening. *Monroe?*

"Eden, are you there, *ma chérie*?"

It was Celeste.

Eden started sobbing, her mouth wide open in a way that reminded her of Chance. She held her forehead as Ava had done, running into the corn. She sounded like HoundDog when the lightning took her life. Tears and spittle drenched her face as she howled and screamed her pain.

"*Mon Dieu*, oh, my God, are you alright? Eden, what's wrong? What happened?"

Eden hung up the phone and passed out before Celeste could call back.

Chapter 16

Loud banging roused Eden where she was lying on the mattress. Shouts. She wondered if Meadow's attacker was back. She sat up, thinking she needed to protect Meadow and Chance, then flopped back down. Meadow and Chance were gone. And she had no strength to fend off attackers.

Then she heard thumping on the bedroom window and tried to cover herself with the sleeping bags. She noticed the bags were soaked with vomit. Her hair was matted with vomit. She cowered on the mattress, unable to move.

"I see her in there! Oh, God, Maurice, I think she is dead!"

A moment later, Eden looked up through bleary eyes at Celeste and Maurice standing in the bedroom doorway. Celeste assumed the bossy manner she used whenever there was work to be done.

"Maurice, go back to town and get coffee. Lots of coffee. We have some cleaning up to do around here."

She pulled the sleeping bags away. Eden lay quaking on the bare mattress, trying to cover her body with her hands. She was naked.

Celeste kept up a steady stream of exclamations as she hauled Eden to her feet and guided her to the tiny bathroom. She set Eden on the toilet and ran hot water into the tub.

"*Ma chérie*, how thin you are! I don't see bruises, and I pray he was not beating you! Why did you not call for help? I had a feeling—a feeling something was wrong! So, I called! Bless Maurice, bless him for bringing me here! Now you get in the tub, and I will help you clean up! There's a girl! There's my beautiful Eden!"

Celeste tackled Eden's hair first, pouring water over her head with a plastic margarine container she found on the edge of the tub. Then she gently swabbed her body as if bathing a child. Eden's flaming shame gradually sputtered into gratitude.

Finally, Eden spoke. "It would have been better... if she had died. Like your baby."

"No, no, *ma chérie*," Celeste soothed. "With life there is hope. The hope of Jesus. We cannot look back, only forward."

After briskly towelling Eden off—Celeste was completely at ease with her nakedness—she led her to the bedroom and extracted jeans and a clean bunny hug from the closet. Scanning the scattered clothing and items from the drawers, she spotted a bra and panties that looked relatively clean. Eden let Celeste dress her with quick, expert hands; after all, she was a big sister to seven. A small smile bloomed in Eden's heart.

Closing the door firmly on the stench, Celeste held Eden's hand as they walked the few steps to the kitchen. Maurice was waiting with four large paper cups of coffee.

Much later, Eden sat in the back seat of Maurice's Skylark, feeling nauseated. They had spent the night in the rundown motel in town, watching reruns of *One Day at a Time* and *Welcome Back, Kotter* on the fuzzy black-and-white television until it was time to sleep. In the morning, they stopped for eggs and bacon at the diner before embarking on the long journey back to the South Country. Eden felt both drunk and horrendously hungover. Her stomach was just as confused as she was.

Celeste and Maurice murmured to one another occasionally, holding hands like they always did. Eden remembered Celeste had asked her to be the maid of honour at their wedding. It was highly unlikely she would want her now.

As they passed the turn that led to Meadow's foster home, Eden shook herself from her stupor.

"I know where Ava is," she said quietly, staring in the direction of her baby. Celeste looked back at her, startled. They listened without interrupting as Eden explained how she knew. Hands shaking, Celeste lit a cigarette for herself and then one for Maurice. She asked with a gesture if Eden wanted one, but Eden shook her head.

Eden noticed Celeste and Maurice were careful not to look at one another. *No one will ever believe me. And I can't blame them.* She had a sudden longing for Meadow and Chance; a tear slid along her cheek. *God, please let them be safe.*

The next major intersection led in one direction to Regina and the other to the South Country. "Eden, do you want a ride into the city?" Maurice asked, looking at her in the rearview mirror. "Or are you going home to the ranch?"

This was the first time Eden had considered either possibility. She didn't hesitate. "Home to my dad's," she said. With her emotions so close to the surface, she was unable to hold back tears of gratitude. "I will never be able to pay you back, but I'll try."

"Oh, believe me," Celeste said, "you will have your work cut out for you next month. I will need lots of help getting ready for the wedding, and you can pay us back by being at my beck and call. Right, Maurice?"

"Oh, yeah, Odette is writing up a list of things to do," he said. "A long, long list."

"You've seen nothing until you have experienced a Sainte-Marie wedding," Celeste said happily. "Ours is going to be huge—over two hundred guests at the reception!"

As horrifying as it was to contemplate standing before two hundred South Country guests, she felt the iceberg in her soul melt just a little. *It will be a good party. By then, I will be able to drink again.*

She took a deep breath. "You're on," she said, and Celeste smiled.

The sun was setting when they pulled into the English's farmyard. Golden light streamed through the trees on the west side of the yard, throwing gnarled finger shadows on the rough grass beside the house. Eden saw her father's truck parked beside the porch and Skylar's truck in the shop. Skylar stepped out of the shop and stared at them with his hand shading his eyes.

Barbie's prize-winning vegetable garden—she always won ribbons at the country fair—was planted with potatoes. The old potato patch was littered with stubble and weeds. Eden tore her attention away from the garden to look at the house, which seemed stark and sad. She grabbed her backpack from the trunk, gave Maurice and Celeste hugs, and climbed the steps to the porch, steeling herself for the changes she knew she would find inside.

She stepped into the smelly mudroom. She almost tripped on the manure-caked rubber boots littering the floor. The slop pail was overflowing in the corner. She swallowed and opened the door to the kitchen.

A gaunt George Senior was sitting at the kitchen table, drink in hand. Days of beard growth covered his saggy jowls.

"Barbie?" George said, looking startled.

"It's me, Daddy. Eden."

"Well, bless my soul," George said, struggling to his feet. "Eden, honey?"

She dropped her backpack and went to her father. Face pressed into his plaid shirt, she inhaled the comforting mix of sweat, leather, and whisky that had always meant Dad.

"Are you back? Are you back, honey?" George said, stepping away from her and looking anxiously into her face. "It's been about a year, hasn't it? Since you left? You back to stay?"

Eden felt a trickle of alarm along her spine. "Well, it's been a bit longer than that," she said. "But I am back now. Don't worry."

She patted his shoulder as he slumped back into his chair. Her stomach recoiled when she looked at the bottle of Canadian Club on the table.

Skylar burst into the room. In his face, she saw a tug of war between the old Skylar, who would never hug her, and the new—the new won the contest. Skylar lifted her off the ground in an embrace that cracked her bones.

"You are one skinny sight for sore eyes," he said, placing her back on her feet. "Back for a visit?"

Eden took a deep breath. "I think I'm back for good if you'll have me." She looked around at the unrecognizable kitchen. "I could lend a hand around here, housekeep, clean... even cook?"

"Oh, boy, could we use the help, eh, Dad?" Skylar pulled out a chair and lit a cigarette from the pack in his shirt pocket.

"What about Mom? Have you seen Mom?" George mumbled, scrabbling for the cigarette pack in his own pocket, which was empty. Skylar offered him one of his.

"No, Daddy. I haven't seen Mom in years."

"She comin'? She comin' home, too?"

Eden flicked a question at Skylar with her eyes. He shrugged.

"Let's get some coffee on," she said. "Or maybe some supper? What are you having tonight, Skylar?"

"Oh, who knows? There might be leftovers; Donnie was here a couple of days ago with a lasagna. Might be some left."

Eden opened the fridge and then closed it quickly. *Something's oozing in there.* She opened a cupboard. "Let's have tomato soup and grilled cheese sandwiches. Got any cheese?"

After supper, George took a tumbler of whisky, went into his bedroom, and closed the door. Eden noticed that the television had been moved into his room. As he passed, her father patted the top of her head. The gesture made her wonder where Barker was.

"Oh, he got hit by Loren's truck last year. That was the end of the barking," Skylar said.

"You guys didn't get another dog?"

"Nope. Things have changed around here. You may have noticed." Skylar eyed her cautiously. "So, what's your story?"

Eden was spared from answering when an unfamiliar truck drove into the yard. George Junior jumped out and walked toward the house. *George Junior has a new truck!* When he saw her sitting at the table, he looked confused for a second and then deeply shocked.

"Hey, George," Eden said tentatively, forcing her face into what she hoped was a friendly smile. Of all the members of her family, she feared George Junior's disfavour most. She rose to meet him as he stepped toward her.

After their hug, George wiped his eyes and said, "So, you're not done growing?" His head barely cleared her shoulder.

"Apparently, a lot of growing still goes on between the ages of sixteen and twenty," she said, relieved. "Except maybe not in your case."

Eden warmed up more soup and made another sandwich for her brother, then sat happily at the table watching him eat.

"How was Dad tonight?" George Junior asked Skylar. "Did the shock do him in?"

"He was pretty good, actually. Kept asking Eden where Mom was and when she was coming home."

George Junior rolled his eyes. "He asks us that about twenty times a day," he told Eden. "I'll bet you noticed a big change in him."

"What is wrong with Dad? Beyond the obvious," she said, nodding at the whisky bottle on the counter.

"Dr. Christianson thinks it's wet brain," George said. "Happens to people who drink a lot for a long time. He has trouble talking and can't remember shit."

Eden was silent, her worst fears realized.

"Yeah, we can't get much work out of him these days," Skylar said. "He has to be watched continually. I left him alone in the barn one time and found him wandering around in the corrals, no clue where he was."

"Oh, my God!" Eden said, clasping her mouth with her hands. "Can they do anything for him?"

"Well, if he quit drinking, it would help," George Junior said. "But even if he did, he'd forget that he quit and just drink again."

"Maybe if we took all the whisky out of the house, he'd forget about it?" Eden suggested, knowing as she spoke that it was wishful thinking.

"Dad still drives, so he'd just go into town and get more. We tried that once," Skylar said.

"He has good days and bad days," George added. "If you are here to stay, that would be an incredible help to us. We are renting out all the land now, and we sold all the cattle. Skylar fixes vehicles in the shop, and I work at the lumberyard. It's hard to keep an eye on Dad at all times."

"We might not be here much longer," Skylar said. "Mom and Dad's court case has been held off until October, but after that... Dad will probably have to sell out."

Eden looked at the filthy floor and piles of junk on the counters and on top of the refrigerator. "I am here to stay and to help as much as I can," she said. "But we can't let Mom take this farm away from Dad!"

"She wants her half, and Dad doesn't have the cash to buy her out."

Eden started washing dishes while George put Elton John on the stereo. She was grateful her brothers hadn't asked her too many questions. She spent the rest of the evening cleaning the kitchen, listening to the stereo, and making small talk until she was too exhausted to go on.

A cloud of fine dust drifted from the chenille bedspread when she sat down, but the second she slipped between the cool sheets, she fell deeply, dreamlessly asleep. Home.

The next day, after breakfast and her brothers' departure for work, Eden tackled the fridge. George Senior sat at the table, smoking and drinking coffee with "just a splash" of whisky in the cup. The room filled with the gag-inducing stench of rotten food when she opened the fridge door.

George flapped his hand in front of his face. "What the hell's that smell?"

Eden ignored him as she dumped dripping bags of vegetables and green-tinged leftovers into a garbage pail. She held her breath until she got everything outside, then filled the sink with hot, soapy water to begin the rehabilitation of Barbie's kitchen.

George was amused by her swearing whenever she encountered another horror show in the kitchen, chuckling as if immensely pleased the house was being put back in order.

Suddenly, he spoke up. "I can do whatever the hell I want to, you know!" he declared, glaring at Eden. "A man can have a little drink once in a while! Work hard all my life and now you're telling me I can't have a drink? I built you the biggest goddamn house in the district and you're still not happy!"

At that, he stormed out of the house and walked toward the barn. Eden shrugged and went on with her work. *If he gets lost in the corrals, at least he's out of my hair for a while.*

By the end of the day, she had sorted through all the papers and unopened mail on the top of the fridge, scoured the oven and stovetop, and swept mouse turds from beneath the sink. The fridge was sparkling, and the floor was mopped.

"River and Stacey are coming for dinner," George Junior announced when he got home from work. "I saw River at the lumberyard and told him you were home."

Eden had thawed a package of ground beef from the deep freezer downstairs and was planning to make goulash. She found the recipe in Barbie's greasy, dog-eared *South Country Kitchens*, a recipe book compiled by the Kinette Club to raise money for the curling rink. It had been Barbie's favourite.

"Hmm, I'll throw in some extra macaroni, and we should have enough," she mused.

"And, by the way, happy birthday," George Junior said. Eden's head snapped up. She had forgotten that today was her birthday. She had lost track of the days. She had lost track of who she was.

River, Stacey, and six-month-old Daniel arrived an hour later. River was holding Daniel, and Stacey was balancing a birthday cake. Eden rushed over to grab the cake as they took off their shoes at the door.

"This is beautiful, thanks, Stacey," Eden said, placing the cake on the counter.

Stacey reached out to hug Eden. Both Stacey and River had gained weight. Of course, Stacey just had a baby, but what was River's excuse? *Marriage agrees with him.*

River hadn't spoken, and Eden could sense his hostility. She ignored it, stepping forward to take Daniel in her arms. The solid little boy looked around curiously, his head wobbling a bit on the soft folds of his neck. Eden struggled mightily not to cry. *He is so cute!*

Eden realized that she had not had an Ava-vision for several days. She felt relieved but also worried. *What if I never see her again?*

George Senior was playing host, beckoning everyone over to the table to sit down and have a drink. He gestured for George Junior to grab glasses, but River and Stacey adamantly refused.

"No, Dad, we're good," River said. "Nothing for us." River and Stacey sat across from Eden, who lowered herself into a chair with Daniel.

"Hey, little guy, come to Grandpa!" George Senior coaxed, so Eden relinquished the baby, who waved his arms and beamed happily on his grandfather's lap. George carefully moved his whisky glass out of Daniel's reach.

"He looks like you, River," Eden said. River didn't respond, although Stacey looked at him expectantly.

"So, where's the Jesus freak?" River asked, bringing everyone in the room—even the baby—to a shocked silence.

"River!" Stacey exclaimed, glaring at her husband. "We haven't been here ten minutes! Leave it alone."

"I'm not leaving it alone!" River snarled. "She runs away with some freaking draft dodger coward and now she shows up here four years later like everything's hunky-dory. Well, I'll tell you—things are not hunky-dory around here, in case you haven't noticed."

Eden felt slapped. She also felt angry. *You don't know what it's like to be me.* She took a deep breath.

"I have noticed," she said quietly. "That's why I am here, to help Dad. Monroe... Monroe left me a few days ago, and Maurice and Celeste brought me home. I won't see him again, I'm pretty sure. I don't even know where he went."

River scoffed. "You'll go back to him the minute he shows up."

"Hey, man, cool it!" George Junior said. "Look at her! She's been through a lot."

Eden looked down at her lap. She knew she was thinner than she'd ever been. *Do the past four years show in my face?* She went to the counter to finish preparing supper. Stacey jumped up to help her.

"Don't mind him, the old grouch," Stacey said quietly. "We are both glad you are home and safe."

Eden smiled at her. "Daniel is just gorgeous," she said, tears clouding her eyes. "I miss *my* baby."

"Well, don't bring that up in front of River," Stacey advised, grabbing the plates.

The awkwardness around the table dissolved as everyone prepared to dig into the food. Skylar came in from the shop and washed up in the bathroom. Stacey took Daniel from George Senior and held him on her lap. Daniel pounded the table with both fists; Stacey staunched his demands with an arrowroot cookie.

"I'll nurse him later," she said. The baby quickly turned the cookie into brown mush.

After they'd eaten, Stacey handed Daniel to River and slipped away from the table. She reappeared carrying the cake alight with candles.

"Sorry, I didn't quite have twenty candles," she said, placing the glowing cake in front of Eden as everyone sang "Happy Birthday." Eden blew out the candles, surrounded by family, her mother and daughter mere ghost shadows on the wall.

A Monroe-shaped shadow was notably absent.

* * *

Eden had borrowed her father's truck to get groceries in town. As she was unpacking the last of the paper bags—moving with satisfaction around the transformed kitchen but ignoring for now the rest of the house that cried out for a thorough cleaning—she saw Maurice's Skylark drive into the yard. She ran outside as Celeste and Maurice stepped out of the car.

"Come in for coffee!" she exclaimed, linking arms with Celeste and guiding her into the house. It felt odd to be the hostess in this home, taking Barbie's place in the kitchen. She knew that with George drinking to this extent, Barbie would never come back. And Eden decided that as long as her father was alive, she would stay here to make his days—perhaps his final days—easier.

244

Celeste's chatter was all about the wedding. Invitations were sent, Odette was working on the wedding dress, the Catholic Women's League had provided a menu for the reception, and many hands were at work making delicacies and storing them in deep freezers until the big day. Today, Celeste was going to take Eden's measurements for her maid of honour dress. They went into Eden's bedroom.

"*Mon Dieu*, you have no bust!" Celeste exclaimed as she weaved a measuring tape under Eden's armpits. "And no hips! You are a stick!"

"Good, you won't have to use so much fabric in the dress," Eden said tolerantly, blushing as she remembered that Celeste washed, dried, and dressed her like a child in the trailer.

"And I love the haircut you have now," she went on, running her fingers through Eden's hair. "But we need a little trim, *non*?"

Eden rolled her eyes. "I suppose, if you must!"

"Now I must ask you two questions," Celeste said. "Are you drinking so very much anymore?"

Eden bristled. I can do whatever the hell I want, she thought, realizing that those words came directly from her father's mouth. Then she calmed down.

"No, I haven't touched the stuff since I came back to the South Country," she said. "I'm off the sauce. Maybe for good."

"Because there will be times in your life that won't go so well. And more times that will be very good! But drinking is not an answer. It's more like a question," Celeste said, looking through the window at the yellowing trees.

"It is like asking God over and over why things are the way they are, instead of changing them for the better yourself. It's like falling down the stairs over and over and never fixing the broken step. You know? I know, because I have seen my papa fall down those stairs. Finally, he is picking himself up. He has promised *Maman* he won't drink again!"

Eden pondered these words. "But you don't have stairs at your house," she said. "You don't even have a basement."

Celeste hit Eden with the measuring tape. "You know what I mean!" They laughed and sat down on the bed.

"And now I have to ask you a hard thing," Celeste said, sobering. "What are you going to do about Ava?"

Eden was dumbfounded. She stared hard at Celeste but detected no irony or mockery in her clear blue eyes.

"You believe me?" she whispered.

"*Oui!* Of course. A mother's love for her child is very mysterious and very strong. But I don't think Maurice understands. He does not want to help you take Ava back."

"What... what do you mean?" Eden clutched her throat with both hands.

"I'm sorry that he won't help, and he doesn't want me to, either. You must find another way."

It was Eden's turn to watch the waving poplar trees cast flickering shadows on her bedspread. There was no one else on the planet who cared enough about Ava to help her. Once again, Eden felt like she was scaling an uncharted mountain alone.

She took a deep breath, fraught with uncertainty. "Don't worry. I will find a way."

A few days later, after washing the supper dishes, Eden went to the shop to look for George Junior. She had barely slept since Celeste's visit; she hoped that after talking to her brother, she would finally get some rest. Her father and Skylar were watching television and unlikely to interrupt them.

"Hey, George," Eden said, trying not to startle him. He was staring intensely at his truck's engine, tapping his fingers in a way that indicated to Eden he was deep in thought.

"Oh, hi," he answered, reaching for a rag to wipe his hands. "Thanks for supper; it was good."

Eden wiped her own sweaty palms on her jean cutoffs. She sat on an upturned five-gallon Texaco oil pail, and George, taking her cue, pulled one up for himself. The sharp edges of the pail cut into her bare legs.

"So, ever since I had my baby," Eden said, not looking at her brother, "I have been having these weird visions about her that are kind of like waking nightmares. I see her and basically, it doesn't look good. She's not in a good place.

"When I lived with Monroe, we had this neighbour who lived in a foster home most of her life. It was a crappy place, and she couldn't wait to get away.

"I started telling her about my visions and she's pretty sure that, from what I described, Ava is at that same foster home. Just before she left four years ago, Meadow said that the family adopted a little white girl. A baby. So, I'm going to go there and try to get Ava back, and I need you to help me."

George sat silently for a few seconds, then leaped up to pace around the shop. He wouldn't look at Eden. His face turned bright red.

"I'm going to take Dad's truck and drive there and kind of get the lay of the land. Then I'm going to try to... take Ava and bring her home." Still no response from George Junior. "George, this is a matter of life or death!"

George threw his arms in the air. "Eden, you have been smoking too much of the Jesus freak's weed! You are effing crazy! You need your head examined! Don't even talk to me about this!"

"George," Eden said calmly, "I need you to help me save Ava."

"You're going to steal somebody's baby? You'll go to jail for that. And you want me to help you?"

"She's *my* baby, and she was stolen from me. Please, George!"

"And since when do you have visions? They could mean nothing. There's no way the kid is in that foster home. This isn't a magical world!"

"I know it sounds crazy, but George, these visions almost do me in. They are so strong sometimes I can't even breathe. I don't know how to explain it! But when I told Meadow that I saw Ava playing in the dirt beside two border collies, she immediately knew that was Myrtle's and Bernie's place. The farm where she grew up."

"Myrtle and Bernie," George said. "Shit."

"Okay, what if I can prove there are people called Myrtle and Bernie who had foster kids living east of Regina? I don't know exactly where, but I can find out from Meadow. Would you help me then?"

"No! Don't even ask me! Don't include me in your bat-shit plans! You have always been trouble, you know that, Eden? You have caused so much turmoil around here, you don't even know how much! Just leave me the hell alone!"

George stomped off towards the house. Eden gently lowered the hood, turned off the shop lights, and followed him through the cool evening.

The next morning, Eden clutched the telephone nervously. The men were gone for the time being; George Junior was at work, Skylar was in the shop, and, to her knowledge, her father was in the barn. She had to do this quickly.

"Hello, is Harry Bird there, please?"

"Yeah, just hold on," said the voice at the other end of the line. Eden imagined Harry in his office at the Friendship Center.

"Harry Bird speaking."

Eden smiled at the formality.

"Harry, this is Eden English? I was the one who brought Meadow and Chance to the city?"

"Hello! How ya doin'?"

"I'm fine. I was wondering if I could speak with Meadow sometime."

"Meadow's here, playing bingo! I can get her to talk to you. Wait a minute, the game's not over. Can I get her to call you back?"

"Well, um, it's kind of important."

"Oh, okay. Just hold on."

Eden stared anxiously out of the kitchen window while she waited. The potatoes will need digging soon, she thought.

"Hello?" Meadow sounded hesitant, and also whole. Safe.

"It's me, Eden!"

"Oh, hi! Are you okay?"

"Well, I need your help. I want to go to Myrtle's and Bernie's place and check on Ava. Can you tell me where they live?"

Meadow paused. "I went there. Harry—I mean, my dad—took me and Chance and my cousin there last weekend. I just… I wanted to see if they had that little girl still. The one you think might be yours."

Eden gasped. "Did you see her?"

"Yeah, we went in, and I just said I wanted to apologize for leaving without saying goodbye before. So, they made us coffee. The little girl played with Chance for a while."

"Was she okay? I mean, is she alright?"

"She didn't look all that great. I mean, she was dirty, and her hair… she didn't talk much. But she liked Chance. She seemed kind of backward. I don't know."

"Oh, God," Eden said.

"Myrtle and Bernie are even worse than before. Bernie was drunk and the house was just… horrible. So dirty. Have you had any more of those visions of yours?"

"No, not really. I'm planning to go there as soon as I can."

"Their last name is Schultz, and they live about two miles north of Orsen Bridge. It's a little town east of Bent Lake. Do you know where that is?"

"Yes, I think so. Thanks! But how can I prove to my brother that these people really exist? He thinks I'm crazy," Eden said, laughing a little. "I want him to help me."

"You could call the operator and ask for their phone number?"

The minute George Junior got home from work, Eden impatiently waved him to a chair. "Sit down! I'm calling directory assistance. I can prove there really are people named Myrtle and Bernie Schultz living near Orsen Bridge."

George scowled exactly like their mother when she wasn't getting her way. Eden dialed zero. "Hello, Operator, could I get the number for Bernie Schultz in Orsen Bridge? Or it might be Bent Lake," she said into the receiver, staring hard at George, who seemed about to flee.

In a moment, the operator said—Eden held the receiver out so George Junior could hear—"Yes, please hold for the number." She hung up.

"So, you see! That place does exist! That's where Ava is, I know it."

"I don't see how that proves anything!" George exclaimed. "Sure, maybe your friend was a foster child there, but how do you know that Ava... your baby is there. They could have adopted another kid four years ago!"

"If I could just get a glimpse of her, I'd know for sure. And I am going as soon as I can. When's your next day off?"

George threw up his hands and walked to the stairs.

"Friday," he said.

Eden wrapped her arms around him before he could escape, standing on tiptoes to kiss the top of his head.

"Love you, man!" she said, laughing but crying, too.

George shrugged out of her embrace and shuffled up the stairs, but not before Eden noticed his tears. George Junior and Dad are the only men I know who cry, she thought, her heart beating wildly at the thought of what he was willing to do to help her.

Chapter 17

Eden loved everything about the Saskatchewan prairie, but today the landscape was a dreary movie on fast forward. Combine harvesters spewed up long windrows of grain, crows orbited like vultures, and deer skimmed the highway a heartbeat before the truck struck them down. Instead of elation, Eden felt only dread at the thought of seeing her daughter for the first time.

George Junior had been shaking his head and muttering as he drove. When the Schultzes' farmyard drew near, he turned to her.

"So, here's the plan," he said. "I'll take the jerry can and knock on their door, pretend I ran out of gas. You walk over to the yard and see if you can see her from there. If I see her in the house, I can let you know how she looks. And that's it. That's the plan. As you say, you just want to check on her. So, today, that's what we are going to do, got it?"

Eden nodded.

"We are not stealing a child today, do you understand me, Eden?"

Eden leaned forward as they crested a small hill. Below, they could see the farm—an unpainted two-storey house, border collies lolling on the step, a weathered barn, abandoned vehicles in the field. A garden in the yard, corn wavering in the wind. A rickety outhouse beside the garden.

"This is the place," Eden said.

George threw her a doubtful glance, then turned his attention to the house as they drove slowly past. No sign of life. The truck proceeded along the road until hidden behind another hill. George pulled onto an approach, jumped out, and grabbed the jerry can from the truck box.

"Stay out of sight, you hear me?" he said to Eden, who was struggling not to vomit. He strolled over the hill, swinging the jerry can casually. As soon as he disappeared, Eden cautiously stepped out.

As she inched along the road toward the yard, she heard them. The border collies were losing their minds. She crouched in the ditch and looked down on the yard. The yapping dogs swarmed George as he tried to approach the house.

Bernie Schultz appeared in the doorway; Eden sank deeper into the weeds. Hollering at the dogs, Bernie stepped out to greet George. He gestured at a rusted fuel tank on a six-foot scaffold beside the barn, then at the house. George entered and Bernie closed the door. The dogs flopped in the dirt beside the step.

Forgetting to breathe, Eden sidled along the ditch, slipped through the barbed wire fence, and crept to the edge of the garden, hiding behind the corn stalks. Deep in the rows, she glimpsed a flash of white. A little girl was sitting in the dirt. Big eyes, long, tangled hair. A pointy chin, a dirty face. Ava.

Eden stopped worrying about the Schultzes, George, or the dogs. She stared for a long minute, then she smiled.

"Hello, my sweetheart."

Ava stared back, unsmiling.

"Ava, it's me. Your mom. Your real mom."

Ava didn't move.

"I'm Eden. I'm your real mom. I missed you." Eden started to cry, wiping her tears and hair away with the backs of her hands.

The little girl approached tentatively. She extended her right hand to touch her mother's tears, then stepped into her arms as if the past four years had never happened.

Her tiny body was shivering. It was cold but the child wore no coat or sweater. She was startlingly dirty, and she stank. There was no other word for it.

"It's going to be okay now. I'm going to take care of you." Eden tried to draw her closer, but the child winced and cried out when Eden squeezed her left arm. The arm hung motionless, a dead thing. Panic surged through Eden. *We have to get her out of here!*

"Okay, Ava, I'm going to pick you up and take you to the truck. Be very, very quiet, okay? I'll try not to hurt you."

She grasped Ava under her arms and hoisted her to her left hip, careful not to touch the sore arm. Ava slipped her right arm over Eden's shoulders in a trusting manner that broke her mother's heart.

Eden had to stand upright to carry Ava; she prayed George was still in the house. At the fence, she set Ava down, slipped through the barbed wire, and reached back to lift the girl over. Ava cried out again when Eden jostled her arm.

"Okay, let's go find the truck." The child was a featherweight and Eden jogged in the ditch, hoping desperately the tall weeds would hide them.

And then the dogs started barking.

Eden glanced over her shoulder; George and Bernie were walking to the fuel tank, the dogs weaving and bobbing at their feet. Eden turned and ran as fast as she could. The farmyard disappeared behind the hill and Eden could see George's truck on the grassy verge. She opened the passenger door and placed Ava gently on the bench seat, climbing in beside her.

"Don't worry, honey, it's going to be okay."

Ava started to cry, then quickly suppressed her emotion. She wiped mucus from her nose and stared at her mud-encrusted runners, avoiding Eden's eyes. Eden was horrified. *This child has learned not to cry. This child has learned to disappear.*

They listened to the dogs without speaking. Eventually, the barking stopped, and George opened the driver's door. He stopped short when he saw Ava and glared at Eden.

"We have to get going," she said.

George was frozen in place, staring at the child.

"Get in the goddamn truck and drive!"

George jumped in and turned the ignition. With another resigned headshake, he stomped on the clutch and accelerated in a cloak of dust.

"Where to?" George asked, gripping the steering wheel with white knuckles as he stared straight ahead. Eden wrapped her arm around the little girl. She wanted to take her daughter home and hide her. She wanted to run with her as far away as possible. She considered Ava's useless arm.

"Straight to the hospital in the city," she said, and George nodded. For once, he had nothing to say.

"So, how were the Schultzes?" Eden asked after miles of silence. Ava's head was drooping.

George shrugged. "That place isn't fit for pigs."

"I'm sorry if this gets you in trouble. I'm really sorry."

George shrugged again. "What's wrong with her?" he asked.

"Her arm is injured. Useless. Maybe they beat her. Maybe they broke her arm."

"I think you did the right thing," George said quietly. "I don't know for sure if this is your kid, but you did the right thing."

As they came to the outskirts of the city, Ava woke up.

"Pee," she said.

"Sweetheart, do you have to go to the bathroom? Okay, George, find somewhere to stop!" After frantic searching, Eden spotted a Pacific 66 station. She rushed Ava to the toilets in the back.

Ava was wearing a flimsy cotton dress, panties, socks, and runners. As she perched on the toilet like a baby bird, Eden noticed feces caked on the little girl's buttocks. Without Eden's support, she would fall backwards into the water. *Where do you usually go to the bathroom? Squatting in the corn patch?*

Holding her hand, Eden led her through the gas station toward the door. She could see George waiting anxiously in the truck. Ava hung back as they passed the candy shelves.

"Want something to eat? Pick anything you like." Ava pointed to an Aero chocolate bar, and Eden quickly purchased it. The cashier gave them a quizzical look. Could she smell Ava? Eden hustled her out of the door.

By the time they got to the hospital, broad strokes of smeared chocolate covered Ava's face and dress. Swabbing her desperately with a licked thumb, Eden met George's eyes; they doubled over, unable to stop laughing. Ava eyed them warily—she didn't get the joke.

On that note, I begin the rest of my life, Eden thought. She carried Ava, smelling distinctly of shit and chocolate, into the emergency department.

In the examination room, the doctor tried to slip Ava's dress over her head, but the child screamed in pain. The nurse reached into a drawer for scissors to cut Ava free. She sat on the table in her panties, shivering and crying, once again reminding Eden of a scrawny baby bird out of its nest.

"What is your relationship to this child?" the doctor asked, deftly feeling Ava from head to foot despite her wriggling.

Eden took a deep breath. "This is my daughter. She was adopted by another family at birth. But I was worried about her, so I checked on her, and I think she has been abused. There's something wrong with her arm, and she's filthy. My brother and I found her wandering on the side of the road." *One little lie won't hurt.*

The doctor looked sharply at Eden, then at the nurse. "Call Social Services," he said quietly.

Eden tensed, thinking of Agatha Browne. *Don't take my baby away from me again. Please.*

256

Ava reached out, and Eden moved close to comfort her. "Don't worry, this nice doctor won't hurt you. Remember, I'm your real mom." Eden turned to the doctor. "She's cold."

"We will look for something for her to wear. There might be a wait until we can get her arm X-rayed. Do you want to stay with her?"

"Yes, please."

The doctor continued his examination, trying to get Ava to open her mouth to no avail. Ava screamed and kicked when he pulled down her underwear and took off her shoes and socks, but he skillfully did what he had to do, and within minutes, it was over.

The nurse returned with a cotton nightgown and a blanket. Eden quickly dressed the little girl and wrapped her in the itchy blanket. They were sitting in a chair when the doctor returned. Ava was drowsy again; the warmth of the blanket and Eden's body was lulling her to sleep.

"We can take her to the X-ray department now, but first I'm going to take some photos," the doctor said. "If nothing else, this appears to be a case of neglect. We have also called the police and child welfare. They will want to interview you."

Eden placed Ava on the table. The doctor stripped her nightgown off as the nurse took photos of her arm, buttocks, face, back, and hair.

"Lice," the nurse murmured, and the doctor nodded. Eden reflexively scratched behind her ear. The nurse gently set Ava on a scale.

"How old is she?" the doctor asked.

"She was four in March," Eden said.

"First percentile," the doctor said as the nurse took notes. They were both shaking their heads.

"We have a gurney here to take… your daughter up to X-ray," the doctor announced. "Would you like to wait in the waiting room?"

Ava screeched when she saw the gurney, then ceased abruptly to stare stoically at the floor. She's trying to disappear again, Eden thought.

"I'll go with her. She trusts me."

After the X-ray, Eden and Ava joined George in the waiting room. It had been more than two hours since they had arrived at the hospital and George looked extremely worried. Eden sat in an orange plastic chair with Ava on her lap.

"They X-rayed her arm. They also called the police."

George looked alarmed.

"I told them the truth. I told them Ava is mine."

"I can't see them giving her back to the Schultzes," George said. "I really can't. Someone should call the SPCA by the look of those dogs. It's a hellhole."

"We need to find something for her to eat," Eden said.

George offered to go down to the cafeteria. "What do kids like?" he asked.

"Think about it! What did you like as a kid?"

"Tapioca pudding."

"George! You're so weird. Nobody likes tapioca pudding."

That was exactly what George brought back; Ava slurped it happily from a spoon.

"See?" George said triumphantly. "Like uncle, like niece."

Eden looked up, surprised, but George swatted her gratitude away. "She looks just like you. Same rat's nest hair."

The emergency department doors slid open, and two police officers strode in. After a quick consultation at the triage desk, they turned toward Eden, Ava, and George. The female officer smiled down at Ava, who shoved her face under Eden's armpit.

"I'm Sgt. Sorenson." The male officer shook George's hand. "Let's go into another room, shall we?"

When they had settled in an adjoining room, Sgt. Sorenson said, "We understand that you found this child wandering along a road and brought her here this afternoon. Where exactly did you find her?"

George glanced at Eden, sighed, then said, "She was walking along a deserted stretch of Highway 617. Just north of Orsen Bridge."

"Not a highly populated area. Did you try to find out where her parents lived?"

"No, sir, we just thought we should bring her to a doctor."

"And what time was that?"

"It was about ten thirty, maybe closer to eleven?" George glanced at Eden, who nodded.

"And what brought you to Highway 617 this morning?"

Eden spoke up. "This little girl is my daughter, Ava. I recently found out who adopted her, and I wanted to... drop in to see if I could meet her. And if she was alright." Eden started to cry. "She's obviously not alright."

Ava's dirty face peeked at the officers, then disappeared into the folds of the blanket. The female officer handed a tissue box to Eden. Ava pulled tissues out by the handful.

"Whoa, baby," Eden said. "One at a time." Everyone laughed.

"Have Ava's adoptive parents been looking for her?" George asked.

The female officer—Sgt. Kravets, by her name tag—shook her head. "There have been no missing persons alerts of this description yet today. Let's see," she looked at her watch, "it's been six hours since you picked her up. No one has reported this child missing in that time."

"Not surprised," George muttered under his breath.

"We will dispatch a car to that location and do some door knocking," Sgt. Sorenson said.

"She can't go back there!" Eden's voice rose with her panic. "Can't you see that she can't go back? She's injured and neglected!"

"Ma'am, Social Services will be here shortly," Sgt. Sorenson said. "Once we determine who her legal guardians are, a decision will be made as to what happens next. Hang tight here with Sgt. Kravets and I'll go talk to Dr. McCall."

Sgt. Kravets took their names and address, then settled down to wait for Sgt. Sorenson to return. Ava peeked at her, enthralled by the uniform. Sgt. Kravets smiled and wiggled her eyebrows from behind her thick glasses, but the smile wasn't returned.

"Serious little thing, isn't she?" she said.

Eden wrapped the blanket protectively around Ava and snuggled her close. *Butt out! You'd be serious, too, if you lived with the Schultzes for four years.*

A nurse walked in. "We can take her up to the pediatric ward now," she said, reaching for Ava. "There's a bed all ready for her!"

"What, no! I mean, can I go with her? Why are you admitting her?" Eden stood with Ava, holding her defensively.

"I'm sorry, but I understand you are not her legal guardian," the nurse said. "We can't divulge her medical condition to you."

"I am her mother," Eden cried. "Her *mother!*"

"Hold on, Eden," George said. "Just calm down."

The nurse grabbed Ava by the left arm, and she screamed like a wounded animal.

"You're hurting her! She has an injured arm. Do your homework!"

At that moment, Sgt. Sorenson walked in, followed by Agatha Browne.

Eden was so shocked she loosened her grip. The nurse efficiently snatched Ava and placed her on a gurney outside the door; an orderly wheeled her toward the elevator. Ava stopped screaming abruptly, choking down her tears. The silence, for Eden, was harder to bear than the screaming.

Sgt. Sorenson said, "This is Agatha Browne from the Department of Social Services. She will be handling Ava's case."

"We've met," Agatha said, staring at Eden. "Yes, several years ago. Hello, Eden. How are you? And this, I presume, is your child's father?"

"God, no," George said. "I'm her uncle. George English."

He reached out to shake her hand, which gave Eden a moment to collect herself. Waves of hatred for Agatha Browne radiated from her skin.

"You! You let my baby go to the Schultzes! You told me Ava was going to a good home. You sent her to a cesspool."

Agatha's ruddy face grew pale, and she took a step back. Eden took a step forward.

"You knew! Didn't you?"

"No, I..." Agatha quickly recovered. "Officer, have you been able to determine who is the legal guardian of this child?"

"Not yet, but we're working on it, based on where Eden and George found her. Hopefully, within a few hours, we will know."

Agatha's lips, which had been trembling, now tightened into a straight line.

"Eden, I assure you that your daughter was adopted by a loving family shortly after she was born. This whole thing must be some kind of unfortunate misunderstanding. Officer, let's get this cleared up as soon as possible so this child can be reunited with her family."

"Heartless bitch." Eden spat the words but controlled her urge to grab Agatha by her nonexistent neck and shake her. Agatha scurried out of the room, followed by the sergeants.

"Calm down, for Christ's sake," George said. "These people are the decision-makers here. It won't do you any good to come off as a hot-headed lunatic!"

Eden angrily slashed at her tears. Her chest was heaving, and it took all the self-control she could muster to stop herself from running after Ava, who had disappeared behind the elevator doors in forlorn silence.

"Okay, what now?" she asked her brother.

"Now, we go to Mom's," he said, gently steering her out of the room. "I called and she is making supper for us."

One of Mom's suppers would hit the spot right about now, she thought. Neither of them had eaten since their pre-dawn breakfast. Eden followed George toward the outside doors. When they passed a gift shop, Eden took a detour. *If I could just find something to help her feel a little better.*

She was drawn to a shelf stuffed with plush animals. Wedged among multi-coloured teddy bears, she saw the googly-eyed, twisted grin of... Squirmy Worm! Eden plucked the toy out of the pile and clutched it to her chest. It was a pristine version of Chance's well-loved snaky toy. She felt certain Ava would love to have a Squirmy Worm of her own.

"George, do you have four bucks? I want to get this for Ava."

George sighed and reached for his wallet in the back pocket of his jeans. "How are you going to get it to her?"

"Don't worry, I know my way around this hospital. Remember, Ava was born here!"

* * *

Barbie flung the door open at George's soft knock. She stared at Eden as if she had never seen her before.

Eden's mother was still petite, still feisty. Her hair, always wavy, was now coiffed in the latest poofy style. *A perm?* She wore tight flared jeans and an oversized white cable knit sweater with wide shoulder pads. She didn't look like a South Country farm wife anymore.

She stood back from the door to let Eden and George enter her apartment. A familiar figure rose from the sofa. Donnie!

Eden felt confused and torn. Her mother had not reached out to hug her. Donnie stepped forward tentatively, then held out her arms. Eden ran into them and buried her face in Donnie's soft neck, shaking uncontrollably. Donnie had gained weight, and Eden sank gratefully into her plump, sheltering arms.

Eden pulled out of the hug, wiping her eyes. "How's Curtis doing?" she asked, smiling through her tears.

"He's doing pretty good," Donnie said. "He's still at the group home. He wears glasses now when he's in the mood. He really likes the new pair we got him. Anyway, I heard you were home," she added. "I'm sorry I haven't dropped around to see you. Angie and Carol are both playing ball, and it's such a busy time..."

"Alright, supper's getting cold. Let's eat." Barbie walked to the table and pulled out a chair. "Come on, Eden, sit down!" *Back to following Barbie's orders.*

Eden sank into the chair where she sat trembling as Barbie and Donnie carried platters of food from the kitchen. Macaroni and cheese. Meatloaf. Fresh buns. Salad. All of Eden's favourites. She filled her plate quickly, not meeting her mother's eyes.

Once the platter-passing had subsided, Barbie spoke.

"George told me what happened," she said. "I think it was very impulsive and dangerous of you to take that child away from her home. However, from what George tells me, you may have... saved her life."

Barbie's voice broke. "You are going to need a very good lawyer. I happen to know one."

"Well, your family certainly likes to be on the cutting edge," Barbie's lawyer, Dot Melnyk, said from behind her desk. "First, matrimonial property law and now the rights of birth parents."

Eden, Barbie, and George sat across from her, speechless. Eden's anxiety had permitted her less than two hours of sleep, and George looked equally shattered from his night on the couch. Barbie was imperturbable.

"You know, don't you, that your mother was instrumental in bringing about Saskatchewan's Matrimonial Property Act, which should become law within the year?" Dot said. She was a large-boned woman with white-streaked, bluntly cut black hair that swung at her shoulders.

Eden shrugged, thinking of her father and his diminishing empire on the farm.

"By sharing her story and working with women's groups to pressure the government, your mother has helped this province emerge as a leader in protecting spousal rights. You should both be very proud of her."

Barbie waved an impatient hand. "Let's get on with this."

"Interestingly," Dot went on, ignoring her, "a feminist movement originating in New Zealand is taking root across the world and here in Canada." She picked up a book from her desk. *Death by Adoption.* Eden gasped.

"Listen to this," Dot said, reading from the book. "'Adoption is a violent act, a political act of aggression towards a woman for committing the unforgivable act of not suppressing her sexuality, and therefore not keeping it for trading purposes through traditional marriage.'"

Barbie squirmed, her mask of calmness deteriorating.

"We have no interest in being another test case for your law firm," she said harshly, glowering at Dot, who merely smiled. "We just need to know what chance there might be of regaining custody of Eden's daughter, as quickly as possible."

"Okay, let's take a look at what's happening here," Dot said, all business. "Eden claims that a four-year-old child named Luellen May Schultz is her biological daughter. Luellen has been removed from her adoptive parents' home and is now hospitalized."

She looked at her notes. "My contact at Social Services says that Luellen is undergoing surgery today for a pulled elbow, also known as nursemaid's elbow. It appears this injury happened quite some time ago."

Eden groaned and looked at her mother. Barbie's eyes bored into Dot Melnyk's forehead.

"The good news is that Social Services is applying for a protection order for Luellen. The hearing is in three days."

"What does that mean?" Eden said, her voice rising in intensity despite her effort to control it. "Where will she go?"

"She will go to a foster home until Social Services decides what action to take, if any. If the court determines that she has been abused or neglected, it seems unlikely that Luellen will return to her adoptive parents. She will then become a ward of the government."

"Not another foster home! She's mine! I will take care of her!"

George touched his sister's arm. "Take it easy, Eden. Just listen to what Ms. Melnyk has to say."

"My first step is to confirm that Luellen is your biological daughter, which is very difficult to do. Adoption records are permanently sealed. This is an unusual case, so I might be able to get to the records.

Without them, we don't have much of a case, I'm afraid."

Dot looked at Eden's anguished face with sympathy. "But it is not impossible. Let me work on it for a day or two. You are going to be called to the protective custody hearing as a witness, and I am going to go with you, but you must promise to let me do all the talking unless you are called upon. Do you understand?"

As they rose to leave, Dot had one more piece of advice.

"Before the hearing on Tuesday, it might not hurt to go shopping," she said, staring at Eden's faded, baggy jeans and stretched-out t-shirt. "And get a haircut."

George left for home right after the meeting; he had to get back to work at the lumberyard. He dropped Barbie and Eden off at Barbie's apartment, where they sat self-consciously on the couch, barely speaking.

"Well, I'm off work today, so let's make the most of it," Barbie said finally, slapping her thighs and rising to her feet. "Let's go to the mall."

When they returned to the apartment carrying a new wardrobe for Eden, the ice had thawed. The two of them had always loved shopping together. And Eden carried less weight in terms of hair; the stylist had cut off six inches and shaped her mane into a layered waterfall tumbling to her shoulder blades. Eden admired herself in a mirror.

"Celeste will be happy with me," she said. "I'll look great for the wedding."

Barbie looked sharply at her. "When is the wedding?"

"In three weeks, in Sainte-Marie," Eden said. "Wouldn't it be great if Ava is home by then? She could come to the wedding."

Barbie sat at the table and motioned for Eden to join her. She began biting her fingernails, starting with the right thumb.

"Eden, anything involving the judicial system moves very, very slowly. One exception is child protection, and I hope and pray that your daughter is removed from that home permanently. But then... God knows what they will do with her. It will be hard to find another family to adopt her at her age. You will somehow have to convince them that a 20-year-old unemployed high school dropout can make a good home for a child who likely has any number of mental deficiencies due to her upbringing."

Eden sat dejectedly, her hair falling over her face as she looked down at her feet. Mom's right, she thought. What do I have to offer Ava compared to a married couple? I should have been making something of my life, instead of lying around smoking dope and drinking whisky with Monroe for the past four years.

Eden longed for a drink and a cigarette. Since leaving Monroe's place, she had been living clean. She had a feeling that was about to end.

Barbie went on. "If anyone can help you, Dot Melnyk can. She is a brilliant lawyer who will take on cases that she feels will further the feminist cause. But she needs to be paid. And that's a problem. I assume you have no money."

Eden thought about the cash box hidden under the trailer. Long gone, along with Monroe. She shook her head. Barbie took a deep breath.

"I have been paying Dot as much as I can as she prepares my case against your father. It has been a long process, and in the meantime, the law is changing to recognize matrimonial property rights. By next year, men will be obligated by law to split everything equally with their wives after a divorce. I'm not sure a court case is necessary now."

Eden looked up, startled.

"Part of Dot's work was done on contingency, anticipating a payout after the trial that I could use to pay her. Now I am thinking of retaining her solely for your case, rather than taking your father to court. I will file for divorce after the new Act is granted royal assent."

Eden felt a simultaneous surge of gratitude and dismay. *A little part of me has been hoping Mom will change her mind and go back to Dad.*

And then, anger leaped in her soul.

"You will help me get Ava now, but when she was born, you forced me to give her up! We wouldn't be in this situation if you had let me keep your granddaughter in the family. Your *granddaughter*!"

Barbie didn't look surprised by this outburst. "Back then, I was a different person. I trusted the system. And I didn't realize that society was changing. I didn't want society to change. Now I do. It has to."

"If I was having Ava today, would you let me keep her?"

Barbie looked sad. "If the circumstances were the same and you were fifteen years old? Probably not. Then again, if there was a baby girl in the house, maybe your dad would have stopped drinking. Who knows?"

"Mom, Dad is in bad shape. The doctor thinks he has wet brain. He can barely stand up even when he's sober. And his memory is shot. Half the time, he thinks I'm you!"

"I know. And I'm glad you've come home to help out. Those men need a woman in the house. And maybe, if we're really, really lucky, they will have a little girl in the house, too. Assuming your father goes for that."

"He'll go for it."

Eden had forced herself to stay away the day of Ava's surgery, but the next morning she took the bus downtown. The brown-brick hospital squatted gloomily, unchanged despite everything that had happened to Eden within its walls. And now Ava was here again, almost four-and-a-half years after she was born.

Ava was lying on her back, her left arm angled awkwardly away from her body in a plaster cast. In her right arm, she cuddled Squirmy Worm. She appeared to be talking to the toy. Eden approached cautiously. There were three more cage-like cribs in the room, but no patients or families. They were alone.

"Hi, Ava, how are you doing?" Eden said, pulling the yellow curtain closed around them.

Ava looked up and—Eden was sure it was the first time she'd seen this—smiled at her mother. A sweet, tentative smile. Her hair was clean and spread out across the pillow; a pretty blonde colour. Like Curtis.

"Does your arm hurt, honey?"

Ava nodded. Her smile disappeared.

"Do you want Mama to kiss it better?"

Ava just stared at her.

"You know I'm your real mom, right? And when you get all better, you're going to come live with me. And guess what? I have horses. Their names are Patches, Blackie, and Diamond. Do you like horses?"

Ava continued to stare.

"Here, give me Squirmy Worm. He can kiss you all better. Okay?"

Ava released her grip on the Worm, her serious, curious grey eyes searching Eden's face. Eden gave Squirmy Worm a big smack on the nose, then touched the toy gently to Ava's arm, head, stomach, and knees.

Then a miracle occurred. Ava laughed.

"Well, that's a sound for sore ears!" It was Dr. McCall from the emergency department, pushing the curtain aside. Eden scrambled to her feet.

"She's come through surgery well, but she'll have to wear the cast for about a month," the doctor said. "I understand you are not her legal guardian, so I won't be able to tell you more. However, I can see that this visit has improved her spirits. I'm going to advise the desk to allow you access for visits, as long as you keep it between you and me."

"Thank you, Doctor," Eden said, tears rising to her eyes.

"Just keep it on the Q.T. Don't bring attention to yourself." The doctor smiled kindly, quickly examined Ava, and shuffled out of the room.

Eden spent the rest of the day with Ava, helping her eat from the food tray. Ava preferred soft foods, which made Eden wonder about the state of her teeth. She spent time holding her in a chair while she napped, combing her hair, and playing quietly with Squirmy Worm.

When she had to go, she hugged her little daughter. "Remember, I'm your real mom. I'll be back tomorrow. Don't be scared."

Ava nodded solemnly and clutched the Worm to her tiny bird chest.

Chapter 18

"This District Court, Family Law Division hearing is hereby called to order, Judge Samuel Evans presiding."

Myrtle and Bernie Schultz were sitting two rows in front of Eden and Dot Melnyk in a cramped hearing room at the courthouse. Myrtle wore a flower-patterned cotton dress and thick stockings; her swollen feet were squeezed into black dress shoes. Bernie's hair was slicked back but untrimmed; he wore a worn black suit and tie.

Eden sniffed. *Is that booze?* Years of practice had honed her ability to detect alcohol lingering under the cover of shaving lotion.

The judge shuffled papers. He looked as worn out around the edges as Bernie's suit. He ran his fingers through his thinning grey hair.

"We are here to deliberate an Apprehension Order for Luellen May Schultz, a four-year-old child who, as I understand it, presented at the hospital on August 31 with injuries. Agatha Browne from the Department of Social Services, will you please summarize the situation for us?"

Eden bit her lip. Agatha Browne was not in the room. Instead, a short woman with long red hair in a ponytail rose from her seat.

"Your Honour, I have been assigned to this case because Agatha Browne is on a medical leave."

"State your name."

"It's Josey MacMillan, sir." Eden stared at Josey MacMillan's back. *Who is this? Do I know her?* The young woman pushed her large plastic-framed glasses up the bridge of her nose. *Josey from Wheatland Manor!*

Eden bit her lip again, trying not to make a sound. A little squeak escaped; Dot glanced at her quickly, then re-focused her ferocious gaze on the judge.

"Proceed," the judge said.

"Your Honour, on Friday, August 31, concerned citizens saw Luellen Schultz walking alone along the side of a secondary highway. The concerned citizens decided to bring the little girl to the hospital immediately. Luellen was assessed in the emergency department and admitted to the hospital. The next day, she underwent surgery to address a radial head subluxation of the elbow, which the doctor determined had occurred some months past. Luellen is still in the hospital, recovering from her surgery and awaiting the outcome of this hearing."

"Is there more?" the judge asked wearily.

"Yes, sir. I submit Luellen's medical report to the court. In addition to the pulled elbow, Luellen presented as dirty and unkempt. She had a urinary tract infection and head lice. Her weight is at the first percentile for her age and a speech therapist has determined that she speaks at the level of a typical two-year-old. A child psychologist also assessed Luellen and reported that she is significantly delayed in terms of social skills. He described her as 'withdrawn, fearful, and unwilling to make eye contact with adults.' In addition, she has several decayed teeth which must be removed as soon as possible."

Josey paused to squint at the judge through her glasses. "Based on these assessments, the Department of Social Services is applying for a temporary custody order for Luellen Schultz."

"Indeed," the judge said. "Anything else?"

"Yes, sir. One of the concerned citizens who took Luellen to the hospital, Eden English, is attending court this afternoon. Her legal counsel has advised that she would be willing to respond to questions from the court."

"Alright, stand forward," Judge Evans said.

Dot nudged Eden. "Stand up and answer his questions," she whispered.

Eden stood, shakily at first, then defiantly, not looking at Myrtle and Bernie, who slumped like lumpy potato sacks in their chairs.

"State your name."

"Eden Holly English."

"Please describe the incident in which you encountered this child on August 31."

"Well, me and my brother George were driving along Highway 617, and we saw... Luellen walking along the road. There were no houses or farms in sight."

"What did you do then?"

"We picked her up and put her in the truck. We noticed that her arm was hanging useless, and she seemed to be in pain. She was dirty and smelled really bad. We decided to head into the city and get her to a doctor."

"You didn't try to find out where the girl lived?"

"No, sir. We thought it was kind of an emergency. We thought someone just dropped her off at the side of the road."

"And what brought you to Highway 617? Do you live in the area?"

"No, we went there on purpose. I am Luellen's birth mother. Her real name is Ava. I was worried about her and thought I should check on her."

Everyone in the room gasped, including Myrtle and Bernie, who turned arthritically to stare at her. Josey turned too, winked at Eden, and pushed her glasses aggressively up her nose.

The judge straightened in his chair. "That is highly unusual. Adoption records in this province are sealed permanently. What leads you to believe that Luellen is your biological child?"

273

Eden faltered. *How can I explain this?* She raked her hair away from her face and let it settle on her shoulders.

"I always knew Ava was in a bad place. Then a friend of mine who was a foster child at the Schultzes told me that they had adopted a baby girl and... I just knew it was Ava."

Dot stood up. "Your Honour, I am prepared to provide proof that Eden is Luellen's birth mother. We will be petitioning the court for custody of the child to return to Eden as soon as possible."

At that, Myrtle Schultz stood up.

"No one is taking my baby from me!" she shouted. "I won't have it! Luellen is legally ours!"

"I take it that you are Luellen's legal guardian, her adoptive mother. Please state your name for the court."

"I am Myrtle Matilda Elizabeth Schultz. This here is my husband, Bernie Schultz. And we want our baby back now!"

"Mrs. Schultz, have you retained legal counsel?" the judge asked.

"N-no," Myrtle stammered. "We don't have money for no lawyer. But Luellen is ours!"

"Eden has testified that she and her brother found your four-year-old child walking alone on the highway. How do you explain that, Mrs. Schultz?"

"She must have wandered away from the yard when we weren't looking. It happens. Kids like to explore. I don't think that's any reason to take her away from us!"

"And how do you explain her medical conditions, Mrs. Schultz? It seems that you did not seek medical treatment for her injured elbow."

"That must have just happened! Maybe they yanked on her arm when they pulled her into the vehicle and stole her. And kids get grubby when they play outside. Luellen wasn't *dirty*. She was just outside playing with the dogs. She has regular baths."

"Mr. Schultz, do you have anything to add?"

Bernie shook his head. "No, Myrtle said it all," he mumbled, looking at the floor.

"Anything else from Social Services?"

"Yes, sir. I have asked Sgt. Bruce Sorenson to attend today. He headed the investigation after Luellen was brought to the hospital."

Eden had noticed Sgt. Sorenson sitting at the back in his uniform. The sergeant stood and removed his hat.

The judge nodded and Sgt. Sorenson approached the head table. He explained that he had interviewed Eden and George at the hospital. "By that time, Luellen had been with the Englishes and in the hospital for six hours," Sgt. Sorenson said. "There had been no missing person of her description reported to the police, and we suspected we had a case of abandonment on our hands. We drove out to take a look."

He glanced at the Schultzes. "Our first stop was the farm of Bernard and Myrtle Schultz on Highway 617. It was the closest residence to the approximate location where the Englishes said they had found Luellen at the side of the road."

The judge rotated his hand. "Go on."

"We knocked at the door for several minutes but there was no answer. Sgt. Kravets went to the barn to see if she could find someone, and I circled the house. I noticed the front door was open, and inside I could see Mr. Schultz lying on a sofa. I banged on the door, but he did not respond. Concerned about his health, I entered the house on a welfare check."

"He came in without our say-so. We've got you right there, Officer! That's not allowed, right?" Myrtle waved her arm as if to rouse the judge to indignation. He ignored her.

"And what did you do then?"

"Sir, Myrtle Schultz entered the living room from the adjoining bedroom. She said she had been sleeping. She tried to wake Mr. Schultz by shaking him, but she was unsuccessful. She said he had been drinking and had passed out. I checked his vital signs, and he seemed to be stable. I then asked Mrs. Schultz about Luellen. Had she seen a four-year-old girl in the area? Mrs. Schultz acknowledged that the child was theirs and then went to the kitchen door to call out for her. I told her their daughter was in the hospital in Regina."

"Mrs. Schultz, please explain to the court why you did not report your daughter missing after not seeing her for more than half a day," Judge Evans said.

Myrtle lurched heavily to her feet. She stood quietly for a moment, then burst into tears.

"Sometimes Luellen plays outside all day. She loves to play in the yard. We have the dogs to let us know if anyone comes near her. She was okay."

"I've heard enough," the judge said. "I grant the Department of Social Services' application for a temporary court order for custody of Luellen May Schultz for a period of ninety days. Mr. and Mrs. Schultz, I suggest you get a lawyer. This court will reconvene at a scheduled time to address this matter. Court dismissed."

Eden felt like she was wading through mud as she left the hearing room. She turned in a daze to Dot Melnyk, who was saying something Eden could not understand. Her ears were ringing, and she thought she might faint. Dot rushed to a fountain and filled a paper cone with water. Eden gulped it gratefully.

"The good news is that Luellen is safe, and we have time to prepare a case," Dot was saying.

"Ava," Eden said. "Her name is Ava."

Josey MacMillan approached them. Eden turned to her. "Ninety days? *Ninety*. Where will she go?"

"I am going to arrange for her to be placed in one of our most trusted foster homes here in the city," Josey said. "And I am going to keep an eye on her myself. You have my word."

"Can I see her? Can I visit?" Eden asked.

Josey shook her head. "I wouldn't recommend it. I wouldn't do anything to rock the boat at this point. Let

Luellen heal and settle into her new home. Her adoptive parents will not be able to see her, either, unless the court approves it.

"Don't worry," she added, staring sympathetically into Eden's wild eyes. "The Department won't be recommending that Luellen return to her adoptive parents under these circumstances."

"Ava. Her *name* is Ava."

* * *

Eden's head bobbed uncontrollably. She could not summon the strength to stay awake during the winding five-hour Greyhound bus trip from Regina to Everview. She was exhausted from all that had transpired since she and George found Ava ten days ago.

A few days after the apprehension hearing, Josey had taken Eden to Ava's foster home. The two of them waited in Josey's car, staking out the place like undercover cops. The lawn in front of the bungalow was neatly cut and geraniums were smiling in the weakening summer sunshine.

Eventually, a station wagon with faux wood side panels pulled up to the house, expelling a trove of children of various ages. As the kids dashed to the front door, the woman driver extended her hand into the back seat. Ava grabbed her hand and climbed awkwardly out of the car.

Eden held her breath. Ava's cast was in a sling, and she clutched the woman's hand tightly as they walked to the house. Her fine blonde hair—washed and combed—swung prettily at her shoulders. The woman gave her a sideways hug when they got to the door and encouraged her to enter. The door shut behind them.

Eden wiped her eyes with the backs of her hands. "She looks okay. Clean. I hope her arm doesn't hurt too much."

Every day for more than a week, Eden traveled on two city buses to the suburbs for a glimpse of Ava. She learned that the foster mother picked up the kids from school around three o'clock and that Ava was always along for the ride. Eden found a convenient caragana bush to shield her from view during these spying sessions. She watched and yearned but controlled her impulse to approach her daughter. There was nothing she would do to jeopardize the work Dot Melnyk was doing to bring them back together.

"I see here that you did not name a putative father at the time of your daughter's birth," Dot had said during their final meeting, as she examined Ava's hospital birth record through her reading glasses. "Are you prepared to do so now? It might strengthen your case."

"Um... no. I will never reveal who Ava's father is. It's no one's business but mine."

"Yes, that is true," Dot said. "The term 'putative father' is an affront to women. It implies that even if a woman names the father of her child, it is not assumed that he actually is. It is assumed that the mother might not be telling the truth."

She shook her head sadly. "Without a judge's order, I cannot access Ava's adoption records, nor can you. However, I might be able to persuade the court that these are extenuating circumstances. You would be prepared to swear in court that you did not sign a consent for adoption when Ava was born?"

"Yes, of course, I will swear to it on a mountain of Bibles!" Eden said. "I am sure that if you can get the records, you will not see my signature on it. I wanted to keep my baby, Ms. Melnyk, and I was forced to give her up."

"Well, it will be interesting to see that adoption order, then," Dot said. "No court would issue an order without full written consent. Someone must have signed it."

Sitting on the Greyhound bus, Eden wondered who could have signed the adoption papers. She remembered the mounting pressure from Agatha Browne before and even during her lengthy labour, but despite her dim memories of that time, Eden was sure she did not put pen to paper.

As she stared at her downcast reflection in the window, Eden was overwhelmed with the immensity of the task ahead. How could she ever persuade the court or anyone else that Ava belonged with her? I am nothing, she thought.

George Junior was waiting for her at the Everview bus stop. Eden tossed the bag of clothes Barbie had purchased for her into the truck box, then crawled into the passenger seat. Her brother looked at her with concern.

"What's the latest on Ava?" he asked, putting the truck in reverse.

Eden shrugged. "The lawyer is working on it. More power to her."

"And how is Ava doing?"

"She's in a foster home that at least looks clean and orderly. I get a good feeling about the foster mom. I can't imagine how confusing this must be for my baby."

"Hey, she'll be okay. She's a kid. Kids bounce back. In the end, she might not even remember this."

George Senior was sitting at the kitchen table nursing a glass of whisky when they got home. The skin on his face and jowls was slack on his bones. His plaid work shirt fit loosely, and he was wearing suspenders. Eden grabbed a glass from the cupboard and pulled up a chair beside her father.

"Hey, Dad, got some for me?" she asked, gesturing toward the Canadian Club bottle on the table. Her father looked uncertainly at George Junior, who was hovering at the bottom of the stairs.

"Eden, what the hell?" he said. "We don't drink with Dad."

"I don't know about you, but I need a drink." Eden poured her glass half full and raised it in a toast to her father. "And a good man shouldn't drink alone."

* * *

Eden stood with her arms extended as Odette poked pins in the bridesmaid dress. Eden feared becoming a human pincushion under Odette's frenzied hands but had obviously underestimated the seamstress's skill. Celeste looked on with amusement as she stirred cake batter at the Tremblays' kitchen table.

The kitchen door swung open, and Denis and Maurice stepped in. But it wasn't Denis. It was Gilbert. He looked so much like his father that Eden felt dizzy, keenly aware that she was standing in a strapless gown on a chair—Odette was pinning the hem—wearing no underwear. *Celeste at least has breasts to hold her dress up. Mine is going to fall down around my knees!*

Gilbert and Maurice stared up at Eden as if she was a stone goddess.

"Put your eyes back in your heads and wash up for supper!" Celeste exclaimed, snapping a tea towel at Gilbert and kicking Maurice in the shins. Maurice grabbed her by the waist and spun her in a circle while Gilbert grinned up at Eden with crinkled eyes, as if he couldn't quite believe what he was seeing. He reached up gallantly to help her down. Eden clutched the front of her dress, blushing under his scrutiny.

"Well, you're all growed up," he remarked.

"You, too," Eden said, regaining her composure. "Boy, did you ever! You're even taller than I am!"

Everyone laughed.

"You two will look fantastic together at the wedding," Celeste gushed. "Gil is Maury's best man, and you are the maid of honour. And I'm going to wear six-inch heels, so I don't look like the little sidekick!"

Odette scoffed. "You are going to be the most beautiful bride Sainte-Marie has ever seen!" she exclaimed. "Go change, Eden, and we will get supper over with. I want to do some more sewing tonight."

After supper, endless piles of dishes were washed, dried, and hidden behind the cotton curtains Odette had strung across her doorless cupboards. Eden and Celeste looped the sodden towels over the curtain rods and joined Maurice, Gilbert, and Alain where they were smoking on the back step. Eden overheard Maurice grumbling about the length of his engagement to Celeste—apparently, a sore point.

"Oh, Maury, enough!" Celeste said, cracking a beer for Eden. "He doesn't understand modern women! I had to finish high school, didn't I? And then go to beauty school?"

"You finished beauty school a year ago!" Maurice grunted, grinding his cigarette into the ground.

Maurice and Celeste had saved enough money to buy a small house in Sainte-Marie. Gilbert—Celeste said her brother "had a way with a hammer"—had renovated the house and built a beauty salon in one of the bedrooms. After the wedding, Celeste was going to quit her job at the hair salon in Everview and start her own business in her new home. She vibrated with excitement whenever she talked about it.

"Pshaw!" Celeste said, dismissing Maurice and his complaints with a wave. She grabbed Gilbert's cigarette pack from the ground beside his foot, helped herself to one, then offered the pack to Eden.

"Hey, buy your own damn cigarettes!" Gilbert snatched the pack from Celeste, then smiled and offered it to Eden. She extracted a cigarette, leaning forward as Gilbert flicked his lighter. She had started smoking again since returning from the city. She inhaled the cool mentholated smoke deeply, feeling herself relax as the earth tipped an inch to extinguish the sun.

"Maury, take Eden home. It's getting late." Celeste curled against Maurice's body in response to a sudden chill in the air. He kissed her as if they had been commissioned by God to populate the earth.

Alain slipped away hastily, although Eden suspected he was accustomed by now to displays of sexual affection in the Tremblay household. Gilbert and Eden stared at Celeste and Maurice for a moment, then Gilbert nodded his head toward his truck.

"I'll take you home," he said without looking directly at her. Eden obediently followed him to the truck.

Both windows were open, which made it difficult to talk as Gilbert sped in a dust cloud along the gravel road toward the blacktop. Eden leaned her head partly out of the window, enjoying the cool air as her hair streamed out of the truck. Gilbert glanced over, amused.

"You remind me of a dog with its tongue hanging out of the window," Gilbert said.

"Gee, thanks." Eden laughed and threw her cigarette butt out of the window, cranking it closed with some effort. Gilbert's Chevy pickup was creaky and ancient. She swept her tangled hair away from her forehead and glanced at him.

His denim shirt sleeves, rolled to the elbows, revealed slender, tanned arms. She caught herself staring at his wrist bones, how they flexed as he steered casually with his right hand. His left elbow extended out of the open window, two fingers lightly touching the steering wheel. Something about his faded, too-long jeans and dusty cowboy boots reminded her of Jason Pedersen. She tossed that thought out of the window, too, and sat back to enjoy the ride.

They nestled their beers in the crotch of their jeans. Gilbert tilted back to kill his bottle, then hurled it at the stop sign as they turned onto the highway. The glass bottle shattered in a satisfying explosion. To keep up, Eden slugged back her beer, forced the recalcitrant window open again, and threw the bottle out. From the side mirror, she watched it roll along the road and come to a stop in the weeds.

Swallows dived in front of the truck as they passed, then settled back into the ditches to resume their evening rest. Eden felt content; an emotion she had not experienced for... well, years, really.

"So, what's your plan?" Gilbert asked suddenly.

Plan? I've never had a plan. "Well, first and foremost, I am going to get my baby back, somehow," she said. "And then she and I are going to move in with Dad and hopefully give him something to live for. And I'm going to raise horses at Dad's place and make a decent living at it."

This pronouncement had come out of nowhere. She was shocked and slightly breathless in the wake of it.

"And if you don't get your daughter back? Will you still raise horses?"

"I can't even think past that. Everything depends on that."

To her deep embarrassment, Eden started to cry. She couldn't wait to get home so she could have a nightcap with her father. Gilbert reached across the seat and squeezed her arm. His touch was warm and kind.

"Actually," Eden said, wiping the tears away, "I don't want to live in the house with Dad and the boys. I want to fix up my grandma's house for Ava and me, to get away from the cow manure they track in."

"Maybe I can help you with that," Gilbert said. "I mean, I have the tools and all."

"Well, I have no money to pay you. I'll show you the house when you drop me off."

Eden shoved her weight against the sticky door of Grandma Doris's cottage. Doris had died three years ago, but Eden could still smell her grandmother as she turned on the overhead light. The house held the scent of furniture polish and lavender toilette water. Gilbert looked appraisingly into every corner.

"Do you think the place is livable?" Eden asked him.

Gilbert scratched his nose. "Looks like the roof is leaking," he said, pointing at stains in the ceiling and the living room carpet. It hadn't rained for a few weeks, but the carpet stain was still damp. "The windows need caulking and painting. In fact, the whole place could be painted, inside and out." He moved into the bedroom. Grandma Doris's furniture had not been moved.

"Mice sign everywhere." He glanced into the bathroom. The fixtures were brown from leaky taps. "If your dad didn't turn off the water, there are probably burst pipes in the walls. It could be a hell of a job."

Eden felt defeated. "Oh, well, it was a good idea while it lasted."

"No, no. It is possible. Totally possible. Your friend Gil is a talented dude. You'll see."

Eden's father was sitting at his usual place when she walked into the house. She could hear Gil's truck backfiring faintly on the grid road. She examined an empty glass on the table—unwashed since yesterday— and deemed it clean enough. She splashed a healthy pour of whisky into the smudged glass.

"Hey, Dad, do you have any money? And if so, can I have it?"

George Senior chuckled. "Have it all!" he announced with some of his former swagger. "Take it goddamned all!"

Chapter 19

Eden saw Gil every day the week before the wedding. Around nine o'clock, his truck would shamble into the yard; through the kitchen window, she watched him reach into the truck box, grab his red metal toolbox, and head towards the cottage. As soon as she had cleaned up breakfast and tended to her father—he needed encouragement and supervision to wash and shave every day—Eden would gather up her cleaning supplies and head down the path.

She liked to clean where Gil was working, despite the messes he invariably made that she had to go back and clean up again. Their best conversations happened when they painted the exterior of the house. Gil wanted this done before the weather turned cool and damp. So far, the harvest weather had held.

On one of those days, she told him about Monroe.

"If he ever shows up here again, he'll have to deal with me!" Gil said with passion, slopping paint on the eavestrough. Eden worried that he would topple off the ladder.

"I really doubt that he will come here. It's over between us. I don't want to see him again."

"I can't believe he let you live like that when he had plenty of money. And then to leave without saying goodbye! Asshole!"

Eden laughed. "Yes, he could be that. I guess I was just a convenience for him. A bed warmer." Gil winced and Eden laughed harder. "I needed to get away from here, and Monroe kind of showed up. I used him, too, in a way."

Then came the day when she told him about the moment at the Indian Friendship Center when she found out where Ava was. It left Gil speechless. Eden looked sidelong at him as he continued to scrape peeling paint from the wooden siding. *Why did I tell him about my visions?*

Finally, Gil shrugged and turned to look at her. His brow was dripping from the heat, and his dark brown hair curled even more vigorously than usual.

"I'll never be a mother, so I don't really get it," he said. "But I've watched my mother perform miracles. When Amelie was a baby, *Maman* insisted Papa drive her into the city with a fever, even though *Tante* Sylvie and everyone else said it would pass. Turns out she had meningitis.

"Then there was the time Hugo got lost. He was only three, and we couldn't find him anywhere. *Maman* was screaming at Papa to go to the neighbours and form a search party, but he was embarrassed and hated to do it... anyway, suddenly *Maman* got this weird look on her face and ran out of the yard, and we all followed her. There's this old willow tree down by the creek, and she found him sleeping in its roots. Everyone swears they looked for him there—I know I did—but there was Hugo, stretching and looking for his mama. *Maman* didn't speak to Papa for two weeks after that. It was awful quiet around the house."

Eden laughed, relieved. Gil shook his head. "But you have some balls, fighting that guy in the trailer! Sure hope you never get mad at me!"

"Meadow was the hero when she hit him in the face with the stroller. He didn't stand a chance."

Eden hadn't discussed this with anyone before. Celeste knew the stories, but Eden had the distinct impression her friend did not want to dig too deep. And she sensed Gil was humouring her, trying to get closer to her. He wasn't hiding the fact that he still had a crush on her, even after all these years.

He dated a girl from Sainte-Marie in high school, but since she moved to the city, he had not sought another girlfriend. Eden was enjoying the attention but told herself not to start depending on it. Gil needed someone with fewer ghosts; an unencumbered girl longing to be a carpenter's wife and raise a big, rowdy French-Canadian family.

The time was coming when Eden would have to discourage Gil's affection. But not yet, she thought. Let me enjoy this for a little longer.

* * *

On Celeste's wedding day, Eden felt like royalty in her shimmering pale-yellow dress. Odette had reconsidered the strapless design, fearing recriminations from the priest. She had attached spaghetti straps to the dresses and produced matching bolero jackets to cover their shoulders and upper arms. Eden was relieved that she didn't have to worry about the dress slipping down to her knees.

While Maurice's sister Rosaleigh, Celeste's sister Gisele, and Eden were resplendent in their bridesmaid gowns, they did not eclipse the bride. No, that would never have been possible. Celeste was ethereal, floating in a voluminous train of satin and lace down the aisle, her bosom proudly displayed, priest or no priest.

Walking out of the church on Gil's handsome arm—the men were wearing powder blue tuxedos rented from the city—Eden had felt a strange mix of belonging and alienation. The Tremblay family accepted her completely, despite all that she had done, or not done, in her short, complicated life. But she would never belong with them; she did not deserve them. Did not deserve Gil.

She was enjoying her third rye and ginger at the wedding dance. Denis brought her the first one,

Maurice noticed she was ready for a second, and Gil showed up with the third, not aware of the other two. Earlier, they had shared the first dance—"We've Only Just Begun" by The Carpenters. Eden secretly thought it was a corny choice, but it was Celeste's favourite. Now the deejay was playing "Tragedy" by the Bee Gees, and Gil wanted to join the gyrating dancers on the floor.

Eden danced with abandon, feeling her drinks and the celebratory joy of the evening. Gil was more reserved; Eden hadn't noticed him drinking as much throughout the day as the rest of them. Sparkling wine before the ceremony. Beer after the ceremony, while they were sequestered for photographs beside the creek near the Tremblay home. More wine during the reception. Highballs during the dance.

When the song finished, Eden swayed toward Gil, taking his hands. "Come on, let's dance," she said, but he was turning away from the dance floor. From her.

Gil placed his hand on the small of her back and steered her toward the tables. "I think I'll take you home," he said, pushing her a little too possessively.

"Not leaving!" Eden exclaimed, twisting away from his hand. "My best friend just got married! What's your problem?"

"You're drunk."

"Maybe. It's a free country. Celeste doesn't get married every day." Eden continued dancing to the music, swinging her hips and raising her hands above her head. "Let's party a little, okay?"

Gil turned on his heel and disappeared. Eden decided to visit the ladies' room, noting as she washed her hands that her updo was falling apart and her mascara was smudged. *Oh well, I don't need to look good anymore. Time to have fun!*

When she emerged, Celeste was preparing to throw her bouquet. Eden joined the group of young women gathered in front of the stage, but the bouquet sailed over her head into the arms of Rosaleigh, who was seriously dating a young man from Elder Valley; she was next in line to get married, it seemed. *I'll never get married. I don't even want to. There's no one out there good enough to be Ava's dad.*

"Ready to go now?"

Gil was holding the jacket she had brought for the drive home. Eden shrugged into it and followed him out of the hall. As she tried to climb into the truck, she caught the hem of her dress with her heel and crashed to the ground. She laughed and kicked her bare legs in the air, brushed the dirt from the dress as well as she could, and completed her awkward clamber through the passenger door. Gil was sitting silently in the driver's seat.

"Gee, thanks for the help, Gil. *You* try walking in a dress like this all day. Sheesh."

Gil put the truck in gear and headed west. Eden couldn't stand the silence.

"What is your problem? Thanks for ruining the day," she said.

"I won't go with a drinker, Eden," Gil said tightly. "Not after watching my dad practically drink himself to death."

"Buddy, you're not going anywhere with me!" Eden was suddenly sober and deeply angry. *Who does he think he is?*

Gil was speeding along the dark road, both hands on the wheel like a race car driver.

"Stop the truck, I want out!" Eden reached toward the door handle, and Gil swerved onto an approach, stopping the truck with a jolt. Eden jumped out and walked through the open barbed-wire gate into a swathed wheat field. *Dress is ruined now anyway.*

She stopped walking to look up at the sky, her heels sinking into the soft dirt. The Big Dipper tilted dangerously, pouring dim light onto her uplifted face. Gil came up behind her and they gazed at the stars.

"We're not going together," Eden said. "What gave you that idea?"

"It's what I want," he said. "But not like this. Sober."

"You think I'm a drinker."

"I smell you in the mornings. You're a drinker."

A sob bubbled in Eden's chest. She turned violently toward Gil. "You don't know what it's been like. You don't know what it's like to be me."

Gil looked as wild as she felt, standing in the starlight with messy hair and stained trousers. "You're right. I don't know. You will have to tell me."

"You don't want to be with me," Eden said, taking a step away with another guttural sob. "I'm ruined. I'm wrecked. I can't have any more children."

"What do you mean?"

"I mean, I was with Monroe for four years without using any protection. I can't have kids."

Gil laughed. "Asshole probably can't breed. Too much dope will do that to a person."

Eden laughed, too. "You might be right. And seriously, we didn't do it all that often. But still..."

"You didn't do it all that often?" Gil wrapped his arms around her.

"No, and it wasn't good, Gil. It was always about him."

"I'll show you what's good." Gil tipped his head and kissed her more tenderly than Monroe ever had. Monroe hadn't been big on kissing.

"Once we get married," he added.

"What the...! You are out of your ever-loving mind!"

She pounded him impotently on the chest before they turned back toward the truck. Gil tried to carry her through the stubble, but they soon realized she was too heavy to be carried far, so they stumbled together, holding each other up and laughing.

Eden had never felt so terrified.

Kissing Gil became the focus of her daily life. Well, she had to admit, the second focus. Hiding her drinking from Gil and her family was her first priority.

Every morning when she arrived at Grandma Doris's house, Gil would stop what he was doing and reach for Eden. They would kiss passionately yet chastely for several minutes. It felt like hours—her mind was emptied of everything but the visceral experience of this man, his searching mouth and respectful hands. It was an escape from reality that even booze couldn't achieve.

Eventually, he would pull away and go back to work like nothing had happened. Eden was beginning to suspect that he was indeed waiting for marriage before making love with her. It was exquisite torture.

So far, her strategy to switch to odourless vodka seemed to be working. Eden kept a bottle in the barn and one in her room, sometimes imbibing during the day and always at night to calm her skittish mind and ensure a good night's sleep. She stopped drinking whisky with her father, to George Junior's great relief.

George Senior was sinking deeper into his sodden brain and didn't seem to notice that he lost a drinking buddy. Eden spent most of her time helping her father with his basic needs and making meals for him and her brothers. On her weekly trips to town for groceries, Eden stopped at the liquor store to replenish both her father's and her own supply. Eden and her brothers agreed that it was better for her to buy whisky for their father than for him to drive into town for it.

Skylar was building a good business for himself. All day, vehicles passed through the yard as local farmers sought his mechanical skills. Skylar's oily kingdom in the shop attracted a sizeable coffee klatch in the afternoons. George Senior sipped coffee laced with whisky and hovered silently at the edges of the men's conversations. Eden provided a steady supply of baking for the men to enjoy with their thermoses of coffee. It was something Barbie would have done.

One thing she would never have done was buy whisky for her husband.

It had been a long time coming, but Barbie finally served divorce papers on George. The package from Dot Melnyk's office lay ripped open and abandoned on the kitchen counter. Everyone averted their eyes when they entered the room, but the brown manilla envelope remained in plain sight as a painful reminder that something had to be done.

"If only I could convince Mom to leave the home quarter out of the settlement," Eden said to Gil, yanking on her hair in frustration. Gil had ripped the stained carpet out of the living room and was now measuring for new carpet. The original wood floor lay starkly bare and accusing beneath their feet. Do something, it seemed to be saying.

Gil was slowly transforming the little homestead shack into a modern home. Eden was buying supplies and paying Gil out of a secret slush fund her father was hiding from her mother. Eden had a feeling the slush would soon dry up.

"She's paying the lawyer to help get Ava back, so I hate to ask her about this. But Dad will have to sell all his land and machinery to pay Mom out. He won't be able to keep any of the land back, according to George. If we could just keep this quarter, then Skylar and George can live here and work, and maybe I can raise horses. We would get by. It could work."

Eden paused to look out of the window toward the barn and granaries. "If we have to sell everything, then all the work we've put into Grandma's house will be for nothing."

Gil held her silently. She drew his strength and delicious scent deep into her lungs, feeling her anxiety retreat for the time being.

Despite Gil's comforting presence, she longed for the end of the day when she could shut her bedroom door and retrieve her bottle from the closet. Without a few drinks, the future would swamp her mind with all its horrifying possibilities until she felt she would be sucked under. Gil thought she had quit drinking—and she would, after she got Ava back. The minute she had her baby back she would stop drinking forever.

* * *

Gil cleaned his truck cab before their trip to Regina. It made Eden smile to herself. She also noticed Celeste had cut his hair, and he was wearing new jeans.

"What are you smiling about?" Gil asked. Eden was sitting close to him on the bench seat, her thigh pressed against his. His right hand was entwined with her left as they sped along the highway.

"Oh, I don't know," she said. "I guess this reminds me of Celeste and Maurice when they first started dating. They couldn't keep their hands off each other. Do you want a smoke?"

Eden pushed the cigarette lighter in, took the pack from Gil's shirt pocket, and proceeded to light a cigarette with what she thought was a good imitation of Maurice's sensual ritual with Celeste. Apparently, she failed because Gil hooted with laughter. Eden laughed too, but then tears came to her eyes. This easy rapport with Gil filled her with happiness but also foreboding. *How long can it last?*

Gil was taking Eden to the city to meet with Dot Melnyk. She also wanted to stop in to see Josey and try to get a glimpse of Ava at the foster home. And, if there was time, she should go see her mother. It was going to be a long, difficult day.

"This is my friend, Gilbert Tremblay," Eden said as they walked into the lawyer's office. Dot rose to shake Gil's hand.

"Have a seat, you two," she said. "Eden, how have you been?"

"I've been well, but worried about Ava. I have never lived through three longer months in my life."

"Well, we have a hearing date on November 26. Only six weeks to go. Now I have two things I want to discuss with you today. Did you ever receive a copy of the adoption forms that, I realize, you say you never signed?"

"No, I never received anything. Maybe my parents did?"

"Yes, you must ask your mother about this. Will you be seeing her today? Also, I am going to have you fill out permission forms to allow me to access your hospital chart and notes on your file at the Department of Social Services. Unfortunately, I cannot access the sealed adoption records through any legal means. No one can."

"Of course, I will sign anything. Do you think the hospital records will show anything?"

"It is possible, although unlikely, that efforts by your social worker or hospital staff to coerce you into signing the adoption forms will be noted. It is certainly worth a try. I will also try to access records at Wheatland Manor, but they are notoriously ill-kept."

Dot changed tack. "As we prepare for the hearing, it would be beneficial to show the court that you are fully capable of raising Luellen should you gain custody. Have you obtained a job since we last spoke?"

Eden squirmed. "Well, no, but... I'm taking care of my father, who has dementia, and housekeeping for my two brothers, who bring in good money. They will help raise Ava, I'm sure of it. And I want to start raising horses," she added.

"Hmmm, do you have experience in raising horses for profit?"

"Well... no... umm, but I can maybe get a job at the grocery store. That's what I did before I moved back home." Eden was feeling more desperate by the minute.

"Without a putative father on record, who could perhaps be compelled through the courts to help support you and your daughter, I'm afraid the judge might not look favourably on your situation."

Gil cleared his throat. "I am the father," he said.

Eden clapped a hand to her gaping mouth. Dot stared at Gil over her reading glasses with blatant hostility. "Young man, you are a little late to the party," she said.

"Gil, no... what are you doing?" Eden grabbed his forearm as if to pull him out of the office.

"And I can tell the judge that I will help support Ava as she grows up. Will that help, do you think?"

"And what do you do for a living?" Dot said, scanning Gil's faded western shirt, shiny new jeans, and scuffed boots. "Are you a farmer?"

"No, ma'am, I'm a carpenter. A handyman, sort of."

"A handyman. Do you have any formal training?"

"No, but I've got lots of work. More coming in every day." Eden knew this to be a lie.

Dot looked at Eden. "I assume that you are in an established relationship with Gil," she said.

"Yes, she is," Gil said firmly. Eden was still speechless. "We are getting engaged."

"Well, congratulations. Yes, it might make a difference if you both appear at the hearing. Yes, it could help."

When Eden and Gil exited Dot's office building at street level, Eden grabbed Gil's shoulders.

"Gil, this is insane. No one will believe you are Ava's father. You were thirteen years old when she was conceived. It's impossible!"

Gil grinned. "Oh, I don't know about that. I was an early bloomer."

"Your parents will hate me. The whole community will hate me." Eden threw her hands up in despair.

"Hey, I only have to convince one person that I'm Ava's dad, and that's the judge." He put his arm around her waist. "Don't worry. Let's go find coffee."

Gil dropped Eden off in front of the provincial building. She was still in shock as she watched his truck drive away. Shocked, but also hopeful. *He can always change his mind about marrying me. We just need to get Ava back, one way or another.*

She climbed the stairs to the third floor and entered the Department of Social Services office suite. Several people were sitting in the gloomy waiting room. She approached the reception desk. "Is Josey MacMillan available?" In a moment, Josey appeared and, with a nervous glance at the waiting clients, gestured to Eden to follow her.

"I'm glad you're here. I've only got a couple of minutes, but I've been meaning to call you. Sit down," Josey commanded, sliding behind her cluttered desk.

"Anyway, I could get into serious trouble for this, but I decided to look at your file in Agatha's office. She's off on medical leave, and I was here late one night. Made me nervous as shit."

Eden was flabbergasted. Josey went on. "Because no one should be forced into giving their baby away. It's inhuman! It's just wrong! I don't care how young they are."

"I know, I know, but what did you find?" Eden said impatiently.

"Well," Josey said, leaning forward and lowering her voice to just above a whisper, "she made notations each time she asked you to sign the adoption papers, but she didn't make a note when you finally did."

"That's because I didn't sign them. But what does that prove? Maybe she could say she forgot?"

"No, adoption files are audited by our superiors, including our client notes. They are super careful about this. I don't know how this could have slipped through. It's just weird."

Eden was thinking furiously. "My lawyer is going to try to access these files. Maybe she'll find evidence that things weren't done properly with Ava's adoption. Wow."

"Agatha's notes were pretty descriptive of you. She called you belligerent, uncooperative, stuff like that.

It's clear from her notes that you did not want to give up your baby. That might help in court."

"Yeah, thanks." Wringing her hands, Eden looked into Josey's kind face. "How is Ava doing at the foster home?"

"She's doing well. She has gained some weight and seems stable. She's still super shy and the foster mom says she doesn't know how to play with the other kids. She says she's really clingy."

A new fissure opened in Eden's bludgeoned heart. "Poor kiddo. I hope she doesn't get too clingy with that foster mom. Maybe she won't want to come home with me."

"She'll do fine. Don't worry about that. And her arm is healing nicely." Josey stood up. "I'm going to have to let you go now. My caseload gets bigger every day."

Eden's next stop was the Women's Emergency Center a few blocks from the provincial building. The center was housed in a small bungalow with a steep gabled roof, squatting bravely between four-storey brick apartment buildings.

Eden entered a wood-panelled room filled with grey metal desks and filing cabinets. At the back of the room, a pamphlet stand overflowed with handouts printed on coloured copy paper. An ancient mimeograph machine lurked in the corner. There was no one in the room.

End the Silence about Domestic Violence. We Will Not Be Beaten. Five Myths About Domestic Violence. Battering and the Indian Woman. Counselling the Abuse Victim. Eden scanned the titles of the handouts in awe. She was reaching for *Alcohol Abuse and Domestic Violence* when Barbie appeared at an office door.

"Eden!" Barbie clutched her heart in surprise. "I didn't expect you."

"Hi, Mom." Eden stuffed the pamphlet back into its slot. "I had a meeting with Ms. Melnyk, so thought I'd stop by."

"How did you get here?" Barbie asked nervously. "Did your father come with you?"

"Mom, Dad can barely walk to the barn. He would never be able to drive up to the city."

Barbie's office was barely large enough to hold a desk and two wooden swivel chairs. Eden spun in one of the chairs.

"So, you're on your own today?" Barbie asked.

"No, I came up with Gil Tremblay. He gave me a ride."

"Gil? That's Celeste's brother, right? Why him?"

Eden shrugged. "We're kind of going out." Although it didn't look like Barbie was biting her tongue behind her tight lips, Eden guessed that's what she was doing.

"What did Dot have to say?"

"She's trying to find evidence that I never signed the adoption papers. Hospital records and stuff like that. I know I never signed anything. If we can find proof, maybe the judge will let me have Ava back. Because I was forced, you know."

Barbie met Eden's eyes defiantly. "At the time, it was the only option for our family. And you know exactly why," she said flatly.

Eden's emotions flared but she forced herself to bite her own tongue. "All that is ancient history. The important thing is to make sure Ava doesn't go back to the Schultzes. And to get custody of her myself. That's all I care about!"

Eden's armpits were damp. She took a deep breath. *Just ask the damn question and get it over with!*

"Did you and Dad sign the adoption papers? Did you forge my signature or something like that?"

Barbie shook her head. "No, Eden, we did not. That social worker—what was her name?—assured us that you had signed it the day before Ava was born."

"Agatha Browne. That was her name." Eden slumped in her chair. She scratched at a streak of dust that had stained her clean jeans. "Did they ever give you a copy of the adoption records that I supposedly signed?"

Barbie shook her head, chewing worriedly on her left thumbnail.

Eden stood up. "Okay. I believe you. Just one more thing before I have to get going. If Dad has to sell the home quarter, he will have to move out of the house, George Junior, Skylar, and I will have to find somewhere to live, and Skylar might lose his mechanic business because he won't have a shop. I'm pretty sure River and Stacey won't take us all in! It will be way harder to get Ava if I don't have a decent home to raise her in. So, I'm asking you to take the home quarter out of the divorce settlement."

"Fair is fair," Barbie said. "Half means half. That is matrimonial property law in this province."

"I want Ava to be able to run around on the farm with dogs and horses and have a childhood. I don't want her in town where everyone will talk about her behind my back. If she can live on the ranch for a few years before she goes to school, she will be... I don't know. Healed, maybe."

Barbie continued chewing on her fingernails. "I'll think about it," she said.

When Eden and Gil pulled up to Ava's foster home, they saw her sitting on a blanket holding Squirmy Worm and a baby doll while the foster mother tilled a flower bed with a shovel. Ava's hair beamed like sunshine on the warm October day; the leaves strewn on the lawn were the same golden hue.

Gil parked the truck across the street. He gazed intently at Ava as if trying to imprint the child's image on his retina. Eden noticed that his palms were sweating; she disengaged her hand from his and wiped it on her jeans.

Ava and her foster mother did not notice the truck. Eventually, the woman picked up the blanket, and Ava followed her into the house, clutching her toys under one arm.

Gil leaned back in his seat and closed his eyes. Eden glanced at him nervously. *What is he thinking?*

To break the silence, Eden said, "She's cute, isn't she?"

Gil smiled. "Yeah, she's cute, alright. She looks like you." Eden felt a rush of relief, but then Gil turned to her, looking more serious than she had ever seen him.

"You don't have to do this today, but you will have to tell me who Ava's father is," he said. "I have to know, but not today. We've had enough stress for one day." He started the truck and made a U-turn in front of the house.

Eden silently fumed. *I will tell no one who Ava's father is. That is my secret to carry to the grave.* Then, surprising herself, she said, "It is so embarrassing. I'm not sure I can ever talk about it. It should never have happened."

Gil said nothing, a trait Eden found annoying. She felt compelled to keep talking to fill the void. "I mean, it was all my fault. I've done a lot of stupid things in my life, but that was the stupidest." She slapped her forehead with the palm of her hand. "Stupid!"

Eden could tell from Gil's profile that he was completely stumped. *He's wondering how a fourteen-year-old girl could be responsible for what happened. He's wondering, Who? Everyone is wondering, Who?*

Finally, he spoke. "Don't beat yourself up," he said, grabbing her hand and pulling her closer. "God has a plan for Ava. Otherwise, she would never have been born. *Maman* says babies make their grand entrances on their own schedule, and it's our job to run along behind them cleaning up the mess."

Eden rested her head on Gil's shoulder. "Even your *Maman* has never had to clean up a mess this big."

Chapter 20

It was obvious to Eden that Patches and Blackie had not forgotten her. Whenever she approached the horses for an ear scratch or a ride, Patches was her usual affectionate and cooperative self while Blackie resumed his old air of reluctance and resignation. With them, at least, it seemed she had never left.

Diamond was another matter. During Eden's four-year absence, Diamond had been turned out to pasture. She was halter-trained but otherwise unschooled. Eden was trying to pick up where they had left off.

Eden hadn't seen Gil for three days. A neighbour's barn had burned down, and the men were taking advantage of the mild weather to rebuild it before the snow flew. Eden missed Gil but also enjoyed having time to herself.

For the past couple of weeks, Diamond had been tolerating the saddle blanket as Eden led her around the corral. Today, Eden decided it was time to try the saddle. While the horse was busy pulling massive chunks of hay from the bales in the corral, Eden approached, the saddle at her hip. Diamond snorted at the flapping stirrups, folded her ears back, and tilted one rear hoof in alarm.

"Easy, girl, that's a girl." Eden rubbed her free hand along Diamond's back and hindquarters. The horse calmed down, and Eden gently lowered the saddle on top of the blanket. Diamond's nostrils flared, but she was soon distracted by the bales.

"This calls for a celebration, eh, girl?" Eden reached for the mickey of vodka that she had tucked between two bales. She returned the mickey to its hiding place and stroked the horse's neck, crooning praise into her velvety ear.

Suddenly, Gil stepped into the corral. Diamond twisted to the right, dumped the uncinched saddle to the left, kicked the bales, and galloped to the fence. Trying to avoid the rogue hooves, Eden toppled backwards. It took a few seconds to catch her breath, then she laughed. *What a spectacle that must have been*! She was still laughing when Gil grabbed her arm and hauled her to her feet.

"Are you *drunk*?" he asked, scowling at her. "What the hell's this?" He kicked at the mickey, which was now in full sight beside the jostled bales.

Oops. Busted. Eden was still laughing. She rubbed her backside where she had landed in the soft dirt.

"Wasn't expecting you today," she said as she walked over to the gate to let Diamond into the pasture. "How's the barn raising going?"

"It's three o'clock in the effing afternoon!" Gil exclaimed. He picked up the mickey and dumped its contents into the dirt. "You told me you quit drinking! You lied!"

Eden shrugged. "I exaggerated," she said. "I'm going to quit drinking the minute I get my baby back. Until then..."

"Doesn't work that way, Eden," Gil said, flinging the empty bottle over the fence. "You can't lie to me. You can't."

Eden picked up the dusty saddle and blanket and lugged them toward the barn, trying to ignore him. Trying to get away from his words.

"Alcoholics lie, Eden. They hide booze. They're so sick they can't even see why that's wrong!"

She turned on him in a fury. "I am not an alcoholic. I just like a drink now and then. Who do you know who doesn't drink? How dare you call me an alcoholic!"

She dropped the saddle and ran toward the house, hoping he was not following her. She slammed through the mudroom and burst into the kitchen, where her father was sitting at the table. He looked up, surprised by her abrupt appearance. Eden was vibrating. She picked up the unwashed dishes on the counter and put them in the sink.

The mudroom door crashed against the wall as Gil stormed into the house. He walked up to Eden and grabbed her shoulders.

"Whoa, what the hell?" George Senior said, pulling himself up to stand. "What's the trouble?"

"Get the hell out of here!" Eden screamed, pushing Gil in the chest. He stumbled backward and took a deep breath.

"Eden, it is entirely possible that you won't get Ava back. Are you telling me that if you don't, you'll keep on drinking? What about us, Eden? What about *our* lives?"

"There is no us, Gil. Can't you get it?"

Gil was silent. George Senior was silent. Skylar stepped into the kitchen and stood silently. They were all watching her.

"There is no us, Gil, because what you see is what you get. A drinker. The mother of an illegitimate child who was stolen from her. A dropout. A hothead. A goddamn loser. That's what you get, Gil, if you marry me. And if that's not what you want, then get out. Get out now!"

Eden screamed her last words so loudly that her throat burned.

Gil turned toward the door, then stopped.

"Eden," he said, not looking at her, "do you want to move Ava from one alcoholic household to another? What chance do you have to get Ava and then keep her if you go on drinking? What chance does she have?"

He turned to stare at her, his gaze softening. He gestured toward her father.

"This is the legacy we pass on to the next generation unless it stops here. Eden, it has to stop with us. Our families can't go on like this. We are the generation that can turn things around. We have to."

He walked through the door and quietly closed it behind him.

* * *

Feeling wearier than she had thought possible, she wrenched herself out of bed to make breakfast the next morning. She was startled to see her father sitting fully clothed at the table.

"Dad, you're up!" Eden usually had to have coffee perking and bacon sizzling to coax George Senior out of bed, and he needed help getting washed and dressed. Today, although his shirt was buttoned crookedly, he looked remarkably presentable.

He was mumbling to himself and barely looked up when she came into the kitchen.

"Enough is enough," she heard him say as she put the coffee on.

"Poorest family in the goddamn South Country!" he exclaimed loudly, then resumed an incoherent stream of words until Eden placed a full coffee cup in front of him. "He's a good kid, that Gil. Hasn't a pot to piss in. Those Tremblays never did."

"Yeah, Dad, you're right. But at least their family is in one piece. At least they stick together. Better than we can say."

Eden sat beside him with her own cup. "Don't worry, you won't be seeing Gil around here anymore," she said. "Pretty sure I drove him away for good yesterday. Probably for the best."

George Senior drained his cup and pushed himself to his feet, swaying slightly as he stood by the table. Then he took a deep breath, squared his thin shoulders, and walked toward the door.

"Dad, where are you going?" Eden said in alarm. "Don't you want breakfast?"

Through the window, she watched him careen slowly toward the barn. Shrugging, she made breakfast for George Junior and Skylar. George Junior made a hasty appearance, grabbed toast, poured coffee into a thermos, and rushed away. He was driving a school bus this year and often ran late. Finally, Skylar trod heavily down the stairs and sank into a chair.

"Glad somebody wants breakfast this morning," Eden said, placing a plate of fried eggs, bacon, and toast in front of her brother. Skylar, who hated mornings, didn't reply.

The dishes were washed, beds made, and floors swept before Eden heard her father's step on the porch. With difficulty, he shoved the door open, his arms laden with bottles. Eden was shocked to realize that her father had raided her secret stashes of vodka around the ranch.

Speechless, she watched him tip each bottle over the sink. She wanted to grab his arm to stop him, but then remembered how often Barbie had poured his booze down the drain. It had only served to inflame him, and the ensuing fight could go on for hours. *Now you know how we felt, Dad. Little ironic, don't you think?*

"There," George said, clattering the empty bottles into the garbage can. Pleased with himself, he sat down at the table and looked at Eden expectantly.

"Sorry, buddy, you missed breakfast," she said to him, annoyed. "Not sure what you think that little display achieved."

Eden filled her day with housework and baking. She couldn't bring herself to go over to Grandma Doris's house and continue cleaning and organizing over there. It was impossible not to think about Gil every minute of the day. Time crawled like a garden slug, and she didn't even have a drink to look forward to that evening. George had found every one of her bottles, even excavating her closet when she wasn't looking. She watched him pour the last twenty-six ounces down the drain with feigned detachment. She wanted to scream.

Shortly after supper, George again roused himself. He rubbed his cheeks as he walked to the bathroom.

"Need a shave," Eden heard him mumbling.

"Hold on, Dad, I'll help," she said. *What has gotten into this man?*

Then, to her astonishment, Eden's father retrieved a good shirt out of his closet, one he probably hadn't worn in years. The plaid western shirt sagged on his body as he attempted to tuck it into his jeans. Eden helped him button and tuck, then set his suspenders back on his shoulders.

"Where ya headed, Dad?"

"Going to a meetin'" he said. "And you're driving."

Eden glanced at George Junior, who was watching in amazement. "I'll take you to town, Dad," he offered, reaching for his keys on the hook by the door.

"Nope, this is a lil' father-daughter trip, thank you very much."

Eden was perplexed. Was he going to an AA meeting? That was the only kind of meeting he had ever attended to her knowledge.

Eden shrugged. "I'll take you, Dad," she said. *I can go to the liquor store if we get into town before they close.*

She grabbed her coat, combed her fingers through her hair, and stood at the door as her father struggled to pull on his boots. Soon they were driving in silence through the bleak, late-autumn evening.

The tiny United Church in Everview was brightly lit when they parked beside it. Several vehicles were huddled in the cold; snow was accumulating gently on hoods and windshields.

"I'll let you out here," Eden said to her father. *The liquor store closes in five minutes!*

"Could you at least help your old man down the stairs?" George said, concentrating hard on opening the passenger door and stepping out into the snow.

"Oh, alright!" Eden said irritably. She helped her father walk up three steps into the church, then down the narrow stairs into the basement. The bubble of conversation and laughter floating up the stairs burst abruptly when they entered the large room at the bottom.

About a dozen men stared silently at them. Eden was overwhelmed as she scanned the familiar South Country faces. *Is everyone in this community an alcoholic?*

Then one man stepped out of the crowd. It was George's AA sponsor Loren, tears streaming down his cheeks. He embraced George, then wrapped his arms around Eden.

George grabbed Eden's hand for support as he was greeted by each man in turn. Some of his old bluster resurfaced as he hollered out the names of his friends. If he didn't remember their names, he just yelled, "Hey, guy!" or "Whaddya know!" Many of the men were in tears.

The men babbled, laughed, and cried for several minutes. Then, before she knew what was happening, Eden and her father were steered to a circle of wooden chairs and practically forced to sit.

"I've got to get going," Eden said to Loren. "What time do you want me to pick him up?"

"You can be our guest tonight!" Loren said. "I'll get you both a coffee. Just sit tight."

George grabbed her wrist. "Hold on, sister. Can't you give an old man a couple hours of your time?"

Eden looked at her father suspiciously. *What is this 'old man' garbage?* Even when she helped him get ready for a bath or clip his toenails, he never lost his dignity. He hadn't once referred to himself as an old man or asked for help.

Loren brought them Styrofoam cups of coffee heaped with Coffee-Mate and sugar, and the meeting began. The first to speak was Denis Tremblay. Eden hadn't noticed him among the men. He winked at her as he took the floor.

"'Allo, my name is Denis," he said redundantly. "I am an alcoholic."

Each man spoke in turn. They talked about families, forgiveness, faith, fear. They revealed personal details of their lives that made Eden's eyes widen. *Now I know why they call it Alcoholics Anonymous.* She wondered how much of her own family's heartache had been shared in this room. She became increasingly uncomfortable as her father's turn to speak drew closer. She wanted to run out into the snow and disappear in the darkness.

Finally, it was George's turn. He began to mumble into his chest and Eden feared that he wouldn't be able to express his thoughts. Then he stopped mumbling and looked up at the other men.

"Goddamn wife left me," he said. "One of my sons won't talk to me. All 'cause of booze."

Everyone in the room was motionless. The coffee percolator burbled and sighed on the side table. George went on.

"I'm losin' the goddamn farm 'cause the goddamn wife wants a divorce. She's sending me to the poor house!" he shouted, waving one arm in the air. Eden grabbed the arm and lowered it for him.

"But I got two grandchildren now," George said, ignoring her. "Might be more, you never know. So, I've gotta straighten up. Gotta straighten up."

He turned to Eden and looked into her face.

"This one here, she's home now," he said. "Thankin' the good Lord for that. I thank Him every day."

Eden felt an enormous lump in her throat—so large it was almost impossible to breathe.

"But she's hidin' booze all over the yard and in the house. She learned lotsa lessons from her old man."

Eden heard a stirring among the men but was unable to look up from her lap, where her hands were twisting painfully.

"She's a chip off the old block!" George chuckled softly and began mumbling again. In a moment, he said, "We got two English alcoholics sittin' here tonight."

George appeared to be finished. Eden looked up; everyone was gazing expectantly at her. *I'm not an alcoholic! What do they want from me?*

Then she remembered Gil's words. Did she want to bring Ava into another alcoholic home? Were they any better than the Schultzes? She felt her father nudge her arm. She stood up to gaze into the kind and worried eyes that were following her every move. She raked her fingers through her hair and burst into tears.

"My name's Eden," she said. "And I'm an alcoholic, too."

* * *

Eden was silent as the snowy fields skimmed past George Junior's truck. Her brother had offered to drive her to Regina for Ava's hearing the next day.

Eden had not heard from Gil for two weeks. A barn-sized ache pressed on Eden's chest, making it difficult to sleep or eat. Despite constant craving, she had not taken a drink since the AA meeting. Her father had not taken a drink. To his children's relief, George Senior had not experienced severe alcohol withdrawal. He was becoming more like his old self with each passing day.

Unfortunately, the cobwebs he was beginning to brush from his mind were taking hold of hers. Her sobriety-fueled anxiety about Ava had reached maximum intensity. Eden thought she might explode at any moment.

"Dad signed the divorce papers," George said suddenly, breaking a long silence. Eden turned to look at him, surprised. "I'm taking them to the lawyer today. It's the end of an era, I guess."

"Will Dad have to sell this winter?" Eden asked. This relatively ignored problem suddenly reared up; Eden, her father, and her brothers would soon be homeless. *Where will I live with Ava? I don't have a hope of winning this court hearing.*

George shrugged. "Dunno. Maybe Mom will let us stay until spring. It might be a little easier to sell the land in the spring. Prices are still good. Nice for her."

"So, if Dad has to pay off all the ranch debt, does that come out of his half?"

"No, the debt gets taken off the top. But what's left won't be enough for Dad to buy her out and keep the land. Like I said, it's the end of the English ranching era. Grandpa would roll in his grave."

"Yeah, him and Grandma Doris."

That evening, Eden and George Junior were sitting on the couch digesting Barbie's supper—braised spareribs, scalloped potatoes, dilled carrots, coleslaw, homemade buns, and apple crumble with vanilla ice cream—when Eden told her mother that George Senior had quit drinking. She did not add that she, too, had stopped drinking forever. Or that forever felt like a promise she could not keep.

"Well, good for him," Barbie said, curling her feet beneath her in the armchair and biting her thumbnail.

Eden looked at George, who avoided eye contact.

"Mom, he's doing really well. He's even going to AA meetings."

"Like I said, I'm glad for him. But it's too late for us, you know that, Eden. I have a new life now."

Eden looked at her mother's tiny apartment. Streaked windows reflected the three of them sitting in the drab room. Barbie switched on all three of the lights on her dilapidated pole lamp. Mom must shop at the thrift store, Eden thought. She soldiered on. Difficult conversations seemed easier now that she attended AA meetings.

"Dad signed the divorce papers. George and I dropped them off at Dot's office on the way here."

"Good," Barbie said, biting her other thumbnail.

"I was just wondering when Dad has to sell the land. I mean, I have to figure something out because Ava will be coming home with me soon. Gil... he helped me fix up Grandma's house so Ava and I could live there and still help Dad out every day. Skylar still needs a lot of support, too, right, George?" Still no eye contact. *Help me out here, you coward!*

"Didn't you get the revised divorce documents?" Barbie asked, staring from her daughter to her son. Eden and George Junior shook their heads.

"Dot sent them to your father weeks ago! Do you even pick up the mail? Good Lord!" Barbie leaped up to pace around the cramped room.

"Dot and I figured out a way to keep the home quarter in the family. It was your grandfather's homestead, and I just didn't have the heart... So, you two and Skylar will become joint owners. It's kind of like an early inheritance. Not really fair to River, but... Also, I like the idea of... your daughter growing up there. I'm not sure what you'll all live on, but I guess that's your problem."

Eden jumped to her feet. "Mom! Are you serious? Thank you!"

Without thinking about it, she wrapped her arms around her mother. Barbie's eyes filled with tears as she held her daughter. When she pulled away, she gazed at her children sadly.

"I've been offered a job in Ottawa with the Canadian Advisory Council on the Status of Women," Barbie said. "I'm going to be supporting a committee that is researching violence against women in Canada. I'm moving in February."

Eden felt waves of shock rock her body.

"Wow, that's great, Mom," George Junior said. "I'm proud of you."

"Thanks! I'm a little scared, to tell the truth. But the money from the farm will help me get settled there, maybe buy a little house or something." Barbie continued pacing. "But there are more important things to think about right now. We've got to get our little girl back!"

The next morning, Eden, Barbie, and George Junior arrived at the courthouse an hour before the hearing. Barbie and George would not be permitted to attend the proceedings, but they promised to sit outside the courtroom and wait to hear the outcome, no matter how long it took. Barbie had taken the day off. Eden was tearful with gratitude.

When the elevator doors opened on the third floor, Eden saw Gil standing at a window looking down into the street. She stopped so suddenly her mother and brother had to squeeze past her before the doors closed.

Gil turned slowly toward her. He was wearing a navy suit and a wide diagonally striped necktie. His dark curly hair was slicked behind his ears.

"You're here," Eden said as he approached her.

"*Oui. Je suis là.*" His eyes were serious and kind.

"I appreciate that," she said. "I'm going to AA."

"I know."

"I thought it was anonymous," Eden said, smiling a little.

Gil shrugged. "I have my spies."

"You look good," Eden said, fingering his silky tie.

"You, too." She was wearing a brown corduroy skirt and a red blazer, gifts from Barbie.

The elevator doors opened, and Dot Melnyk stepped out. She looked them up and down, nodded her approval, then gestured toward a small adjoining room. When they emerged half an hour later, Eden was in an agony of anxiety. Her armpits, forehead, and palms were glazed with sweat. She felt that she could vomit at any moment.

"You doing okay?" Gil asked, bending to look directly into her eyes. "It's going to be okay, you know. We've got this. That's a good lawyer right there." He took Eden's sweaty hand, and they walked past Barbie and George Junior, who looked deeply bewildered. Why was Gil Tremblay allowed into the courtroom while they were not?

Eden and Gil sat in the front row. Eden kept her hand in Gil's as she watched Josey MacMillan enter the room. A young man in a rumpled suit also took a seat. There was no sign of Bernie and Myrtle Schultz. Dot entered, the court reporter and clerks walked in, and the hearing was called to order.

Judge Evans took his seat, his balding head shining under the harsh fluorescent lights. He seemed to carry the weight of a weary world.

"To summarize," the judge began, "a four-year-old child named Luellen May Schultz was committed by this court to the Minister for a period of ninety days under the recommendation of the Department of Social Services. The temporary committal has expired, and it is now upon this court to determine future custody of the child."

Judge Evans looked up from his notes. "We will now hear from the Department, which has undertaken to further investigate this case. Miss MacMillan, will you please step forward?"

Josey stood up and walked to the podium. "Your Honour, after the apprehension order for Luellen Schultz was issued, I attempted to arrange a visitation to the home of Myrtle and Bernie Schultz, Luellen's adoptive parents. After trying for several weeks to reach them by telephone, I decided to drive to their farm. I thought the place was deserted when I first arrived, but finally Mrs. Schultz opened the door after I had been knocking for several minutes. Mrs. Schultz refused to let me into the house. There was no sign of Mr. Schultz. From what I could see, the home was suffering from significant neglect. Two dogs on the property appeared to be in distress, so upon returning to the city, I called animal welfare to report the situation."

"Did you continue to try to set up a scheduled appointment with Mr. and Mrs. Schultz?" the judge asked in a monotone.

"Yes, sir, I did, but they did not answer my calls. The last time I tried, the telephone number had been disconnected."

"From what you ascertained, would this be a suitable environment for a young child?"

"No, sir, I would state adamantly that it is not."

"Are Mr. and Mrs. Schultz in attendance today?" Judge Evans asked, glaring nearsightedly through his glasses at the smattering of people in the room.

The rumpled young man stood up. "Sir, I am Leslie Lafontaine of the Legal Services Commission. I was assigned to this case at the request of the Director of Social Services to represent the Schultzes at this hearing. I, too, was unable to get in touch with them, after trying their telephone number multiple times and sending them a registered letter by mail."

"Has the Minister received a petition from the parents seeking to resume custody of their child?"

Josey stood up. "No, sir, there has been no communication between the adoptive parents of Luellen Schultz and the Department of Social Services."

"This child appears to have been abandoned," Judge Evans said sadly. "Under Section 29, subsection C of the Family Services Act, I declare Luellen Schultz to be permanently committed to the care of the Minister of Social Services."

Eden gasped and was only prevented from jumping to her feet by Gil's strong hand on her arm.

"Miss MacMillan, please review for the court the status of Luellen Schultz today," the judge said.

"Your Honour, Luellen is currently housed at a foster home in the city. Her health status has improved.

I have visited the foster home regularly and Luellen appears to be settled. However, the operators of the foster home have indicated to me that they are not in a position to adopt her. They have three biological children of their own. We will have to try to find another adoptive home for this little girl, which may be a challenge due to the developmental delays she exhibits. The pediatrician says that without significant improvement, she will not be ready to attend kindergarten next year due to her speech and social impediments."

Judge Evans shook his head morosely. "Are there any other parties in attendance today who wish to address the court?" he asked, looking pointedly at Dot Melnyk.

"Yes, Your Honour. Thank you. I represent Eden English and Gilbert Tremblay, the biological parents of Luellen Schultz, known to them as Ava English. I wish to present evidence that Eden was coerced into giving Luellen up for adoption in 1975 and that the adoption of the child by Bernie and Myrtle Schultz was not legal from the beginning."

"Go on," Judge Evans said impassively.

"I present to you the hospital birth record of Ava English, signed by her mother Eden English on March 5, 1975. I also present a copy of Luellen Schultz's birth certificate. As you will see, the documents are both dated March 5, 1975."

A clerk took the documents from Dot's hands and presented them to the judge. He placed his glasses on the top of his head, squinted at the papers, then set the glasses back on his face.

"No putative father is indicated on the hospital record," Judge Evans said.

"Yes, Your Honour," Dot said. "Ava English's parents were painfully young when Ava was conceived. At the time of her birth, her mother refused to reveal the identity of the father."

"And now?" the judge said, looking over the top of his glasses at Eden and Gil.

"Sir, Gilbert Tremblay has stepped forward as the father."

"Very interesting, but what does this have to do with Luellen Schultz? What proof do you have, beyond the birth date, that this is Luellen's birth record?"

"Sir, I present to you a list of live births at Regina General Hospital on March 5, 1975. On that day, only one female child was born at the hospital. You are holding that birth record in your hand. Now I would like to present documents from the Department of Social Services obtained via a subpoena duces tecum."

She handed a sheaf of papers to the clerk. Judge Evans started leafing through them, looking more interested by the second.

"You are looking at client records for Eden English from 1974 and 1975. You will note that Eden's social worker, Agatha Browne, asked and failed repeatedly to obtain consent from Eden for the adoption of her child. Consent forms were presented to Eden on five separate occasions and on each occasion, she refused."

Dot went on. "The last request was made on March 4, a day before Eden's daughter Ava was born. As you can see, Miss Browne made a notation that day indicating that she spoke with a couple who were standing by to adopt Eden's child. That is the last entry in Eden English's client file."

"Hmm," said Judge Evans.

"I would put to you, Your Honour, that Eden's daughter was indeed adopted shortly after her birth in March 1975. I would like now to call on Eden to testify before the court."

After she was sworn in by the clerk, Eden stood nervously at the podium. She glanced at Gil, who winked at her with his right eye, then with his left. It made her feel like laughing and she relaxed slightly.

"Miss English, please tell the court in your own words what happened," Judge Evans said.

Eden took a deep breath. "I blame myself for everything," she said. "It was all my fault that Ava was conceived. It should never have happened. But I loved her from the moment I knew she existed. That must count for something."

"Miss English, please stick to the facts. Can you explain to the court how you knew where your assumed daughter was living? All adoption records are permanently sealed and may only be opened under a judge's order."

"Well, if you looked at those records, you would see that I never signed them. Everyone wanted me to—my parents, the matron at Wheatland Manor, the social worker, everyone. Especially the social worker. She was always browbeating me about it. But I kept on refusing. Why would I give up my daughter just because I was young? Young people can be good parents, too."

"I repeat, how did you know where your daughter was living four years after her birth?"

"It's really hard to explain. But I kept getting these visions that showed me she wasn't in a good place. One day, I told my friend about the visions, and she said it sounded like Ava was in the foster home she lived in when she was a kid. So, my brother and I decided to check it out."

Dot said, "Judge, I apologize..."

"No, let her go on," the judge said.

Eden glanced back at Gil. *I sound like a crazy person, don't I?* Gil resumed his erratic winking, and Eden smiled.

"Now I'm back home, living with my dad and brothers on a ranch in the South Country. My... fiancé and I have fixed up my grandparents' house to make a nice home for Ava. I have lots of support now, which I guess I didn't have when Ava was born. There's nobody in the world who wants Ava more than I do. There's no one else in the world who even wants her, period. And I've wanted her more than anything since the day she was conceived."

Eden started to cry. "Please give my baby back."

"Okay, Miss English, you can take a seat." The judge stared into the space directly in front of his face for several long minutes. Gil draped his arm around Eden and pulled her close, trying to quell her quaking. Dot Melnyk was fidgety and silent. The fluorescent ceiling lights roared overhead. A door slammed loudly in the hallway.

Finally, Judge Evans spoke. "For the first time in my twenty-three years in family court, I am compelled to open an adoption file. I don't see any other way to get to the bottom of this case. I hereby order that the order of adoption for Luellen Schultz, which was filed in 1975 in this judicial center, be opened for examination by myself and the counsel for Luellen's presumed biological parents. This hearing is hereby in recess and will recommence in one week's time."

Eden was still crying when she burst through the courtroom doors and flung herself into her mother's arms. Barbie's face was grey; she wrapped her arms around her sobbing daughter and looked at Dot with trepidation.

Dot threw her head back and laughed. She slapped Gil on the shoulder. "Well done, folks. This is all good news. Don't worry," she said to Barbie and George Junior. "The judge has issued an order to open Ava's adoption records. If Eden didn't sign them, as she claims, we have a good argument to make that Eden's daughter was adopted illegally, or that proper procedure was not followed when the adoption was processed."

Gil and George Junior left for home after the hearing, but Eden decided to stay in the city with Barbie. She realized that these few days with her mother might be her last in a long time. When Barbie moved to Ottawa, would she return for visits? Given her financial circumstances, it seemed unlikely that Eden could travel to see her.

"Of course, I'll visit!" Barbie exclaimed when Eden expressed these thoughts. "I have a couple of grandchildren to see—not to mention you guys." She poured tea into Eden's cup. "When the committee travels across the country to do its research, I will be going with them, so that's at least one time that I will be in the province. Ottawa's only an airplane trip away these days!"

The thought of stepping onto an airplane to fly through the skies—something no one in Eden's family had ever done—made Eden queasy. Already, her feet longed to be stuffed into rubber boots to check on the horses. Already, her hair longed to be whipped and tangled in the wind. City life wasn't for her.

"I miss the ranch, sometimes," Barbie mused. "I even miss your father, believe it or not." She looked at Eden, a small smile teasing her lips. "Oh, we had so much fun in the early years. Your dad... well, he made me laugh so hard, every day. Everyone teased us because we were so mismatched in size, but we were a good match in other ways." Barbie wiped the moisture from her eyes, smearing her blue eye shadow. She looked at Eden, who had turned pale.

"But all of that laughing, the good times with friends... it was always fueled by booze. Everyone drank, no one thought anything of it. We were young. And in love. But drinking every day gets old, mighty fast. After we were married, I took a look around and realized that not everyone's husband drank daily. Your dad was a good man, and I know he loved me. But he never gave me all of himself. He always held back because drinking was more important than anything else."

Barbie picked up their empty cups. She stood for a moment, looking down at Eden thoughtfully.

"You know, we work with women every day who have escaped the worst situations you could imagine. Lots of men drink, but some are bloody mean bastards. Your dad wasn't mean, but some of them, my good

God... and then these women go back to their husbands. The staff at the shelter get so upset when that happens, but on some level, I get it. It is just so, so hard to leave your life."

Barbie set the cups down beside the sink in her galley kitchen, then sat down again across from Eden.

"Dad never hit you or anything like that," Eden said. "He wouldn't hurt a mosquito."

Barbie chuckled, perhaps remembering the hordes of mosquitos that plagued them on the rare rainy summers on the ranch.

"No, he did not, and when he was verbally abusive... I know you heard some pretty wild things as a child... it was mainly because I provoked him. I wanted to get through to him that he was ruining our lives, but I never could."

Barbie shook her head. "But then I came to the city, and the director at the women's center took a chance on me. And I ended up working in the sort of professional job I'd always envisioned for you one day. Something dignified and important, something meaningful. Life is ironic, isn't it?"

"I don't want to work in an office," Eden said. "I want to work on the land."

Barbie's eyes glazed as she looked out of the dusty window. "For women, farm life can be drudgery—endless, repetitive, tiring work. Unless a wife is an equal partner in the farm operation, but that's a rare thing. Women don't make any of the decisions; they just support their men. With your dad drinking so much... well, I just couldn't stand it anymore.

"Maybe it will be different for you. Eden, whatever you choose, however you decide to live your life, get an education. Finish high school, take correspondence courses, do something to make the world better."

"Well, Dad and the boys need me right now. I think that's meaningful. And when Ava comes home, I'm going to give her everything I have. Everything she has been missing since birth."

Chapter 21

On days when Barbie was working, Eden took the inconvenient bus trip to Ava's foster home at the edge of the city. November had burrowed into the prairies, and the days were bitterly cold and dreary. It was difficult to get a glimpse of Ava at this time of the year; the foster mother hurried her charges from the car to the house after her afternoon school runs.

Sometimes, all Eden could see was the top of Ava's head—a pink and white pom pom bobbing on a white knitted toque with long pom pom-endowed ties. She was wearing a pink parka and white fuzzy mittens. *Cute, but they'll be dirty in two seconds once I get her back to the farm!*

Gil returned to the city the afternoon before the hearing. It started at nine o'clock in the morning, and he needed time to get spiffy in his suit. Eden and Gil went on what he called a date that evening. It occurred to Eden that this was their first official appearance together as a couple. She wondered if it would be their last.

After burgers at the New Utopia Cafe, Eden and Gil went for ice cream at A&W, enjoying their cones while driving along Albert Street.

"So, are we back together?" Eden asked between licks, trying to be casual. She was sitting as close to Gil as the laws of physics would allow, so it seemed to her that they must be.

Gil captured a drip as it escaped down the side of his cone. He swung the truck into a Ford dealership to fully attend to his dessert.

"You must have felt so helpless, those years with Monroe," he said. "Knowing Ava was in trouble and having no way to help her."

Eden concentrated on her ice cream.

"I might have drank too, in that situation. Being away from family and all. But you chose to run away with Monroe."

Channelling superhuman strength, Eden said nothing.

"And every day going forward, you are going to have to choose whether or not to drink. I don't see any other way around it. Like my Papa. He says he gets up in the morning and makes a decision every day. We are all praying to Jesus that he makes the right decision."

Gil crunched the cone with his teeth.

"Maybe back then, when you lived up north, you didn't have much to live for. But now you do. You have Ava, and you have me. I don't know if that means much to an alcoholic, though. Our dads had families and farms—they had lots to live for, it seems to me—and they still drank their faces off."

Eden looked up into *his* face. Gil was staring blindly at the traffic streaming before them.

"I swore to myself that I would never become an alcoholic and that I would never marry one. But I want to marry you. I want it more than anything. Eden, if you quit drinking, I would like to marry you next year. Sorry to put a condition on it, but I have to. I'm like your mom, I guess. I know my limits."

Eden smiled. "If you're asking me to marry you— and I think you are—the answer is yes. Yes, to you and no, to booze. Forever." *Forever? Maybe for a while. Forever is a long time.*

"And we can tell our grandchildren that you proposed to me in a used car lot," she added. "It's a good story."

Then Gil kissed her like he was drinking a tall glass of water in the desert. And she kissed back with gratitude, love, and doubt mingling fiercely in the deep well of her heart.

She would try not to drink. For this man, she would try harder to do this one thing than she had ever tried to do anything else in her life.

The next morning at the hearing, Eden was shocked when Agatha Browne walked into the courtroom; she looked much older than she had three months ago at the hospital. It seemed Agatha's self-certainty had been checked at the door. She sat in the back row, fidgeting and staring nervously at the front of the room, looking neither right nor left.

Eden dug her fingernails into Gil's hand when Myrtle Schultz took a seat beside the legal services lawyer. Myrtle turned and glowered at Eden. There was no sign of Bernie. Eden noticed Josey MacMillan sitting in the back. Josey's red ponytail swung as she nodded and winked at Eden.

The hearing was called to order as Judge Evans walked in.

"Luellen May Schultz is a four-year-old child who has been permanently committed to the care of the Minister of Social Services due to the failure of her adoptive parents to provide adequate care as well as their decision not to petition the court to resume custody of her within an allotted time."

Judge Evans looked up from his papers. "As a result of a highly unusual petition by a young couple claiming to be the biological parents of Luellen, and their assertion that Luellen's adoption in March 1975 was illegal, I have ordered the adoption records to be opened."

The judge looked at Dot Melnyk. "As counsel for the petitioners, would you please summarize the contents of the adoption records for Luellen May Schultz?"

"Yes, Your Honour, I will, indeed." Dot rose from her seat and stood at the podium. Eden noticed her hands were shaking as she looked down at her documents.

"The record shows that the child known as Luellen May Schultz was born on March 5, 1975, at Regina General Hospital. Her original birth certificate confirms that she was born Ava Celeste English, daughter of Eden Holly English and an unnamed father. Ava was adopted by Bernard and Myrtle Schultz on March 9, 1975.

"Your Honour, my client, Eden English, claims that she did not participate in the signing of the adoption order. She claims that she did not give her consent to the adoption either verbally or in writing. Yet, as you can see, this order has been signed and witnessed. I hold here the original copy of the order, which appears to have been signed by Eden. I also hold Ava's hospital birth record, which was previously entered as evidence in this case. These two documents are dated on the same day, March 5, 1975, the day of Ava's birth. As you will see, the signatures on these documents are vastly different."

A clerk transferred the documents from the podium to the judge's desk. He held them up, side by side, to examine the signatures. Eden held her breath.

Judge Evans looked up. "Will Eden English approach the bench?"

Eden walked to the judge's desk, her knees weak. He placed the two documents on the table in front of her.

"Can you confirm that the signatures on these documents are indeed yours, and if so, explain why they are so different?" Judge Evans said.

Eden looked at the hospital birth record. She remembered signing it; it was the moment when she decided that Ava's middle name would be Celeste. Her fat-lettered, childish signature appeared in blue ink at the bottom of the record. This was definitely her signature.

The scrawled, difficult-to-read signature on the adoption order was not hers. Eden's handwriting was rounded and curlicued to this day.

"This one is mine," Eden said, pointing to the hospital record, "but this is not! I would never sign my baby away. Someone else signed this document, not me."

When Eden had returned to her seat, Dot said, "Judge, I would like to ask the witness to this signature, Miss Agatha Browne of the Department of Social Services, to answer a few questions."

Judge Evans nodded, curiosity intensifying behind his spectacles.

After she was sworn in, Agatha Browne was asked to sit in a chair behind a small table to the right of the podium. Eden and Gil had to lean to the right to see the back of her head—a tight bun of grey hair, a pudgy neck. Tense shoulders under a black sweater. *Agatha.* Eden shivered with revulsion.

"Miss Browne, please state your position with the Department of Social Services and explain to the court how you know my client, Eden English," Dot said, towering over Agatha at the podium.

"I am currently on leave as a social worker with the Department. I have worked for the Department for twenty-one years. I have a good record and lots of commendations from my superiors, just take a look at my personnel file!"

"Miss Browne, you were the social worker assigned to work with Eden English when she was a resident of Wheatland Manor, a home for unwed pregnant women, in September 1974. Am I correct?"

"Yes."

"Please describe your relationship with Miss English."

"Well, all of us who worked with Eden found her... uncooperative. She was belligerent at times and prone to leaving the property without permission. She selfishly refused to make plans for the relinquishment of her baby. By the way, she was the youngest of all the girls I ever worked with there. She was barely fifteen when she came to the Manor."

"And what was your concern when she told you that she wished to keep her baby?"

"Well," Agatha said, jerking her head in irritation, "everyone knows that a fifteen-year-old can't provide for a child like an established, married couple can! I mean, it's only logical. Eden had no education, no job, and no family support. How was she capable of raising a child?"

"What led you to believe that Eden was incapable, other than her age?"

"Becoming pregnant at fourteen is proof enough for me! Believe me, most young women at Wheatland Manor are just waiting for their pregnancies to be over so they can put their children up for adoption and get on with their lives."

"Based on Eden's testimony, and on your case notes, which were subpoenaed and read by this court one week ago, you knew who would be adopting Eden's daughter. In your notes, you indicate that a couple from rural Saskatchewan was staying in the city, ready to adopt the child shortly after it was born. How did you know the Schultzes, Miss Browne?"

"Well, they went through all the proper channels, of course, and... it's not unusual to have recruited and screened couples waiting to adopt long before they get a baby. The Schultzes were properly vetted, just look at the records! Plus, they were longtime foster parents. They took some of the worst Indian kids off our hands, the drug addicts, the promiscuous..."

"I asked you how you knew them," Dot Melnyk said firmly. "What is your relationship to Myrtle Schultz?"

Agatha took a shuddering breath.

"Myrtle is my sister. And... and I thought they would give a good home to this illegitimate, unwanted child, a good start! Something a fifteen-year-old could never do!"

Eden bolted to her feet. "*I* wanted her," she screamed.

"Let's take a recess for fifteen minutes. Counsel, please get your client under control." Judge Evans rose to his feet and hastily left the room.

Dot handed Eden a paper cup of water. "Drink all of this and listen to me!" she said. Gil was standing behind Eden, his hands on her shoulders. "They are hanging themselves in there! Just let them do it. Don't say anything more unless you are asked to by me or the judge. Do you understand!"

Barbie was standing a few feet away, her face red. She had no idea what was going on.

"You both want to give the judge the best impression you can possibly project. So, rein it in! I know it's hard," Dot said. "But this is going in our favour, believe me."

She looked at Barbie, who smiled tentatively. "And here's your mom, all worried."

Eden turned to her mother, who extended one arm for her while encircling Gil with the other. The three of them stood quietly for a few moments, drawing strength from one another.

"The hearing will resume in five minutes, please take your seats!" the clerk called from the door. Barbie patted Eden and Gil on the back and shoved them gently toward the courtroom.

"Miss Browne, I remind you that you have revealed a serious conflict of interest that should have been declared long before the adoption took place," Judge Evans said when the hearing resumed.

"I also remind you that you are under oath and that perjury has very severe consequences. As well, the Family Services Act establishes harsh penalties—fines up to five thousand dollars or imprisonment for up to one year, or both—if a person is found guilty of procuring a child for the purposes of adoption. Do you understand?"

Agatha was snivelling. She wiped her nose with the back of her hand. "Yes, Your Honour."

"Did you falsify Ava Celeste English's adoption records so that it appeared that her biological mother had given consent? This, Miss Browne, is a yes or no question."

"No!" she blurted. "I mean, yes... sort of. I don't know." She was weeping openly now.

"And if you did falsify the records, did your sister Myrtle Schultz know about it? Because if she did, she too is liable on summary conviction to the fines or prison sentence I have just described!" Judge Evans pounded the desk with his fist.

Myrtle pushed herself to her feet. "I never knew nothing about this," she said. "Agatha never said nothing about consent to Bernie or me. You have nothing to hang on us for this mix-up. We are innocent parties here!"

Judge Evans turned his glistening eyes to Myrtle. "Mrs. Schultz, I hardly consider you innocent in this matter. Your neglect of your adopted child is what brought us to this point."

"I never neglected Luellen. She is my precious little girl! That Eden and her brother stole my baby right out from under my nose. It's them that hurt her. They got her all dirty and pulled her arm out of its socket. And now because of you," she pointed at Agatha, "because you can't do your job properly, I'll never get my Luellen back!"

Agatha shot back, "I never thought you'd raise her in a pigsty. I never knew Bernie was so far gone, or I wouldn't have helped you!"

"All right!" the judge roared. "Everyone in your seats." He took a deep breath and regained his dignity. His lethargy had evaporated.

Eden and Gil were gaping at Agatha and Myrtle. Dot Melnyk had a triumphant look on her face. Eden felt a trickle of hope as the iceberg of dread she had carried for almost five years started to melt. Gil lifted her clammy hand to his lips and kissed it.

Dot broke the silence. "Sir, it appears that a great travesty has occurred. Our system has failed a helpless child who has known only neglect and uncertainty since birth. Our society has failed a young woman who dared to want to raise her own child despite the obstacles and judgment she faced. Now we are left to pick up the pieces and try to right these wrongs in a way that will create a stable, loving home for Ava Celeste English.

"Eden English and Gilbert Tremblay, Ava's biological parents, have stepped forward to take responsibility for the child they regrettably conceived when they were still children themselves. They, too, want to put things right. They have the will and the means to raise Ava, and I implore you to let them do it."

The judge said, "Does anyone else in this courtroom have anything to say?"

Leslie Lafontaine from the Legal Services Commission stood up. "Sir, I have been retained to represent the Schultzes in this matter. They deeply regret their failure to petition for their daughter's return to their home and for not meeting with Social Services to facilitate that return. They have been going through a rough patch, which has resulted in Bernard Schultz's admission to an alcohol rehabilitation program, which is the reason he is not here today. On their behalf, I ask the court to grant them time to make the changes they so desperately want to make in order to regain custody of their child."

"Mrs. Schultz, could you explain in your own words the changes you plan to make in order to create a wholesome environment for your daughter?" Judge Evans asked.

Myrtle clutched the back of the chair in front of her and stood. The seams of her black dress were stretched to the limit; she looked to Eden like a sausage bulging in its casing.

"Well, I'm going to be a better housekeeper, that's for sure." Myrtle tittered and waved her hand. "And Bernie... he's working on it. He's been to rehab before... but this time, I'm sure he'll sober up. He's been such a good father to Luellen. You should just see him on Christmas morning, playing Santa Claus." She wiped her eyes. "The house is so quiet without him and Luellen, and now they even took away our dogs!"

"Thank you, Mrs. Schultz. You may be seated."

Judge Evans cleared his throat and looked myopically around the room. Eden prayed harder than she ever had in her life. *God, wherever you are, please let me take Ava home! I'll go to church. I'll stop drinking. I'll do anything. Please.*

"This certainly has been a travesty, a situation that has caused great suffering for everyone involved. But we are here to ensure that a four-year-old girl known as Luellen May Schultz is heretofore protected under the law. We cannot be hasty in removing her from what I consider to be the safest circumstance possible at this time. Luellen will remain under the full care and custody of the Minister of Social Services."

"But..." Eden leaped to her feet, pulling her hand violently from Gil's.

"Hold on. Young man, could you please stand?" Judge Evans said to Gil. He stared at them for a long moment. Then he said, "It is my understanding that you are engaged to be married."

"Yes, sir, we are," Gil said loudly.

"Then I suggest that you enter into the legal process of declaring that the child is your biological daughter, in which case you will be forevermore responsible for her welfare and maintenance, no matter what your relationship with her mother may be.

"And I suggest to you, Eden, that you apply immediately to the Department of Social Services to become your biological daughter's foster parent."

"Yes, sir!"

"This court will consider your petition for custody only after thorough and frequent supervision of your foster home over a period of one year. Josey MacMillan, can you see that this process is expedited?"

Josey called out joyfully, "You got it! I mean, yes, Your Honour!"

"I will further call for an investigation of the procedure breaches evident in Luellen's adoption in 1975, which may result in criminal charges for those closest to the matter, including Miss Browne's supervisor at Social Services."

Agatha and Myrtle moaned. Agatha lowered her head to her hands, and Myrtle glared at Leslie Lafontaine. "You call yourself a lawyer?" she shrieked.

Judge Evans said, "This hearing is now adjourned *sine die*."

* * *

The day was ebbing when Eden, Gil, and Ava pulled up to the house. The string of lights Eden had looped around the kitchen window glowed softly against fresh snow. The yard was full of vehicles.

"I hope she's not overwhelmed by all this," Eden said to Gil.

Ava lifted her head from Eden's lap and rubbed her eyes. "Hey, cutie, we're home," Eden said. Ava gazed impassively around the yard.

Eden zippered Ava's pink parka and placed the pom pom toque on her head. She noticed Gil's smile. "I know, it's not far to the house," she said. "But I don't want her to catch cold." Now that she was responsible for Ava, she was beginning to feel the weight and worry of motherhood. I'm going to be one of *those* parents, she thought.

Ava grabbed Squirmy Worm, and they were ready to face the welcoming committee.

Ava hid her face in Eden's shoulder when they walked into the steamy kitchen. Donnie, Vic, Angela, Carol, and Curtis were sitting in the room. River, Stacey, and Daniel were there, plus George Junior, Skylar, and her father, who was holding court at the head of the crowded table.

Everyone except Curtis turned to them and called out a greeting. George Junior jumped up to give Eden his chair. She pulled Ava's parka off, tucked the toque into the parka's sleeve, and placed Squirmy Worm into her arms. Ava's fine, blonde hair danced with static electricity from the toque, so Eden licked her fingers to smooth it down.

Ava was peeking around the room, so Eden said, "Ava, this is your Grandpa George."

Her father hollered, "Now, that's a pretty little girl!" His loud voice made Ava jump, but she smiled a little.

George Senior plucked Daniel from Stacey's lap. He had a full cup of coffee on the table; George was drinking several pots a day now. It had become his whisky substitute.

"Hey, Ava, you want a horsey ride, too?" George Senior asked. Daniel was giggling and squirming as his grandfather galloped with his knee. Ava shook her head imperceptibly, then wiggled out of Eden's lap, abandoned Worm, and touched Daniel's chubby leg. Daniel was irresistible. George Senior set Daniel on the floor near his chair so the kids could play with the toys scattered there.

"You guys want coffee?" Donnie asked, rising from her chair to grab the pot. "I've got supper in the oven. I hope Ava likes chicken."

I have no idea what Ava likes, Eden thought. *She has put on weight, but still looks like a starving baby bird.*

Eden scanned the table—her brothers, verbally poking one another; Vic and Donnie, faithful to the end; Angela and Carol, leggy teenagers who still liked to irk one another while the others talked. And Curtis, looking very grown up in his glasses, sitting quietly at the table with the other adults. She could not catch his eye.

Eden noted Stacey's gentle arbitration when Ava took Daniel's block and he howled; Skylar's battered hands wrapped around a giant ceramic mug labelled Uncle; and George Junior laughing compassionately at one of her father's garbled jokes.

Her father, sober. Eden, sober.

And Gil Tremblay, floating on the edges of her family, completely at home in her kitchen.

Two phantoms hovered outside their warm circle. Barbie, tousled hair in a ponytail, hands rough from gardening, wearing boy-sized jeans. And the faceless one—Ava, Eden's womb sister, lost to them but still clinging to the periphery of their lives.

Donnie was refilling coffee cups around the table when she froze. She stared at Ava, glanced at Curtis, then looked at Eden with horrified eyes. Eden looked away quickly. *Yes, Ava looks just like Curtis when he was a kid.* She wondered if anyone else would notice.

Donnie set the coffee pot down with a shaky hand and left the room. Ava was crawling back into Eden's lap, so she picked her up and followed Donnie into the living room, where she was standing at the window, weeping. Eden and Ava joined her there.

"I'm sorry, Donnie."

"You could have told me, you know. You should have."

"I was afraid to. I knew it was wrong, what happened. I was afraid everyone would be mad at me."

"Did he... hurt you?" Donnie's hands were shaking as she fished for a tissue in her sleeve.

"No! No, Donnie. It was my fault. I did it. I don't know what came over me."

Donnie's eyes flashed. "Eden, how could you? Don't you understand that people like Curtis can't... live like the rest of us? They need to be protected."

"It was just stupid! I thought it would be a way to break through to him." Eden tore at her hair. "But I can't regret it, I can't. I have Ava now."

Donnie took a deep breath and looked at Ava, who had tucked her face shyly into Eden's neck.

"She's beautiful," Donnie said.

"I know."

Donnie reached for the little girl. "Come to me?"

Ava twisted away at first, then extended her arms to Donnie. With a sob, Donnie held her granddaughter like a fragile doll, but Ava squirmed and reached back toward Eden. Donnie handed her to her mother, and they walked to the kitchen.

Gil smiled at Eden as they approached the table. I'm going to tell him tonight who Ava's father is, Eden thought. Right after we give her a bath and tuck her into bed. Just like a real mother and father.

Eden sensed Ava was anxious. "Hey, you want to go outside and look around?" The outdoors had always been Eden's solace, and she expected it would be Ava's, too.

Snow crunched under their feet as they stood in the yard, crisp air tingling deep in their lungs. Eden heard footsteps and turned; Curtis had followed them. They walked together toward the barn.

When they reached the path to Grandma Doris's house, Eden asked Ava, "Do you want to see your new house? And your new bedroom? Or do you want to see the horses first?"

Ava scrutinized Eden's face, searching for the correct answer in her eyes. Then she hopped up and down. "The horsies, the horsies!" she cried, bouncing along the path holding her mother's hand. Curtis was close behind them.

Patches, Blackie, and Diamond were in the corral, taking shelter beside the barn as the temperature dipped. Curtis hurried over to Patches and grabbed her halter. One little tug and she was all his; she poked her nose into his armpit and inhaled happily.

Ava hid behind Eden's legs, her eyes stretched with wonder. Eden picked her up.

"Let's go see Patches," she said. When they approached, the little girl reached out tentatively. Patches snorted, and Ava laughed. *Sweet music.*

"Do you want to ride on Patches?" Eden asked. *Pink parka or not, she's got to start riding, and it might as well be now.*

Curtis held Patches's head while Eden swung Ava onto the horse's broad back. Her bird legs were splayed as wide as they could splay. Eden had to laugh at her expression, a mixture of abject terror and jubilation. Eden showed her how to hold on to Patches's mane.

"Mama?" said Ava, her fists full of brown and white horse hair. "You're my weal mama, wight?"

"Yes, baby, I'm your real mama." Tears seeped from Eden's eyes, but she didn't bother to wipe them away. Ava reached out to touch Eden's wet cheek.

"And, Mama? Is Patches my weal horsey?"

Curtis started leading Patches around the corral, taking great care where he placed his feet. In the dimming light, he wisely avoided anything that looked like fresh manure. Patches was wheezing a bit. We have to get her out for more rides, Eden thought. She's getting so fat.

Eden looked at the winter sunset—violet and soft pink, like Ava's coat.

"Yes, my baby," Eden said, reaching up to swing her daughter to the ground by the armpits. "She's all yours."

The End

Born and raised in Saskatchewan, Katherine Matiko now lives in the Canadian Rocky Mountain foothills where she finds daily inspiration for fiction and poetry. Her work has been published in Canadian and American poetry anthologies. *Eden's Daughter* is her debut novel.

BWL Publishing

bwlpublishing.ca

www.ingramcontent.com/pod-product-compliance
Lightning Source LLC
Chambersburg PA
CBHW011114100726
47898CB00011B/3084